LIVING NIGHTMARE

The hall seemed bathed in a blue light. That was all he needed as confirmation that he was still dreaming.

He reached the door and pushed against it gently, then stepped quietly into the room.

He approached the bed softly, tightening his grip on the knife as he moved nearer.

He knelt at the side of the bed and studied Sylvia's features for a few seconds. They seemed so real. Perhaps too real. Maybe he should try to wake up. But nothing made any sense except the knife in his hand and the hatred he knew he must purge from his soul.

He stood up, trembling.

He raised the knife, hesitating only a second when Sylvia's eyes blinked open. Then he plunged the blade into her side, and he kept on hacking at her, again and again, until she was still.

Strange, she hadn't struggled much. Nor had she cried out. But she couldn't be expected to react normally, since this wasn't real.

Or was it?

NIGHT GLOW

NIGHT GLOW

MARTIN JAMES

PINNACLE BOOKS
WINDSOR PUBLISHING CORP.

PINNACLE BOOKS

are published by

Windsor Publishing Corp.
475 Park Avenue South
New York, NY 10016

First printing: April, 1989

Printed in the United States of America

"In every one of us, even those who seem most respectable, there exist desires terrible in their lawlessness, which repeat themselves in dreams."

—Plato, *The Republic*.

One. Reality in Reverse

For a while, the world seemed to go backward.

The cat padded backward around the couch. The digital clock registered time in retrograde, counting back from midnight. Dust in the air swirled the wrong way and flew up from the carpet. Light retreated from the corners of the room.

The world outside, viewed from the big bay window, was equally awry. Shadows seemed to wither away from the landscape and the moon seemed to shift uneasily in the sky. Clouds rolled across the face of the moon in a halting, haphazard blur.

William Myers turned from the window and glided through the dimness of his living room, feeling himself pulled from behind, watching the reverse order of events in rapt awe. His breath went and came slowly, in the wrong order. His eyes seemed to dry every time he blinked.

He tried to resist the motion guiding him, but his limbs would not respond to his will. After a few seconds, he didn't even try to struggle, realizing finally that getting himself into a state of panic wouldn't help anything.

After all, it's only a dream, he thought. *I'll wake up soon enough.*

That thought comforted William momentarily. Though he still couldn't enjoy the experience, he could at least resolve to let it flow around him.

Hadn't the doctor said dreams were a form of spiritual exorcism, a way of playing out the stress that so many people had imprisoned inside them? That meant it was okay to live through your dreams, to ride them out and see what happened. It was actually healthy to have dreams—even bad ones, even horrible ones.

Going backward wasn't so terrible, anyhow.

William was cold. He wore only the bottoms of his pajamas, though it was cool enough in the house to turn the furnace on. He watched himself move past the mirror in the hall and almost laughed, though his muscles were pulling against the corners of his mouth. His sparse gray hair was going in every direction and the bags under his eyes seemed so dark they might be painted on; he looked like a grotesque clown. He even had the red nose, though it seemed more gray in the semidarkness.

He bumped through the swinging doors in the kitchen. Then he was by the counter next to the stove. A drawer opened, and his right hand reached behind him while a long knife slid into his grasp.

A memory flashed into his mind of taking the knife out earlier and putting it back. He had intended to do something terrible with the knife but had changed his mind. In the reverse logic of the present moment then, the knife should go back in the drawer of its own accord, and he would eventually float back up to the bedroom to slide in next to his sleeping wife. Then he would wake up, clammy and sweaty, and tell Sylvia about the dream.

She'll think I've really gone around the bend this time. This is the weirdest yet.

A chill went through him as he realized the knife remained in his grip, almost as if it were refusing to play out the scenario. The knife was warm, causing heat to spread up his arm, radiating through his muscles. He twitched and tried to let go, but the knife wouldn't fall.

Let it flow.

His whole body was reacting now. As the heat from the knife

10

tingled in his limbs, he was filled with the dark thoughts again, the sinister ideas he dreaded coming to him in every dream.

William was no longer at the end of the reverse dream but at the beginning of a nightmare, one he recognized only too well. It was the familiar nightmare he had at least once a week, the awful dream that caused him sometimes to run screaming out of the house—the dream that had him so sick in mind and spirit he needed medical attention.

But I took the pill! I shouldn't be having this dream at all.

His thoughts were jumbled and confused, but he was still reasonably certain he had taken one of the little blue capsules that somehow blanked out the dreams and gave him rest. He remembered distinctly swallowing it and washing it down with cool water.

He licked his lips and it seemed like the taste of the gelatin the capsule was made of still lingered in his mouth.

He also tasted something else: the bitterness that came over him in waves, the contempt he had for his own life and the absolutely dire hatred he felt against his wife.

As he considered his wife and what she was, he felt suddenly feverish. He wondered, as he always did in his dreams and never in his waking life, what had attracted him to her. She wasn't a loving, giving person at all; she was a major disappointment, a kind of lie in the flesh to which he had succumbed when his reasoning faculty was clouded by youth and lust. Marrying her and, more to the point, staying with her was the most foolhardy decision he had ever made in his life. Now he was paying for it—with his life and the sacrifice of his mental health.

What had Sylvia ever done for him? Nothing. She had held him back for years, first by bearing children, then by saddling him with debt and other circumstances that kept him from being what he really wanted in life—to be a man independent of care. A free man. A man who could do whatever the hell he wanted without having to answer to a snivelling bitch or a couple of ungrateful brats. Now he was too old to pursue his youthful goals. Too damn old to do anything but watch the rest of

11

the world get ahead of him while he languished on the sidelines of life.

It was all Sylvia's fault. She had enticed him with beauty, then gotten fat; appeased him with sex, then gotten pregnant; teased him with cuteness, then gotten old and dull. Now he had to spend the rest of his days with her!

The knife seemed to pulsate.

Was she ever kind to him? Not lately. Did she really care about him? Not likely. What was she good for? Not much.

The knife was distorted in his vision now, reaching out before him like a harpoon.

If only he could get rid of her. If only she would die. Then maybe he'd have a chance to repair his wasted life.

Why not?

He could do it himself, couldn't he? Take care of her for good, so he'd never have to watch her mincing gestures or see her dour face again. She deserved to die. All of them did. All of the people who ever wronged him had no right to live.

His dream-logic posed the question again: *Why not?* Since it was a dream, it would be okay to act out his feelings. There was really no danger. The doctor had told him things that happened in a dream were totally unreal. Thoughts, dreaming or waking, did *not* create, even if they were driven by fierce emotions. Why not, indeed, act out his dream thoughts and thereby release them?

That's what dreams were for.

Thus convinced, William ascended the stairs to the second floor and padded down the carpeted hallway to the master bedroom. He didn't notice anything as he crept toward the room, not even the bloodstains that decorated the walls already. Nor did his peripheral vision register the horrors lying in the other bedrooms where his teenaged daughter and son had been alive only moments before. William didn't even pause when he came to the other knife lying on the floor, the one he had used earlier, in the dream he had already forgotten. He just stepped over the bloodied blade and kept going.

12

Now that he knew it was *okay*—okay to kill Sylvia—he was filled with excitement, his apprehension having drained away with his new resolve. He'd feel much better after he did this, even if it were only in a dream. He had almost done it before, in the other dreams, but the horror of the deed had always stopped him and made him wake up at the last moment. Not tonight, though. Tonight he would go through with it, and that would mean an exorcism and a purging of his personal demons.

The hall seemed bathed in a blue light. That was all he needed as a confirmation that he was still dreaming.

Let it flow.

Time lurched along with his steps. Put the right foot down, lift the left foot, put the left foot down, lift the right—left-right, left-right, left-right, left-right, marching to the bedroom, marching to the scene of the crime, marching to the sweet release that could only be accomplished in this unreality.

He reached the door and pushed against it gently, then stepped quietly into the room. Moonlight coming through the big windows next to the bed illuminated the room. Sylvia was lying on her side, the covers half off her, wheezing lightly in her sleep. She wore a flannel nightgown, one that covered everything and disguised her womanhood while effectively discouraging desire.

As if he *could* desire her anymore. As if anyone could want her. She was better off sent to hell, where she belonged.

He approached the bed softly, tightening his grip on the knife as he moved nearer. Sylvia's face in repose was ugly as ever. Her lips were pursed, as always, on the verge of a sneer. Her dark, gray-streaked brown hair was spread out behind her head. Why didn't she dye it? Why wouldn't she make even the most minimal effort to look young?

William was sweating heavily now, and the pulse in his forehead was throbbing so hard it ached.

Do I really hate her this much?

He knelt at the side of the bed and studied Sylvia's features for a few seconds. They seemed so real. Perhaps too real. Maybe

13

he should try to wake up. He tried to sort out his thoughts again, but nothing made any sense except the knife in his hand, the hatred he knew he must purge from his soul, and the idea that all of this was ultimately for his own good, if only he would let it flow.

He bent over and kissed Sylvia on the forehead. Her sleeping breath smelled foul and her flesh felt clammy on his lips. "It's only a dream, dear," he whispered.

He stood up, trembling.

Should I wake her first?

He smiled. That was a silly idea. Best to get it over with.

Let it flow; let it go.

He raised the knife and hesitated only a second when Sylvia's eyes blinked open. Then he plunged the blade into her side, and he kept on hacking at her, again and again, until she was still.

Strange, she hadn't struggled much. Nor had she cried out. But then since this wasn't real, she couldn't be expected to react normally.

After he was finished with her, William took a deep breath. His pulse was no longer racing and the feverish feeling had disappeared. He felt much better now, as if a massive weight had been lifted from him. He felt relieved and relaxed, and a bit weary. Perhaps he could go on with his life and never have to experience this particular dream again. Maybe his life would be totally different from now on.

He studied Sylvia briefly. The dark blood pooling under her didn't seem very real at all; it looked like the fake stuff they used in the movies—too red to be convincing. But maybe that was the point; it wasn't supposed to be absolutely real. There was always something to call attention to the illusion, some little detail that reminded the moviegoer—or the dreamer—that he was, after all, only participating in a fantasy, so he wouldn't take it all too seriously.

Satisfied with the comfort of that thought, William wiped his hands on the blanket and carefully draped it over Sylvia. Then

14

he let the knife fall on the carpet as he went around to his own side of the bed and crawled under the blanket next to his wife's body.

He lay on his back and closed his eyes. It seemed as if a great calm was snuggling with him, warming him with a vast peace he had never felt before.

He listened for the sounds of the night that would lull him to sleep, but there was little to hear. All he heard were the faint echoes of the dream-world lingering in his awareness: the sounds of a knife going into flesh, the sounds of muffled screams, the sounds of life leaving the house, perhaps borne on the wind to another world.

It was all so unreal, yet too real at the same time, a contradiction of abstracts, a tapestry of events perceived in a reverse reality that made sense only momentarily—only in the uncharted universe of the nightmare.

He reached out in his mind for more mundane thoughts but they were elusive, and after a few seconds nothing seemed to matter. Sleep came, enwrapped in a velvet, comforting darkness.

It was a wonderful, deep, refreshing sleep, the best William had known in months—the only sleep he knew that night.

Two. Late for Class

It was a bright, shimmering May day. It was much hotter than usual for this early in the spring, and there hadn't been any rain for days. The weather wasn't much good for anything except causing lethargy and rampant spring fever. It was difficult to think and even harder to concentrate on such mundane tasks as driving, but Marian Turner didn't have a choice.

She was late again.

She cursed as she darted in and out of traffic on the I-65 inner loop on her way through downtown Indianapolis, accelerating and braking as she tried to make up for lost minutes.

Just when she seemed to be gaining on the traffic she would find herself behind some old fart who was going too slow in the fast lane—usually an elderly man hunched over the steering wheel of a car at least a decade old, wearing one of those stupid nylon caps and hanging on as if the car would go out of control if he let go. Marian always felt trapped when she came upon one of these geriatric menaces. She was afraid a semi would come up and crush her beneath its massive wheels before she could get out of the way. Her old Dodge Omni didn't respond as well as it used to, either, which made her even more nervous.

Today there seemed to be more old farts on the road than usual. The highway was full of them. The sun seemed to bring them out, or maybe there was a convention for doddering old drivers in town.

Marian beat on the horn as she changed lanes abruptly, just missing a 1972 Buick being driven by a withered old man wearing a nylon cap that said "Coors" on it and a pair of thick glasses. He stared vacantly at the highway before him and didn't even acknowledge Marian's presence. He just kept on poking along, creating a hazard for every unwary driver out that afternoon.

Christ, he must have been doing thirty-five!

She honked again and merged into the far right-hand lane to take the West Street exit off the freeway. She barely braked in time to make the light, which seemed to turn red just to spite her and slow her down even more.

"What kind of asshole designed this stupid exit?" She had asked herself that question hundreds of times and never received a reasonable answer, although in her heart she knew: It was the kind of asshole who worked for the government, and those guys rarely had any sense. They certainly didn't know where to put stoplights.

This light always seemed to last forever, too. Marian used the time to glance at herself in the rearview mirror. She shook her head and sighed. What would her students think if she ever showed up in class looking like a human being instead of some damn harlequin with smeared lipstick, mostly unplucked eyebrows, and hair that was only semi-combed? They probably wouldn't recognize her.

She checked her watch. If the light changed in her lifetime, she might still make it to class basically on time.

She reached behind the seat and felt around to make certain her briefcase was there. She had forgotten it twice the previous week. Just as she touched it, someone behind her blew his horn, startling her into noticing the light was now green. She glanced at the impatient driver in the rearview mirror, considered giving him the finger, then pressed the accelerator to the floor, deciding the best insult was to make him eat her dust.

Of course, the recipient of the insult was an old man in a nylon cap. And he didn't seem to care.

By the time Marian walked the block and a half from the faculty parking lot to the main campus, she was already five minutes late. If she was much later, her students could leave without penalty, and if that happened one more time, the department head would chew her out again. She might even be suspended.

She decided to run. It was a perilous exercise in her high heels, so she took them off and stuffed them in her briefcase, not caring if anyone saw her. She sprinted across the vast expanse of concrete between the library and Cavanaugh Hall in just under twenty seconds. Her bare feet ached from slapping the hot concrete and she had a rip in her pantyhose, but those were trivial concerns if she could get there before her students started leaving.

She dashed up the front steps, pushed through the front doors, still in a run, and yelped as she saw the elevator doors just about to close.

"Hold it, damn it!"

A male student stuck his umbrella between the doors and they bounced against it before opening again. Marian slid in just as they were about to re-close, silently thanking God for making nerds who carried umbrellas on sunny days.

"Thanks," Marian managed breathlessly. "Three, please, someone."

"Sure thing, Dr. Turner."

She recognized the voice. It belonged to a student in her class. He turned to face her, blushing slightly. "I'm late too."

Marian smiled and looked away, her face also a trifle red.

The elevator was crammed, and just about everyone was sweating. At first, the crowded conditions made Marian uncomfortable, but when she realized her own blouse was wet under

18

the arms, she decided the smell wasn't so bad if she was contributing to it.

The elevator stopped at two, then labored to the third floor. The sound of gears grinding somewhere and the cables straining against the load made the trip seem longer than it was. Marian wondered when the elevator had had its last safety check and couldn't help but feel relieved when the doors finally opened—in agonizing slowness—on the third floor.

Three students got out first. Then Marian. She watched the student from her class walk ahead of her, considered running after him to get there first, then decided it wasn't worth the effort. He would tell the class she was on the way. Her job was secure again.

She paused and leaned against the wall to slip her shoes back on. She was conscious of her skirt hiking halfway up her thighs but couldn't figure a way to put her shoes on gracefully. She wasn't that concerned about being ladylike even on a good day, and on a day like this there was no reason to waste effort on any of society's pretenses.

At that moment, Jack Daley chose to come along the hall. He was an associate professor of botany and a general pain in the ass. He was also, he made it clear, very interested in anatomy.

He whistled. "Hey, there, Marian, is that a threat or an invitation?"

She slipped the other shoe on and stood up quickly, almost losing her balance as a result. "Christ, Jack, I'm late for class. I don't need any of your harassment right now."

"Who's harassing? I'm just expressing my genuine appreciation of the female form." Jack was twenty-eight and a typical young professor—always on the make. At least he was typical of most of the specimens Marian had encountered at Indiana University.

"If I had the time, I'd show my fighting form, but I have young minds to nourish. Beat it."

"I love tall and sassy broads."

19

He walked on by, chuckling under his breath.

"Pissant," Marian muttered. She composed herself and made it the rest of the way to her class without further incident.

After forty minutes of lecturing on abnormal psychology, Marian wondered who was less interested—herself or her students. Thank God there were only two more classes left this semester! Then after finals she wouldn't have to worry about students for three whole months. She could spend the summer on her research and not give a thought to grading papers or faculty meetings.

At thirty-two, Marian had decided teaching wasn't that fulfilling. Her research project on dreams and nightmares was much more satisfying and promised to make her well-known in the right circles. She was already planning a book as a result of her work, and its publication would definitely get her noticed. With that kind of recognition, she could write her own ticket at one of the major universities out East—where she yearned to live.

Indianapolis was much too dull for her and its men were not the type she wanted to attract. Even on campus most of them were of the rather low caliber represented by Jack Daley. In the East she could meet someone whose mind operated on the same level as hers. She wouldn't mind getting involved with a man who had more going for him than an uncontrollable sex drive. Sex was okay, of course, but it didn't really fill the emptiness in a person's life like it was supposed to.

After dismissing the class, Marian didn't linger behind to take student questions. There just wasn't time. Besides, nothing she could tell anyone this late in the semester would make any difference in grades. She gathered up her papers and left quickly, barely nodding at the inquisitive students gathered around her desk.

She took the elevator downstairs, then she trekked back to the faculty parking lot, climbed in her car, and started for Shodale Drugs. She was in a pleasant hurry now, eager to face the challenges her research provided her.

Shodale Drugs was housed in an expansive complex of buildings located in the northwest quadrant of the county, just above the suburb of Zionsville. Its various structures included the corporate offices, two manufacturing facilities, and a long four-story building where research was conducted.

Marian pulled up to the security shack at the south edge of the Shodale complex and flashed her ID badge. The guard knew her, but it was a matter of policy to check everyone who came through no matter how familiar the face. Marian didn't mind complying; the badge gave her a sense of importance she never felt on campus. It said she was really somebody—somebody who belonged and who knew what she was doing.

She parked the Omni in the lot nearest the research building and walked briskly to the doors, where another guard checked her badge. The second checkpoint gave her a fleeting sense of paranoia, even though she realized it, too, was necessary. She had heard there were things going on in certain rooms in the research building that could affect national security and, though she had a vague uneasiness about what such research might be concerned with (drug warfare? recombinant DNA?), she realized it was a necessary endeavor, not only for business but for keeping up with the rest of the world in science.

Of course, most of the research was being conducted on new Shodale products, such as cough and cold preparations, birth control pills, and antidepressants. There was also research on consumer products from Shodale's Chemical Division, which produced everything from plastic wrap to herbicides. Research in these areas was not so much a security risk as it was a matter of keeping ahead of the competition, many of whom would pay dearly to know what Shodale planned to put on the market next.

Marian's project was connected with one of Shodale's "ethical" pharmaceuticals—known to the layman as prescription

21

drugs. She was helping to test a new drug for the treatment of sleep disorders. In return for her help, Marian was allowed the use of a modern lab and the latest equipment—which was much more advanced (and expensive) than anything she had access to on campus.

She walked past the guard and stepped into a waiting elevator, one that moved her quickly and efficiently to the fourth floor. Its pristine walls were remarkably free of graffiti, which was really a change from the campus elevators. She even liked the way it pinged when its doors opened.

As she walked through a maze of halls that led to her lab, Marian gradually began to feel more centered. Her dark brown hair bounced and her hazel eyes brightened with the prospect of tackling her real work.

The research was going well. Marian felt she was on the verge of a breakthrough, especially in the area of nightmares. Who knew, today might be the day something really significant would happen.

Marian nodded politely at the white-coated men and women who passed her in the hall. Some of them knew her by name and acknowledged her with due respect. That made her feel proud to be there, proud to be part of the Shodale team. She was in her element and loving just about every minute of it.

She came to a door labeled: "Sleep Disorder Lab, Rooms 415–419." Next to the door was a plastic sign that warned: "Research on Product #4155A; Security Clearance B Required for Entry." She took a key from her briefcase and unlocked the door. A young woman was sitting just inside, typing correspondence on a word processor.

"Any messages for me, Sue?" Marian asked, reaching for a white lab coat from the rack behind the desk.

"Lots of them, Dr. Turner." Sue was about twenty, a dull-looking blond woman with a pockmarked face and too much makeup. She was the standard security-cleared clerical type Shodale sent over from the main offices, pleasant enough, but not exactly a brilliant conversationalist.

22

"Anything I have to answer right away?" She pinned her badge to the lapel of the coat, then backed away to peer at herself in the mirror next to the coat rack. She patted her hair in place and tested her face with a brief smile. Pleased with the way she looked, she turned to the secretary.

"Let me see." Sue ruffled a stack of pink phone memos. "Here's one from Mr. Morton across the way in corporate."

"I know where he is. What did he want?"

"Something about your grant."

Marian sighed. She didn't want to tangle with Morton today if she could avoid it. The only way he knew how to handle people was by applying more and more pressure, and Marian didn't like being handled like that. "What did you tell him?"

"That you weren't in yet."

"What did he say to that?"

"Mostly expletives." Sue prided herself on affecting what she considered a "good" vocabulary around Marian. She liked to appear educated, though her only education beyond high school was a short stint at secretarial school.

Marian smiled in spite of herself, imagining what some of the "expletives" might be. "Typical. Anything else urgent?"

"This, from a policeman."

Marian took the pink slip of paper and regarded it quizzically. "A cop? What would a cop want with me?"

"He wouldn't say. He wanted to talk to you real—I mean, really—bad. Or should that be badly?"

"I'm not an English teacher. You don't have to watch your grammar around me."

"I thought all teachers had to speak correctly." She frowned, running the variations over her tongue a few seconds to herself: really bad, real badly, really badly. "None of them seems right." She shook her head, then handed the rest of the phone memos to Marian and returned to the word processor.

"If Morton calls again, tell him I'm still out." She stuffed the phone memos in her pocket.

"Yes, Dr. Turner."

"And bring me some of the strongest coffee you've got when you can. Get some of that stuff that's been sitting in the pot a couple of hours."

"No problem."

Marian strode past a series of numbered doors toward her office. Behind each door was a sleep chamber full of equipment for tracing brain wave activity. No one was in any of them at the moment, since most of the research was conducted late in the evening and all through the night. Marian usually stayed past one or two in the morning herself, making sure her assistants set everything up exactly the way she wanted it before going home. She allowed no margin for errors in her research; too much of her future depended on it.

Marian's office was a small unnumbered room at the end of the hall. Once inside, she put her briefcase on the floor, sat behind her desk, and stretched. It would be a good afternoon for a nap.

It was ironic. She was doing research on sleep, but she never got much of it herself. Maybe she should be in one of those chambers with electrodes glued to her scalp. At least that way she might catch up on her rest.

She took a deep breath, held it to a count of ten, then let it go slowly. She would get her second wind soon and be able to accomplish something.

But before starting in, she took the bundle of phone memos from her pocket and reread the one from the policeman. His name was Carl Nolan. A plain-sounding name yet somehow familiar. Wasn't there a Nolan in her high school class back in Mishawaka, Indiana? Was his first name Carl? No, that was Nolen, and his name was Fred or Ted. Ed Nolen, maybe. Or maybe she was thinking of the actor Lloyd Nolan.

She tried to recall anything she might have done that could make the police interested in her. She couldn't remember any unpaid parking tickets. And she hadn't been stopped for speeding in three or four years; that probably wouldn't even be on the record by now. Anyhow, she had paid the fine. Maybe it was nothing. Probably this guy was asking for donations to send a poor kid to one of those concerts.

But why did the police want to contact her at Shodale? Why hadn't they called her at home or the university?

She glanced up at the clock above the observation window to her left. Christ, it was almost three-thirty! No time to worry about cops now. Her first sleep subject was scheduled for four o'clock, and she had a lot to do before he arrived.

She went to the file cabinet for the electroencephalographs from the last session with the subject. She studied the EEG's for several minutes and when she looked up again, it was four-fifteen. Her subject was late. She buzzed Sue on the intercom.

"Any sign of Myers yet?"

"No."

That wasn't like Myers at all. He never missed a session and was seldom late. "Did he call?"

"He didn't call."

"Well, give him a few more minutes, then call his home. And where's my coffee?"

"Sorry. I'll get it right away."

She switched off the intercom, then returned to the EEG's. Damn, she hated no-shows, but this one was particularly irritating.

William Myers was her best subject. He had the worst nightmares.

Three. Lawn Care

Carl Nolan awoke to the sound of trucks rolling past his house. He turned over to ask his wife what the hell was going on, but she wasn't next to him. She had apparently been up for a while; her nightgown was lying on the chair next to the bed, and there were no sounds of her in the bathroom.

He sat up, woozy from not having slept quite enough, and looked at the Emerson clock radio. Nine o'clock. Too early to get up, but he didn't really feel like going back to sleep. He massaged his temples, trying to get the blood circulating.

"Laura!"

Where was she? She didn't have to work on Wednesdays and normally slept in with him.

He twisted around and put his feet on the floor, shivering. The air conditioning was already on and he had fallen asleep in his underwear again. A T-shirt and briefs didn't protect him that well from the frigid temperatures Laura insisted on sleeping in.

Maybe she kept it cold to preserve herself, he thought. But it sure didn't do much for his sex drive.

He bent down and looked under the bed for his deerskin slippers. He spied one of them lying in the landscape of dust bunnies and plain old dirt beneath the bed. The other one was nowhere in sight.

26

"To hell with it, then." He picked up the single slipper and flung it across the room. It bounced off the wall and landed in the wastebasket next to Laura's dresser. "Two points!" On impulse, he peeled off his T-shirt, rolled it in a ball, and tossed it at the wastebasket, too. "Crap! Missed by a mile."

He went across the room to the window and parted the curtains to look outside. There was a small tank truck of some kind sitting at the curb, its identity obscured by the leaves of the maple trees in the front yard. He could hear workmen opening and closing doors on the truck. One of them was shouting something. The only word Carl could make out was *fucking*.

He lost interest and left the window. He'd ask Laura about the truck later. Right now, he needed a shower. He walked across the carpet, managing to roll his briefs down his legs and drop them on the way to the bathroom. He kicked them into the air, watching with satisfaction as they landed on Laura's side of the bed. "A gift for you, madame! Dirty underwear for the queen."

It felt good to walk around naked. It gave him a sense of freedom and a little thrill. It was nicer when he had an audience, of course, but Laura wasn't that appreciative of his body lately, so he was doing it only for himself.

"How's it hanging?" he asked himself. "Long, loose, and full of juice."

He smiled grimly. Some day Laura might discover there were women in the world who weren't so squeamish about the male body. Some day he might even find one of them.

He stepped into the bathroom and swore at the cold floor. The little blue rugs that were usually lying in front of the sink and toilet were missing. Laura had probably forgotten to take them out of the dryer. He took a dirty towel off the rack next to the medicine cabinet and placed it on the floor as a temporary measure, then stood on it while he brushed his teeth.

Carl was forty-two. His brown hair was thinning, but there were no signs of gray yet, and if he combed it just right, his small bald spot was effectively camouflaged. His dark brown eyes brooded under shaggy eyebrows, and his nose was straight and a bit too large for his face, though not to the point of distraction. In fact, when viewed in profile, it was a rather handsome nose, a nose with character. His jaw was basically square and his jowls were only beginning to sag. His beard grew quickly; he could shave twice a day if he cared to.

The overall effect of his face was that of a man slightly older than he actually was but not so much older that Carl worried about it, because he generally felt younger than he appeared. He often told people he might look like he was fifty but he felt like he was thirty-nine.

After rinsing his mouth, Carl shut the door and looked himself over in the full-length mirror attached to the other side. He was six feet one, trim, and muscular. He hadn't let his stomach go to pot like so many men his age and could still run a mile in under five minutes when he wanted to.

He flexed his muscles, pretending he was Arnold Schwarzenegger. "I can take you, Arnold. Don't mess with me."

He flipped a towel at his own image, then stepped into the shower and turned the radio and the water on. The radio was tuned to a local FM rock station, and the *Bob and Tom Show* was on. Bob and Tom were morning jocks who entertained their listeners with risqué humor that often got them into trouble with the more prudish segment of the Indianapolis radio audience. One of them made an oblique reference to fellatio and Carl laughed. The prudes would be shocked by that one— assuming any of them understood the joke.

As Carl scrubbed vigorously, his mind wandered and he no longer paid attention to the shower radio. His thoughts turned to his most recent case—that guy Myers who had killed his family for no apparent reason. Carl wondered what caused a nice, "straight" middle-class man like that—a man with a nice home and a good income—to go berserk. The murders were extremely brutal, too, enough to turn even a seasoned cop's stomach, and Myers was a quiet, unassuming man of fifty or so who didn't seem capable of harming anyone.

28

Carl's experience told him, however, that the man's looks meant nothing. Often the most hideous of criminals was hiding beneath a veneer of normalcy and respectability.

Myers had even turned himself in. He was very cooperative and more than willing to confess his crime. In fact, he seemed anxious to be taken away, as if going to jail was the real payoff for murdering his wife and two teenaged children. He didn't even want a lawyer. At one point he had said he hoped they gave him the electric chair, because he knew he deserved it.

On the other hand, maybe Myers was just being crafty. He could be pretending he was just a normal guy who went crazy on the spur of the moment. Maybe he was trying to set up an insanity plea, which, if it worked, meant he'd be walking the streets again eventually. That might be why he was claiming he committed the murders while he was dreaming. If a smart lawyer convinced a jury Myers was incapable of telling dreams from reality, the insanity angle would pay off. Myers's story was a variation on hearing voices or not remembering what you did, that's all.

Then there was the bit about the doctor Myers had been seeing, something they learned about after Myers was finally convinced to hire an attorney. The lawyer came out after consulting with his client and told Carl about some kind of "therapy" Myers had been going through and the drugs he had been taking, supposedly to "tame" his nightmares. If that wasn't laying the groundwork for an insanity plea, or at the very least extenuating circumstances, then Nolan would turn in his badge.

"Therapy, my ass," Carl said. "What crap!" It seemed like every asshole in the universe was going through some kind of therapy. To Carl, it was just a way of not taking the blame for what you did. Therapy taught people they were not culpable, that their bad childhoods were responsible, that their mothers had given them complexes, that it was PMS, drugs, or some other bullshit that impressed the public and gullible juries.

At least Myers's reason for insanity showed a little imagination. Carl couldn't recall any case he had ever worked on where the criminal used having nightmares as a motivation for murder. It could be an interesting case to watch. At least the media would have some fun with it. They loved to make a spectacle of nut cases.

Carl turned off the water and stepped out of the shower. He shaved, then returned to the bedroom to dress. Considerations of the Myers case could wait till later; right now he had to find out what his wife was up to.

He barely trusted her out of his sight.

Downstairs, Carl looked out the front door and saw the tank truck still sitting there. A sign on its side said: "Dwyer Lawn Treatment." Long black hoses led from the truck to two men in white jump suits, wearing helmets and goggles, who were spraying his lawn.

"What the hell? Laura!"

"I'm in here."

He confronted his wife in the kitchen, where she was fixing toast and scrambled eggs.

"What are those men doing to our lawn?" Carl sat down in the breakfast nook, grabbed a piece of toast off a plate, and munched it angrily.

"Spraying it."

"I can see that. But why?"

"It needs it, that's why."

Laura was five years younger than Carl. She was five feet six, a plumpish woman with frosted light brown hair and blue eyes. Her nose was turned up a fraction, just enough to be irritating when seen head-on. She usually wore a lot of pancake makeup, but this morning her face was pale and colorless because she didn't have to go to work. She was a nurse at St. Vincent's Hospital.

"What do you mean it needs it?"

She was wearing casual attire, a sleeveless blouse and a pair of baggy shorts. She poured herself a cup of coffee without offering Carl any and sat down across from him. "You know it hasn't rained in days. The grass is dying and the weeds are

30

taking over. It's also pretty obvious to me that *you* have no intention of taking care of our lawn, so I called some professionals in."

"I'll bet it was one of those rip-off companies who called you on the phone."

"No, it wasn't," she said, blushing at her own lie. She dumped two heaping spoons of sugar and a spoonful of powdered creamer in her coffee, then stirred it nervously.

Carl found the concoction she drank repulsive; it certainly wasn't coffee. "We can't afford 'professionals' to do our lawn. You've run up so many bills we can barely afford the sugar for your coffee."

She sneered and took a big gulp from her cup. "It's okay. I'll put it on American Express."

"Oh, great. That makes it fine. You don't have to pay American Express. They're a charity organization."

Carl stood up and went to the sink. He found a cup in the pile of dishes that wasn't too dirty, rinsed it out, and went to the coffee maker to fill it. "When the hell are you going to do these dishes?"

"I'll get to them." Laura took a bite of scrambled eggs, grimaced, and shoved the plate away. She picked up a leather case next to her plate, snapped it open, and took out a cigarette. "I work, too, you know. If you'd get me a new dishwasher, the dishes wouldn't be such a hateful job."

He took another piece of toast from the plate and ate it while sipping the coffee that was, as usual, too strong. "That's what we need, another goddamn bill. While you're at it, why don't you bounce some more checks? I love getting nasty phone calls from the bank."

She blew smoke in his direction, knowing how much he detested her habit, especially since he had quit smoking himself over two years ago. "I can't help it if it takes money to live. I do my part and I deserve to have some of the money spent on me. I don't know why you think that's wrong."

He calculated she must spend twenty dollars a week on cigarettes but resisted mentioning that. It was trivial compared to the rest of her spending.

"We can't afford all this extra shit. Can't you get that through your thick head? Our house payment is too damn high, the utility bills eat us up, and we've got car payments—not to mention the Penney's charge, Sears, Ayres, Lazarus, and charges at just about every other fucking store in this town."

"Well, we have to have things. Things break. Clothes wear out. . . ."

"Bullshit." He set his coffee down without finishing it. "I guess it's too late to tell those lawn guys to leave," he said more calmly, having already exhausted himself. The argument would never come to any kind of reasonable conclusion, no matter how much he ranted and raved. Laura was immovable.

"I guess." She blew more smoke and seemed smug; she probably felt she had won.

"How much are those professionals, anyhow?"

"Couple of hundred."

"Jesus." He turned to leave, afraid that if he stayed any longer he might be tempted to hit her. He didn't even go through the motions of kissing her good-bye.

"Where are you going?"

"None of your damn business."

"We'll have the best-looking lawn in the neighborhood in a couple of weeks," she called after him. "Think of that."

Carl didn't want to think of it. He muttered a final curse and slammed the door on his way out.

There certainly wouldn't be any sex with Laura tonight, but then why should it be different than any other night?

Carl wasn't scheduled to go to work until the second shift began at three o'clock, so he had a lot of time to kill. First, he stopped and ate breakfast at the Waffle House Restaurant on 30th Street, then browsed around in a used book store where he bought a couple of back issues of *Playboy*. That brought him up to the lunch hour. He couldn't think of any more time killers, so he decided finally to just go on into work and find something—anything—to do there to keep his mind off his domestic troubles.

The Homicide Division was located on the second floor of the Indianapolis Police Department's headquarters. Carl checked in with the lieutenant in charge, who was used to seeing him come in early, and discovered there wasn't really much for him to work on at the moment, except the Myers case. There had been a shooting on the city's near east side that morning, but other men were already on that one.

Carl sat at his desk and fiddled around with his paperwork for a few minutes, then checked his sidearm, a .357 magnum, to see if it needed cleaning. It hadn't been fired for a couple of weeks and that had been at target practice at the police shooting range. He had cleaned it then, so it was still in good shape. He replaced it in his holster and considered his next move.

Actually, the Myers affair was pretty much closed as far as Carl could tell. The man had confessed, after all, and the extenuating circumstances—insanity or whatever the attorney came up with—could be taken care of by the prosecutor's office. Besides, the man was safely in jail where he could perpetrate no further mayhem with no bail set.

But Carl had a gnawing feeling there was more to it than what lay on the surface. He couldn't actually define what it might be; maybe it was just a hunch, or intuition, or plain old instinct, but he couldn't let the Myers thing go that easily. This wasn't just a case of some drunken lowlife getting crazy and killing everyone in sight. Myers was a respectable person, a man with no real motives that Carl could see.

The nightmare angle continued to intrigue him, too. Maybe he should try to contact that doctor Myers's lawyer had mentioned again. Dr. Turner.

According to his notes, she was supposed to be at the university this time of day. He started to call her, then decided it would be better to see her in person. The university was only ten minutes away and he might learn more by surprising her.

Marian kept an office in the psychology building on campus, where she was obligated to keep hours twice a week for handling student problems. Most of her hours there were used to grade papers, because students rarely came to see her. She often wondered if it was because they considered her aloof and unapproachable, or because they considered themselves too smart to need additional help. Maybe it was just that most of her students comprised a feckless lot who were taking abnormal psychology as an elective and not seriously considering psychology as a career.

Today, however, a student had decided to visit. His name was Tod Corey, and he wanted Chapter 21 of the text explained to him in more detail. After a few minutes of his earnest questioning, though, it was obvious to Marian he was more interested in trying to make a date with her. He'd probably seen too many of those teenage sex comedies where the young man learns about love and life from an older woman.

Marian was polite but uncomfortable, though she was used to students getting crushes on her. It happened to most teachers, but she herself still didn't know how to handle it with the proper aplomb. It was flattering to an extent, she had to admit, but it wasn't the sort of thing she wanted ever to pursue. It could get real messy. She didn't really like young men that much, either. They weren't much better than the older ones.

This boy Tod (could she really accept him as a man?) was not bad-looking; he would probably do well with the coeds if he had more confidence. But he was too shy. Why did the shy ones feel they could be attractive to their instructors but not to women their own age? It didn't seem to make much sense.

She could tell he was about to approach his real reason for coming to see her, when there was a knock at the door.

"Excuse me, Mr. Corey," she said, not bothering to hide her feeling of relief.

Marian rose from her desk and went to open the door. A tall, well-built man with rough features was standing there, who appeared somewhat ill-at-ease. He was wearing a gray lightweight suit with a strange bulge around the shoulder.

"Can I help you?"

He showed her a badge. "I'm Carl Nolan, with the Indianapolis Police. I called you yesterday."

"Oh, yes, I remember. Sorry I didn't get back to you. I got involved in my work."

"That's okay. Could we talk now?"

"Just a minute." She turned to Tod, who looked as guilty as a person could who hadn't actually done anything. "Mr. Corey, you'll have to go now. This is important, I think. You can talk to me after the next class or on Friday."

"Yes, Dr. Turner," Tod said, obviously disappointed. Equally obvious was the fact that he had lost his nerve and would not approach her again, for any reason. He gathered up his books and papers, stuffed them in a big satchel, and departed hastily, showing deep embarrassment as he brushed by the big man at the door.

"Well, come in, Mr. Nolan. I have a few minutes before I have to leave. I hope we can get this over with—whatever it is. Did I double-park or something?"

"No. It's something more serious than that. I'm with the Homicide."

"What? You'd better have a seat." She returned to her desk chair and motioned for him to take the seat where Tod had been.

Carl watched her closely. He didn't know what he had expected a "Dr. Turner" to look like, but Marian certainly wasn't it. He had anticipated a dumpy older woman with gray hair, not an attractive young woman with dark hair and the kind of pale complexion Carl admired.

It was the damn movies, of course. Movies provided all the

35

stereotypes by which people were judged. A woman doctor of any kind was not supposed to be attractive. She was supposed to be old and dried-up. On the other hand, this woman probably had a stereotype of "cop" in her mind, which unfortunately Carl lived up to all too well, at least in appearance. Stereotypes worked against the police officer; people always expected you to be some kind of gruff asshole with no feelings. Even though recent movies and books tried to make cops out to be human beings, people still carried the old stereotypes they had grown up with around with them. Carl had seen that cold appraisal of himself as a cop in people's eyes many times, but he didn't see it in Marian's. Her eyes possessed a spark of intelligence that was very appealing. She looked real and vital.

He liked the confident way she had about her, too, and the way she moved. It wasn't really sexy, yet it wasn't exactly sexless, either.

"Okay, what's this about? A student? Did one of the faculty murder somebody?" Her voice had lost its edge of surprise. Now she was merely inquisitive, almost clinical.

Carl took out his notepad and pretended he was about to write. "No. It's one of your patients—William Myers." He noticed she wore no wedding ring—or any rings for that matter. He was suddenly painfully aware of the gold band on his own finger. He reminded himself he was here on business. Having an argument with his wife was no reason to start appraising every woman he met.

"Myers?" She seemed confused. "He's not a patient. I'm not a medical doctor. I have a Ph.D. in psychology."

"Well, what is he then?" Carl tried to sound pleasant but realized it wasn't coming out that way. He sounded like a cop and was thinking like one now. His mind was already racing with suspicions, such as the possibility Marian could be Myers's lover. "I mean, I assumed that was your relationship with him."

"Christ, what's he done?"

"I'm afraid he killed his wife and children."

"I don't understand."

36

"He said he couldn't help himself, because he was having a nightmare. He mentioned you were treating him—if that's the right word—and I'm just following up on that."

She paused and took a deep breath. "He's a test subject, a volunteer in my research. I'm not sure I can tell you much more than that."

"Can you tell me what the research is?"

"I could, but ... well, I think I'd have to get clearance from Shodale. I've never been involved in anything like this." Her face was suddenly pale, as the full import of what they were talking about finally hit her. "Did I hear you right? You say he—he killed ... his family? I can't believe he'd do anything like that." She recalled Myers's descriptions of his nightmares. The worst always involved his doing harm to his family.

"That's another thing I need to ask you. What does Shodale have to do with it?"

"We're doing research on sleep disorders. Shodale is providing the financial backing. We're leading up to testing a new kind of drug, a kind of anti-hallucinogen. It's all in the experimental stages right now, and extremely sensitive and confidential."

"You wrote prescriptions for Myers?"

"I can't administer drugs. I ... what do you mean? Are you saying Myers was on drugs?" She seemed dumbfounded.

"Little blue capsules. He said they were supposed to control the nightmares."

"I didn't know anything about that." What was going on here? Myers wasn't supposed to have access to the capsules; they weren't ready for testing on human subjects yet. She frowned, then realized Nolan was still watching her. She had to regain her composure and be careful what she said until she found out more on her own. "We deliberately kept him off medication," she said quietly. "Maybe his family physician gave him something."

Carl sat back to evaluate her. Her cool manner was more than was required for mere professionalism; it was a studied

37

aloofness deliberately designed to put people off. He could imagine that she didn't like men, yet, contrary to the effect she wanted, her attitude was strangely attractive—which probably confused her.

"Do you know who his family doctor is?"

"No, I can't recall. You'll have to ask him."

She didn't react as he expected. Most people at this point would become flustered, because most people were threatened by a police officer's questions, even when they had nothing to hide. This woman was a cool one, though, almost frosty.

"I want to be cooperative. It's just that I have many factors to consider. Career considerations. Legal considerations. And, of course, the welfare of Mr. Myers. Even though it's not a doctor-patient relationship, there are confidences. I don't know the legal ramifications. I'll just have to get back to you."

Damn, she was closing up on him. "Maybe I could come out to Shodale and see what's going on for myself."

She glanced at her watch and sighed again. "I'll see what I can do. I guess you could get a court order or something, if I refused."

"If I had to."

"All right. Maybe you'd understand better if you saw what we were doing firsthand at that."

He took a card from his wallet and handed it to her. "Call me at this number. I'm on from three to eleven. If I'm not in, just leave a message."

"I'll call you as soon as I can." She shifted papers on her desk and waved at him as if dismissing a student. "Now, if you'll excuse me, I have to get back to work. I'm a very busy person."

"We need to get moving on this," he said, though he sensed she didn't respond to pressure. "I want to wrap it up."

She looked down at her papers, made a scribble, and said nothing. Carl sighed, thanked her for her time, and left.

He was confused as he drove back to headquarters on Alabama Street. He had hoped to learn a great deal more from this Dr. Turner; instead, he had learned virtually nothing and had more questions than ever.

Maybe the source of his confusion didn't have anything to do with the case. He hated to admit it to himself, but maybe he was confused because he hadn't encountered such an attractive woman in some time, and he didn't know what to do about it.

In any case, he planned to see a lot more of her, whether she wanted him to or not.

Marian also had many unanswered questions as a result of the conversation with Nolan. The most perplexing one concerned the revelation that Myers was taking drugs—apparently drugs that weren't even on the market yet.

There was only one man who could answer that one for her, but it wasn't that easy to get the truth out of him. He had built a career on lies and double-dealing.

Still, if anyone could get John Morton to talk, Marian could. She might know things that could ruin him and she certainly had something he wanted.

Four. Baboon Attitudes

Dr. Stephen L. Richards watched the baboons writhe.

Their silent screams did not move him, nor did the frantic straining against their tethers. If anything, their efforts to escape amused him.

He was fascinated by the large blood vessels popping out on their hairy forearms and marvelled at how their veins seemed to have a serpentine life of their own, pulsating under the baboons' skin as if they were burrowing, or perhaps ready to burst through. That would be a pretty sight, indeed: veins ripping themselves from the monkeys' flesh and spraying blood all around like the out-of-control firehoses seen in old-time comedies.

Even if something that bizarre did happen, Richards would be unaffected, emotionally or physically. He was observing the baboons from a very safe position, peering at them through the glass in the door to the chamber where they were unwilling participants in one of Shodale's many experiments with animals. There were four baboons in the chamber, each securely strapped to a wood and metal chair. They sat on grounding pads to prevent their being electrocuted by their own bodily secretions, and electrodes were glued to their scalps under metal caps that looked like stainless steel yarmulkes. Large needles, attached to syringes that automatically injected them with a calibrated amount of an experimental drug, were stuck in their arms.

The spectacle of the animals was particularly intriguing because they were, according to the instruments to which the electrodes were connected, asleep, though their eyes were open and darted about as if seeking a way out.

And in their sleep, the baboons weren't struggling or screaming because of pain, even though the needles in their veins were certainly uncomfortable. They were screaming because of the drug being forced into their bloodstreams—controlled doses of Product 4155A—and the demons it was apparently unleashing in their minds were causing them excruciating torment.

Richards chuckled softly to himself. What kind of demons would be conjured up in a baboon's mind, after all? Did baboons think? Did they really have any idea what was going on here?

Yes, they were intelligent beasts, as far as beasts went, but could they really have any conception, any actual awareness of what they were and what their position in the scheme of the universe was?

That they dreamed was evident, if the studies were correct. According to the countless EEG's collected here at Shodale and in other studies, baboons showed evidence of REM sleep, just like humans, and if they went into REM, then they must dream.

But what would a baboon dream be like? What would be a monkey's worst nightmare?

Richards stared into the gaping maw of the baboon nearest the door. As it screamed, its massive canine teeth, murderous spikes that could rip any enemy (save the man who was well-armed) to bloody shreds, seemed almost unreal. Was this animal having a nightmare now—as a result of the drug? Is that why it wanted so desperately to break free?

Maybe baboons dreamed of this exact situation—of being trapped in a laboratory, subjected to nameless tortures for the benefit of mankind. Perhaps, if they had a race memory, as man was said to have, such a nightmare would even be recorded as part of their genetic code, as the most fearsome thing that could happen to a member of their species: to be experimented upon.

It would be a nightmare for any sentient creature to be reduced to the status of a piece of meat into which needles and probes were stuck with absolutely no regard for their effect. For a man, it was so outrageous a prospect that laws prevented such experimentation except under the most extraordinary circumstances, which was why baboons were necessary.

Of course, there *were* times when the laws could be circumvented, but it was a perilous business to contemplate.

"You have a great purpose on this earth," Richards said, grinning. "In fact, you have more purpose than most human beings, the majority of whom just occupy space." His grin broadened into a smile as the baboon seemed to renew its struggles. "Perhaps you hate me, then? You don't want to be better than a human? I suppose you're only interested in running through the jungle and rutting. I'm afraid there won't be any more of that, dear boy. Soon, you'll be going under the knife, so all your hatred of me means nothing."

The animal's eyes seemed to go wide, as if it could hear and understand him.

"That, too, is part of your purpose."

Suddenly bored, Richards took a clipboard from a hook next to the door, turned away, and strolled through the lab to his desk.

He was in his middle fifties, a tall, slender man over six feet, with thinning brown hair streaked with gray. His eyes were cold gray-blue and hid behind silver-colored wire-framed glasses with yellow-tinted lenses. His chin was slightly pointed and his cheeks somewhat hollow, giving him a gaunt appearance that matched his pale complexion. In dim light, he seemed cadaverous; in bright light, he seemed beyond that, almost certainly undead, even to those who thought they knew him well, though no one knew him well enough to see past his faults. His hands were broad and thick and bore calluses that belied his status as a member of the medical profession, and he would not discuss how he'd gotten them.

He was clean to the point of distraction, insisting on keeping his lab coat immaculately white, even under the messiest of circumstances in the lab. He sometimes changed the coat half a dozen times a day, and because he seemed to know what he was doing, he was allowed that and other eccentricities.

He sat down and made notes about the behavior of the baboons, appending to them a few speculations about the apparent effects of Product 4155A. Then he removed the notes from the clipboard and locked them in the file drawer at his right.

He wanted desperately to know how the new product would affect human beings, but the only subject on whom it had been tested had apparently failed to show up at his scheduled session in the sleep lab, so he didn't yet know what had happened. He hoped he would not have to find someone else to experiment upon.

He sighed and went to another corner of the lab to check on the cats. They had been given purpose, too; the tops of their skulls had been removed and electrodes implanted directly into their brains. They were acting out their dreams.

But as far as Richards could tell, all cats dreamed of was being cats.

John Morton tapped his fingers impatiently on the edge of his desk. He knew Marian had deliberately ignored his page and it angered him when anyone defied him. To his way of thinking, Marian was, ultimately, a mere employee of Shodale, no matter how lofty she considered the purposes of her research, and an employee was supposed to drop everything and come running when summoned by the boss.

Above all else, Morton *was* the boss and it frustrated him that the doctors in his charge did not defer to his authority more. Their being doctors didn't make them gods, though some of them seemed to see themselves that way. Here he had spent the greater part of his career climbing to a high position in a major pharmaceutical company, and he was still treated like shit by people—just because they had more degrees than he did. And Marian wasn't even a goddamn *medical* doctor!

That bitch was difficult to manage, but he vowed to get to her someday, somehow, no matter what it required.

Morton's office was large, thirty feet across by twenty-five feet deep, and furnished with leather chairs, a sofa, and a scattering of expensive glass-topped tables. There were brass lamps on each table and plants everywhere. A remote-control color TV sat on a long credenza, which was also equipped with a stereo and compact disc player. Morton never used any of the electronics in his office, but their presence was an indication of his status with the company.

The wall behind his vast walnut desk was glass from ceiling to floor and overlooked the Shodale complex, providing him with a panoramic view of the company that made him feel like a king, though he was currently only a vice president. Beyond the Shodale buildings, he could see the wooded green hills of the surrounding countryside, and in the distance even further beyond, he could watch the progress of a new housing development being built to accommodate the growing population of nearby Zionsville.

Morton grimaced as he sat watching a parade of cars leaving the parking lot. It was lunchtime and here he was still waiting for Marian to appear. His stomach was growling, too, and the timbre of the growl told him it was in dire need of a steak sandwich.

He slouched in his chair and put his feet up on the edge of the desk, still managing to maintain his view out the window. He was forty-nine, though his tendency to overweight made him appear a little older. His reddish-blond hair bore no traces of gray yet and his eyes were deep blue, set in circles of fat that gave him a slightly porcine look from a certain angle, which was accentuated by a square nose that turned up slightly on the end.

As always, he was dressed in a conservative gray suit, with a dark blue rep tie and a white-on-white shirt with French cuffs. He looked like somebody important—a force to be reckoned with. His attire also reflected his ambitions; he entertained notions of being the president of Shodale someday, if the old guard of the company ever got over its ultra-conservative attitudes and recognized just what an innovative thinker Mr. John Morton really was. And because he wanted to be president, he dressed as if he already held that position. He knew looking the part was half the battle in going up the corporate ladder.

What power he would have if he actually ran Shodale! He smiled to himself. If things went his way, it wouldn't be too long before he realized his ambitions.

Morton's smile faded when his secretary buzzed him to announce Marian's arrival. He considered making her wait for him, but he didn't have the patience to make an object lesson of her at the moment.

"Tell her to come in."

Marian came through the door and strode across the room.

"Have a seat, Marian," Morton said, stressing her name and the fact he had not used her formal title.

Marian seated herself primly in the chair facing the desk. She wondered now why she had decided to come. He was a hard man to confront, and she had put it off until the last minute. She didn't like to talk to John Morton under any circumstances, and these were far from ideal. Yet she had to talk to him, if only to see if she could somehow gain the upper hand. She knew things about him, but she wasn't sure if what she knew would be enough to make a difference.

She looked over at him, deliberately avoiding his eyes. He seemed to her to exude a kind of palpable evil, based on a presumptuous lack of conscience that was difficult for her to understand. His manner hinted at a latent, dark sexuality that frightened her, even though she realized it might not be directed at her specifically, but was a weapon he used on everyone, especially women.

"Well, you took your time coming to see me," Morton began. "I guess your grant isn't that important to you."

"I'm not here to talk about the grant." She tried to sound forceful, but her words lacked punch.

Morton tilted his head and gazed at her under half-closed eyes. "Oh?"

"I have to talk to you about—about one of the sleep subjects we're responsible for. William Myers."

"The name means nothing to me."

"I know that. But what he's done will." She took a deep breath. "He ... well, he's accused of murdering his family."

"Oh?"

She rankled at his apparent indifference. "Didn't you hear what I said?"

"Yes. It sounds bad, but I don't see what it has to do with us—with Shodale."

"You will."

"Will I? It seems to me the man must have been crazy. Too bad we didn't know that when we took him as a subject." He paused as he often did, merely for the sake of being irritating. "I hope the publicity doesn't impact on our project."

Marian's face began to turn red. "I think it will do more than that. Damn it, publicity is the least of our worries. Don't you realize this thing could stop the research entirely? But that's not even the most important part. We're talking about a human being who may have gone berserk because of a Shodale product! Does that spell it out for you?"

Morton appeared bored. "You're not implying Shodale had anything to do with it, are you? I mean, how? . . ."

"Myers took some of the new drug. At least that's what it sounds like from what the police say."

"You mean 4155?"

"Yes. As if you didn't know. As if you weren't behind him getting it."

"That's preposterous. We all agreed it wasn't ready for human testing yet, though personally I still think you're being unnecessarily paranoid about it."

"I knew that's the way you thought. . . ."

"Let me finish," he said, putting an edge in his voice. "Even if a human did get some of 4155, I'm convinced the risks would be minimal. You've read Dr. Richards's papers. The tests on animals are going quite well. We have more than enough documentation to apply to the FDA. Your insistence on more research is just slowing things down. We could have the drug on the market in a couple of years."

He leaned forward, his breath wafting across the top of his desk and hitting her in the face. It was an unpleasant sensation.

"I've heard that song before, Mr. Morton."

"You'll keep hearing it, too. We need to move ahead on this project. After all, Shodale has other projects to develop."

"I get it. You're saying it's Dr. Richards, then. He gave the drug to Myers."

Morton leaned back and made a temple of his fingertips, through which he peered at Marian. His face wore an expression of utter innocence, which was a difficult condition for Morton to affect.

"Now, I know you don't like Dr. Richards, but that's no reason to accuse him of breaking the law. He's a man of high ethics."

"You told him to do it, didn't you?"

"I did no such thing!" He seemed truly indignant. "If Dr. Richards administered any of the drug, he was acting on his own. Entirely. I wouldn't sanction any such action."

"Like hell you wouldn't."

"You can believe what you want." He broke eye contact with her and swung halfway around in his chair. He now seemed to be staring at a series of framed architectural drawings on the wall. They depicted a proposed Shodale facility to be built in South Bend, Indiana some time within the next three years. He already imagined himself there, sitting in the main office, directing the corporation.

A sudden thought occurred to him. "What you're really worried about is your grant, isn't it?" he said, turning back to her. "You're worried your own career will be fucked up. That's it. You don't care about this Myers fellow or the drug or anything—except what might happen to you."

47

Marian felt a cold chill at his casual use of *fuck* in her presence. To her it showed how little respect he had for her. For a moment, she was unable to reply to his accusation.

Morton looked her over thoroughly, and her skin crawled under his gaze, as if she could feel his eyes lingering over her body, somehow seeing it through her dress.

She gulped and regained her composure. "That's outrageous, and I think you know better. There are some people whose ambitions aren't the only motivating force in their lives. I'm not worried about my career now. I'm worried about another human being and what might happen to him as a result of *our*—of Shodale's involvement. Any person with *human* sensitivity would feel the same way."

He almost laughed out loud. "Maybe. But you would sure hate to lose that grant, wouldn't you? And it wouldn't look too good on your resume if it said you had anything to do with a non-approved drug being given to a man. After all, a good case could be made for your knowing exactly what was going on. You had access to the drug, too. You could have taken it upon yourself to test it on a human subject—to further your own career. Isn't that right?"

Marian was appalled. "That's absolute nonsense! I wouldn't jeopardize anyone that way!"

Morton's voice was becoming more gleeful with each new possibility. "In fact, Dr. Richards might even be prevailed upon to tell the authorities just that—that you came to him, since you're not a doctor yourself, and begged him to administer the drug."

"You bastard!"

"You see, Marian, things aren't always so clear, are they? It's hard to draw the line between guilty and not-guilty, especially when there's so much more at stake than the fate of a nonentity like this Myers fellow. In addition to your own career, there's Dr. Richards's career to consider. Would you have him in jail?"

"Maybe that's where he belongs."

"Do I sense some professional jealousy there? I think I do. You hate Richards, because he's not only a physician but a good one, and he—"

"Stop it."

"And, of course, you have a loyalty to Shodale. You've been collecting grant money from us for almost two years now. You owe us something."

"I don't owe you a thing," she managed to say.

"You'd better rethink that. You *do* owe us loyalty, because if you don't realize you owe us that, then things could get rather nasty. Do you really think you can fight a multimillion dollar corporation? Do you really think the police or a jury is going to believe the word of a neurotic psychologist over the staff of a major research facility that is respected for its many contributions to the good health of mankind? Do you think you can find a lawyer who can beat our lawyers?"

"Maybe I could. There are precedents. There are cases of the little guy winning. . . ."

"Perhaps, but the little guy isn't always concerned with a career. Suppose you did win. Suppose you beat us and Dr. Richards goes to jail, and 4155 is prevented from going to market. Don't you realize what that would mean to your career?"

"I don't see what you're driving at."

"It's this, little lady: You'd never get into research at another drug company. I'd see to that. The best you could hope for the rest of your life is to become—let's say, for the sake of argument—maybe an associate professor at some no-name, jerk-off school, where you'd have to teach psychology to snot-nosed kids who don't give a shit. That's assuming, of course, that any school would want you. I know lots of people in lots of high places."

"That's persecution."

"I don't give a fuck what you call it. You're not in charge of your life as much as you think, are you?" He smiled triumphantly. He was an expert at reducing people to quivering hulks, and it always made him feel good to do so. "But all this nastiness is so unnecessary. All you have to do is think things over." He sat back to admire his handiwork. Marian look duly subdued; indeed, she was obviously on the verge of tears. But it was time to turn things around a bit, so he wouldn't seem a total son of a bitch.

"Now, I agree this Myers thing is a tragedy, but nothing we can do is going to bring back his family, is it? Now, you like to help people. If you get involved in this mess, then you'll be pulled away from your research and the ultimate result will be that no one gets helped."

"I guess I didn't look at it that way," she said quietly, agreeing in order to end the confrontation.

"And there's one other consideration, Marian."

"What?"

"You may be wrong about the drug. I mean, even if Myers had access to it, that doesn't prove anything, does it?"

"I don't know."

"Think it over."

"But the police know about it."

"Don't you worry about the police. Just keep things to yourself and it will all work out."

"I may be asked to testify."

"We'll worry about that when the time comes. If the police come around again, be cooperative but don't offer anything. Besides, the way courts move nowadays, we may all be dead by the time anything comes to trial. Just don't do anything without consulting me first. And those attorneys I mentioned can help out, too, you know. You'll have powerful allies, if you need them."

Marian frowned at the implication she might need the attorneys—as if she was the one guilty of something.

"Can I have your assurance that you won't act without consulting me? That's not too much to ask."

"I guess so."

"Good. Now, you just let me worry about everything else. Okay? And, Marian?"

"What."

"Next time, don't let your righteous anger get in the way of your good sense. That's no way to run your life."

"I—"

"Don't say anything more now. Just go back to your research. Things will work out. I'll take care of you. Trust me."

As Marian left Morton's office, she never felt less like trusting another person in her life. She was hurt and she knew she had been manipulated, but she was also confused. What if Morton was right? What if the drug had nothing to do with Myers going insane? *Was* she just being a self-righteous fool?

Damn it! Why did things have to be so complicated?

She walked slowly down the hall to the elevator. All the way there, she had a creepy sensation of being watched, and when she turned back she saw Morton standing in the doorway looking through her, even from that distance. A terrible expression was etched on his face, and she read his thoughts and shuddered.

Cats without tops to their heads danced to the beat of electricity. Guinea pigs and white rats ran in their cages. Baboons lurched in their chairs and drooled. Machinery pumped and ground, and instruments recorded the animals' heart beats, their brain waves, and the rate of their various secretions. But the instruments couldn't record their terror.

From behind the glass, one of the baboons looked out on the world of humans. Symbols did not register in his brain but forms and colors, smells and sounds did. His eyes were glazed over with pain, but the features of the man who watched him were marked in his memory forever.

The man was part of the nightmare.

Five. Dead Puppies

"Elizabeth!"

The old lady's thin, frail voice cracked with the effort of shouting, but she kept on, because she just knew the maid was ignoring her.

"Elizabeth! Come here. Now!" The echoes of Mrs. Snodgrass's voice dissipated quickly in the corners of the mansion. It was as if a mouse had cried.

She sat up in bed and reached clumsily for the glass of water on the nightstand, intending to wet her lips, but she missed the glass and knocked a bottle of pills on the floor. Frustrated, she laid back against the pillow and gasped. Summoning the maid was exhausting her.

Ida Snodgrass was a withered seventy-two, a shrunken and fluttery woman with no one to care for her except the person she called the maid, who was really more of a nurse. Her long silver hair was fastened in a haphazard bun behind her head, out of which stray strands radiated like frayed wires. Her eyes were dark brown and lost in a network of wrinkles. She wore a pink nightshirt with lavender flowers on it.

"That maid is impossible," she muttered. "She never answers my calls." A white Persian cat was curled up next to her on the bedspread, purring. Ida reached over and stroked its thick fur and was immediately calmed. "Ah, Miranda, you'd never ignore me, would you? You'll never not come when I call. That's a good little kitty."

She fondled the cat's left front clawless paw. Touching the limp paw was a weird sensation. But the animal had to be declawed; it had been ripping up the Queen Anne chair in the foyer.

"I wish to God people were as dependable as animals, Miranda. But you can't depend on them a bit. Elizabeth is just as sassy as she can be, and I ... well, I hesitate to say this, dear, but I'm not sure she's as God-fearing as she should be."

Ida sighed and shook her head. She shut her eyes and breathed in the luxuriousness of her perfumed coverlets. Since people were so undependable, money and animals were her main comforts.

"Do you believe in God, Miranda?" She leaned forward, breathing on the cat's whiskers, then laughed thinly. "Of course you do!" The cat yawned widely.

"You called, ma'am?"

Ida looked up with a dark frown on her face, evidently flustered at having been caught talking to her cat. Elizabeth stood in the door, hands on hips, a slight look of disapproval on her dark face. She was a tall, solidly built woman with chocolate-brown skin. She wore a white uniform with a light green apron.

Miranda meowed a greeting, then proceeded to lick herself.

"You know I did. Why, I had to just scream and scream to get your attention!"

Elizabeth walked briskly across the vastness of the bedroom, her steps effectively dampened by the thick carpet. The room was done all in garish pink; it was, in fact, so pink it almost sickened her, though she figured it was the old lady's business if she wanted her home decorated like a whorehouse. White people could be so tasteless sometimes, especially rich old white women.

"Why didn't you use the intercom, Mrs. Snodgrass?" Elizabeth asked as she approached the bed. "I was down in the kitchen preparing your breakfast."

53

"I did use it. You ignored me." She sniffed haughtily.

Elizabeth's lips began to form a protest that the intercom had not been used, but she decided not to irritate Mrs. Snodgrass any further. "What did you want, Mrs. Snodgrass?" The cat got up and went over to sniff the fingers of her left hand, which dangled close to the edge of the bed. Elizabeth bristled slightly as its cool nose brushed her flesh. She bent over to pick up the bottle of pills on the floor and set them back on the nightstand without comment. "Did you want me to help you to the bathroom?"

"No," Ida said indignantly. "I don't need anyone to help me go potty! I can take care of it myself just fine, thank you."

"Then what did you want?"

"Why, I wanted—I wanted—" Ida seemed suddenly perplexed. That was strange; she could not recall why she had summoned the maid. Yet it had seemed so important only a few seconds before. Surely she was not getting senile as that high-priced doctor had implied.

Some doctor he was. Only a young pup barely out of medical school! But he was all she had since her own good Dr. Mellencamp had died on her. Dr. Mellencamp never would have hinted she was becoming senile, which was really doctor talk for "going crazy." Her mind was as sharp as ever. Only yesterday she had been reading the Bible, and she was surprised at how crystal clear some of its passages were to her. It took a keen wit to understand the Bible in all its wisdom, and her understanding proved just how bright she really was.

"I guess I wanted my breakfast," she said at last.

"I'll bring it up immediately."

"No. I want to come down. I'm tired of staying in bed half the day."

"But the doctor said—"

"I know what I can do, I tell you. I'll not remain in bed any longer. Now, scoot out so I can get dressed."

"Don't you want me to help?"

"No! I'm perfectly capable of dressing myself, too. You go take care of the family. I'll be down directly. Now skedaddle!"

Elizabeth withdrew quietly. She remained out of sight in the hall, however, just in case she was needed.

"Damn colored! Sassiest woman I ever saw." Ida uncovered her legs and eased them slowly over the side of the bed. "Watch out, Miranda." The cat jumped off the bed, scampered across the rug, and left the room.

She felt for her glasses and found them in the drawer of the nightstand, then set them on her nose. "That's better." Looking at the clock radio, she made an angry little sound. "Nine o'clock! Why, that Elizabeth would let me just sleep all day, so she can carry on any old way."

She stood up on unsteady legs. She was barely five feet tall and resembled an uncertain child as she made her way over to the closet. After wrestling with the mirrored sliding doors a few seconds, she finally got them open and selected a long purple house dress.

It was a seemingly endless struggle but she finally managed to get the nightgown off and the dress on. It hung crookedly, drooping somewhat off one shoulder, but Ida nevertheless felt a sense of accomplishment at having dressed herself. She put on a pair of white house slippers and left the bedroom.

Out in the hall, Elizabeth met her and helped her down the stairs where the family awaited: Miranda the cat, Giorgio the parrot, the fish in the big tank in the living room, and the newest additions to the family, the bull terrier puppies, Gog and Magog.

Ida went out on the sun porch to eat breakfast, where she could look out on the green expanse of the backyard and watch the puppies romp and play in the sunshine. She felt especially good this morning; she had shown Elizabeth she was perfectly capable of doing things for herself.

After breakfast, Ida spent the rest of the morning reading her Bible. She was particularly impressed by *Leviticus*.

It all seemed so clear to her now.

* * *

God spoke to Ida that night.

Of course, God had spoken to her many times before, but that had been in dreams. This time it was for real.

At first, she thought God was standing at the foot of the bed, and He was a tall, shadowy figure in a long white robe. But when she blinked, He had gone away. Or maybe He had just turned invisible.

His voice was still there, though, telling her things.

It was a marvelous voice, God's voice was. It was deep and resonant and majestic and it reverberated through the house. It was exactly a perfect kind of voice for God to have.

God had a lot of work for Ida to do.

Get up, Ida, God told her, His voice dropping to a warm whisper.

She switched the bedside lamp on and rose from the bed slowly. There was a chill in the air and she wrapped herself in a pink robe.

Elizabeth is a no-good shiftless woman.

"I know."

She has turned the family against you.

"Yes, yes. It's true."

Suddenly aroused by her mistress's stirring, Miranda bounced off the bed, ran sideways toward Ida, and spun around, chasing her tail. Ida bent down to pet the cat, but she arched her back and hissed.

"Bad kitty! Why did you do that?"

Miranda backed away, then began scratching at the carpet as if she were going to defecate.

"Stop that!"

Miranda is no longer a good kitty. Elizabeth turned her against you. Don't you see? They're all out to get you now. The whole family.

"Oh, whatever shall I do?"

You must kill Miranda.

56

"Oh, no, I couldn't do that!"

A haze seemed to fog her vision.

Ida looked up and saw a figure standing in the doorway. Its lips moved, but no words were heard. God was back.

No, it wasn't God. It was the doctor.

"What are you doing here?"

"I've come to tell you to do what God says." His words were barely audible. "He will guide you to the Light."

"Go away, you young pup."

"Do what God says, old woman, or you'll burn in eternal hell."

"Don't you call me old woman, you pup!" She rushed at him, her fingers stretched out like angry claws, and then fell through him. He was gone.

Miranda was rubbing up against her legs, purring. She picked the cat up and stroked her absentmindedly, then spikes of cold went through her. Miranda no longer seemed real.

Elizabeth has corrupted the cat and it is evil now. She will take you to eternal hell.

She shivered and held the cat out at arm's length. Its deep blue eyes did seem sinister now that she really looked into them. There was an agency lurking behind those orbs that was not of this world.

Somehow Satan had taken residence in the cat. It was no longer warm and loving; it felt like a piece of corruption, something that had to be destroyed.

You must kill her. It's your only salvation.

"Oh, God, Miranda!" She closed her eyes and wrapped her bony fingers around the cat's neck. She squeezed hard, finding strength she didn't know she had. The cat's ineffectual front paws fought against her, then it lashed out with its back paws, which still had claws. It kicked and clawed, ripping tiny tears in Ida's arms, but she still kept squeezing its neck harder and harder. The cat made a choking, meowing noise, then it became silent.

"Bless you, Miranda."

She laid the cat's limp form on the bed and went out into the hall.

Now you must take care of the rest of the family.

Ida had tears in her eyes. "I can't."

They have all been corrupted by Elizabeth.

"It's God's will, then," she said to herself. She wiped her eyes with her sleeve and descended the stairs.

Accomplishing God's will in the living room didn't take much time at all. She uncovered the parrot's cage and easily wrung Giorgio's neck. She ladled each of the fish from the big tank into a bowl and carried them out to the kitchen, then dispatched them by means of the garbage disposal.

As the last fish was chewed up by the disposal's blades, Ida began to shake with rage.

"Damn that Elizabeth! Damn that Elizabeth! Damn her!"

You must take care of Gog and Magog now.

"But, Lord, they're only puppies!"

Elizabeth has already corrupted them.

Ida sighed and went out to the sun porch, where the puppies were sleeping. They whined as she entered. Gog was all white with a tiny brown spot near his tail. She hesitated before killing him, but God was giving her the strength of purpose she needed and she finally managed to crush his head under a flowerpot. Magog, upon seeing this, cowered in the corner of the room and barked—a tiny whimpering bark—as she approached. He was completely white, the most beautiful bull terrier pup she had ever seen.

But he was evil.

He was corrupt.

He had to go, too.

She had to chase Magog around the room a few times, which almost caused her to collapse, but she finally scooped him up in her arms, which were still bleeding from the cat's claw marks, and carried him, struggling, out to the kitchen. She put him in the oven and turned the gas on.

She pressed her body against the oven door and gasped,

wondering why she hadn't thought of this *easy* way to take care of the others.

The pup whined pitifully, but Ida remained steadfast, though it seemed an eternity before he finally became quiet. She peeked in through the glass of the oven door and the tears came again. Even dead, the pup was lovable; it was hard to believe that he was infected with evil.

But God wouldn't lie about a thing like that.

She was very tired, but there was one more task to perform. *And now Elizabeth.*

Elizabeth deserved to die more than any of the rest of them, because she was responsible for the death of the family. That damn no-good shiftless woman with her evil ways; she was too sassy and had no respect for her mistress. She didn't fear God. She was evil. Hadn't Ida overheard her talking to her boyfriend in a very nasty way on the telephone? Didn't they talk about sex and other indecencies? No wonder the woman was so evil. She was downright depraved.

But how would she handle Elizabeth? She was much younger and stronger than she was, and even though God was tonight endowing her limbs with a special reserve of strength, she wasn't sure it was enough to subdue the maid. Doing a person in wouldn't be easy at all. As if any kind of killing was easy, no matter how necessary it was.

She pondered the problem as she trudged up the stairs, gasping for breath with each painful step.

"Lord, I'm running out of steam. I can't do any more."

My work must be done.

"But how?"

Pillows.

Ida wondered what that meant, then realized God was telling her how to do it.

At the top of the stairs, she turned and crept down the hall to Elizabeth's room. She pushed the door open quietly and walked softly across the room to the bed. Enough light spilled in from the hall for her to see Elizabeth's face clearly, and that

59

face, even in repose, was definitely twisted with evil. Elizabeth's arms lay on top of the quilt, which was pulled up just below her large breasts, the dark nipples of which, oddly erect, were visible under the white nightgown she wore. An odor of scented talcum powder permeated the air around the sleeping woman, and for a scant second smelling it was a pleasant sensation that disturbed Ida and almost undermined her resolve.

Then she felt her arms tingle. A rush of feelings pumped up and down her small muscles: anger, apprehension, and dread. Yet all of them were tempered with an absolute righteousness that could rend mountains. And just as faith could move mountains, it could also move a withered woman to do what God had determined was right and just.

She leaned over and picked up one of the extra pillows. She held it over her head as if it were a kind of soft bludgeon, considering one final time what she was going to do. A fly crawled over the black woman's nose and, somehow, that seemed to be a kind of signal. To get it done. Now.

"Yes," she whispered. Then she placed the pillow carefully over Elizabeth's face and pushed down hard.

Elizabeth's arms began to wave about. Her body bucked wildly, and muffled screams came from under the pillow.

Ida's own arms became rods of steel, but Elizabeth was still much stronger than she was, and she knew she would not be able to hold the pillow down very long. Then, suddenly inspired, she jumped up and sat on the pillow. Elizabeth scratched at her legs for a few seconds, then stopped moving altogether.

It had been easier than Ida ever thought it would. She slipped off the pillow and stood there, watching and listening.

God was silent, but the room was not. The fly that had triggered her buzzed its approval. A clock ticked on the table next to the bed. The air-conditioning was running, producing a low hum that suddenly annoyed Ida. It made her think of a dying breath.

Elizabeth was still. Ida took a deep breath and went back to her own room to sleep.

It had been a hard night, but God's work had been done, and she felt very good about that.

When Ida awoke the next morning, she felt particularly refreshed. She didn't even feel the aches and pains that usually assaulted her the first thing in the morning.

It was going to be a bright, sunny day. Ida started thinking of all the things she might do and called out for Elizabeth.

As usual, the maid ignored her.

Suddenly, she remembered part of a dream she had had the night before and trembled at its recollection. It was an awful dream, even though God was in it, and it made her slightly queasy even to think about it. She couldn't imagine why she would dream of harming her family.

But surely dreams couldn't hurt anyone. Still, she felt guilty at having participated in such a dream.

She saw Miranda at the foot of the bed and leaned forward to pet her. As she reached out, she noticed scratches and claw marks on her forearms. The cat was cold and stiff. She drew back and cried out.

Ida screamed for Elizabeth again.

But no one in the vast old house could answer her.

Six. Marian's Demon

Marian dismissed her last class for the semester and went down the hall to pick up some papers before going out to Shodale. As she walked, she mulled over the events of the last few days, trying to straighten things out in her mind.

She was paranoid and distraught, unable to think clearly, so she didn't look forward to going to Shodale this evening. Her meeting with John Morton had upset her to the point that she was barely functioning and anything connected with Shodale was a sore reminder of that disaster. Much of what she was feeling was anger, but she was also so frustrated that her every waking minute was an exercise in living on the edge.

Perhaps the way things had turned out was her own fault, but then she hadn't expected Morton to thwart her so effectively. Here she had gone into his office thinking she would put him in his place once and for all, and she had ended up allowing the man to twist her words around and make her seem the one culpable—and she wasn't even sure what she was guilty of.

What had she hoped to accomplish, anyhow? She didn't really know that much about Morton with which to intimidate him. Yes, she knew about his affairs (or had heard of them) with various women, she was reasonably certain he had played fast and loose with sales figures (but that was thirdhand information), and she felt his sense of ethics was somewhat less

veloped than that of a gorilla (perhaps an insult to all primates everywhere), but what did she have against him that was positive, that would hold up under close scrutiny? Admittedly, not much.

Yet her every instinct screamed that the man was a monster!

Now, because of Morton's machinations, she was uncertain what she would tell the police and how she would avoid implicating herself in the Myers case. Because that's what it came down to—self-preservation, which meant she was, ultimately, no better than Morton himself. At least in her own view of things.

But then Morton was just being Morton, and in *his* view of things he was acting morally. His life was driven by his own ambitions and by the fact that business came first, emotions and human beings second, if they were to be considered at all.

The fact was, Marian admitted to herself at last, she had lost her courage, and at a time when she really needed it. That wasn't Morton's fault; it was hers and she had to own up to it, though taking responsibility for her loss of courage didn't make her feel better, nor did it help her avoid the possible consequences.

Worse than that realization, was the awful feeling of déjà vu that accompanied her sudden cowardice. This sort of thing had happened to her before, and it made her feel she was a weak-willed, ineffectual person, someone who was not really in charge of her life, no matter how much lip service she gave to the idea of independence.

The first time—the most important instance she could think of, at any rate—she had found herself without the necessary moral fortitude to make the right choices in her life had, of course, been when she had decided, at the last moment—on the day she was to register for classes—not to pursue her career through medical school.

She had allowed herself to be intimidated by her college counselor, Joe Brewer, a man who in retrospect she recognized as a typical male chauvinist. He had cast doubts on her ability to succeed as a physician, even though she had the academic standing and the resources to be accepted to medical school. His doubting attitude was based on her being a woman, and he apparently did not believe women had any place in the world of medicine.

Prior to that time, Marian had not encountered such sexism; indeed, she had assumed, with the naivete typical of many of her generation, that such thinking no longer existed, that certainly all educated males were enlightened about the equality of the sexes.

But Joe was not that blatant. Like many modern men, he was practiced and subtle in the ways he sabotaged a woman's self-confidence. He dropped hints, raised his eyebrows, and gave her strangely quizzical looks when she mentioned her desire to become a doctor. The result was he slowly eroded her ambitions. Or at least she had permitted him to, and she found herself choosing the path of least resistance, agreeing to continue her studies in graduate school where things would be much easier for her.

So just like that, in a moment that was born neither of whim nor of caprice, Marian had denied her life's ambitions. Those four years of premed studies were basically wasted: the organic chemistry, the anatomy, the biology, the anthropology, the Latin, and the myriad other brain-breaking courses she had taken in preparation. She had readily overlooked her emotional and psychological investment in her chosen future, just because she could be manipulated by a raised eyebrow.

Her only consolation was that she did extremely well in graduate school, earning her doctorate in psychology with an A-plus performance that impressed more than one professor.

Of course, she had been compensating; she had tackled the non-medical courses with the enthusiasm she had reserved for medicine, and she had much to be proud of. Except she wasn't really the person that voice that had hounded her all through the years had urged her to be.

Perhaps, she realized, she had been looking for someone to

say no to her. Her parents, her sister Connie, and even her older brother Roger had all been supportive of her medical aspirations. And even Joe would have backed down if she had really asserted herself. He wasn't God; he was only a counselor. He was only supposed to help.

She had wanted someone to say no, because deep down inside, there was a knot of self-doubt that told her she could not really succeed.

It didn't matter now; she was what she was, and she tried to be the best in her field. She could still be a very important person, even if she wasn't an M.D.

But after that early sudden shift in her life's ambitions, it gradually became easier for her to lose courage when she needed it. It was a like a demon, always lurking beneath the surface, ready to spring on her. And, through the years, the demon of self-doubt, of fecklessness, often reared its ugly head to interfere in the direction of her life.

The next most important time the demon made itself felt was when she had the affair with the English professor. It had almost resulted in marriage, and it could have been a comfortable life. But he had been married himself, and at the last moment, Marian's demon had asserted itself and made her feel less worthy than the man's wife—who abused him and didn't respect his intelligence.

There had been many other times through the years when Marian's fortunes were seemingly determined by caprice rather than reason, though it was always by the demon of cowardice. Now here it was again, keeping her from asserting herself with Morton. Only this time, not only her career but her whole life could be at stake.

If only she had someone to help her sort things out! But who could she talk to about such serious matters? Who could help her overcome the demon?

She suddenly felt very alone.

* * *

65

Carl was rereading his notes on the Myers case. He could see where the case was heading—temporary insanity or something to that effect. The man's defense was going to rest on the drugs he had taken, though he could produce none of them, and the blood test to which he had submitted showed nothing. Still, his lawyer might be able to prove something if he could pin Myers down as to how he obtained the drugs.

Carl wished he knew more about the drugs himself, but so far he hadn't heard from that Turner woman at Shodale, and the man's own physician denied any knowledge of drugs, therapy, or even the fact that Myers was a subject in the sleep research. But his intuition told him there was something to the drug aspect of the case, and he was confident some kind of evidence would surface eventually, though how it would affect the case was still a matter of speculation.

In the meantime, he had another homicide to occupy him. This case also had a few odd angles. It involved a wealthy elderly lady on the east side, an Ida Snodgrass, who had killed her maid. The strange thing was that she had also killed all her pets. She would probably cop an insanity plea, too, assuming she lived to stand trial. She was past seventy and very frail, and she apparently had a heart condition. She would seem more a victim than a criminal, though, and even a mediocre lawyer would be able to get her at the most a very light sentence.

However, the fact remained that she had gone berserk, just as Myers claimed he had, only she said God had told her to commit the murder—in a dream.

Carl had to marvel at people's lack of invention some time. Why couldn't the old lady have just said the maid had pissed her off? Why did she have to blame it on a dream?

Maybe she had picked up the idea from a TV show. Lots of older people took what they saw on the tube literally. Many of them didn't realize the tele-dramas were not real—not even close to reality, actually.

Something in this case made Carl uneasy, though. It wasn't

something that could be readily dismissed. It was something that had his instincts roused.

Maybe there was more to this dream thing than he realized. It might be coincidence that two cases should come to his attention with basically the same motives—if you could call them motives. Such coincidences did happen, but it was unusual for the motives to match so closely.

He needed to know more about dreams, if only to satisfy his own curiosity. Maybe he ought to go to Central Library and check out a couple of books.

Better yet, why not talk to someone who was an expert on the subject? Like that Turner woman.

He could learn a lot from someone like her. And it *was* in the line of duty.

Marian removed her skirt and blouse and wrapped herself in an orange flannel bathrobe, then she popped a frozen dinner into the microwave and sat at the kitchen counter to wait.

She was supposed to have worked in the lab tonight, but she just didn't feel up to it and had left early. Her head truly ached, and she was hungry and wanted to care for herself for once, instead of looking out primarily for Shodale's interests. Let someone else stay there half the night working to further the career of John Morton. She was not in the mood.

"The son of a bitch," she said. She sighed and watched idly as the time on the microwave ticked off the seconds. It seemed it was also counting down the seconds of her life, and that was a most depressing prospect. She turned away and thumbed through a *People* magazine, trying to take her mind off everything, if only briefly.

Marian lived in a efficiency apartment on the northwest side of town, in a complex located at approximately the midpoint between the I.U. campus and Shodale, which meant she could go to either place with as little hassle as possible. The place was modestly furnished and decorated, because Marian believed in "traveling light." The most she had of anything was books.

When the microwave buzzed, she tossed the magazine aside, removed the dinner, and turned on the television. Her meal was turkey and dressing with corn and a dessert that was supposed to be a combination of apples and cranberries, but it tasted like neither. It was her usual bland evening repast, and TV helped distract her from its nothingness.

There was not much happening in the news: local politics, a fire on the east side, and a story about a rich old woman accused of killing her maid. Nor was there anything earth-shattering transpiring on world fronts.

She finished her ersatz food, turned the TV off, stretched out on the couch to study the report Dr. Richards had prepared concerning the effects of 4155A on animals. It was difficult to read it without wanting to fall asleep; Richards was a pompous, obdurately dull person, and his writing was as turgid and stolid as he was. He seemed unable to make a point clearly, but as far as she could figure out, his analysis of the data collected to date showed 4155A was not adversely affecting animals, though it was unclear how he could determine what *psychological* effects it could have and how that could be extrapolated to apply to humans. The question remained in her mind: Would Richards take it upon himself to do human experiments without telling anyone?

He might. She knew very little about the man's background, except for a rumor about his having been involved in a scandal in a private practice out west somewhere, in Arizona or New Mexico. Whatever the nature of the scandal was, he had apparently convinced Morton he was not blameworthy, or he would not have a job with Shodale, a company that usually turned its potential employees inside out before hiring them. Unless he had somehow covered up his past.

If Richards had decided to conduct human experiments on his own, Myers would have been a perfect choice. He was a very vulnerable human being. His nightmares seemed so severe that he would easily be persuaded to try something to control them, despite the risks involved, especially if Richards, a rather imposing figure who took advantage of his presence to get what he wanted from people, convinced him the drug would help. Indeed, Myers might have begged for the drug, once Richards intimated he could make it available to him.

Still, there was no proof of anything. If Morton denied any wrongdoing, Richards certainly would as well. So it would be a matter of Myers's word against that of Richards and Morton. Marian couldn't even help that much, since she had actually seen nothing. Maybe she could find something in the report that would provide a clue—if only she could keep reading it.

The type seemed to blur before her eyes; the charts and graphs ran together nonsensically; the words and ideas became a swirl of meaningless jabber. Her eyelids drooped, then closed.

The report slid from her fingers and dropped to the floor.

An insistent ringing jarred her awake. She staggered to the kitchen and fumbled for the wall phone. She lifted it from its cradle, almost dropped it, juggled it briefly, then grabbed it as if it were a snake that was trying to get away. Finally, she got it up to her ear.

"Yes?" she said groggily. She glanced at the wall clock; it was past nine.

"Dr. Turner?" a man's voice asked.

"Yes," she said hesitantly, expecting a sales pitch.

"This is Carl Nolan. Indianapolis police."

"Oh, sure. I kind of recognize your voice now. It's kind of late, isn't it?"

"This is my shift. The city never sleeps, you know. Am I disturbing you?"

"No. I was just asleep."

"I'm sorry. I can call back tomorrow, if you like."

She yawned and blinked her eyes. "No, I'm wide awake now. I needed to get up. So, what can I do for you?"

"You said you'd get back to me."

"I guess I forgot. I've been really busy. . . ."

"What did you find out about the drug Myers said he was taking?"

"Well . . . nothing, really." That was basically true, though it bothered her to say it with such self-assurance.

"You think there's something to it?"

"I don't know. I guess so." She expected him to see through her, but his voice betrayed no suspicion. Yet.

"Well, you will let me know if you find out anything?"

"Sure."

There was an awkward pause during which she thought the conversation was over, then he came back on the line.

"You know, I need some insights into this whole dream thing. I was wondering if it's really possible for someone to do something like that—in a dream—and not realize it. I don't know much about psychology, except what I've picked up on the street and dealing with people."

"Well, it's not something you could learn overnight."

"I'd really like to understand it better."

"I could suggest some reading, maybe." She realized she was talking to him like a student, and it didn't feel right. Besides, did she really think she could put him off that easily?

"Oh, I can do that, I guess, but it's better to talk to someone who's actually working in the field. Textbooks can't give you any real insights. Besides, you said you'd show me around Shodale."

"I guess I did at that." Marian seemed to recall it wasn't as simple as he was making out, but she decided not to press it. "Our work at Shodale is really pretty interesting."

She considered putting him off, then decided it was better to get it over with. Also, the sooner she saw him, the more cooperative she would appear. Self-preservation again. Couldn't she ever stop playing games? Or was it the demon's game? "Well," she said, "how about tomorrow afternoon?"

70

"I can swing that. As long as there's no major crime wave between now and then. Would about three o'clock be okay?"

"Yes, that would be fine. I'll make sure I'm not too busy."

"Where do I go?"

Marian had to smile. This was beginning to sound like a date—or even more to the point, considering the way she was feeling, like a clandestine meeting between two lovers. It wasn't like part of a police investigation at all. "Just come to the research building. The guard will show you. I'll leave a message for him to watch for you."

"I'll find you. But be prepared for a lot of dumb questions, doctor."

"Somehow, Mr. Nolan, I don't think any of your questions would be dumb."

He laughed. "See you tomorrow."

After Nolan hung up, Marian was overcome with the strangest feeling. She should have been feeling guilt because she thought Nolan could tell she was being cagey, but she felt, instead, a vague sense of relief, as if she might have been given a second chance somehow.

The sound of his pleasant laughter still echoed in her ear, and Marian realized she was actually looking forward to seeing the policeman.

71

Seven. Dream Machine

"This monstrous contraption is a polysomnograph," Marian said, pointing to a large console that came up to her chin. "We have four of them in the lab, one for each of the sleep chambers."

"Very impressive," Carl said. "What does it do?" He seemed genuinely interested in the machine. At least he pretended to be. He had been extremely pleasant ever since his arrival at Shodale, and it was driving Marian crazy.

She didn't know whether to take him at face value or not. To her his interest, feigned or not, was suspect, but she had to go on, if only to show how "cooperative" she was. She had decided a matter-of-fact, no-nonsense approach would be more effective than any cutesy bullshit—of which she was barely capable at any rate. She didn't think a policeman used to dealing with hard-bitten types would be swayed by a cute act, anyhow. But even though her approach was apparently working, she was still uncomfortable.

She leaned on the polysomnograph console and waved her hand across its face. "It has three major functions." She indicated a large roll of paper positioned on a flat surface at the front of the console. Twenty thin metal arms, each with a ball-point head, hung down to touch the paper at one end. "It makes recordings of brain waves, which we call an electroencephalogram, or EEG; it makes an electromyogram, or EMG, which is a recording of electrical currents arising in muscle fibers; and it makes an EOG, or electrooculogram, which tells us about eye movements. Each of these is recorded on this continuous sheet of paper by these pens. This is part of a recording made last night."

Carl was watching her every move. "How do you get the recordings? Needles in the arm?"

"No. The subject lies down on the bed in the chamber—you can see one of them through this observation window—and electrodes are glued to the scalp and other strategic places."

"And they go to sleep with all these wires coming out of them?"

Marian replied with a smile that she hoped didn't seem too professorial. "It's a little uncomfortable at first, but it's not painful, and most of our subjects get used to the electrodes very quickly. If you came here later in the evening, when our subjects check in, you could see how we hook them up."

"I'd like to see that." He smiled easily, his dark eyes sparkling. "Now, what do the recordings tell you?"

Marian found herself wondering just how old he was. He was obviously fortyish, but he didn't really seem middle-aged. He was also more attractive than she remembered him from their first meeting, and that disturbed her—that and the wedding band on his left hand.

"Well, the EEG and EOG are the most important for our dream research. The EEG gives us brain wave activity so we can judge whether the subject is in the alpha, delta, or theta stages. The EOG—eye muscle movement recording—tells us when the subject is in REM...."

"You're losing me with those acronyms."

"Sorry. I guess I'm used to talking in shorthand. I must sound like a real snob."

"Don't apologize. We use initials a lot down at headquarters, too, but they're just different. If I started talking in *my* acronyms, you'd think I was a snob."

He accidentally brushed against her and she felt a chill. She couldn't determine whether it was borne of fear or of excitement. His presence was beginning to affect her quite differently than she could have predicted. His policeman persona was beginning to be replaced gradually by that of a regular male human being.

"Okay," she said in a low tone of voice. She cleared her throat. "I'll back up. REM is Rapid Eye Movement. When that stage of sleep happens, usually later in the sleep cycle, dreams occur."

"Or nightmares?"

"Or nightmares."

Now Marian felt self-conscious. She was sure he was concentrating on watching her, studying her facial muscles, looking for a sign of her nervousness. Was this what the third degree felt like? Did he act like a regular person so he could catch his victims off guard—by trapping them in lies, or even worse, by trapping them into telling the truth?

"Rapid Eye Movement . . . what does that mean literally?"

"Just what it says. During that stage of sleep, the eyes are moving rapidly under the lids—as if the sleeper is involved in activity. Some people think it's a way of acting out the dream."

"Do you think that's what's happening?"

"Maybe."

"So why don't they get up and *really* act it out?"

"They can't."

"Why not?"

"Because the brain secretes a chemical that blocks the neurotransmitters that control muscle movement. In a sense, the dreamer is semi-paralyzed. I suppose it's a survival thing. If we actually acted out our dreams, we could be in big trouble."

Carl started to say something, then seemed to think better of it. His face betrayed no particular emotion.

She led him from the chamber back to her office, continuing to speak as they walked. "You know, sleep itself is a dangerous exercise."

"How do you mean?"

"Science has yet to come up with a valid reason for our having to sleep. I mean, when you think about it, every night we go into a kind of coma and become totally vulnerable. Doesn't that sound dangerous as hell?"

"Yeah, but we need the rest, don't we?"

"We don't really need it from a physiological point of view. In fact, the brain and the body functions are all active when the body is supposedly at rest, especially during the dream period."

Having reached the office, Carl sat down in a folding chair next to her desk. Marian had her assistant bring them coffee, then sat down opposite him.

"So what do you think sleep does, Dr. Turner?"

She handed him a cup of coffee. "You don't have to be so formal. Call me Marian." She didn't know why she had said that. Was she flirting? What the hell *was* she doing? His wedding band seemed to gleam maliciously at her; she glanced away.

"All right, Marian. What do you think sleep does? Surely you have your own theories."

"I think we need sleep because we need our dreams. And we need our dreams for reasons we haven't discovered yet. I think our psyche needs replenishing—not our body. The dream world offers us a solace, a kind of respite from daily cares, that we can't get otherwise. In short, dreams are truly beneficial."

"Then what about nightmares? They don't seem to fit it."

"Nightmares are beneficial, too, though it's difficult for most people to see that. In a nightmare you confront your worst fears, and often that's the way you come to grips with them. In fact, we tell our subjects who have particularly bad nightmares to try to go with them, to let them play themselves out—no matter how horrible they may seem."

"Sounds dangerous."

"It isn't. You can't harm yourself in a dream—or anyone

75

else, for that matter. Despite the old wives' tales, you can't die in a dream and be really dead, either."

Carl reached over for the Styrofoam cup of coffee and thoughtfully took a sip. Marian could almost hear the wheels turning in his head.

"Is that what you told Myers?"

She was taken aback, though she had been expecting him to bring up her former subject. "What do you mean?"

"Did you tell him nothing in his dreams was harmful?"

"Yes. Of course I did. Why shouldn't I?"

Carl set the coffee back on the corner of her desk. "Because in his case, it would seem you were wrong. If he's telling the truth, he did exactly what you said is impossible—he acted out his nightmare."

"He may claim that, but I still think it can't happen."

"All right. Let's let that drop for the moment. You say nightmares are beneficial, but the work you're doing here is for a drug that will control nightmares. That's contradictory, isn't it?"

"Not entirely. The theory is that controlling really intense nightmares might have therapeutic value in the long run. Lots of people have nightmares that are so terrifying they are afraid to go to sleep. They need some kind of help and therapy doesn't always provide it—at least not immediately.

"The patient wants quick relief. If we can calm the patient who has bad nightmares, we can get to the root of his problems. The idea is to alleviate some of the suffering. That's what 'good' drugs should do. I believe the patient will ultimately cure himself; we're just helping him or her along the way."

"You're losing me again. It seems drugs could just worsen the problem."

"Sure, that's current thinking, because drugs are abused so much in our society." Marian paused, trying to gather her thoughts. She was dangerously close to revealing proprietary information. "It's like prescribing antidepressants—which are used to correct a chemical imbalance in the brain. They are

76

prescribed only as long as it takes to get the patient back in balance. Then, eventually, they can handle depression on their own. The drug we're working on will do much the same thing. It'll control nightmares, so the patient can get a grip on his life and gradually face up to the things that might be causing the nightmares. It's treating the pain until the wound heals."

"So that's why Myers took the drug."

"I still don't know that he did." She hesitated, then continued. "He might have wanted the drug, but I don't think ... even if he did get it, it wouldn't have caused him to act out his nightmare. It would have suppressed it."

"You mean it was supposed to."

"Honestly, I don't know what you want me to say." Was he trying to trick her into admitting something? She considered telling him it was all too complicated for the layman but sensed he wouldn't accept such a facile, obvious evasion. If anything, he would be insulted. He had already shown himself to be an intelligent man, more than capable of grasping complicated concepts.

"The chemistry of the brain is very tricky and unpredictable," she said, recovering nicely. "Just when we think we know what a certain neurotransmitter does, we discover its function is different from what we expected. Sometimes it's the exact opposite of what we thought. The human body manufactures hundreds of different chemicals, and the brain has its own little pharmaceuticals factory, too. We can't predict what will happen all the time, especially when science is constantly discovering new brain-made drugs every day."

"Can't you be reasonably certain?"

"Maybe," she said slowly, only barely cognizant of what she might be implying, "you should talk to a real brain technician, like our Dr. Richards." Now that she had mentioned his name, she expected something magical to happen, as if Nolan would immediately pick up on the possibilities the doctor represented by somehow reading her mind.

"I'd rather talk to you," he blurted, apparently oblivious to any special meaning Dr. Richards might represent. "You seem to know all about it."

"But I don't. I'm not a medical doctor," she reminded him, somewhat painfully.

Carl finished his coffee and tossed the cup in the wastebasket. "Okay. I guess I've grilled you enough for one day."

Marian sighed. She hoped her sense of relief wasn't too obvious. "I hope I helped you out. If it helps Mr. Myers ..."

"It's hard to say. That's up to the courts now. You may be asked to testify, so you'll probably have a chance to help him before it's all over."

She regarded him earnestly. "How do you think it will come out?"

"Who knows? I gave up trying to predict the outcome of trials a long time ago. There are always too many surprises. But my best guess is he'll cop a plea of temporary insanity. A good lawyer should be able to make it work."

He stood and Marian found herself admiring the way his muscles worked. He extended his hand and she took it. "This has been very enlightening, Marian."

She was aware of the sweatiness of her palm and blushed. His after-shave seemed suddenly overpowering.

"I was glad to be of service, Mr. Nolan."

"Carl."

"Okay ... Carl." It seemed he was holding onto her hand longer than professionally necessary, but she was afraid to say anything.

"Is it okay if I call you again? I may have more questions."

"As if you had to ask. I want to cooperate."

"I know you do." He was staring into her eyes intensely. She wanted to break contact but couldn't. He let go of her hand and went to the door, then suddenly turned back. "I almost forgot. . . . Do you know a woman named Ida Snodgrass?"

She didn't even pause to think. "No. Should I?"

"I guess not. You should've read about her in the news. She

says she committed murder the same way as Myers—in a dream. Strange coincidence, isn't it?"

"Is it?"

"I don't know. You're the doctor." He smiled mysteriously, then left.

After Carl was gone, Marian rushed into the rest room and splashed cold water on her face. Trembling, she looked into the mirror above the sink, but she didn't see herself at all.

She saw a red-faced demon.

Eight. Shodale The City

The Shodale trucks kept rolling, hour by hour, day by day, year by year.

Shodale Drugs, like Indianapolis, was a city that never slept. Over two thousand people worked at Shodale around the clock, in three shifts, producing drugs, both ethical and over-the-counter, to treat society's many physical and mental ills.

A Shodale preparation existed for virtually every part and function of the body. There was a whole line of cough and cold preparations, some with codeine requiring a prescription, others with less potent ingredients for purchase by anybody; there were pills for arthritis and bursitis; pills for dental pain, back pain, post-partum pain, and menstrual pain; pills for nasal congestion, diarrhea, constipation, hay fever, and other allergies; pills for cuts and bruises; thinning the blood, lowering cholesterol, controlling triglycerides; pills for heart disease, stomach ailments, infection, earache, headaches, body aches; pills for athlete's foot, ringworm, tapeworms; pills for the liver, the spleen, and the pancreas; pills for hemorrhoids and birth control. There were drugs for general practitioners and specialists, for use in cardiology, oncology, gynecology, psychology, neurology, otolaryngology, ophthalmology and dermatology; and in podiatry, osteopathy, obstetrics, and pediatrics. Drugs were made to be inhaled, injected, swallowed, and absorbed, in the form of salves, emollients, suspensions, solutions, suppositories, tablets, capsules, and caplets.

But Shodale considered the mind its major province, for in producing preparations designed to help moderate and modulate brain function, the company was without peer. Shodale manufactured antidepressants, MAO inhibitors, antianxiety preparations, and tranquilizers, among many other substances designed to alter brain activity and help the patient achieve a level of sanity that was comfortable, more or less. In a society where psychological ailments were increasing, business was very good and getting better. The company's production of diazepam, a generic form of Valium, was double that of its nearest competitor, and that was only one example of Shodale's massive output of mind-altering drugs.

Producing pharmaceuticals naturally led to related chemical endeavors, such as the manufacture of pesticides, herbicides, fertilizers, and other chemicals that helped control and/or alter the environment. And beyond these products, but within the scope of the same enterprise, were such derivatives and logical extensions as plastic wraps, sandwich bags, trash bags, window cleaners, oven cleaners, and toilet bowl cleaners. All Shodale's products were sold in both consumer and industrial strength; thus, every sector of every market was covered, so the housewife, the janitor, and the government employee were served.

Such were Shodale's overt concerns. There were many secret enterprises, mostly for the military, to which only the most select, high-security-clearance Shodale personnel were privy. It was rumored, though, that the secret enterprises included the continued manufacture of napalm, poisonous gases, and other warlike materials; research in germ warfare, eugenics, and genetics; and experimentation with recombinant DNA.

It was as if there was a vast chemical/pharmacological stew to which Shodale had unlimited access and from which any magical potion, drug, or chemical substance might be created. Yet everything ultimately was all chemical; and it was all drugs; and it was all plastic.

Shodale's products affected America and the world. It was virtually impossible for anyone to live a normal life without coming into contact with at least one Shodale product every day.

Such wide-reaching influence meant more than mere money; it meant power, and the men who were part of the Shodale billion-dollar-plus empire could wield it—as they pleased—with only minimal regard for the consequences. So if a drug didn't work, or even worsened the condition it was designed to ameliorate, the worst that could happen to the people responsible was a lawsuit against the company, and possibly a settlement. But that was mere money, and there was no moral restitution.

The Shodale machine was inexorable, changing the face of the world and the makeup of the universe. Nothing apparently could stop it. Nothing dared.

The Shodale trucks kept rolling, hour by hour, day by day, year by year.

John Morton had summoned Dr. Stephen Richards to his office for a good chewing out. The man was getting out of control and had lost sight of his true position in the company; he was, whether he considered himself one or not, just another staff researcher, and Morton intended to remind him of that little fact of life.

Though Morton did not care much for Richards, he had to admit he and the doctor were very similar in many ways. At least Morton had come to that conclusion. They both craved power; they both put their careers above human considerations; and they both were basically ruthless individuals. It was possible, even, that they both shared similar sexual tastes.

Morton was amused by that possibility. He couldn't really imagine Richards cultivating sexual practices as bizarre as his own. That took imagination and Richards had little of that commodity in his personality. He was cruel and insensitive, which made him an asset sometimes, but he was essentially a dull fellow, and the dull were not creative in the sexual arena.

As he awaited Richards's arrival, Morton thought back on his meeting with Marian Turner. It had turned out just as he had wanted, with her not knowing, at the end, whether she was coming or going. Controlling her mind, orchestrating her thinking processes for her, was just another step in making the Great Conquest—getting to her body.

Because that was the ultimate plan Morton had for Marian: to seduce her and then make her participate in one of his fantasies. He often imagined her stripped naked and spread-eagled in a motel room somewhere, forced to submit to sordid acts of twisted love. He could see her lying there, totally open and vulnerable, her breasts taut and sweaty. He could see her eyes pleading with him. He could see her wince with pain as he made her flesh sting for his pleasure. He could almost smell her fear.

Yes, a stuck-up college woman like Marian was an awesome challenge, but she would be ideal, and a fitting replacement for that dumb secretary he'd been taking to the Signature Inn. If he could get rid of that stupid woman, he vowed never to do anything fancy with such a low, uneducated, uninteresting person again. Because even when she let him do anything his fervid imagination could conjure up, there was little pleasure in it. She was too willing, too submissive to really satisfy him.

He smiled crookedly as he visualized Marian and him together, then realized he was getting an erection. He was tempted to do something about it, to go in the bathroom and quickly self-consummate his fantasy, but just then the secretary buzzed him to announce the arrival of Richards.

His smile and his erection subsided at the same time.

"Shit! All right. Tell him to come in."

Richards came in, looking imperious, and sat down in one of the leather chairs across from the desk without being asked.

"You're looking smug today, doctor."

Richards's glasses caught some of the glare of the afternoon sun, making it impossible to see the man's eyes. He seemed to be staring straight ahead, barely acknowledging his superior.

"But then you're always smug."

"Did you call me here for that—for an analysis of my character?"

Morton shifted uneasily in his chair; it looked like it would be a battle of wills. As usual. "No. I wanted to talk to you about this 4155 project."

"You mean 4155A; 4155 is no longer in use. The two formulations are completely different, though the effects—"

"Shit, you know what I mean," Morton interrupted. "Don't get so damned technical. Anyhow, do you know about that one test subject—the guy that killed his wife?"

"What do you mean?"

"He was one of your sleep subjects." He looked at a note scribbled on his desk pad. "His name was Myers. You gave him some of this 4155A stuff, didn't you?"

Richards was relaxed, apparently unconcerned. "Of course. Why should I deny it?"

"Well, you fucked up." Morton glowered. "And this time it's serious."

"It's presumptuous of you, Mr. Morton, to place the blame entirely on me. Do I have to remind you that it's what you wanted?"

"Maybe it's what I wanted, but you chose the wrong man. Now the police might get involved, and it could affect the project adversely. We have a lot of time and money invested in this thing, and I don't need any screwups. We want to get this product on the market—not put it on trial."

"How was I to know the fellow would go berserk?" Richards said simply. "I don't think anyone can prove 4155A was the cause, even if it did come out in court."

"It could've been a factor, couldn't it?"

"The man was inclined to violence in the first place, as his dream profile indicated. I was only trying to help him out— and help you out, Mr. Morton—by obtaining results of the drug with human subjects. My only error was in misjudging just how much violence Myers was capable of. Normally, I know what violent people are like. . . ."

"You don't have to remind me of your years in the loony bin, doctor."

"You say that like I was a patient and not a doctor."

"Sometimes it's a very fine distinction."

Richards acted as if he were going to leave. "I refuse to stay here and take your insults."

"Cool yourself." Morton decided to bring out the heavy ammunition, more as a test than a real intention. "What would you say if I asked you for your resignation?"

Richards was ready for him. "I'd say you'd be going with me."

"You think you could take me down? Really, doctor, you have delusions of grandeur."

"Perhaps. But if you want to test me, go ahead."

Morton reconsidered his strategy. "All right. Let's forget about anybody resigning. Let's just think how we'll handle it, if things come out during Myers's trial. We have a lot at stake here. All of us do. Surely, you realize that much."

Richards was unflappable. "We can always deny any involvement. Myers is unstable and unreliable. It would be easy to turn his testimony against him. He couldn't stand up against me. I should think the real problem is with Dr. Turner. She's full of ideals that might compel her to talk about things she had no business being concerned with. I feel she's already interfered."

A familiar mental picture flashed into Morton's mind. "Don't worry about that bitch," he said. "I'll take care of her." He was having little success manipulating Richards, he realized suddenly, and it made him feel resentful. He would remember this episode, if Richards ever needed anything from him.

"Dr. Turner doesn't know her place," Richards continued. "She needs, shall we say, a lesson on her position."

The picture grew more vivid in Morton's imagining, and his face reflected a measure of satisfaction, though it wasn't as much fun with Richards maneuvering him into the fantasy. "I can take care of her, all right."

"I thought you could," Richards replied, and it seemed he might almost smile.

Morton grimaced with displeasure. "Wait a minute, Richards!

85

You can't get off that easily. You know damn well Marian is the least of my worries. I want to know *you* won't fuck up anymore."

"I'm not stupid, Mr. Morton. I have everything under complete control. In any case, I will be discreet." He stood and started for the door.

"Discreet, my ass. I don't want discreet. I want you to stop! I want you to confine all experiments to animals only from now on, until I say different—until this thing blows over."

Richards frowned but nodded assent. "Certainly."

"It better be certain, because I'm the one who's running things around here—not you or any stuck-up bitch with moral delusions. I'm the goddamn boss. Don't forget that."

"Was there ever any question?" Richards bowed imperiously, still managing to appear smug, then slipped through the door before Morton could stop him.

"Son of a bitch!" Morton growled. He wondered briefly how he might get to Richards, then assured himself the man wasn't as smart as he thought he was; no one could stand up to John Morton.

Thus comforted, he turned in his chair to look out the window at the bustling activities below that made Shodale a potent force in the world. Fascinated by the sheer vastness of the company's enterprises, he found himself lulled into a sense of well-being and warmth, because he knew that every Shodale product sold increased his wealth and contributed to his power.

He leaned forward and could see the big semitrailers at the loading docks being filled with cases upon cases of Shodale products. He watched until he was almost hypnotized by the grandiose monotony of it.

Then he closed his eyes and returned to his fantasy—in which a woman screamed, and Morton was fulfilled.

Nine. Parks and Recreation

After the Bundy family came home from their Sunday outing in Christian Park, they expected the rest of the day to be dull and uneventful as Sundays usually were. They had had fun in the park, but now it was time to wind down and start thinking about what Monday would bring.

Alan Bundy relaxed while waiting for his wife to prepare supper. He felt very much the man-of-the-house, or more aptly the Lord of the Manor, whose responsibilities had ended when he discharged his parental duties by taking the family out. He sat in front of the television with a cold beer in one hand and the remote control in the other, and started watching the second half of an old John Wayne war movie on Channel 4.

Wayne was leading the marines in an attack against the Japanese on Iwo Jima. Alan had seen the film many times before, but this time it was a different experience because the movie had been colorized. He marvelled at the way the technicians had gotten most of the colors right, even the eyes, though after a while he noticed that all blue eyes were exactly the same shade of blue. Same with brown. And everyone's teeth were uniformly white. The weird colors didn't really detract from the film, but they didn't add anything, either, and Alan wondered what the point of it was.

Still, the movie was entertaining in a mindless sort of way, and it was fine for killing a Sunday afternoon.

Faith Bundy hummed as she worked in the kitchen. She was fixing one of the family's traditional Sabbath meals: fried chicken with mashed potatoes, fresh green beans, corn on the cob, and Dutch apple pie for dessert. The best thing about this particular meal was that there was absolutely no part of it any member of the family would complain about. Even the kids would enjoy it, especially since she had splurged on real butter for the corn. It made her feel good to see her family really enjoy the meals she made for them.

She turned the chicken, then went to the counter to finish peeling the potatoes, pausing occasionally to blow her nose. She hoped she wasn't getting a cold. But her nose had been running constantly since they came home from the park. That was strange, since it hadn't been cold at all today.

The children had watched a couple of minutes of the Wayne film, which quickly bored them. Sue was six and went into her bedroom to play with her dolls. Her brother Jeremy was eight and he liked movies that had more graphic action in them, such as a Rambo flick or something with that blond-haired guy who always did kung fu and karate on people's heads, that Chuck Norris guy. That was the kind of movie Daddy rented from the video store every now and then, and those old movies like they showed on regular TV just couldn't measure up in Jeremy's estimation. They didn't even have cussing in them.

Jeremy took one of his guns, a replica of an automatic like Rambo carried, and loaded it with a fresh roll of caps. Then he went out in the backyard to pretend he was one of the hard action men. He would be Chuck Norris, because with his blond hair he imagined he must look just like him.

The yard was small, since they lived in a double and were allowed to use only half of it, but it seemed big enough for a boy's war on imaginary enemies. He aimed at one of them and fired. The caps exploding made a very satisfying noise, and a Viet Cong guy toppled in the dust.

Alan yawned. He was having trouble becoming involved in the movie, since World War II didn't mean anything to him. He was only thirty-eight, so he hadn't even been born when the war was on. His old man had been in it and had often told him stories about the action he had seen, but it still left him cold.

No war meant much to him. He hadn't even gone to Vietnam, having lucked out with a high lottery number during the days of the draft. Of course, some of his friends had gone and some had even been killed, but it had been so long ago that even that part of it had little significance for him now.

He did wonder, though, how he would have done in Vietnam. It seemed, in some ways, he had never been able to prove himself as any kind of man. He was a small person, and though he had once or twice shown his mettle in a fight, there still seemed to be an emptiness where his masculinity should be. He went hunting with his friends occasionally and practiced shooting at Don's Guns about once a month, but handling guns didn't really make him feel as manly as he thought it should, either. Even his job was wimpy; he was a dispatcher for a trucking firm and didn't even flex his muscles. His hands were soft and uncalloused, like a woman's, and it was hard to get respect when you sat on your ass all day.

Maybe people would notice him and realize there was more to his personality if he bought himself a better car, something more powerful and impressive than the old Plymouth station wagon he drove to and from work. Maybe he could get a loan from the credit union for something sportier, like a red Fiero.

Yeah, it definitely had to be red. Something like that would be a real pussy wagon.

Sue sat on the floor of her room, frowning and holding a headless Barbie doll in her lap. All she had done was twist its head just a little to see what would happen, and it had come off in her hand. She was thoroughly disgusted. Nothing seemed to last very long.

She made several attempts to pop Barbie's head back on. Her face turned red and she pushed with all her strength, but the head refused to return to its body. Frustrated, Sue tore Barbie's wispy yellow hair out and threw her head and body across the room, where they landed next to a broken Teddy Ruxpin bear lying in the corner. Keeping the bear and Barbie company were a Ken doll with one leg, a chatty Kathy that couldn't talk any more, and a scattering of Smurf figures and Strawberry Shortcake dolls, all damaged in one way or another.

Sue went over to the window and looked out on her brother, who was obviously having a lot of fun. Boys had better toys. They had guns, and guns were much more fun than silly old dolls.

It wasn't right that she had only toys that broke every time she played with them. She wanted to have fun, too, and she was going to do something about it—right now. She stamped her feet and returned to the living room to confront her father.

"I want a gun!" she told him.

"What?" Alan shook his head. He had almost fallen asleep in the chair. "You're a girl. Girls don't play with guns. Now go back to your room until supper's ready."

"I want a gun now."

"Well, you ain't going to get one."

"I want a gun!" She took a big breath and held it.

"That ain't going to work on me. All it's going to get you is a spanking."

She continued to hold her breath. Her face was already purplish.

"I guess I got to show you I'm not fooling." He started to undo his belt.

Seeing her father was not going to be intimidated, Sue let out the breath. Then she grunted, turned around with a toss of her blond curls, and marched back to her room.

"I'm getting me a gun," she said, and threw herself up on the bed. "I'm getting me a gun, so I can be mean, too." Then she began to cry.

Alan quickly forgot the incident and went back to watching

the movie. He finished his beer and dozed off, the fumes of the frying chicken tickling his nose as his stomach growled.

Chuck Tripper made sure all the lights were out and locked the doors to the clubhouse. It was sundown and the park was officially closed to the public. He could go home.

It wasn't a bad job, working for the Department of Parks and Recreation, even on a day like today when people kept complaining about the chemical smell that had hung in the air all day. He had handled their complaints pretty well, he thought, telling the people the smell was coming from the plastic processing plant over in Beech Grove, though he didn't really believe that himself. His own eyes were burning, and he guessed it was because of the park being sprayed on Friday—probably to control mosquitoes.

He figured it was better to fib a little than complicate matters with a probable truth. Besides, he couldn't do anything about it, and the smell would go away after a couple of days.

His job didn't include handling complaints, anyhow. It didn't pay well enough. Chuck had hopes of landing something better and had applications in at the gas company, the Allison plant, and several other companies in the Indianapolis area that paid better wages, but so far he had heard nothing. He had read in the paper United Parcel Service was hiring, so he'd put an application in there some time next week, but he didn't really think anything would come of it. What did he have to offer a prospective employer? He had a strong back and a desire to work hard, but so did a lot of young men his age. You had to know somebody to get a good job if you were an unskilled laborer.

He had to admit it was his own fault he wasn't earning decent money. He should have learned a trade as his father had told him many times. But he hadn't listened to him when he was a kid, and now he was seeing what it meant not to have

91

real spending money. It meant having virtually nothing and no hope for the future.

He could enroll at IVY Tech or Lincoln Technical Institute and learn computers or something, if he could get the money up for the tuition. After all, he was only twenty-four; he wasn't too old to get an education. If he knew any kind of trade at all, he could move out of his parents' house and get a place of his own. He could even get a newer car, instead of driving around in that old rusted-old Oldsmobile his uncle had sold him. It was a beat-up junker with faded blue paint and one fender covered with gray primer, and he was ashamed to drive it.

Computers might not be that difficult. Some guys he went to high school with were in the computer field and they were no smarter than he was. It sure would beat being a welder, like his father was. Welding was hard work and didn't take any brains, though the money was good once you got in a union somewhere.

Welding or computers—it didn't matter. It would be some time before he could change his life. He just had to get by somehow and bide his time. He sighed and walked wearily toward the parking lot.

Chuck's shorts and short-sleeved shirt were uncomfortable now that the sun had gone down and it was no longer so hot. There was also a breeze coming through the trees that cooled his legs and made him wish he had brought a pair of trousers to change into. The breeze also brought with it more of that smell, which stung his eyes, and he quickened his pace.

Halfway to the lot, he heard something rustling in the bushes that lined the walk. He approached cautiously, since in Christian Park a person had to be ready for anything, especially in the evening. The surrounding neighborhood had more than its share of weirdos.

"Who's there?" he called. He heard a sound like water hitting the ground. He parted the leaves and saw a skinny, short old man standing there, urinating.

"Hey, I told you bums not to hang around here after dark."

The man looked about sixty. He was wearing a torn shirt, a ragged jacket that was evidently the top half of a suit, and baggy work trousers. In the twilight, the man and his clothing were virtually colorless.

"I ain't bothering nobody," he said in a voice garbled by phlegm. His stance was unsteady and he weaved back and forth as he continued to add to the urine that was pooling at his feet.

Chuck pinched his nose and turned away. "The park's closed. You have to get out of here."

"Can't a man piss in peace? Shit."

Chuck took out a handkerchief and dabbed his eyes. "Don't give me any trouble. Just finish your business and go home. That way, I won't have to call the law on you."

"Ain't got no home." The stream seemed to be diminishing, though the smell was not.

"That's not my problem. You can't stay in the park, that's all."

The man was finally finished. Chuck heard him zip his fly. "What the hell is it to you, boy?"

"I work here. I'm in charge." He was growing impatient. He hated dealing with drunks.

"Hell, I ain't going to hurt your damn old park."

"Look, I can have the fuzz here faster than you can get away. So why don't you give me a break and take off?"

He mumbled a few obscenities and staggered out from behind the bush. "Okay, I'm leaving. I don't like it here noway. Smells like a big fart been let."

"Well, it doesn't smell any better with you around."

The man's eyes grew wide and he snorted like an animal. "Insults! You snotty-nose asshole. I can beat your ass. C'mon, I'll take you any day of the fucking week." The old man put up his fists and swung at Chuck. He missed by several feet.

"Hold off, old dude!" Chuck said, smirking. He put his hands on his hips and shook his head.

"Take them insults back." He swung again.

Chuck flinched involuntarily. The man's breath was fouling

the air and threatened more harm than his fists. "All right. All right. I take it all back."

Apparently appeased, the man dropped back and let his arms fall to his sides. "You better. Fucking yim-yam, snotty-nose whistledick. Fucking kid with no hair on your chin. No fucking balls, neither. You chickenshit."

"Look, I took it back. I'm sorry I said it. I'm sorry you don't have a home, but you've got to leave the park. That's a rule. Do you understand that?"

"Sure. I ain't no fucking moron."

"Good." Chuck pointed to the street. "Now you go on over there and take off."

"Where am I going?" He started swaying and looked as if he might fall over.

"I don't know. I don't care, either. Just leave. I have to go home." He started to touch the man to get him moving, then hastily withdrew his hand.

The man seemed startled. "Don't you touch me! I'm going! Ain't no need to hit me."

"I'm not going to hit you. See? I'm getting out of your way." He crossed his arms and waited.

"I'm going. By Jesus, I am." He picked up his feet slowly, then shuffled toward the street. "I'll get out of your way so you can go home, little boy. I can tell when I ain't wanted. Whole fucking park smells like shit, anyhow. I don't want to stay around here and . . ."

His voice trailed off abruptly.

Chuck accompanied the man till they were both by the parking lot. Then Chuck turned off and went to stand by his car while the old man continued toward the street. He watched until he was out of sight down the street. "Have a good evening," he yelled.

"Fuck you!" he heard the old man shout from the shadows.

Chuck shook his head sadly and climbed into the car. "Jesus, I need a better job," he said. Then he started the engine and drove away.

After the car was gone, the old man cut back through the trees and returned to the park, a defiant smile on his wrinkled, sallow face. He sprawled on the first bench he found and curled up, falling asleep almost immediately.

Alan Bundy dreamed he was John Wayne. At first it seemed he was black-and-white, just like in an old movie, but then the color sort of bled back into everything.

He was still John Wayne, though, and he had to go looking for Nips. Funny, he never realized before that Japanese were outside the house. Fortunately, he was prepared for them.

Careful not to disturb Faith, Alan rose from the bed and got dressed. A man couldn't win the war in his pajamas. He went out into the hall and turned on the lights. At the end of the hall was a metal cabinet where he kept his gun collection. He reached in his pocket for his keys and found the one to the padlock on the cabinet. He unlatched it and opened the doors. Which weapon should he choose? What would be most effective against the onslaught from the Orient?

A long wailing roar sounded overhead, somewhere outside. Then there was machine-gun fire. The dirty bastards were strafing the house! He threw himself to the floor and huddled behind one of the metal doors.

The strafing started again. It was a Jap Zero. They must be attacking Indianapolis. Why would the Japs want Indy? Unless—that was it—they were after RCA! If they got RCA, everyone would have to buy nothing but Japanese TVs, because there wouldn't be any American ones left.

He heard explosions in the street outside. They were dropping bombs. Goddamn it! Why did he have to live so close to RCA? The plant was just a couple of blocks over, on Sherman. If they got RCA, they'd get the whole damn neighborhood.

Another plane went over so damn close he could hear the pilot cussing in Japanese.

Where were the rest of his men? Where were John Agar,

Forrest Tucker, and Richard Jaeckel? Where the hell was Arthur Franz? Had they all chickened out on him?

The planes strafed again. He could hear chunks of pavement flying up as they ripped the street.

Alan almost wet his pants, but he felt his bladder straining just in time and was able to hold it.

Suddenly he realized how cowardly he must appear, hiding behind the cabinet door. A man didn't do that. A man stood up and fought, and he was more than a man. He was John Fucking Wayne and John Wayne didn't run from a fight.

His courage restored, Alan jumped up from behind the cabinet door, reached in, and grabbed the first weapon he touched. It was a snub-nosed Smith and Wesson .38, one of his older pieces. It would have to do, because he didn't have time to be picky. He loaded the weapon quickly, racing against time as the house was strafed again and again. The Japanese weren't going to let up—unless he did something to stop them.

With his pistol loaded and cocked, Alan dashed into the living room, grabbed his camouflage cap off the closet shelf, and ran out the front door into the street.

But the Japanese were gone.

At ten-thirty that night, Teddy Cobb and his girlfriend Debbie unrolled a blanket between two trees behind the clubhouse.

Teddy was seventeen, a tall, gangly youth with brown hair and blue eyes. He smelled of his father's English Leather aftershave and had Scope mouthwash on his breath. He was wearing Nike athletic shoes, white socks, a black muscle shirt, and faded cutoffs. In anticipation of the possible outcome of the evening, he wasn't wearing any underwear.

Debbie had a round pale face set with blue-green eyes, framed by short red hair. She was fifteen and only five-feet-three. Her breasts were large in proportion to the rest of her, which caused her some embarrassment and attracted too much attention. She smelled of Charlie cologne, rose-scented talc, and lipstick. She was wearing lavender L.A. Gear shoes, a pastel blue T-shirt with matching shorts, and white underwear. She clutched a small vinyl handbag in her right hand.

Teddy plopped down on the blanket and patted the space next to him. "Come on, Debbie."

She joined him with some hesitation. "Teddy, I just know we're going to get caught." She set her handbag in between them to form a kind of barrier.

"No, we're not. Nobody comes around here much at night."

"But it's kind of scary. And I'm getting hay fever. My nose is already running."

"Chill out, Deb. I'll take care of you." He moved the handbag out of the way and scooted next to her, wrapping his arm around her as he did. "It's a nice night. We don't want to waste it." He let his hand drift to her right breast, which he squeezed lightly.

She shivered in response. "Don't do that," she said without much conviction. She didn't attempt to move his hand.

"You let me do it before." He kissed her on the cheek.

"That was different. It was in the living room, and—"

"I know, you didn't worry about going all the way with your folks upstairs." His voice wasn't quite angry, but there was a definite edge in it.

"Well, I—" She turned her face from him, just as he was about to kiss her on the lips.

Now he was angry. He withdrew his arm and moved away from her. "That's it, isn't it? You didn't even mean to go all the way with me. You're just—you're just a prickteaser!"

"Don't use language like that around me!" She was genuinely outraged and tempted to slap him.

Teddy sighed. He hadn't meant to use such words, but his frustration was talking, not his reason. He had to use a different approach with a girl like Debbie. She was nicer than most of the others he had been out with. Being rough with her was not going to work. A guy had to show her some respect.

"I'm sorry," he said as he searched for other strategies in

his mind. He pretended to sulk and fell silent for several seconds, during which he could hear Debbie's breathing; it was becoming heavier. She wanted to go all the way as much as he did. He was sure of that. It was just that she needed persuading. Finally, he thought of what to do and cursed himself for not thinking of it sooner. It was so obvious.

"Debbie," he whispered.

"What?"

"I thought you loved me."

"Well, maybe I do."

"That's not what you said before."

"Okay, I guess I do."

Teddy repressed a grin. *Love* was the magic word, after all. "And you said you'd ... you know. If you love a guy, you should go all the way with him."

Her reply was breathless, but he could tell it was honest. "I'm scared to."

"You shouldn't be scared. I won't hurt you." He moved close to her again.

"That's not it. I'm not scared of you. It's just that you'll tell the other boys and soon everybody will know all about it."

He was about to touch her breast again. "I wouldn't do that," he said, evidently surprised. "You should know me better than that."

"That isn't what Linda said."

"Linda!"

"She said you did it to her and then you told that nasty Billy Weaver, and he tried to get her to do it, too."

"That's a bunch of lies and bullshit. I never did it with her." He blushed in spite of himself, recalling that time with Linda after the church picnic. He never dreamed she'd actually talk to other girls about it. Guys bragged, but he thought women kept their sexual adventures to themselves.

"She's just jealous," he said, "that's all. She's jealous of you and me being together."

If Debbie knew he was lying, she chose to ignore it. She had even forgotten she brought the matter up as she inhaled the musky-sweet smell of his after-shave. "I've never done it with anyone at all."

"I know, because you're saving it for the right boy." He tried to say it gently. He had to contain his anger if he was going to get anywhere with her.

"How am I supposed to know if you're the right one?"

He leaned over and pressed his lips against hers, thrusting his tongue in. She resisted at first, then parted her lips and let him go deeper. He kissed her like that for as long as he could, and when he finally broke away he could see she was flushed and could barely get her breath.

"See?" he said. "I *am* the right boy." When she didn't reply, he kissed her again, sliding his hand down the soft curve of her stomach at the same time. He drew his fingertips across her flesh, lingered briefly at the waistband of her shorts, then shoved his hand in slowly. His whole body tingled when his fingers brushed the edge of her pubic hair. He pulled the blanket up over them, although there was no one around to see.

"C'mon, Debbie."

"I don't know . . ."

He reached further down, touching her with growing urgency. "I am the right boy," he said between kisses. "I am. I am."

Debbie must have agreed, for she started helping him.

Sue Bundy dreamed she had a gun of her own. It wasn't as much fun as she thought it would be, though. The trigger was real hard to squeeze.

She went into the bedroom to show it to Daddy.

There were monsters in the park. The old man could hear them talking in the distance. And since they were talking, they couldn't be bats or giant rats like he usually saw. No, these

99

were people monsters, and they were making plans to kill him. They would succeed, too, unless he did something to defend himself.

He rolled off the bench and stood up on shaky legs. "God-damn monsters, everywhere you go." He reached in his back pocket for the whiskey flask and brought it out. He unscrewed the cap and took a short swallow. There wasn't much in the flask and he wanted to conserve it until he could get the money to buy more. The liquid burning his throat fired him with the courage he needed to fight the monsters.

He walked, somewhat bowlegged, toward the sounds the monsters were making. He kept wondering how he could subdue the monsters. What if they were bigger than he was? They might try to eat him.

He had almost been eaten once. It was that time he had encountered a rat that was six feet tall. He'd also seen a bat with wings that stretched wider than a Buick. People monsters might be even bigger!

He shuddered at that thought and took another swallow of courage from his precious reserve. Then he realized he was a people, too, so a people monster couldn't be much bigger. That made sense, didn't it? Of course it did. All he needed was a big old rock.

There were plenty of rocks lining the walk to the water fountain. If he could lift one of those, it would be an effective weapon. He ambled to the edge of the walk, bent down, and tugged at one of the large stones. It took some straining, but he managed to wrench a stone loose. He carried it with both hands to the place the sounds were coming from.

He was sweating with the effort of walking and carrying the stone, but he couldn't retreat now. He was almost upon them.

He stepped as lightly as he could, hoping they wouldn't hear his labored breathing.

There were no voices now; only the sounds of grunting and moaning. He thought he heard one of them say, "You're hurting me!" in an almost childlike, high-pitched voice. One of the monsters hurting the other?

He found them behind the clubhouse. It was very black back there, but he could make out the vague outline of the weird form lying on the ground, writhing and squirming. It was a horrible sight to behold.

He crept up on them cautiously, working the stone up over his head, then holding it high above him.

The people monsters didn't seem to notice him.

In fact, there was only one ... and ... Good God! It was a thing with two heads!

It had to be killed.

He brought the stone down on the heads, first one, then the other, as quickly as he could before it could react. He smashed and smashed until the heads were a big smear of nothing and the loathsome body stopped moving. Then he threw the rock away.

He bent over, hands on his knees, to inspect the monsters. They were unmoving. They had to be dead. He straightened up to listen. There were no more monster sounds.

Even so, he decided to run.

Daddy didn't like it when Sue showed him the gun. And when it went off, it hurt him, and Mommy, too. It made her ears hurt, too, and it made her cry.

It was such a terrible dream. The only thing that was good about it was that there were no monsters in it. But dead people were scary, too. Especially when they looked like Mommy and Daddy.

After the shooting part, the dream got kind of silly. Jeremy came running into the room. He yelled at her and tried to take the gun away from her, but she didn't want him to have it. It was hers and he had plenty of his own.

The gun made a big hole in Jeremy.

It wasn't much fun being so mean, even in a dream like this

one. So Sue dropped the gun and went back to her bedroom. When she got there, she went over and picked the headless Barbie out of the pile of hurt toys and took her to bed with her. A Barbie with no head was better than no Barbie at all.

She cried for a while, until the sleep-man came. Then there were no more bad dreams that night.

Monday morning, Chuck Tripper found quite a mess behind the clubhouse in Christian Park. Actually, a stray dog had found the mess and Chuck only went after him when he whimpered and whined.

Chuck had never seen naked dead people before. In fact, he had never seen anyone dead except in the movies, and that wasn't real.

At least in the movies you could get up and leave if things got too gross.

Ten. Marital Bliss

Carl Nolan had often considered another woman as an answer to his marital problems. He had even pondered how he might go about finding another woman. In his line of work, there were opportunities for women, and he could create additional opportunities by merely saying he had to work late on a case. But, even though there was the potential for bringing a new woman into his life, he wasn't usually attracted to other women that much.

It was simply that Laura had spoiled him for other women. Not because she was better than any other woman he could imagine, but because she was worse. Whenever a woman seemed attractive to him or she seemed attracted to him, he had only to conjure up the hell that was his married life and he turned cold. He didn't want to repeat the same mistake he had made with Laura. Life was too short.

Yet he was still a human being, and a human being needed something in his life, something beyond physical love, though even unadorned physical satisfaction would be more than he was getting now—which was basically nothing. Sex was a necessity for a man, but he had learned that sex alone meant little, especially at his age, when the magic surrounding sex was what really aroused him. By the time a person turned forty, he had participated in enough sexual acts to know it was the mind that made the difference in sex, not the gonads. The human male needed sexual interaction with the human female, but he also needed much more.

He longed for the touch of another person who would attempt to understand him, who would be there when he needed her, who would share in his life and not be only a bystander who happened to live in the same house. Sex with such a person would be a magical thing, not a dull duty.

Maybe that type of person was hard to find; maybe there wasn't such a person in the world for Carl Nolan. In any case, he knew it wasn't Laura.

Laura didn't love him. Not now. Perhaps not ever. He and she were essentially disparate partners in a relationship of convenience. They coexisted as husband and wife, and that was about it.

It had taken Carl years to admit he wanted, even needed, love, and now that he realized it was a true human need, that even the toughest man might benefit from it, he despaired of ever finding it, inside or outside of marriage.

He couldn't believe that everyone lived in a hell such as his; surely there were marriages—relationships—where love—and satisfactory sex—flourished. Why were these things denied to him?

He lay awake in his bed, staring at the ceiling in the dark, pondering his needs and his lacks. He glanced at the clock radio. It was almost two in the morning, and he wasn't sleepy yet. His legs ached and he couldn't get comfortable no matter what position he assumed.

He looked over at Laura. It was ironic that they still slept together—or at least slept in the same bed. Of course, it was a matter of routine more than anything. Their cohabitation was a vestige of their former relationship, a charade of the apparent love they had shared when they were first married, when it was possible for a person to convince himself—and herself—that physical attraction automatically translated into a semblance of everlasting love.

The moonlight coming in the room from the window opposite the bed rendered Laura's features in stark outline, emphasizing the small wrinkles around her eyes and mouth. The texture of her skin appeared harsh and rough, and suddenly she seemed old and undesirable. It was hard to believe she was actually younger than he was. That sloppy nightgown she was wearing didn't add much to her allure, either.

But she was a person underneath those features. She had to have human feelings. She couldn't really be as cold and heartless as she seemed sometimes. Could she?

Why couldn't they get together? Why couldn't they communicate? Why did it always have to be hell for them?

He went over their frequent arguments in his mind. In retrospect, they always seemed so trivial, though when they were in the middle of them they were deadly serious. Like the other day when they had argued over her having the lawn sprayed. There was nothing wrong with that per se, but her ordering it done without consulting him had made him feel like his opinion meant nothing to her. Maybe he would have agreed to it if only she had approached him. That way they could have worked out how to pay for it without going into debt any further. That was logical. Why couldn't she do things that way? Was it because she always assumed he would say no?

And, of course, he usually did. So that meant he was just as guilty as she in creating the argument situations. It took two to tango.

Even so, she could have asked. That wasn't so difficult, was it? She could at least have given him a chance to say yes.

But she never did.

Their relationship seemed hopeless.

Carl turned on his side, deliberately thrashing to disturb her, in the hopes she would wake up and be pissed off.

Let her be pissed off, then! Let her wake up!

There were lots of women in the world. Women who wouldn't mind being awakened by a man like him. Like Dr. Turner. Like *Marian* Turner. She was intelligent and desirable, the type of woman he wished he had known in his younger years, before he had met Laura and settled for her.

He willed himself not to think of her. He had reality lying next to him, and it was the only reality he had.

Laura stirred and the rate of her breathing changed. She sighed drowsily.

He sensed she was awake, and now that he had accomplished her awakening, he drew into himself and pretended to be asleep. He regulated his breathing, in and out, like the most sound-asleep person in the world.

Laura turned on her side. Her left arm came over his waist and reached down to pull at his penis tentatively. A chill went through him. She hadn't touched him like that in weeks.

"Carl . . ."

He stiffened, trying to make his body a stone, an unfeeling rock. *I'm asleep!* he cried mentally. *Leave me alone.*

She pulled at him again. "Carl, honey. You awake?"

Honey?

Her fingers were cold, but they became warm quickly enough.

It was unusual for her to want to make up so soon. Usually she carried a grudge for a couple of weeks, to the point of absurdity. Her sudden decision to come on to him in the middle of the night unnerved him. He felt too defenseless.

But he wasn't going to let it work, not matter how horny he might be.

And he was definitely horny. He could feel himself responding to her touch, getting hard, despite his mental lack of desire. He might not relish making love to her, but his physiology was warming to the idea.

"Carl, let's make up. I don't like to stay mad at you."

"Since when?" He growled with what he considered sufficient menace. Didn't she get the hint?

"You are awake! I knew it."

Of course, all he had to do was to move her hand.

"Come on, Carl, baby. Don't torture me like this. I want to make up, and you're being mean about it."

106

She pressed closer to him, her breasts like two warm loaves against his neck, enticing him. She kissed the back of his neck and nibbled at his ear. It was becoming difficult to even think about taking her hand away now.

He tried to shrug her off.

"Carl, honey." She stroked him and part of him was no longer pretending to be a rock. It *was* a rock.

She maneuvered her head over his shoulder, kissing his cheek as she went. Her breath stank of stale cigarette smoke and he felt a lurching in his stomach. He winced.

But, damn it, he wanted it, too. He needed it.

Christ, no! I don't want to, not with her, not ever again!

"Laura, I . . ." He turned over as she slid her hand away, and before he knew what was happening, he was touching her. She was wet and hot.

But he felt stifled.

Goddamn dick thinks it's in charge. The stifling feeling went away, and he mounted her and let his horny condition take care of itself, though he felt that on some higher plane he was not involved in this act, which was not an act of love at all, but only an act of needful physical release. He could do it, but he resolved to stay angry.

"That's my Carl. That's my baby. Keep going, honey. . . ." Her words burned in his ears, feeding his anger, and he thrust harder, realizing he was suddenly using himself as a weapon, in protest against being forced. He kept his eyes closed and tried not to breathe, tried not to smell her nicotine breath, the traces of pancake makeup on her skin, her hair oil.

Yet even though he knew it was Laura underneath him, it didn't seem like her. She was counter-thrusting just as violently as he was thrusting. That wasn't the way Laura made love. It didn't even begin to resemble the parody of sex they normally had. She was acting more passionate than she had ever been in their entire married life. Maybe it wasn't an act.

No matter what was driving her, it wasn't quite right, and for some reason, that scared him.

She grunted and moaned. They actually came together. Then he rolled off her.

As they both lay there gasping, it seemed something awful had just happened.

Tears were coming to Carl's eyes, and he realized it was because he felt both betrayed and felt he had betrayed someone. He had betrayed Marian and that was stupid, because she meant nothing to him and he certainly meant nothing to her.

Yet the feeling was there. After all, he had been thinking of Marian when he came.

A wisp of smoke curled under Carl's nostrils. He wrinkled his nose and sniffed. Laura was having an after-sex cigarette.

"That was nice," she murmured between puffs. "It can be so good when you want it to."

His eyes still stung from his tears. He mumbled something deliberately unintelligible, which he hoped she would take as a criticism of her smoking.

She ignored his hint. When she inhaled, the tip of the cigarette illuminated her face eerily, making it appear like a painted mask lit by an orange spotlight. She seemed uglier than she had in the moonlight.

"Why do we have to fight?" she asked pleasantly.

Again, that wasn't like her. She should have been satisfied with the forced sex. Did he have to talk to her, too?

"I don't know," he said.

"It's just damn money."

"That's usually enough."

"Money problems can be solved." She reached over to smash her cigarette out in the ashtray on the nightstand. "Any problem can be solved if two people put their minds to it. Even a marriage problem."

"What do you mean?"

"Well, I've been thinking. If you want, we could go to a marriage counselor or someone like that and go over things.

We could straighten our marriage out. We don't have to go on like this."

"You must be dreaming."

"Don't be so cynical."

"I'm not being cynical. I just don't see how we can patch things up—after what we've been through." He tried to sound like he was grumbling but realized he was sounding reasonable in spite of himself.

"But, honey, we can't go on like this forever. Can we?"

"No, I guess not, but . . . well, what did you have in mind?"

"I'll call someone and set up an appointment for us. Unless you'd prefer to do it."

"No, I don't have the time." He turned on his side as a signal that he was through talking.

He expected that to start an argument; instead, she continued talking in a conciliatory tone of voice. "Okay. I'll do it. I'll ask around. We have too much invested in this marriage to let it fall apart."

"I don't know if it can be saved."

"Sure it can. Two people can't love each other like we do—like we just did—and just give it all up so easily. I mean, that doesn't make any sense."

"Whatever you say. I'll do what you want to do. Okay?"

"Good. I knew you wanted it that way, just like I do."

She gave him a sloppy kiss on the neck, which made his stomach turn again. He tried to ignore the feeling, but it burned within him, festering like an ulcer.

"We're going to"—she yawned mightily—"live happily ever after."

Sure, kid, sure.

When he was certain Laura was asleep, Carl put his pajamas on and went downstairs to think. He no longer felt betrayed; he was beyond that and into the guilties, and he didn't much like it.

A goddamn marriage counselor! And he had agreed.

There was no way of getting out of this mess now. He was chained to Laura forever. It was a difficult commitment to resign himself to, but he didn't see what other choice he had. If he objected, he would seem unreasonable and vindictive.

There was nothing to do for the moment but blank the events of this night from his mind, with the hope that maybe they would go away if he ignored them.

He turned the TV on with the volume low and stretched out on the couch. He flipped through all thirty-six channels on cable three times before settling on an ancient rerun of *The Odd Couple* on Channel 9. He fell asleep in the middle of the show.

"What the hell is this?"

A screaming in his ear. He stirred uneasily.

"What?" Where was he? Shit, he remembered now. The couch. That was a mistake. He should have . . .

"I'm not good enough to sleep with! Is that it? Is it?"

He sat up and peered over the back of the couch. Laura was standing right behind him. She squinted at him in a pose of irate righteousness, the effect of which was minimized by the way she looked. Her hair was frizzed out, and her makeup was smeared. Her near nudity didn't contribute much, either; she was dressed only in panties and her breasts shook absurdly when she screamed again.

"You son of a bitch! Get off that couch."

He stood up. "Christ, what time is it?"

"None of your damn business. I want to know why you're sleeping on the couch. What the hell did I do to you to deserve this—this insult?"

"I wasn't insulting you," he said, his throat thick with morning mucus. "I couldn't sleep after last night, so I came down to watch TV. I didn't want to disturb you."

"What do you mean *after last night?* What happened to keep you up?"

110

He shook his head, unbelieving. "You know, after we made it." He tried to think of something plausible. "I was overstimulated."

"*I* didn't overstimulate you."

"Sure you did. We had sex last night. Remember?" He smiled wanly. "It was good, too. The best."

She moved slightly and the bright morning sun streaming in through the picture window radiated from behind her. Carl shielded his eyes. She looked like a grotesque statue in the sunlight.

"You're out of your goddamn mind, Carl. You must have been having a wet dream."

"But, Laura . . ."

"Don't Laura me."

"Now, goddamn it, we did it last night and then we talked for a long time. I know you weren't asleep. You started it."

"I didn't start anything. You must have been whacking off."

"Laura!" He had never heard her say anything so coarse—at least not when she was sober.

"That's what you were doing—jacking off and thinking of some other woman. Then you try to tell me—"

"Listen, you said you wanted to patch things up. I remember every word. You said you'd call a marriage counselor and we'd get our lives back together. Surely you haven't forgotten *everything?*"

He stared at her in wonder. Her eyes were glassy and for a moment her face showed self-doubt, then her features contorted into a cruel expression that was a combination of amusement and sadistic indulgence.

"Oh, that's pretty funny, Carl. Pretty fucking funny!" She laughed harshly. "We're going to put this piece-of-shit marriage back together just like that. That's the funniest thing I ever heard!" She laughed uncontrollably, until she started coughing. "Fuck and make up. Fuck and save the marriage." She hacked and wheezed. "That's all it takes, isn't it? What

111

a—" She doubled over in apparent pain, turned, and ran into the kitchen.

Carl followed her. When he came in the room her head was over the sink and she was dry-heaving.

"Laura, can I do anything?"

She stopped briefly, then looked back at him, her face blotchy. "You can go fuck yourself, Carl. Leave me alone." She returned to the sink.

"But," he began lamely, "I thought . . . you wanted to . . ." He stepped toward her, thinking to placate her, then halted. There would be no reasoning with her this morning. Her hateful mood obviated any further negotiation.

She continued heaving, though nothing was coming up. "Go away . . . let me die in peace!"

Carl knew when he was defeated. He turned and went back through the house to the stairs. There wasn't much left for him to do but leave and kill time until he went into work. Just as he always did after their arguments.

He went up, took a shower, and dressed for work. He felt disoriented. It was as if his special hell had taken on new, disturbing dimensions. Laura wasn't herself. She had turned into a different kind of bitch from the one he was accustomed to. Before, she had at least been predictable.

But the argument this morning was different. Laura wasn't just being contrary; she really didn't remember last night at all. Because even she didn't deny something so *un*deniable just for the sake of being difficult.

Her denial went deeper than mere argument. She actually believed nothing had happened, and Carl sensed that was a symptom of a profound change in her.

It was a change he wasn't sure he could handle.

Eleven. Matters of Law

Being in jail wasn't as bad as William Myers imagined it would be.

He didn't have his freedom, but lack of freedom wasn't the worst thing that could happen to a person. In jail, he was fed regularly and no one bothered him, and that was a freedom of sorts. Being free of people was almost a kind of vacation from the world. He didn't have to worry about business, or social pressures, or much of anything.

The main thing that bothered him when he was first locked in his cell was having to go to the bathroom out in the open, where the other prisoners could see him. It had taken him several days to get used to that, but when he realized the other inmates had to do the same thing, he found himself suddenly without false modesty. Besides, nature wouldn't let him go forever without taking care of his daily business. No one else seemed to care that he had to go the bathroom in "public," so why should he?

He wasn't wasting his time in jail, either. He was catching up on his reading. His lawyer brought him paperbacks, and a variety of magazines was available. As a result he was up on current fiction and world events—more than he had been in years.

He should have felt good about his new enlightenment, but something was missing. Now that he knew what was going on in the world, he had no one with whom to share his knowledge, and when he reflected on that sad fact, he was compelled to remember why: He had no family.

Someone had killed them all.

Well, not all, only his immediate family. There was his brother in Cincinnati and his sister who lived in town, but for some reason they refused to talk to him. His lawyer said they wanted nothing to do with him.

They acted as if it was his fault his family had been killed.

That was one of the strange things about being in jail. He was here because the police said *he* killed his family. That didn't make any sense, but if that was the reason he was in, there wasn't much he could do about it. That was the lawyer's concern, not his.

After all, it was bad enough his family was gone. Wasn't it? He saw no reason for them to implicate him in the crime. What was that supposed to accomplish?

Of course, he realized he would have to face trial eventually. That's why they put people in jail, to hold them until the judge and jury had their say. But he could handle that. After all, he was innocent. He was confident the authorities would find the guilty parties before he was tried. Then they would let him go, and he'd really be free. He would start a new life as an enlightened person without personal encumbrances.

Without a family, that is.

That was another strange thing. He didn't seem to care that much about his family having been killed. He wanted to care—or at least he knew he *should* care—but he just didn't. Maybe that was why they were accusing him, though he didn't know they could punish a person because he didn't show the proper emotions.

It wasn't his fault.

Talking to his lawyer made him very uneasy, though, because it didn't take him long to discover the attorney thought he was responsible for what had happened, too. In fact, the lawyer almost refused to represent him—unless he admitted his guilt. William realized the best thing to do was to play along and tell the lawyer what he wanted to hear. So he told him about blue capsules and nightmares and doctors and sleep clinics, but he was making it all up for the lawyer's benefit, even if it seemed awfully real when he was telling it.

Well, maybe it wasn't all pretending. Actually, when he talked about those things it seemed like it was a different person talking—another William Myers that just happened to live in the same skin with him. It was a fascinating experience, but he understood it was only part of an elaborate game he was playing with the attorney and the legal system. Perhaps it was a game designed for his own amusement. It was difficult to say what its ultimate purpose was. And it didn't matter, as long as he was basically left alone.

That was all he had ever wanted in life.

Besides, he'd have his day in court, and the truth would come out. He'd deny what that other Myers said and tell what had really happened, which wasn't his fault at all.

In the meantime, being in jail got better and better. He didn't even have the awful dreams anymore—those horrid nightmares where things went backward and forward and all over the place, and he seemed to do terrible things.

He could barely remember ever having them.

Marian was glad to leave the confinement of the classroom and be out on the road. That morning she had risen early to give her class in Abnormal Psychology their final exams, and by noon she was feeling strung out, paranoid, and claustrophobic. She desperately needed a break before starting to grade all those final test papers, though she wasn't really looking forward to talking to Victor Cross.

Cross was William Myers's attorney, and there was something about the man that offended her sensibilities—even over the phone. He had an ingratiating, unctuous manner that seemed designed to hide the type of underlying smart-assed attitude Marian abhorred in any man—and especially in a lawyer.

But she wanted to help Myers as much as possible, if she could manage it without getting into trouble herself. Maybe if she told Cross the right things, she wouldn't have to be involved at all.

Cross kept his offices on the northeast side, on 82nd Street, close to the Geist Reservoir area, a trendy section of the city where young people with money lived. His office was located in a six-story building surrounded by three other buildings that were mirror images; they seemed to be all glass with very little steel or concrete showing, the kind of ultra-modern structures that gave progress a bad name.

Marian pulled her Omni into the spacious lot south of Building B, where Cross's office was, and had no trouble finding a parking space. It was the middle of the day and the middle of the week, and there weren't that many people out. She hadn't even noticed very many shoppers parked over in Castleton Square, the giant mall across the street. Usually their cars clogged every street in the area for blocks in all directions.

She locked the car, though the only stealable things were her students' blue books, and went up to the building's revolving doors in a quick, worried pace. She was dressed conservatively, which for her meant a light beige suit and white blouse, with a blue paisley tie at her collar. The outfit was uncomfortable for such a warm day, but she thought it put forth the proper image of a professional woman. She wanted the attorney to think she was all business and no fluff, so he would have no suspicions she harbored any secrets.

She paused at the building directory to check the location of Cross's office, then entered the elevator and rode up to the fifth floor. His office was down the end of a long corridor, and as she walked along, she passed the doors of other attorneys, a loan company, a charity organization, and a market research firm. She saw no other people. Indianapolis didn't seem to be doing much business today.

She pushed the door open into Cross's office and was greeted by an older woman who was sitting behind the desk typing on an IBM Selectric that looked like it was twenty years old. Marian

116

stated her business, then sat down on one of the four chairs in the outer office and halfheartedly scanned a *People* magazine while she waited. The chair was hard and uncomfortable, and she thought her ass would go to sleep if the man didn't call her in soon. It would be difficult to think clearly with a numb posterior.

After a few seconds, Marian laid the magazine aside and stared out the picture window behind the secretary at the Castleton Square shopping center complex, which stretched across the landscape like a vast military camp. Having shopped there before, she felt that was an apt comparison; it was so crowded and the traffic so heavy that going there was like going to war. At the very least it was a formidable challenge, especially on the weekends, and at Christmas time only the most intrepid shoppers dared go there. Marian didn't count herself among such foolhardy souls, especially with her hatred of traffic of any kind.

After ten minutes, Victor Cross came out to greet her. He was probably in his forties, but he had a round baby face that made him appear much younger. His hair was light brown and his eyes very dark and small. He was an inch shorter than Marian and carried about fifty extra pounds on his medium frame. He wore no jacket and his shirt sleeves were rolled up to the elbow, though his tie was securely in place. He looked well fed, confident, and smug.

"Come on in, Dr. Turner." His voice was even more unnerving in person. Perhaps it was effective when dealing with juries, though. They might acquit a man just to get Cross to shut up.

Marian stood up and followed him into the office, pausing briefly to stretch her legs and relax the muscles of her rear end. Once inside, they made the necessary greetings, during which it was established she should call him Vic, but Marian did not offer the free usage of her own first name. When they shook hands she noticed he wore several gold rings, including one with a black cat's-eye sapphire set in diamonds.

The upholstered chair he asked her to sit in was at least somewhat comfortable, and Marian was inclined to rest easier. Then she became conscious of letting her guard down and de-

117

liberately tensed her muscles. She had to be alert—in control of the situation. Cross was a lawyer, and lawyers were slick characters. Everything about him—his dress, his office—was designed to manipulate people, though the environment wasn't as conducive to people games as John Morton's was. Nor was it as expensively appointed as Morton's office.

Marian made a brief survey of the trappings of Cross's profession: walnut desk, fancy wall coverings, expensive wooden bookcases full of law books, brass statuettes of jungle animals. Cross apparently did well for himself, even if he forced his secretary to work on an antiquated typewriter (he probably underpaid the poor woman, too), when surely everyone in the world had word processors by now. No doubt he drove a Mercedes or another ostentatious car.

"Would you like some coffee or a soft drink?" He sat across from her, almost reclining in a big high-backed leather chair. He seemed rather nonchalant.

Her mouth was dry, but she was afraid accepting anything from him might obligate her somehow. "Not really."

"We can get you just about anything. Coke, Pepsi, Dr. Pepper. Pam will be glad to—"

"No." Mustn't get any more relaxed, she thought. Be very businesslike. "I have things to do, Mr. Cross." She couldn't bring herself to call him Vic; the nickname just didn't seem to go with the person who wore it. "Let's get down to it."

She knew it would be easy to compromise herself in this situation, if she weren't careful. As for the possible damage to Shodale, Morton, or Richards, she would worry about them only if it was absolutely necessary.

He smiled easily. "Of course. I appreciate your frankness. No use beating about the bush, is there? It's about my client, William Myers, as you know. I was wondering what you could do to help me defend him."

"I don't know that I can do anything."

"I think there might be a great deal you can do. You can start by telling me what you've told the police."

118

She sighed relief. This was something she could handle easily enough. "Not much. I don't know much."

"Well, tell me anyway."

"I told them Myers was a sleep subject. He had awful nightmares, and our ultimate goal was to help him learn to control them, by therapy and—"

"Excuse me for interrupting, but how do you define therapy in a case like this?"

"Psychotherapy primarily. I was trying to show him he could control his dreams, if he learned to accept them. That's the bare bones of it, anyhow. Of course, he needed to get in touch with some of the feelings that were making him have the dreams."

"How did that relate to your research?"

"We're studying dreams and nightmares for—" She hesitated, unsure what she would reveal if she continued, or how the attorney could use it.

"I think I know. You're studying them for ultimate control by drugs."

"Yes." That seemed noncommittal enough. It was no secret Shodale was in the drug business.

"Doesn't that contradict what you're doing in the psychotherapy?"

"Not at all. The drugs are merely a way of making the subject comfortable until he can control the nightmares on his own."

"That's interesting," Cross said, a strange little smirk on his lips.

"What?" she asked guardedly.

"You call your patients 'subjects.' Why is that?"

"That's what they are. I don't have any patients."

"You don't consider Myers a former patient?"

"No, of course not. I wasn't his physician, if that's what you mean."

"But you counseled him in a patient-doctor relationship."

119

"No, I didn't. I advised him as a psychologist in a research program."

"That's all?"

"Well, of course, I got to know a little about him. We'd been seeing him for about six weeks."

"But you say you didn't treat him?"

"No." She was squirming inside, but she was determined not to let Cross see her discomfort or use it to her disadvantage.

Cross glanced at some notes in a file folder on his desk. "So your relationship to the patient—I mean, subject—my client, was for research only. Is that right?"

"Yes."

"You only wanted to observe his behavior and study his nightmares?"

"Basically that's correct."

"What about Myers's nightmares was different from those of any other subject—or any other person for that matter?"

Marian paused to ponder that question. There didn't seem to be any hidden meaning in it, so she answered, "His nightmares were the worst of the lot at the time. Of course, you realize that's a subjective judgment."

"Would you call them uncontrollable?"

"No. There's no such thing. That's what our research was about, which I think I already told you."

"You don't think a person could have a nightmare that was so real he would confuse it with reality—and actually act on it?"

"No. It's not possible. . . ." She started to volunteer the fact that the sleeping brain prevented a person from doing that, then despaired of explaining it to the man. He was beginning to make her angry, and she wasn't sure why.

"Then why did you give him the drugs?"

So that was what he was leading up to. Everyone seemed determined to link her to the use of the drugs.

"I didn't give him any drugs."

"You didn't?" She almost expected him to say, "You're

120

under oath." Real lawyers certainly weren't like those depicted on TV. Victor Cross was a far cry from Perry Mason.

"No, I didn't."

"You didn't give him a sample of the new drug—I don't know what it's called? You didn't give him some blue capsules?"

"Of course not. Only one of our doctors—our physicians—could give him drugs."

"And you maintain you know nothing about any drugs?"

"Look, Shodale manufactures drugs. There are drugs all over the place, both approved and non-approved. I suppose it's possible Mr. Myers could have gotten his hands on some of them. But the drug they're in the process of developing hasn't been approved by the FDA, so it's unlikely he would—"

"I guess you're trying to tell me there are no experiments with drugs before they're approved."

She chose her words carefully. "No one ethical would get involved with those drugs. Shodale is a very ethical company. They employ only ethical people."

Cross rubbed his chin and seemed suddenly pleased. "No one *ethical*? How about someone *un*ethical?"

"What do you mean?"

"Could there be an unethical person working in the research program with you who might give drugs to a man like Myers— a desperate man, a man so overwrought as a result of his dreams he was afraid to go to sleep at night? Wouldn't such a man be a likely test subject for the drugs?"

"Well ... I guess so ... maybe."

"Don't equivocate."

"I'm not on trial here."

He looked bemused. "Who said you were? No one's on trial— yet."

Watch it! Marian told herself. He's trying to trap you into saying something. She wanted to get up and leave, but she couldn't seem to make her legs obey her. She felt as if she were strapped to the chair, unable to escape.

121

"All right. Myers was vulnerable. If he were offered drugs, he probably would have taken them."

"In fact," Cross said, apparently delighted with this small concession from her, "he had a history of taking drugs for this condition."

Marian was surprised. She couldn't recall Myers ever telling her that. "What sort of drugs?"

"Sleeping pills, Valium, Librium. Antidepressants."

"I didn't know about that," she said meekly.

"Apparently someone did. They—whoever it was—knew Myers was what they call an 'addictive personality.' He was used to the idea of taking drugs to control his emotional state."

"Why are you telling me this?"

"You didn't know?"

"I said I didn't." She realized with a blush that Myers had apparently lied to her in his prescreening interviews. If she had known about his former experiences with mind-altering substances, she wouldn't have approved him as a subject. It was too late to do anything about that now, though; the damage had already been done. If this information came out in the trial, it would cast doubt on the ethics and purity of Shodale's research methods and it wouldn't say much for Marian's research methodology, either.

"That's very interesting," Cross said. "You take a subject into a research program and don't even look into his medical background. Sounds like somebody didn't do his—or *her*—homework. Sounds pretty damn sloppy for an *ethical* company like Shodale."

Marian wanted to scream that it wasn't her responsibility. It was something the medical people were supposed to do, but something in her refused to defend her position, as if she accepted the guilt without question, almost as if she wanted the guilt somehow.

But she wasn't guilty of anything. She started to say something about how busy she was with her teaching and other

122

duties, then looked over at Cross's fat, smug face and realized that would not cut any ice with him.

"What do you want me to say?" she began weakly. "I don't think I should be held accountable for what Shodale did or did not do." She was suddenly very warm. If this were a preview of how it would be in court, she didn't want any part of it.

"Well, my client might not agree with you. After all, he's being held for alleged murder. He'll need a lot of help. . . ."

"Alleged?"

"Well, you know a man's innocent until proven—"

"I thought he admitted his guilt."

Cross smiled knowingly. "That doesn't mean anything. He was on drugs at the time—and he had no idea what affect the drugs would have on him." He studied his manicure. "In fact, I think after I get him off for this murder charge, we may have a good malpractice case here. I wonder what the legal precedents are. It's something to think about."

Marian was confused. Was Cross really concerned for his client, or was he contemplating how taking on a major drug company like Shodale could bolster his standing in the legal community?

Or maybe he was bluffing. She suddenly realized there was something vital missing in this whole line of questioning, a piece of physical evidence that was being conveniently overlooked.

"All right, Mr. Cross," she said, "maybe somebody did screw up, but do you have any of the drug Myers is supposed to have taken? Does anyone?"

The attorney's expression changed abruptly. "Well, no, I'm afraid not. The police apparently don't have it, either."

"Then you have only Myers's word."

"That might be enough, Dr. Turner—if I had the right witness, a person who would corroborate Myers's story."

"So that's what you expected to get from me." Marian didn't think the lawyer knew what he expected to get from her. She could tell he liked to manipulate people for the sake of manip-

123

ulation alone—shake them and see what rattles. She didn't much like such sick little mind games; she had been the plaything in them too often.

"I thought you wanted to help my client."

"I do. I feel sorry about what happened to him. But you don't expect me to lie, do you? I can't corroborate what I don't know."

He sat up straight in the chair, his expression now deadly serious. "I never asked you to perjure yourself. I thought you knew more than you apparently do. I have only the word of my client." He twisted one of his rings up and down his finger absentmindedly, and it distracted Marian for a moment.

"But there is one thing you could do," he said, "if you *really* wanted to help Mr. Myers."

There was a perceptible shift in his attitude; Marian could feel it in the air. "What's that?"

He stopped fiddling with the ring. "You could ... well, this is just between you and me, so let me put it very delicately: You could *procure* a sample of that drug for me. I'd get it analyzed and get a couple of technical witnesses who could testify it would have driven Myers crazy, so he wouldn't have known what he was doing."

Marian didn't know whether to be outraged or confounded; she was a little of both. "You don't really mean that."

"It would help the case a great deal."

"Why don't you ask Shodale? Can't the court subpoena them or something?"

"It's not that simple with a corporate entity. I don't think they would cooperate. Shodale has a lot of pull in this town, you know, and a bunch of attorneys who eat guys like me for breakfast. I don't have the resources—which means I don't have access to the money—to get them to cooperate. It would be so much simpler if someone like you would get the drug for me, and ... well, let's say I do have the resources to compensate you for your trouble."

She could almost see the headlines: ATTORNEY CROSS

124

BRINGS SHODALE TO ITS KNEES—SUES FOR TWENTY MILLION.

She gave him a withering stare. "And you question Shodale's ethics?"

"Ethics has nothing to do with it," he replied indignantly. "I'm trying to save a man's life here. William Myers does not deserve capital punishment for what he did. He was not, *is* not, responsible."

Marian frowned. She didn't know much about matters of law, but she was certain Cross was suggesting something criminal. "You're offering me a bribe and you want me to steal. Is that it?"

"I wouldn't call it that. I'm just offering to compensate you for your efforts. What's wrong with that?"

"What you're really saying is your case is pretty lame without the evidence of the drugs."

"No. I believe I can still get him off. The man's not an habitual offender, and he has some standing in the community. It would just be much easier if—"

"I wouldn't even consider it." She blushed, because in the back of her mind, she *was* considering his proposal, not for the money, but for the satisfaction it would give her if she could somehow implicate John Morton. It would be a fitting reward for the way he had looked at her that day. He couldn't ruin her career if his own ass were in a sling.

But that would be vindictive, and it didn't seem right to help Myers just to get back at someone. It was Machiavellian and made her feel dirty. Still . . .

"Don't answer so quickly, Dr. Turner. Think it over."

"I think this whole thing is bizarre."

He dismissed her statement with a wave of his hand, then tried another approach. "You should also remember this: It's better to be on the winning side than on the losing side. Whatever happens, being on the same side as *me* would benefit you the most."

"Is that a threat of some kind?"

"No. I don't make threats. I'm an attorney, I don't have to make threats." He grinned as if he were sharing his favorite joke with her. "So, what do you say?"

"I gave you my answer."

"You didn't say absolutely no."

"We're getting nowhere. I'm tired, and you're trying to make me say things I don't want to." She got up to leave. "I'll be ready to testify in Mr. Myers's behalf. I owe him that much, but I can't do anything else. I have to go now."

"Please, don't make it sound so final."

The man was insufferable. "I won't promise anything."

"I'm not asking you to." He went to hold the door for her. "Just think things over. We have plenty of time before the trial. We can make any kind of arrangement you want."

She halted in mid-step, her mind rushing with alternatives. She settled on one. "Mr. Cross, I think you have the wrong person here." She hesitated only a second, but it was enough time for John Morton's scowling face to flash into her mind and for her courage to wane slightly.

It didn't wane enough, though; she determined the demon wouldn't win out this time.

To hell with John Morton!

She stared directly into Cross's eyes. "You want to talk to Dr. Stephen Richards," she blurted, already cringing at the possible consequences. "He's the son of a bitch who gave Myers the drugs."

Before Cross could reply, Marian was out the door and halfway down the hall. He might have called after her, but she didn't notice. She didn't even notice she was running.

She was too busy trying to sort out all the confrontations, ultimatums, and other sorry business she had been subjected to recently. She was tired of getting it from Morton, from the police, and from assholes like this lawyer.

She was ready to fight back. All she needed was the opportunity.

Twelve. Movie Madness

God, I hate this!

"Hey, Josh, look at him take that guy's head off! Jesus, that's gross. Pass me some of that popcorn."

Josh Douglas tried not to look at what was happening on the screen. But it was hard to avert his eyes while sitting in the car. His friends would notice and call him "wimp" and "chicken" if he covered his face. His stomach was protesting mightily, though, and he feared he might throw up.

I'm gonna puke!

No, he couldn't let that happen; the guys would razz him endlessly. He forced himself to swallow the bile creeping up the back of his throat.

His buddy Walt, who was sitting up front with him, was really enjoying the carnage. Walt was enthusiastic about every movie he saw, but his first love was horror movies. He went to every new gorefest that came out. It was Walt who had persuaded Josh to go to the Clermont, a drive-in theater just west of Indianapolis, where a triple bill of splatter films was playing. He had also insisted they park in the front row so they could see better—where the splatters on the screen were thirty feet wide.

"Oh, shit, the little girl!" Walt sprayed popcorn spittle all over the inside of the windshield. "Man, everybody in this movie is a fucking zombie. Everybody!" he nudged Josh in the ribs and guffawed. "This is a real gross-out, ain't it?"

"Yeah," Josh responded lamely. "Really gross." The little girl on the screen was attacking her mother with a garden trowel. Josh turned and pretended to be adjusting the volume on the car speaker. He was beginning to get sick of the word *gross*, which he figured he must have heard a thousand times by now.

Terry and Mick were laughing in the back seat. The whole car was shaking with their mirth.

"Goddamn, Sam!" Mick said. "You dork!"

"What's going on back there?" Josh turned around.

"This dickhead spilled my Coke."

"Don't call me dickhead, fuckface."

"Hey, you guys," Josh said, "this is my dad's car. You're going to get me grounded." He was happy for the opportunity to look away from the screen, though he didn't want to sound like he was whining. That was wimpy, too, but it was better than being wimpy because he couldn't stand a horror movie. All seventeen-year-old boys were supposed to like horror films. Such films were made for teenaged audiences.

"Chill out," Terry said. "I'll clean it up. Give me some of them napkins."

"I'll turn the light on."

"Not yet." Walt pulled Josh's hand away from the light switch. "This is the good part."

"But he spilled Coke."

"Fuck it, man. It'll keep."

Reluctantly, Josh faced forward again. But this time he really couldn't keep his eyes open. Instead, he closed his left eye completely and squinted the right, which effectively rendered the film a fuzzy blur in his vision while making it appear to Walt he was actually watching. He agonized through the next ten minutes, then the film was over.

Josh was thankful when the end credits started to roll. The last hour and a half had been torture. Now he sat still, oblivious to his friends as they cut up and joked, trying to catch his breath. The atmosphere in the Honda was stifling; the smell of popcorn, candy bars, and spilled Coke in the close confines of the car was overpowering, and the last bloody images of the film still lingered with him. They seemed to have weight in his mind, as if they could come to life somehow and harm him.

When the playground lights came up and the intermission film was running, Josh told the others he had to go to the bathroom. He got out of the Honda and ran across the gravel to the concession stand, his blood pounding in his temples and his stomach churning. He made it to the men's room before the crowd hit and was fortunate to find an empty stall.

As soon as he closed the door to the stall, he threw up his popcorn, his Coke, and most of his dinner, splattering his shirt-front and jeans. When he came out he felt as if his guts had been ripped out. He must have looked as bad as he felt, too, because other people in the men's room stood away from him and seemed to regard him as if he were some kind of monster. A glance in the mirror told him why: He had puked so hard his face was spotted with broken blood vessels. Snot was running down from his nose, spittle hung from his lips, his cheeks were stained with tears, and his eyes were bloodshot. No wonder people were shying away from him. He looked as bad as one of the zombies in the film.

Shit, he couldn't let the guys see him that way. But they wouldn't know if the light was kept off in the car. Then he sniffed his fingers and inhaled deeply. He smelled like vomit! That would be difficult to hide. The guys would know how chicken he was.

He stood at one of the basins, splashed cold water on his face, and rinsed his mouth out. Then he dabbed his clothes with a wet paper towel and combed his hair. That took care of most of the visual evidence, but he still had the smell to contend with.

Why had he let Walt talk him into going to the damn drive-in, anyhow? He had told him he didn't want to go. He had wanted to see that new Bruce Willis ovie at the College Park Loew's. He liked action movies and he didn't mind a little blood spilling, but he found he could no longer stand the really graphic stuff like in this horror bullshit, where they seemed to delight in rubbing a person's face in the gore.

He had listened to Walt and now he had puked all over himself. He would never live it down. They'd be calling him a wuss all summer long.

He staggered outside and drew some of the cool air deep into his lungs, breathing slowly so he wouldn't hyperventilate. It was still intermission and an animated character on the screen urged the drive-in patrons to rush to the concession stand for a pizza with all the trimmings.

Josh's stomach did a flip-flop; the giant pizza up there resembled the mess in the last few frames of the movie he'd just seen. All it needed was some blond hair to be the face of the little girl's mother.

He ran back into the men's room.

"What the fuck took you so long?" Mick called out the window when Josh returned to the car.

"Open up, you guys. My hands're full." He held a large carton of popcorn and a cardboard tray with four Cokes in it. He had eaten a Milky Way bar and chewed half a pack of Certs breath mints; he hoped that was sufficient to banish the smell of vomit on his breath. However, the candy bar was a mistake; it was not lying on his stomach well. He thought the popcorn might absorb some of the acid crawling up from his guts, but so far it had proved ineffective.

"Did you bring me anything?" Walt asked, pushing the car door open for his friend.

"Coke."

"Hand me one," Mick said.

"Wait till I get in, mo'."

"What were you doing? Jacking off?"

130

"Shut up, Terry. It takes one to know one. Hey, what kind of razor do you shave your palms with, anyhow?"

"Bite me, Walt. At least I get safe sex that way."

Josh took a deep breath and slid in the car. He waited anxiously for someone to say something about how he smelled, but apparently no comments were forthcoming. The Certs must have worked.

"Speaking of sex," Mick said, "did you check out the jugs on that chick in the 'Vette?"

"What 'Vette?"

"That red convertible in the second row. She's sitting there with another girl with the top down."

"I saw her," Terry said. "I'd like to get *her* top down."

"No shit, she's a fox," Mick continued. "A redhead. I could tell she was a natural redhead, too."

"Oh, yeah? How?"

"Well, I could just tell."

"Why, did she pull her pants down?"

"Hey, be cool, man. There are virgins in the car."

"Yeah, and you're one of them."

"Listen," Mick said, undaunted, "I ain't been a virgin since I was twelve. Honest to God. I got more ass than a toilet seat before you guys was shaving."

This brag was met with skeptical laughter.

"I bet them girls would like some company. I could show them where it's at."

"You'd scare them off, dork-breath. They probably like humans." Walt grabbed a handful of popcorn and stuffed it in his mouth.

"Oh, I guess you're one of the higher life forms, Walt. They wouldn't go for a zit-face like you."

"Hey, zits give you personality. It makes the girls feel sorry for you."

"Sure, Walt. They feel sorry for you because of your pencil dick, too."

"What do you think, Josh?"

131

"I don't know." He had just swallowed a bubble of stomach gas, which left a foul taste in his mouth. He popped another Certs.

"Let's go check them out."

"Hey, I saw them first," Mick protested. "Let me and Terry check them out."

"You wouldn't know what to do with a real woman. You couldn't do it if Terry helped you and the girl held it up."

"Fuck you."

"Fuck you very much, too."

"You guys are full of shit," Mick said. He opened the back door and stepped out. "Terry and me are the cocksmen in this outfit."

"Okay, but leave something for the rest of us."

"When I get through, that girl will be spoiled. She won't want nothing with a geek like you. She'll want men. You coming, Terry?"

"Not yet, but I will be." He chuckled nastily.

"Haul ass, then. The next movie's about to start."

Terry got out and joined Mick. Together they walked back toward the red Corvette, which was about ten yards to the left of the Honda and one row back.

After they were gone, Walt leaned forward and belched. "Nothing like a good belch to clear the air. Hey, you know, those guys are full of it. They won't get anywhere with those chicks." He yawned and pressed a button on his digital watch to light the face. "It's ten o'clock already."

"Getting late." Josh was still fighting bile.

"Shit, it's early, man. We got two more movies to go."

"I don't know," Josh said, "maybe we shouldn't stay for all three. My dad might get pissed about keeping the car out."

"Hell, we ain't hurting it. Besides, he'll be asleep by the time we get back."

"I hope I can stay awake that long."

"You have to. The last movie's the best. We got to see it.

Texas Chainsaw Massacre, Part III. It's the grossest of the gross.''

"Okay," Josh sighed. "I guess I can handle it."

"Man, after you see *Chainsaw III*, you'll be awake all right. You won't never go to sleep again."

Josh was not comforted by that thought, but he resigned himself to sitting through that and the next film. He'd get through them somehow. He had to or he would be branded a wimp, and he could suffer the films more comfortably than he could potential loss of status with the guys.

But he knew he'd have nightmares, probably for weeks.

For the next three and a half hours, Josh felt like he was dancing with the dead. The second film was gorier than the first, and the last film made the first two seem like toned-down versions of *Heidi.* By the end of the third movie, Josh had witnessed more larger-than-life scenes of garroting, disemboweling, dismemberment, decapitation, and other mayhem than he could count, all rendered in gushing, vivid colors that went beyond realism into another dimension, into a realm of ultra-horror that twisted his nerves into tangled skeins, knotted in abject terror. Not only could he not imagine what he was seeing, he could not imagine anyone even thinking such things, much less depicting them on film.

He believed the filmmakers had conspired against him in particular by showing every bloodletting gimmick of which the special effects people were capable. They also seemed bent on convincing the audience the world was populated with animated meat that just happened to be human beings. Josh's sensibilities were frayed beyond endurance; he was wrung out, turned inside out, and put back together all wrong; it was like being caught on a roller coaster the sides of which were studded with razor blades.

He was transformed from a boy with an upset stomach to a boy with an upset mind.

But he managed to endure the films. He even refrained from being sick again, though he had to choke back a lot of stomach acid.

At least he proved he was no wimp, and that was the important thing.

At one-thirty, they left the drive-in and headed back to Indianapolis. It was an eight-minute trip to Interstate 465, which would eventually take them to 86th Street and their various homes.

Mick and Terry grumbled for most of the trip about how they had failed to score with the two girls in the Corvette. Terry kept contending they must be lesbians to turn him and Mick down, and Walt had fun taunting them mercilessly with put-downs and insults about their lack of manhood.

Josh remained silent and concentrated on his driving. He was exhausted from the evening's activities and anxious to get home. It had been an especially long day for him, since he had worked in the yard all day, then helped his mom around the house. He never had a chance to get a nap in before going out with the guys, and he was really feeling the lack of that nap now.

Fortunately, he had talked Walt and the others out of stopping at the White Castle for hamburgers. He certainly didn't need any belly-bombs to aggravate his condition. He didn't feel like he'd be eating for days now, nor sleeping very much, either. He hoped he could get out of going to church in the morning somehow, though his mother was usually insistent about that. Maybe he could pretend to be sick; he wouldn't have to pretend very hard, because he doubted he would feel much better in the morning.

Josh dropped his friends off at their respective homes, then drove up Ditch Road to 79th Street, where he turned left. He jogged south on the next street over and followed that to a cul-de-sac where his house was located. It was a two-story four-bedroom house that resembled most of the others in the neighborhood—not quite prefab, but not really custom, either. It was the type of house preferred by most middle-income families in the city; it was also the most affordable.

It was after two when he pulled up in the driveway. He had to stop the car to look for the remote transmitter to the garage door opener. Normally, it was stuck to the dash on a patch of Velcro, but it wasn't there now. He searched under the seats but found nothing but kernels of popcorn and a sticky wet place where Terry had spilled the Coke.

He stopped looking for a moment and sat in the car just resting, hoping to clear his head. The air was cool and crisp, but not unpleasant, carrying with it the smell of new-mown grass. It seemed like ages ago that he had cut the lawn. Tomorrow, he'd have to rake it, but somehow that prospect no longer seemed so daunting. Tomorrow, he'd be himself again, full of pep and energy. All he needed was a little sleep to be rejuvenated.

The blue-gray sky overhead was virtually cloudless and most of the stars were visible. He had studied astronomy as a kid and now some of his young sense of wonder returned to him as he automatically identified the major constellations in the night sky: Orion, the Big Dipper, the Little Dipper. And over there was Venus.

Everything was so peaceful. It was hard to believe that only an hour ago he had been cringing in this very seat, about to wet his pants as old Leatherface swiped at his victims with that chainsaw. The contrast between that moment and now was awesome, yet it was immensely comforting. There was the movies and there was the real world, and they really were different. The real world was actually a very safe place for the most part.

Why had he been so afraid of a movie? It seemed silly now. It was all special effects, anyhow. It was just foam and latex and K-Y Jelly and fake blood and fake plastic body parts. None of it was real at all. He'd read how the guys in the movies did those things; if he thought about how unreal it was, he could dismiss it from his mind.

135

A big illusion, that's what it was. Like something in a dream. Thus having comforted himself, Josh felt secure again. He could even close his eyes now and not see any of it—no more latent images of garish blood and stray limbs flying through the air, no more dancing with the dead. Even his stomach felt better. He suddenly felt very relaxed.

He jerked awake as a drop of rain hit his nose. His neck ached, and he realized he had fallen asleep with his head resting on the edge of the car window. He blinked, looked up, and saw that a few clouds had gathered. The rain was very light, though, nothing like Indianapolis usually had this time of year. It would make the grass grow faster, though, and that meant he would have to cut it again within a few days.

He stretched and yawned. His watch told him it was four-thirty-five; he'd been asleep a couple of hours. He did feel a little better but he longed for the comfort of his bed. There was no way he was going to church tomorrow.

He'd been doing something before he fell asleep. Oh yeah, looking for that thing for the garage door opener. Maybe it was in the glove compartment. He should have thought of that before. Sometimes Mom forgot and put it in there, even though it really pissed the old man off.

He reached out and flipped the glove compartment lid down. A light came on and he leaned over to look inside. No remote transmitter in there. Just a bunch of road maps, repair receipts, and half an old candy bar—that stuff and a hand.

Josh jumped back, looked again, then shrieked.

There *was* a hand in the glove compartment—a severed human hand. Blood was oozing from the jagged end, running down the lid and dripping on the carpet. The drops made soft *splats* as they hit.

God, it was like something from the last movie. Only it was much, much grosser.

He reminded himself how much he hated the word *gross*, but it seemed the only appropriate term in his limited vocabulary.

He took one more look at the thing; it didn't go away. In fact, he could swear it was twitching.

That was enough.

He slammed himself against the door twice before he remembered to use the handle. Then he jumped out of the car, slid on the wet driveway, and scraped his palms and knees. He muttered a curse and ran to the front door. He hammered at the door for several breathless moments, but no one answered.

"Dad! Mom! Wake up!"

He stopped beating the door momentarily to listen. The night was silent except for the muted patter of rain on the grass and in the trees, which under other circumstances would have had a soothing effect. But the sound of his own heart drowned out the rain; it was amplified in his ears, throbbing like the hearts did on the soundtracks in the horror movies before something stopped them.

He sucked in a deep breath and suddenly felt foolish.

Walt had probably pulled this on him. That couldn't be a real hand; it was probably one of those plastic things like they sold at Spencer Gifts in the mall. This would be Walt's idea of a great joke.

"That shithead!"

To confirm that the hand was only a joke, Josh went back to the car. He'd stuff that thing up Walt's ass for him the next time he saw him. It was about as funny as a sore dick.

He opened the door on the passenger side of the Honda and reached in to get the hand from the glove compartment. There was nothing there. The remote transmitter had taken the hand's place.

Josh realized now it hadn't even been a practical joke. It had only been his imagination playing tricks on him. Those horror movies had affected his mind. He promised himself never to go to one again, no matter how it made him look with the guys.

"I guess I *am* some kind of wimp," he said, taking the transmitter from the glove compartment and activating the garage door opener. As the door folded up out of sight, he started the car and guided it into the garage. Then he rolled up the windows and got out.

He started to close the garage door but just then something brushed against his right shoulder.

He froze.

Something tapped him.

"It's my damn imagination. There's nothing there."

It tapped again. Considering it was something he was only imagining, it was very insistent. It was also unnervingly solid.

Josh emitted a sigh of frustration. He was getting tired of screwing around with this imagining thing, but apparently it wouldn't go away unless he met it head-on.

"Okay! Okay!"

He turned.

The hand was hanging there in midair, its index finger poised to tap again.

Josh didn't wait for it to touch him. He turned and ran around to the other side of the car, then ducked down on the floor of the garage.

He lay there on the cold cement a few seconds, trying to catch his breath before standing up again. He peeked over his shoulder to see if the hand had followed him, and it had not. But he felt it was still hovering in the air, waiting for him.

What would it do if it caught him? Strangle him? It was only a hand; it couldn't do that much. Surely, he could overpower it.

His thoughts of how he might defeat the disembodied hand were interrupted, however, by his sensing movement out of the corner of his eye. There was something on the other side of the car, something he knew in his guts was bigger than a hand.

He closed his eyes tight and counted to ten, then to fifty, then to one hundred. He opened his eyes and turned his head, peering underneath the car.

He focused his vision on a spider that was making its way

across the floor. For a brief instant that seemed to be all there was, but when he cast his focus further out he saw something else.

There was a pair of feet over there—feet shod in worn-out black leather boots with run-down heels. The feet were awfully big, too.

"It'll go away. It'll go away! Mom! Dad!" He shut his eyes again. The next time he dared to look the feet were gone. He flipped over on his side and started to get up, then stopped. The tip of his nose was touching a boot.

He glanced up and saw a towering figure dressed in a torn coat. He scrambled to his feet and found himself staring Leatherface in the eye. It was a bloodshot eye that watched him coldly through a mask of human skin.

Leatherface looked just like he did in the movie, only he was holding his dad's new Stihl chainsaw—the one the family had bought him for Christmas last year. The saw was running. Leatherface chortled, making a sound like guts ripping, and revved the chainsaw a couple of times.

Josh let out a cry in which a thousand screams were compressed. He sprang past the masked hulk, leaping over the hood of the car.

When he landed on the floor, he felt something hit the back of his neck. He glanced backward and saw the hand lying on the floor. If Leatherface had used that to get his attention, it had certainly done its job. Now he knew the monster meant business.

Josh skidded to the other side of the garage and pushed through the door that led into the house.

Leatherface pursued him, continuing to rev the saw.

Josh dashed through the living room, wound back through the dining room and family room, then through the kitchen and back out to the hall where the stairs were. He moved like accelerated lightning, urged on by the awful roar of the saw grating in his ears.

He gobbled the air as he ran. In between gulps, he attempted

139

prayer, promising God and Jesus he would go to church tomorrow no matter what happened.

But Leatherface kept up. For a man—a thing?—his size, he moved quickly.

Josh could hear Leatherface right behind him as he took the steps two, then three at a time.

If only he could get to Dad's room. Dad would know what to do. Dad could stop anything.

He turned at the top of the stairs and started down the hall.

He could feel Leatherface's breath on his neck.

It was only a few feet to the master bedroom, but suddenly it seemed he was running in slow motion, his feet falling leadenly on the hall runner.

Almost there.

In a final burst of energy, he hurled himself against the bedroom door. It flew open and he flung himself facedown on the carpet.

"Dad! Mom! Watch out! Dad? . . ."

It was too late; Leatherface had already been there.

The bed was cut almost in half; so were its occupants.

Josh screamed and covered his face. He waited for Leatherface to catch up with him, waited for the chainsaw to descend.

It didn't.

A few seconds passed soundlessly. Josh rose and started to leave, but he halted when he glimpsed Leatherface in his peripheral vision. He steeled himself for the worst, but nothing happened. Then he realized it wasn't really Leatherface at all. It was only the thing's reflection in the mirrors on the doors to the walk-in closet.

The reflection cradled the still-smoking chainsaw almost tenderly, as if it were a fragile infant.

The reflection was skinny and tall and had blond hair and blue eyes and bloodstained clothing and its mouth was frozen in mid-scream.

The reflection was only seventeen.

And it didn't wear a mask; it wore its own face.

The reflection was Josh Douglas.
That was really odd.
He thought *he* was Josh Douglas.

Thirteen. Getting Together

Laura was getting moodier every day; she was becoming more arbitrary and argumentative. As a result, her behavior was unpredictable, unpleasant and, to Carl's way of thinking, uncalled-for.

Carl felt like he was married to two different women. During the day, Laura was abusive, contrary, and difficult. They couldn't discuss anything without it deteriorating into a vicious fight, whether it was something as simple as what was for breakfast, or something more serious such as how they were going to make the next payment on her car. She kept spending money, too, daring him to say anything about it, and if he *did* dare, she trapped him into another of their seemingly endless arguments that had no resolution.

Yet at night, she continued to make amorous advances, acting as if she had not been Super-Bitch during the day and pretending she wanted to make up. Carl found her sloppy invitations to sex repugnant and had slept on the living room couch more often than in his bed in the last week—which, of course, precipitated more arguments.

If she intended to drive Carl crazy with her oscillating moods, she was doing a good job of it. He didn't know whether to contemplate divorce or suicide.

The one thing he found the most difficult to think about

142

was actually trying to save the marriage. Even though she had denied any recall of her idea the next morning after that night, Laura had planted a seed in Carl's mind and he had been giving serious thought to seeing a marriage counselor.

To save a marriage often required outside help, although Carl's upbringing caused him to view the prospect of a stranger interfering in his affairs as something to be avoided. His father, whose various pronouncements had structured most of Carl's core beliefs, would have scoffed at such a step, asserting that any "real man" could handle his problems on his own, with no one's help at all.

But his father was not forced to deal with the modern female mind-set, with the independent breed of woman who saw herself as not only equal to a man in a relationship, but perhaps, in many cases, even superior. His father had blustered his way through life, demanding the prerogative of all "right" men, that he should be obeyed, that his children should respect and love him in spite of anything he might say or do, and above all, that his wife should accept his every command without question.

But being right hadn't made everything rosy for the old man, either. His marriage had never been all that secure. Before his father had died, he had separated from Carl's mother three times and was considering yet another parting, when he discovered his heart trouble was so advanced he would not likely live another year. He spent that last year a bitter, despondent man, so given to vocalizing his depression that hardly anyone could stand to be around him, making the survivors—Carl, his mother, and his younger brother—feel guilty relief when the elder Nolan finally succumbed.

If he did make the effort and went to a marriage counselor and things were somehow mended between him and Laura, what then? Did he really want to live out the rest of his days with her?

He shuddered at the thought of himself, twenty years hence in his mid-sixties, with Laura, by then herself a sixtyish woman, probably shrivelled and wrinkled, sitting by his side while they reminisced about the good old days that never were. It was an agonizing tableau of the future that made him flinch.

Maybe things would have been different if they could have had children. But Laura was unable to conceive. Their life together was barren in more ways than one.

Going to a counselor might have the opposite effect from what was intended, too. It might serve to confirm the marriage was unsalvageable.

The best thing to do for the moment, which was the course of action he usually took, was to do nothing: to remain ambivalent, make no decision, and let it all ride.

Maybe things would resolve themselves on their own.

Carl was working long hours, not only out of his sense of duty to pursue each case to the greatest detail, but also to keep his mind off the current state of his marriage.

And there was plenty of work for the homicide department to do. In addition to the Myers and the Snodgrass cases, Carl was now investigating a mindless murder that had taken place in Christian Park on the south side of the city. Two teenagers had been viciously killed early Monday morning, and so far he had no clues at all on that one.

He was taking a snack break at the City Market, which was just around the corner from Police Headquarters downtown. He was eating a croissant sandwich with ham and cheese and was surprised it wasn't that bad. Normally, he shied away from what he considered "yuppie food," preferring plain wheat or rye bread, but this afternoon he was feeling adventurous. Besides, he had often wondered what a croissant tasted like. He was washing the strange sandwich down with a diet Pepsi.

As he ate, he glanced over the first afternoon edition of *The Indianapolis News,* and what he read in the letters column disturbed him. The gun control nuts were making a big deal about the case where the little girl had taken a pistol from her father's gun cabinet and shot both her parents and her little brother. It was one of those senseless incidents that happened every now and then, the type of thing that made the blood boil. But Carl didn't believe such occurrences meant guns should be outlawed. The father should have kept the cabinet locked at all times; that was common sense, and not exercising it had cost him his life. He should also have educated his children in the dangers of firearms. Again, common sense.

Carl wasn't involved in the case with the little girl. Someone else in the department was on that one. He had overheard some details, but not enough to make him think this was different from any other of the countless accidental killings that happened every year.

It did strike him that there had been a run of homicides recently in which people killed family members or people close to them: the William Myers case, the Ida Snodgrass case, the case with the little girl, and most recently, in a murder reported only yesterday, the case of the teenage boy who apparently went nuts after seeing too many horror movies. Out of all the homicides reported in the last few weeks, the percentage of people doing in their own people was high. That was unusual, but did it mean anything?

Another similarity was present in at least the first two cases. The perpetrators claimed they were dreaming at the time. Yet there seemed to be no connection other than that. Myers might have been taking drugs (though none were ever found), but the old lady apparently had just gone batty. Aside from her saying she was dreaming God was talking to her at the time, Ida Snodgrass claimed no extenuating circumstances—no drugs, no booze. Nothing. Maybe that was what advanced senility did to a person. Myers and Snodgrass had been dreaming. That was unusual, too.

Carl was always trying to find connections and correlations. He had read once that the state of the economy could be predicted by tracking the sales of peanut butter. If times were bad, people bought more peanut butter; if they were good, they bought less. It had something to do with people's perceptions of how things were going, and peanut butter was a cheap staple that could be stocked up on for hard times. Maybe the nature of this current run of murders reflected another strange correlation. It might not be true cause and effect, but if he could find a common thread in all the recent family murders, it might lead to something—if only a fascinating observation on human nature.

He speculated about the people in the cases he wasn't working on. He wondered what they claimed as motivation, if any. It didn't make sense that people would kill their loved ones so readily. Was there a "peanut butter factor" in those cases? If so, could it be something equally as off-the-wall? Or was it something simple?

Maybe it was because the family unit in America was breaking down. Maybe fluoridated water was finally affecting people. Maybe it was only just a series of coincidences that ultimately meant nothing.

But it wouldn't hurt to ask a couple of questions, if only to satisfy his own curiosity. The answers might be surprising, though as a homicide detective, Carl had stopped being surprised years ago.

He finished his croissant sandwich and went back to the office to talk to a couple of his coworkers. If there was a peanut butter factor, he was going to find out what it was.

Marian was trying hard to think, but her cognitive mechanism refused to percolate this evening. It was six-thirty and she had a long evening ahead of her, and she had no idea how she would get through it without going mad.

She fidgeted in her office at Shodale, trying to do paperwork, though all the words in the various reports she read were a blur to her. She was also drinking too much coffee, which aggravated the jitters she had developed in the last few days.

She knew what was making her so nervous. It was what had

146

happened in the encounter with Myers's attorney. She kept imagining John Morton would find out she had told Cross Richards was responsible for giving drugs to Myers, and she was becoming absolutely paranoid about the possible repercussions. She felt she had jeopardized not only her career, but also her entire life. She had ruined her prospects for the future because of a careless impulse. The dumb thing about it was that she didn't even have any proof that Richards had given Myers drugs. Her saying that he did could even be construed as an attempt to save her own skin.

She expected the door to burst open at any moment and for Morton or Richards (or both!) to be standing there, demanding a piece of her hide. Or even worse, some dark authority figure would come to take her away—to jail or perhaps to the funny farm.

Yet so far nothing whatever had happened. She hadn't talked to Morton for days and the only time she had seen Richards was the other morning when he had dropped off a copy of a new report he had prepared updating the effects of product 4155A on baboons.

Richards had been as inscrutable as ever then. He had given no hints that he had been contacted by the attorney or that he even knew Marian was plotting against him.

Plotting! That's what it was called. She was attempting Machiavellian maneuvers. Unfortunately, as she now discovered, she didn't have the stomach for such machinations.

The feeling of impending doom hung over her, unresolved, affecting her ability to function. She almost wished something *would* happen, and she could get this episode of her life over with. Peace was in knowing; terror was in the unknown.

At that moment, there was a rapping on the door and Marian almost dropped her coffee in mid-sip.

"Yes?" Her voice betrayed her dread. They had come for her at last. Her career was over.

The door opened and the pleasant face of Sue, the blonde

who worked as a secretary and clerk at the desk up front, peered in.

Marian successfully hid her apprehension and even managed to set her coffee down without fumbling. "What is it?"

"Is something wrong, Dr. Turner?"

"No. Nothing. You just startled me."

"I'm sorry."

"Don't worry about it. Now, what do you want?"

"That policeman is here again."

Marian's face went white. Someone had accused her! She started to reach for the coffee, then changed her mind. "You mean Mr. Nolan?"

"Yes. He says he needs to talk to you. Says it's urgent, too. Do you want me to send him away?"

Marian smiled inwardly. Sue was a good kid. Fearless, too, offering to dismiss a police officer as if he were an unwanted salesman. But putting off yet another confrontation wouldn't help anything. There was nothing to do but to face up to him and accept the consequences. "No. I can see him."

"I can tell him you're busy."

"No. I'll have to talk to him some time or another, so it might as well be now."

"Whatever you say, Dr. Turner." Sue closed the door softly and left.

Marian took a deep breath. What could she say to him? What had she been accused of? She gulped coffee and flexed her hands, but that tenseness in her digits would not dissipate.

A minute passed and Carl was at the door. Marian braced herself and yelled for him to come in. As he entered, Marian scrutinized him closely. He didn't seem to have an official air about him this time. The only thing that seemed the least bit official was the portfolio he carried under one arm on which the initials "C.J.N." were stamped in gold. He was wearing a brightly colored tie and his suit looked like it was fresh from the cleaners. As he sat down, she caught a whiff of his after-shave, which smelled as if it had just been applied.

All in all, Carl looked rather friendly, perhaps too friendly. If he had any suspicions concerning her, he wasn't going to be obvious. As usual, she would have to be on guard. She hoped her nerves would hold out.

"Hello, Marian."

"Have a seat, Mr. Nolan." She watched him sit down as if he were one of her test subjects, analyzing his every movement, trying to detect body language that would reveal everything.

"It's Carl, you know," he said.

She didn't comment. She would determine for herself if it was going to be Carl or not. She vaguely recalled telling him to call her Marian, though, so perhaps she should go along with the pleasantries.

"Would you like some coffee, Carl?"

"Not right now."

"I have to cut back. Awful stuff. Bad on your kidneys, pancreas, liver, and God-knows-what-else."

He nodded indulgently, then folded his hands over the portfolio in his lap as if he were applying for a job. She read this movement as a reluctance to get on with the purpose of his visit. It was maddening.

"Well?" she said at last.

He seemed about to smile, and Marian decided she would like him to. It might ease the tension.

"First of all," he said, "I want to apologize for acting like a policeman when I was here."

"What do you mean?"

"You know, that remark I made about Ida Snodgrass."

"I'm sorry, I don't remember ..."

"She's the old lady who killed her pets and her maid."

"Yes?"

"Well, when I made that remark to you about being the doctor, I was just being a smart-assed cop, and I'm sorry for that."

"Isn't that what you're supposed to do? I mean—"

"I know what you mean. I'm supposed to be a policeman

149

not a smart ass, except when it's called for. But it wasn't called for. I was just frustrated. I get that way often when I'm working on a case. So I apologize." He finally broke into a smile and it was very engaging.

"This is funny," Marian said, about to blush. "I've never had anyone apologize to me for being a smart ass before."

"Now you have. How does it feel?"

"It feels good. I accept your apology." She sighed. "But surely you didn't come all the way out here just to say you're sorry."

"No. I came out because I have a kind of—I guess you'd call it a proposition, to make."

She raised her eyebrows. "What sort of proposition?"

"I just discovered something about a couple of cases we're working on and I don't know what to make of it. Maybe it's just coincidence. Maybe it doesn't mean anything at all, but I need an expert's help in figuring it all out. Interested?"

"Keep talking," she replied, suddenly becoming interested in spite of herself. She noticed her fingers were no longer trembling. But his artless manner could be a very elaborate setup, she cautioned herself. Policemen were clever that way. Yet, looking at Carl, she couldn't imagine him not just being open and frank about his business.

"You know about Myers and you know about Snodgrass. Now we have two others to add to what I'm calling 'dream alibiers.' "

"You'll have to explain that one."

"I'll get to it. Have you been keeping up with the news lately?"

"Not really. Too busy. Last week was finals week, and this week I'm on the night shift here."

"The night shift?"

"I'm staying up to monitor the sleep subjects."

"Then you don't know about the little kid and the teenager."

"No, I guess not." The way he said that made her feel something terrible was about to be revealed.

150

Carl briefed her on the Bundy and Douglas killings, leaving out few details, though he didn't relate his theory of the "peanut butter factor." He spoke with an authority and a precision that made her feel as if the police photographs were laid out on her desk. When he was finished, Marian's face was ashen.

"That's horrible stuff. How do you stand it?"

"I don't always. People do sick things, though. You don't get used to what they do, but you learn to expect the worst and people oblige by doing their worst."

"Well, you've certainly caught me up on the news." She took a sip of coffee; it was cold and brackish, but she needed it. "I don't know what to say. What's this leading up to?"

"Well, let me tell you the interesting part about both these cases. They have something in common with Myers and Snodgrass, too. The little Bundy girl said she was having a bad dream about guns when she shot her parents, and the Douglas kid said he was having a nightmare about a horror movie he'd seen when he went crazy. I talked to the officers working these cases and just found out most of these details myself this afternoon. After I got through talking to them, I naturally thought of you."

"Why me?" Marian asked, not attempting to hide her surprise.

"You're still not getting it. The dream connection. We have four cases in which the accused claim they were *dreaming* at the time. I wouldn't think much of it if there was some time between the cases, like a couple of years, but four of them in the space of days is too much to be coincidence."

"Maybe they knew each other?"

"I thought of that, too. But none of them even share a bus line."

"Could it be—what do they call it all the time—'copycat' crime? You know, where the person hears about it in the news and? . . ."

"Nope. The details about the dream alibis were not revealed

151

in the media. The Indianapolis police—and now you—are about the only people who know."

He sat back to let it all sink in for a moment. When a sufficient number of seconds had elapsed, he leaned forward, the beginnings of excitement apparent on his face. "So, what do you think?"

"Well, it does sound unusual. I have no idea if it's statistically significant, though."

"I think it is." He sighed, a bit exasperated. He realized he wasn't making himself very clear, but something in him made him hesitate. Was he questioning his own motives? "Well, do you want to go for it?"

"What?"

"My proposition."

"What *is* the proposition?"

He laughed. "I guess I forgot to tell you. I need your help. You're a dream expert and you have enough medical knowledge to be a real help in this case."

"You want me to help? I thought I'd been helping already."

"You have. A lot. I have to confess I didn't have much respect for psychology, psychiatry, or any of that brain stuff at first. But when you showed me what could be done here in your sleep lab—tracking people's dreams and stuff—well, it changed my way of thinking. That's why I think you could really help me if you got involved—with me, that is—in the investigations."

"Like a cop?"

"Not on an official basis. Not as a cop, but as an expert. You could direct me in finding the right questions to ask and everything else." He wondered to himself how he would define *everything else,* then hastily dismissed the possibilities.

"I don't know if I could really do much," she said.

"Listen, I know we may discover no connection at all, but I think there's something here that I can't put my finger on in my vast policeman ignorance. I don't know much about psychology, remember?"

She had to smile at his earnestness. "Okay—I think, though I'm still not sure what you want from me."

"Don't worry about the details now. You'll be like my psychic on this case."

"What do you mean?"

"Well, we don't like to publicize the fact, but the department does use psychics from time to time, especially when we have a case that's tough to break."

"Really?"

"You don't approve?"

"I don't know. I try to keep an open mind about these things."

"Believe me, in this business, you really need it, too."

"I'm not a psychic, but I'm willing to give you the benefit of my brains."

"Good. I kind of suspected you'd want to help. And, don't worry, I won't interfere with your regular work. In fact, if at any time I get in your way, just tell me to get out of your face and I'll do it without question."

She laughed again. The nervous tension in her hands was now gone. Curiously, it was being replaced by a different type of tension that she felt elsewhere on her person. She recognized the nature of the feeling readily enough and immediately tried to ignore it. But his after-shave *was* persistent, even though his wedding band provided an equally persistent counterpoint to its implicit message.

"Well, Carl, where do we begin?"

He opened the portfolio and brought out several file folders. "I brought along everything we know about each case so far. Statements, witnesses, the works. I have medical histories, profiles and, of course, the descriptions each person gave of his or her dreams. That's where I need your expert opinion." He handed the folders over to her.

Marian laid them aside and looked to him for further instruction.

"I want you to read these at your leisure, Marian. Then we'll get back together—at your convenience, of course. I'll be anxious for your ideas."

"I hope I can offer something constructive."

"I'm sure you can." He glanced at his watch, then stood. "I'd better let you get back to work." He reached over and shook hands with her. "I'm looking forward to working with you."

She smiled graciously and grasped his hand firmly, perhaps too firmly. She wanted to say something, but the words wouldn't come. "I'll be in touch with you soon." That wasn't it. She wanted to tell him about her sense of guilt and how she needed to rid herself of it somehow. No, that wasn't it, either. She wanted to tell him about Richards. That was it.

Pretty smart, Marian, she told herself. Compound your folly. Make a real fool of yourself—just when you have an opportunity to do something. She almost bit her tongue in her effort to avoid saying more. Instead, she offered a lame good-bye as he walked to the door and let himself out.

When he was gone, she allowed herself to feel relieved, but it was with only fleeting satisfaction. The policeman hadn't come to take her away after all; he had come for her help. And she had offered it without thinking of the consequences and how they would be multiplied if Carl did discover she was holding things back from him. She felt like a very deceptive person— like some kind of criminal.

But she knew he didn't regard her that way.

The scent of his after-shave lingered in the air.

He regarded her as a straightforward professional who could really assist the police. Maybe she could compensate for her withholding evidence (was that what it was?) by being especially helpful, going beyond what was asked of her.

The memory of his smile and his easygoing manner also lingered.

Marian dismissed the thought that was trying to surface in the back of her mind, the thought accompanied by the unfamiliar, yet remembered, feelings stirring deep within her. Certain things were not to be; a person couldn't let hormones direct her life.

She wondered idly what the "J" stood for in his initials.

She took the pile of folders Carl had left and set them in front of her. Opening the one on top of the stack, which described the case of the Douglas boy, she glanced at the first page of notes.

At first she felt like a voyeuristic outsider, but as she continued reading, her professional curiosity took over. All her feelings of guilt, dread, and misdirected sexuality began gradually to subside.

She might enjoy playing cop for a while after all.

When Carl returned home that night it seemed the lawn was glistening, even in the dark. It smelled like strong chemicals, too, and irritated his nose. His buoyant mood was almost wrecked.

A bill lying on the kitchen table finished destroying his good feelings. It was from Dwyer Lawn Treatment for a second application on the lawn.

Goddamn it! Laura was deliberately defying him by having the grass treated again.

He considered going upstairs to confront her. But he was too weary. It had been a long day and he just didn't have the energy for another protracted argument. Besides, she was probably already asleep.

He fixed himself a quick snack of milk and Oreos, munching the cookies quietly until his rage dissipated. What was the use? Laura was determined to force the issue, after all. It was obvious she didn't really want to save the marriage. She was interested only in continuing to torment him one way or another.

And what was he doing about it?

Nothing.

Well, not absolutely nothing. He was at least interacting with another woman. He knew it was only a harmless flirtation, that

155

he didn't really have any desire for Marian—beyond a professional relationship, that is. He just wanted her help. What was wrong with that?

Nothing at all. He was a police officer and police officers often called on experts for help. It wasn't his fault that Marian Turner was an attractive, vibrant young woman. It wasn't his fault she was intelligent. It wasn't his fault her skin was flawless and . . .

Damn it!

He returned to the cookie jar, a ceramic rendition of the head of W.C. Fields, and gathered another handful of Oreos. He had always been a nut for W.C. Fields. The cookie jar was a reminder of the earlier days of his marriage, when Laura cared for him and bought presents to please him. She had bought it for his thirty-first birthday. That seemed ages ago now.

He wondered what Marian Turner thought of W.C. Fields.

Yawning, he set his empty glass on the counter. Then he went out to the stairs to go up to the bedroom. Halfway up, it occurred to him Laura might not be sleeping at all.

She might be waiting up there for him, anxious to start the expected battle over the lawn treatment. Her snarling face was going to make it difficult to get a decent rest.

Then an even more disturbing possibility presented itself: She might be waiting up there for sex. He closed his eyes and images of her rolling around assaulted his senses. He could smell her cigarette breath. He could see the many blemishes that mottled her skin. He could hear her raspy voice.

A phrase he'd heard on the Bob and Tom Show on radio that morning popped into his mind: "rubbing uglies." That's what sex with her was like.

The very idea was too nauseating to contemplate.

He decided not to take a chance on either possibility and turned around. He considered sleeping on the couch, but he knew that would make him too vulnerable. Laura would get to him too easily there in the morning, and he had no desire to be awakened by her yammering. The couch was out.

He thought a moment, then went out to the garage and found an old cot they kept around for the rare occasions they had company. It was dusty and smelled a bit of mildew, but he brushed it off with his hands and it didn't seem too bad. As long as there were no spiders on it, Carl could rest easily.

He unfolded the cot and set it out on the floor in between his and Laura's cars, then stripped down to his underwear. Lying down, he felt suddenly claustrophobic, as if the sides of the cars might engulf him somehow. He got up and moved the cot to a space toward the front of the garage, then lay down again.

He felt much better. Now he could relax and replay the day's events in his mind.

It was strange how things had worked out, how he had gone from feeling sorry for himself and his estranged relationship to feeling like he was a young man again, all in the space of a few hours. But the strangest thing of all was when he had discovered the dream link among the four cases. As soon as he had made that connection, the face of Marian Turner had immediately come into his mind.

She sure was a far cry from a marriage counselor.

Fourteen. Richards Reminiscing

The lab was a wreck.

Chemicals were splattered and smeared on the walls. Delicate test instruments had been virtually disemboweled, coils of wire and transistors ripped out of them and strewn across the room. The computer terminals were reduced to worthless rubble, their screens smashed and their keyboards trampled on. Pages had been torn from notebooks, and reams of priceless, perhaps unrecoverable data littered the floor like so much trash. Chairs, tables, and desks were overturned.

A cat with no top to its head lay dead in the corner. Another cat, similarly minus its cranial cap, had crawled behind the bank of cabinets against the wall and refused to come out, hissing and scratching at anyone that approached it. Guinea pigs and gerbils crawled through the debris, darting in and out, looking for secure places to hide.

The air stank of blood and feces; the sounds of fluids seeping and dripping magnified the smell.

There were three dead baboons on the floor. One of them had a leg torn off. All of them had met violent ends.

Only one baboon had survived. It was in the test chamber, sitting in its metal chair doing nothing. It seemed to be asleep.

* * *

When Dr. Richards arrived that morning, three lab assistants were already busy cleaning things up. They didn't even pause when he came in the door, though his entrance usually commanded immediate respect.

"What the hell happened here?" he asked with distaste, directing his question to a small woman with olive skin and dense black hair. She was half bent over, trying to catch a gerbil. Shards of glass from broken test tubes crunched under her feet. She stopped and straightened up; the top of her head barely reached Richards's collarbone.

"We're not sure, Dr. Richards," she said, her accent betraying her Middle East origins. "We think the baboons ... they escaped from the testing ... environment ... somehow." She found it difficult to look Richards in the eyes.

"That's impossible."

"Nevertheless, doctor, that seems to be the case."

"The only way that could happen is if someone left the door unlocked. Wouldn't you agree?"

"Oh, doctor, none of us would do that. No, no, no." The more upset she grew, the more pronounced her accent became. It also irritated Richards that much more.

"I suppose you think the baboons picked the lock themselves."

"No, no, no."

Her voice was really grating on his nerves, so he decided to silence it. "We won't discuss it any further at the moment; just get this mess cleaned up. Get someone from maintenance up here to help, after you've saved the animals."

"Yes, sir."

As she returned to pursuing the gerbil, Richards swept the room with an angry gaze, grimacing as his eyes stopped at various points to assess the damage. He regretted the loss of the baboons the most, not because of any humane concern for them, but because of the valuable research data they represented.

Then he noticed his desk was on its side and started toward

it, picking his way through the mess, trying not to get his clothing or shoes soiled. In this he was unsuccessful. By the time he reached his desk, his shoes and trouser cuffs were both stained with green, yellow, and orange muck. He also just missed mashing a guinea pig.

The desk had a few scratches and stains, but fortunately the file drawer had not come open, which was all that really mattered to him. It was important that no one see what he kept there.

It bothered him, however, that the wrecked laboratory would be impossible to conceal. Morton would cast blame on him, no matter who turned out to be ultimately responsible; after all, he was in charge.

He ordered the woman to stop chasing the gerbil and get him a clean lab coat.

"They've all been ruined, Dr. Richards."

"That is not my problem; it's yours. You go find one somewhere."

"Yes, sir." She bowed slightly and left the room, making a skittering motion that reminded Richards of the gerbil she had been pursuing.

Without asking for help, he heaved the desk back up on its legs, picked a chair up from the floor, and sat down, seemingly oblivious to the labors of the assistants. He pretended to be writing in his notebook, but he was really concentrating on something altogether different.

He was remembering.

Being in charge of a hospital, even a modest mental institution such as Farley, was the biggest accomplishment of Richards's career. He was the Chief of Staff, in charge of everything and everybody. He had worked years to achieve this goal—years spent in toadying and distasteful ass kissing—but it had paid off.

He had a fairly generous salary; he had status in the psychiatric community; and most of all he had power. Nor was it only administrative power, the exercise of which satisfied him rather mildly; he had power of a more significant nature—the power of life and death, which he exercised only rarely, at least in the early part of his career.

This sinecure provided material perks as well. He had the use of a brand new Cadillac, furnished to him as a company car. And he received discounts in many stores in Tempe, Arizona, the town on the outskirts of which Farley was located, a particular perk that made his wife, Fran, very happy. She also shared in the respect he received in the community. She loved attending the many social functions to which the two of them were often invited, especially the banquets. Richards loved seeing her delight and enjoyment as she basked in the light of his success and accomplishments.

She deserved to be a part of it, for in large measure she had contributed to his getting to this position and status at the age of forty-six. She had been his touchstone, the driving force in his life, his impetus to succeed. She had worked extra jobs to help support him while he attended medical school. She had helped him in many other ways, too, guiding him in his manners and the way he dressed, helping him meet the right people and always being the perfect wife whenever she was called upon to participate in the sucking up that was necessary to climb to the top in any profession. She had sacrificed so much so he would succeed. She had even put off having children—until it had been too late.

So it didn't make any sense that she had died only two years after he was appointed to his position at Farley. It didn't make any sense at all. She was stricken with a severe case of bacterial meningitis. It was an ugly, paralyzing malady that made her last few weeks on earth agonizing not only for her, but for him.

He hated watching his Fran turn into a helpless wretch, and toward the end he hated himself for not having the resources—mental, physical, or medical—to help her more. All he could do was watch those pale blue eyes suffer in silence, pleading with him for help or, at the very least, for an explanation.

But he couldn't explain to her why she didn't respond to the antibiotics. He couldn't explain that medical science was sometimes ineffectual and often inept.

He was tempted many times to end her suffering with a simple injection, and he knew Fran would understand how that would be the best possible way he could help her. But every fiber of his being protested against the idea. He felt he'd already done enough to her in this life by causing her to sacrifice so much for his greater good and not for hers.

He had watched her die, and when Fran died, much of what made Stephen Richards a decent human being died, too. Without her as his guiding light, the quality of his life, as well as the disposition of his character, quickly deteriorated.

It began with a series of nightmares in which he cast himself as a specter of death, watching over his wife. These continued for weeks, disrupting his sleep to the point that he was almost unable to function during the day.

He tried taking a leave of absence, flying to Europe for a few weeks' rest, but the nightmares didn't abate, nor did his travel chase away the memories. Seeing the world's celebrated places was a constant reminder of how alone he was.

When he returned to America, he started taking drugs and spent a few months walking through a continual fog.

Then all of a sudden the nightmares were gone, and it was as if he had awakened from a sleep as profound as death. Life had no meaning for him, but life had to go on.

He determined to immerse himself in his work. That would be what Fran would have wanted. He could live for her.

A year after Fran's death, Richards had begun the experiments.

It all started out simply enough. He had volunteered the use of several of his patients for testing a powerful new antischizophrenic formulation. The drug company involved had approached him on several occasions, but he had always resisted their overtures, professing an ethical aversion to testing on human subjects. But with Fran gone, his sense of ethics had taken a new twist. Human beings no longer seemed to matter, and it was suddenly easy for him to compromise his values.

It was then he discovered just how much his power of life and death over people could be used.

Of course, he did everything possible to make it appear the testing was being conducted under controlled conditions that insured nothing would go wrong, that no one would get hurt. With the pretense of ethical practice established, it had been relatively easy to persuade the relatives of the patients there was no danger inherent in the testing.

After all, laymen were generally ignorant of drugs and the motives of drug companies. People assumed drug companies had well-developed senses of altruism, while in reality they were concerned with the bottom line—that is, big profits—above all else, just as any business was. That's why only certain drugs reached the market—not so much because of the FDA's seemingly stringent regulations, but because there was little profitability in producing certain drugs no matter how direly they might be needed by some suffering people.

Drug companies preferred to market drugs that would get people hooked: tranquilizers, antidepressants, uppers, downers, sleeping pills—anything on which a person could develop both a psychological and physiological dependence. Such drugs were gold mines for the big pharmaceutical companies; they paid big dividends. The public even thanked the companies for providing them.

So it was a simple matter to convince the patients' families the new drug would make their loved ones "better." They were already programmed to believe that relief was only a swallow away. Was it so difficult to accept that a miracle drug would keep Uncle Bert from drooling on himself and remove that dull look from his eyes; that it would open up the world of reality

163

for sister Bess; that it would keep young Greg from playing with himself? Of course not! Not if the Chief of Staff at the hospital said it would do those things. Would he lie?

"Yes, Mr. Smith," he would say, "your wife has been selected to participate in a program that will most certainly alleviate many of her symptoms. The prospects are very good."

"Will it cost much more?"

"That's the nice aspect of this, Mr. Smith. It costs you nothing."

And the patient's spouse or parent or relative would sign on the dotted line, theoretically exonerating the drug company, Farley Hospital, and especially, Dr. Stephen Richards from responsibility.

He had withheld certain facts, however. He had conveniently overlooked the results of some of the preliminary testing on animals, just as he had conveniently overlooked the potential side effects, one of which was a violent and immediate death; another, which was even more harrowing, was increased severity of symptoms.

He put himself in charge of administering the drugs. He had selected twelve patients as the guinea pigs, and he started out administering the antischizophrenic twice a day. After two weeks, it was evident this dose did nothing. So he upped the dose to four times a day, then six times a day. When he hit eight, things began to happen.

One patient's heart stopped. Sorry about Uncle Bert.

Another patient tried to kill herself. Sorry, Mr. Smith.

Two patients became comatose. Sorry about Bess and young Greg.

Three patients withdrew into deeply paranoid worlds of their own making and spent the rest of their lives living in their own heads. So sorry about that.

But, remember, it had cost nothing.

The remaining patients went berserk. They went on a trashing spree one night in the special ward that separated them from the rest of the hospital and wrecked everything, leaving behind them a shambles of things and people that included a strangled fellow patient and a raped nurse.

Richards had come upon the scene too late to salvage anything and much too late to cover it up.

A board of inquiry was formed. Richards came before the board and tried to defend himself, but it was clear from the beginning that he was the designated scapegoat. After all, he had been in charge. He was ultimately responsible, no matter what he said.

The nurse who had been molested saw to that. She was only too glad to drive nails in his professional coffin. She refused to keep quiet and told the board all kinds of damning things, damaging his character and reputation irreparably.

"Did you administer this drug yourself, Dr. Richards?"

"Yes."

"Were you aware of the side effects?"

"I took all due caution."

"Did you inform the relatives of these patients of the potential dangers?"

"I did what was necessary."

"Did you monitor the patients' progress on a continual basis?"

"Of course."

Did you compromise your ethics?

Yes, yes, and yes!

If he hadn't had some influence, if he hadn't been able to call in some favors, he would have gone to jail. As it was, he lost his license to practice medicine in Arizona and depleted most of his resources in legal battles with the families of patients.

It was incredible that he could fall so far, so quickly. No sinecure, no Cadillac, no more hobnobbing with the upper crust. The only good thing was that Fran was not there to see it. Of course, if she were there, it might not have happened.

It was some time before he secured another position with a

company that even recognized he was a physician. That was with an abortion clinic in Indianapolis.

Then the opportunity at Shodale opened up, which Richards had heard about from one of the company's salesmen. He interviewed with Morton and discovered a man with many of his own qualities. And Morton didn't care about Richards's past. Indeed, he seemed to *want* a man of the doctor's character, and Richards didn't bother to question his superior's motives. He desperately wanted a position where he could command respect again.

It was good to be back in such a job, even if it was in research, which, upon reflection, promised to be better than an administrative post.

In research, he could play God.

The scene before Richards didn't duplicate the scene of human destruction he had witnessed some years before, but it came close. If anything, the baboons were less destructive than the human crazies had been. Baboons had limited imaginations.

He remembered finding that nurse cowering behind the door in the ward back at Farley. She was a middle-aged woman with graying hair and large breasts, not a likely target for anyone's lust in his estimation. Yet there she lay, not quite in shock, trembling with rage. Her face, arms, and legs were battered and bruised. Her uniform was ripped open down the front and her panties were hanging off one ankle.

"You son of a bitch," she had screamed at him. "Your goddamn loonies raped me!"

"Let me help you," he had said, trying to soothe her.

"Don't touch me."

He bent down to help her up, but she twisted away from him and screamed.

Then he just left her there and walked away, back to his office where he spent the next few minutes shredding documents. There would be no book about the experiments. There would be no praise from his colleagues. There would be nothing but infamy.

If he hadn't destroyed his notes at that precise moment, he *would* have spent the rest of his life in jail. Without them, much of what the nurse said was speculation. He had saved his own life, if not his career.

Fortunately, the present incident involved no humans.

But, like a fool, he was keeping notes again. These documents might not be as threatening, since he was confining his experimentation to animals, but if someone were to find them and it were to come out that he had given drugs to that Myers fellow, it wouldn't be too difficult to predict the outcome.

Damn it to hell! Why did Myers have to screw up everything? He needed to test the drug on humans. And now this fiasco! It was as if the universe were conspiring against him personally.

He would have to start all over—with new animals, a new batch of 4155A, and new parameters.

But before any of that would happen, he had to worry about the investigation that would follow this morning's incidents. He didn't need any more of that kind of misery in his life, not with Morton keeping close watch over him, not with Dr. Marian Turner against him, not with Myers's attorney hounding him day after day.

He had to destroy those notes at the earliest opportunity— before too many questions were asked.

Richards put away his memories and turned his gaze to the lab. Some progress had been made. The surviving animals were safely in their cages and the lone baboon had been locked in the test chamber. The maintenance crew had arrived to assist in the real clean-up work. They were already grumbling and cussing.

The notes could wait; there were too many people around to spirit them away safely now, and there would be too many questions. Besides, he had remained silent long enough. It was time for him to reassert his authority.

"You ..." he began, singling out one of the male lab assistants. He was blanking out on the fellow's name.

"Alex," the assistant supplied.

"Yes, Alex. Mr. Stryker, isn't it?"

"Yes, sir."

"Which baboon survived?"

"I think it's number seven."

"Did you take precautions against its getting out?"

"The door is secured."

"It want it double secured, and give that monkey a shot of tranquilizer. I want it subdued for the rest of the day."

"But ..."

"I know what you're going to say. I'm too concerned about safety now. I can't worry about interaction with the test drugs." He stood and started pacing the floor. "How many animals are dead?"

"Seven, including the three baboons. There's one cat and two guinea pigs. We think we got all the gerbils. Nadjat is doing a head count right now."

"Very efficient. Very efficient, indeed." The words sounded like praise, but the effect was negated by his delivery. "Where are the corpses?"

"In the unused test chamber next door for the time being."

"Prepare them all for autopsies."

"Sir?" Stryker's face showed horror.

"Do I have to repeat myself? Prep them!"

"Now, sir?"

"Yes, now. I want to get to the bottom of this."

Alex looked stricken. A human superior would have given them the day off after all the work they'd just done. Of course, the whole staff knew Richards wasn't human. His bowed head concealed a sigh of frustration. "Who do you want to assist you, sir?"

"No one. I'm going to do them all myself. I'm the only one qualified."

Stryker started to say there were many qualified people around, but he knew better than to question Richards, especially when he was obviously in one of his hellfire moods.

"Don't you want someone to take notes?"

"No, but get me a tape recorder and several blank microcassettes."

"Yes, sir."

Stryker and another assistant started gathering instruments for the autopsies. In a few minutes, the dead animals were prepped and waiting in the room next door.

The scalpel descended and sliced, parting the flesh in the first baboon. The creature was homuncular though disanimated of the antics that made people compare such beasts to humans.

Richards worked steadily, speaking in low, almost hushed tones into the voice-activated microcassette recorder he had suspended from one of the lights. Sunlight intruded from the opposite windows and glittered off the edge of his scalpel, bouncing into his eyes occasionally and impeding his progress. He paid no attention to that or any other distraction. He had left orders he was not to be disturbed for any reason.

After checking the internal trunk organs of the animal, he started on the skull, cutting out the top of it with an electric bone saw. At first glance, the condition of the brain indicated nothing unusual.

He split the brain, then probed deeper.

He found something he wasn't even looking for.

Shaking, he continued cutting and probing, peeling back layers of flesh and muscle, all the while murmuring into the recorder.

A foul smell assailed his nostrils and he almost dropped the scalpel.

He didn't know whether to believe his eyes or not. This was incredible, unexpected—unpredictable.

He worked more quickly now, moving to the next baboon without even stopping to wipe sweat from his brow. On this one, he didn't bother with the internal organs but went directly to the skull.

He labored well into the evening, finding the same thing on every animal.

Then, when he was finished, he cut the thing out of each of them and put the pieces in jars with preservative, then hid the jars in a safe place, planning to pick them up later for further tests.

He almost dreaded what those tests might reveal.

It was near midnight when Richards returned to the lab. His lab coat was soiled, but for once he didn't care. He was tired and distraught. He wanted only to go home and try to sleep.

He stood in the door of the darkened room a moment and took a deep breath. It smelled better now, but certain things would linger in the air a long time.

He switched the overhead lights on, then went to his desk to deposit, with his notes, the tapes he had made. He opened the file drawer and tossed them in, hesitating momentarily.

Should he destroy his notes now?

No, it could wait. He wanted to go over them one more time, if only to see if anything he had observed in the past could offer even a hint of what he had discovered in the autopsies. Having made that decision, he pushed the drawer shut and locked it.

The lab was quiet, as if the surviving animals were subdued. He didn't even hear the skittering sound the gerbils usually made at night, when they would scratch at the walls of their cages for hours on end, while rearranging their environments to suit a purpose only they knew.

He walked over to the door of the test chamber to check on the lone baboon now there and looked in the window at the slumbering animal. He wondered what he would find if he were to open its skull. For the moment, however, he wanted to keep it alive.

The baboon was a male, weighing perhaps seventy-five pounds, easily the largest of the group. Its size might have explained why it was the only baboon alive. There were dark brown-red crescents under its fingernails and scratches on its abdomen, which might explain something, too.

It had a glistening erection.

The beast sat there without moving, its chest rising and falling in a regular pattern. Its eyes were closed, but Richards thought he could detect movement beneath the lids. It was possible the thing was dreaming.

Perhaps, Richards thought with mordant self-amusement, the monkey was dreaming he was a human being.

Fifteen. Whiskey and Twinkies

It was a bright afternoon. The sun was shining so intensely that it made everything sparkle, even trash. It glinted off the pavement, causing points of light to dance before the eyes, and it bounced off the discards of civilization that lay everywhere, rendering aluminum cans jewellike in the brightness.

A grizzled old man pushed an old Kroger bascart down the alley, his eyes squinting in the brightness, his vision fighting the intensity of the sun. He stopped occasionally to pick up the discarded jewels—the aluminum cans, inspecting every trash container for more cans.

He was sixtyish, with a sallow face and a complexion that approached jaundice in its color. His head was square and sloped oddly up the back, as if his mother had never turned him over when he was a baby. He had a large ragged cut running from his right ear to the middle of his chin, which he had acquired when running from a cop a week before; the cut was slow to heal and itched constantly. His eyes looked like black olives, and there were deep, dark circles permanently etched beneath them. His nose was inflamed at the end, had been broken several times, and had healed crookedly. His teeth— what was left of them—were yellow and caked with plaque. His tongue was coated with a phlegmy substance that seemed to grow. His ears were overlarge and stuck out absurdly.

His face gave the impression of a human being slowly turning into an animal—because of the hair. He always had a week's beard, extra hair sprouted from his nostrils, his ears bristled with black hairs, and his eyebrows were so shaggy they produced a kind of dandruff.

His smell corroborated the transformation from man to beast: Filth clogged his pores; he was constantly pissing on his feet; he never bathed; he had trouble remembering to go to the bathroom, and when he did he was not concerned overmuch with the necessary hygiene.

He wore a plaid jacket, which he had bummed from the Salvation Army, and baggy trousers. His shirt was an old flannel on which one pocket was torn. He wore a red baseball cap he had found in a trash bin behind Earl Scheib's, the place where they painted cars, and the cap was splattered with many different shades of enamel. His shoes were run-down at the heels and mismatched—one black, one brown—and neither had shoelaces. The right shoe—the brown one—had a hole in its sole, and he had stuck a piece of cardboard in it to protect the bottom of his foot.

His normal gait was somewhat bowlegged and slow; he walked as Popeye might walk if he were a real person. He had so many physical things wrong with him he barely noticed when new symptoms appeared, though he felt he was coughing and his nose was running more than usual lately.

His name was Larry.

Larry's cart was getting full. Pretty soon he'd have enough cans to cash in so he could buy a pint of whiskey. His progress was slow, though, since the afternoon sun hurt his eyes so much and he was sweating under the jacket.

"When the fuck did summer get here?" he mumbled as he bent over. It was an honest question for him; he couldn't keep track of time or the passing of the seasons, and shifts in the weather always seemed abrupt and surprising to him. It seemed every part of his body ached when he stood up, even his scro-

173

tum. He wiped his nose on his sleeve. "Son-of-a-bitching weather. Fucking nose."

The aluminum-can-picking-up business was doing quite well for Larry, especially since the machine over at the Marsh Supermarket started paying forty cents a pound for aluminum. Forty cents! It used to be twelve. Now he didn't have to pick up so many cans to make a few dollars. Instead of spending all day scavenging, he could collect enough for a pint in about three hours, particularly if he hit Christian Park, where people left lots of cans, especially the teenagers who went there at night to drink beer away in secret.

"Drink and screw, that's all they do," Larry said under his breath, then laughed to himself.

But the laughter quickly subsided as he remembered something he had read in a week-old newspaper he had found that morning. The paper said two dead teenagers were found in Christian Park—*his* park—on a Monday morning. The story disturbed Larry on several levels. First, he didn't like to think the park was no longer safe, because it was basically his home, even though the place smelled so bad lately. Second, the story was very similar to a dream he had had a few nights ago.

In the dream, he had discovered two kids under a blanket, just humping away to beat hell. Except they didn't seem like kids to him. They seemed like some kind of monsters, and it seemed like he had tried to kill them with a rock.

So reading a story that sounded like the dream made him wonder about his brain.

Of course, his brain wasn't ever too clear. He made sure of that, because when it did start to clear up and memories began to rush in, he would do something to fog it up as soon as possible, like chugalugging a half pint of whiskey or tossing off a couple of jugs of wine.

Usually, the alcohol not only numbed the brain but everything else as well. Larry didn't have to worry about his past, his future, or his present, about being sick, about dying, or even about what to do with his dick. And the best thing of all had

174

always been that he didn't dream, because he didn't sleep; he just passed out.

The nightmare about the teenagers had been only one dream. Larry had been dreaming a great deal lately—about monsters, about murderous women, about gigantic squirrels and bats and rabid wolverines, and about things he thought he had erased from his brain ages ago. These dream-things were something like the things he saw when he had the D.T.'s, only much worse—much more vivid and frightening.

No amount of alcohol would make the dreams go away.

Larry judged his cart was as full as it needed to be, and he turned out of the alley and went up the sidewalk on Washington Street, toward the Marsh Supermarket that was three blocks away, on the corner of Sherman. The wheels of the cart kept catching in the cracks in the concrete of the sidewalk, but he continued to push, urging himself on with visions of whiskey bottles. It wouldn't be long now before he'd be plunging into sweet oblivion.

On the other side of the street, he saw a black man carrying a big plastic trash bag that clinked and rattled, and he realized he had been collecting aluminum cans, too. Suddenly, he was inspired.

"Hey, brother!"

The black man didn't stop.

"Hey, man. You there, with the bag."

The man halted and looked across at Larry. He was a thin man, possibly in his late forties, wearing grease-streaked mechanic's overalls.

"What you want?"

"Come on over here. I got a proposition for you."

The man shook his head and continued on his way.

"Hey, brother, listen. C'mon." Larry was having trouble keeping up with him.

"I ain't your fucking brother, honky," he shouted back.

"Listen, I got an idea for some money." All this shouting was making his throat ache.

"Shit, man," the black man said and stopped, apparently deciding to deal with Larry and get it over with. He waited for the traffic on Washington to let up a little, then walked slowly across.

"Okay, man, what the fuck you want?" When he got close enough to take in Larry's general aroma, he pulled back and winced.

Larry fixed a broken smile on his face and cocked his head to one side. "Ease off, brother."

"Quit calling me brother, motherfucker. Tell me what you want and get it over with." He was about two inches taller than the other man, but that didn't intimidate Larry at all.

"You got cans. I got cans. We could put them together and get more money."

"Shit, man, why I want to do that?"

"Well, you get more money that way."

The black man found himself getting interested, but then he thought about it and started walking again. "I got as many cans as you. Maybe I got more. How the hell we get more money that way?"

Larry pushed his cart alongside the man. His mind was racing; for some reason, he felt he had to have those extra cans the man was carrying, but he wasn't sure how to get them. He should have thought this thing out in greater detail. Then another inspiration hit him.

"Okay, what about the odd ounces?" Larry asked.

The black man stopped. "What?"

"The machine screws you if you got odd ounces. Like, if you got a fraction of an ounce, it won't give you the money."

"So?"

"So, if we put our cans together, we can be sure we don't get screwed. I'll split with you fifty-fifty. That way we both get treated right."

The man was still skeptical. "I ain't done picking up."

176

"Now, what have you got to lose, bro—I mean, buddy? Come on down to Marsh with me and we'll put all our cans in together and split the money. Ain't nothing to it."

"I don't know."

"C'mon, man. You ain't got nothing to lose at all."

"I guess it'll be all right. I'm getting tired of picking them up, anyhow."

"Sure you are."

The two of them continued to the supermarket without saying much more, though it seemed to Larry the black man was having second thoughts.

Just hold on, he thought. Be cool. It's going to work.

"Nice day, ain't it?" Larry said as they reached the edge of the parking lot.

"No, it ain't."

"Whatever you say, man." Larry shut up until they got to the collection center.

"Dump your cans in the cart."

"Hey, man—oh, fuck it." The man emptied the trash bag into the bascart.

Larry rubbed his hands like a miser who had found a secret cache of gold.

The big machine that collected the cans stank like stale garbage, but that didn't bother either man much. Larry pushed his cart up to the bin and dumped all the cans in. The machine made an outrageous noise, rumbling as it chewed up the cans, then eventually delivered four dollars and thirty cents in a little metal cup in front.

Larry scooped up the money and counted it rapidly, even though an LED display on the machine displayed the amount. "Not bad, my man."

"I think I got fucked on that one," the black man said. He tried to look menacing, but Larry ignored him.

"No, you didn't. We got rid of them odd ounces. Made it fair and square."

"Give me my half, then."

"Sure. Let's see. Now you don't want all them quarters, do you?" Larry's mind was racing again. Four dollars and thirty cents would buy a good pint. Two dollars and fifteen cents wouldn't buy shit.

"Still spends, man. Give me my half, motherfucker, or I'm taking it all."

"You ain't taking shit," Larry yelled and rammed the bascart into the man's mid-section. The corner of it hit him square in the groin, causing him to double over in pain immediately. He fell back on the pavement and started screaming obscenities.

Larry smirked with satisfaction. He turned and ran across the parking lot toward Sherman Avenue, his legs pumping as they hadn't in months. He was almost hit by a woman driving a van, but that didn't slow him down at all.

He was too preoccupied to worry about his safety; he was thinking of whiskey and its sweet respite.

He also had an incredible craving for a pack of Twinkies. That was no problem; he could get Twinkies at the liquor store.

It was twilight. As evening approached, Larry sat on a bench in Christian Park, feeling good. His stomach rumbled and gurgled as it fought to digest the mixture of whiskey and Twinkies he had forced down his throat, but otherwise his mood was rather mellow.

He smiled as he remembered how smart he had been with that black guy. Maybe having the old brain clear sometimes had its advantages, if it wasn't left clear too long.

Of course the brain felt much better when it wasn't clear. To prove that point, he brought out the pint and took another swig, then held the bottle up to determine how much he had left. It was half full, and that would be enough to blot out the rest of the evening.

He turned the bottle up and drank.

178

Bats hovered in the air. They were looking for Larry and they were patient. They would find him soon.

Larry had crawled under the bench to hide. Bats were bad enough, because they got in your hair, but six-foot-tall bats were impossible to deal with. They could easily devour a person and wouldn't even feel bad about it.

It was not only bats he had to be wary of. There were monsters everywhere tonight.

Out on English Avenue things with lights for eyes sped by. Occasionally a giant bird would soar overhead, its cry rending the night air. There were giant squirrels about, too. And wolverines. There might be snakes, too.

Larry shook uncontrollably. He had no idea how he could escape all the monsters. One of them would surely get him if he showed his face at all.

He clamped his hands over his eyes and moaned. Then he started cussing under his breath, letting fly a stream of profanity that would banish any flying or crawling thing forever. He engaged in this protracted curse for half an hour, and when he uncovered his eyes, the monsters were gone.

He crawled out from under the bench and sat up on it. The cut on his face itched viciously and he clawed at it a few seconds, drawing blood. Finally, the itching sensation went away and he took out the whiskey bottle. There were three, maybe four, swallows left; he gulped them quickly.

The burning liquid made his whole body tingle. He belched and tasted whiskey, Twinkies, and bile on his tongue. He shivered in disgust. Twinkies tasted good going down, but they didn't really mix well with whiskey. He hoped he could keep it all down.

He decided to take a walk, just to make certain all the monsters were gone. As he approached English Avenue, he saw a patrol car coming along the street and turned to run. He didn't need to be hassled by John Law tonight.

There was no moon and it was very dark in the park, back beyond the radius of the street lights. Larry couldn't see where he was going very well and ran into a tree. He stumbled back, then darted around the tree.

His eyes were assaulted as he suddenly found himself standing in a long corridor between the trees, radiating with bright light the source of which was not obvious. Awed and confused, Larry walked along the corridor. It seemed to have no end, and when he looked behind him, he couldn't see the place he had entered anymore.

He kept moving, hoping he would find the way out.

He took a few hesitant steps, then the ground before him started to move.

Snakes, intertwined and writhing, stretching in a vast, living, hissing carpet as far as he could see. There were all types of them, vipers of every hue and description: green, gray, yellow, orange, red, striped and spotted, hooded and non-hooded. Cobras, rattlers, adders, asps, boa constrictors, coral snakes, garter snakes. There were snakes that could bite him and there were snakes that could swallow him whole.

Panicking, Larry broke into a galloping run, his Popeye-gait becoming absurdly exaggerated. Every step fell on a twisting, scaly creature; every other step just missed getting him bit or swallowed.

Suddenly, there were no more snakes. Larry stopped and glanced back. All he saw was a misty area where the corridor had been. He turned, and in the time it took him to blink, he was transported to a large arched room. As he stood, the room began to fill with pews and other furnishings, with an altar at the end and a large crucifix hanging over it. The things just seemed to pop into existence.

Larry now recognized the place as a church he had gone to as a boy. He was all alone in the church. He went up to the altar and dropped to his knees.

He remained motionless several moments, trying to make something happen, then he realized he didn't remember any prayers. He folded his hands and shut his eyes, anyhow. Maybe something would come to him. Nothing did. His brain was fuzzing up again.

"Shit, can't even pray no more."

He got to his feet and looked up at the giant crucifix, which must have been eight feet tall. Only the figure of Christ wasn't spread out on this cross. It was Larry himself, and blood was oozing from his palms.

He averted his eyes and turned, clenching his fists. As he did, he felt something squishing through his fingers; it felt like he had stuck his hands in a big bowl of jelly. He opened his hands and saw round holes in the middle of his palms from which flowed thick, gooey blood. He screamed and ran down the center of the church. As he reached the door, a figure popped up in front of him.

It was a giant whiskey bottle. It had hands and feet and a skull face that was frozen in a bizarre grin. It reached out to embrace him.

Larry opened his mouth to scream, but nothing came out. Then everything dissolved and he was back in the park, lying on the ground next to the tree he had run into earlier. The sun was just beginning to come up.

He sat up and rubbed his eyes. He checked his palms and found nothing, not even a scratch.

The import of his experience struck him in a wave of self-realization that was too painful to endure. He couldn't go on the way he had been. His life had no meaning.

"I ain't no fucking good," he said. "Just a goddamn old drunk with no goddamn reason to fucking live no more." He put his hand on the ground, bracing himself to rise, and jerked back. There was a snake lying there.

Looking again, he saw it wasn't a snake after all. It was a piece of rope someone had thrown away.

The message was clear enough.

At that moment he felt exceptionally lucid and regretted hav-

181

ing drunk all his whiskey. But there was no escape from reality now. There was only one escape from anything.

The rope seemed to glow.

"Okay, Jesus, I'm coming. I ain't that fucking dense."

He picked up the rope and fumbled with it for several minutes before he managed to form a makeshift noose. He looped the noose around his neck and began looking for a suitable tree.

Larry was jolted awake so abruptly he fell off the bench. Every ache in his body was magnified tenfold. The strange, burning smell of the park was overpowering, much stronger than before, and he couldn't handle it. He righted himself, then retched and coughed. Nothing would come up except strands of green phlegm and globules of bile.

He stopped retching and caught his breath. Latent images of his dreams hovered like gossamer before his eyes. It was the worst nightmare he could remember, and the scariest part was when he had dreamed he was awake and he wasn't. Then he had dreamed he killed himself.

"Fuck a duck," he moaned, and put his hands up to his throbbing temples. His fingers brushed something, and when Larry realized what it was, he almost fainted.

His belt was around his neck.

He started running through the park, desperate to get away from his dreams and perhaps from himself. He was almost out when he hit something. It was a person, the guy who had run him out of the park the other night. He threw himself on the man and tried to strangle him.

Chuck Tripper proved much stronger than he was.

Sixteen. Memo to Morton

John Morton fought fatigue as he drove home from Indianapolis International Airport. He had just returned from a conference in New York City and was on the point of collapse after six days of meetings, seminars, and banqueting. The night life had worn on him, too, and the last night had been the most exhausting, because he had spent most of it with a high-priced call girl.

She was a tall redhead in her twenties, who came highly recommended by one of Morton's colleagues at the conference. She lived up to the recommendation very well and proved well worth her price. She had yielded to his every request without question or hesitation, even suggesting a few kinky things he never would have thought of himself. The girl's imagination was admirable.

Morton sighed as he remembered the acrobatics the two of them had indulged in. Why couldn't his wife Kate show that kind of imagination in the bedroom? Or for that matter, why couldn't any woman he knew be as adventurous?

Well, he told himself, you get what you pay for, even in the sack. If you don't pay for it, then you don't get much. Fortunately, he had the money necessary to pay for what he wanted.

He forced himself to stay awake as he cruised up Interstate 465, keeping the big Mercedes sedan at a steady sixty. He listened to WXTZ, the FM easy listening channel, playing Mantovani through the Blaupunkt stereo system.

He exited the highway at 56th Street, turning left to go to the Eagle Creek area, a newly developed section of the city where people with real money were beginning to settle. His neighbors were doctors, lawyers, and other professionals, all of whom lived in houses that cost at least half a million dollars, which was expensive for Indianapolis, where property values hadn't yet reached the outlandish levels of California or New York.

He parked the Mercedes in the three-car garage, where it kept company with a Maserati, which he hadn't wanted to trust to the security of the airport parking lot, and a Plymouth Voyager, the mini-van Kate drove.

It was eleven-twenty-five when he came into the family room. Kate was sitting in front of the Sony console, watching *The Tonight Show*.

"Hi, honey," he said, setting his luggage down.

Kate was forty-seven, trim, and tan. Her face was angular, with a sharp nose and a mouth continually on the verge of a grimace, though she could laugh easily at odd times. Her hair was dark brown and cut short. She was wearing a light blue terry-cloth robe.

"How was the trip?" she asked, not taking her eyes off Johnny Carson, who was in the middle of his monologue.

"Not bad for a business trip."

"How was New York?"

"Same as usual. Crowded and dirty."

"Are you hungry? There's baked ham left in the kitchen."

"No. I ate on the plane, some kind of stuff masquerading as food. They called it beef."

Kate nodded, which was her usual response to one of his jests. She was straining to hear Carson's every word.

Realizing the conversation was basically at an end, Morton went to the bar and made himself a vodka martini, then removed his jacket and sat on the opposite end of the couch from Kate. She didn't seem to mind his not sitting closer to her.

As he sipped the martini, much of his tiredness vanished and for once he enjoyed watching TV. During the commercial break, he inquired about their three children—two teenaged girls and an eleven-year-old boy—and learned nothing was new with them. When the show came back on, they both fell silent.

One of Carson's guests turned out to be Kathleen Turner, who was promoting her latest movie. Watching her made Morton think of Marian—not that she looked anything like Kathleen Turner. But he felt Marian had some of the potential sexuality the actress seemed to exude, even on a talk show. If she had the right attitude, she'd be a more than adequate substitute for Kathleen Turner in his fantasies.

He wondered if Marian had any imagination.

The next morning, Morton arrived at Shodale at nine o'clock, ready to get back to work.

As usual when he had been away from his desk for a few days, there was a stack of memos waiting for him. He picked up the one on top and began reading:

TO: J. Morton
FROM: A. Stryker
SUBJECT: Destruction of property, lab section VII

In accordance with company policy regarding vandalism, or other destruction of company property, I hereby submit the following account of events transpiring June 8, during which much equipment and data was lost. As far as can be determined, the destruction was a result of test animals escaping from their confinement. All animal subjects were being utilized in testing of formulation 4155A. Of these animals, four were baboons, two of which were large males. At this point, we have not yet been able to ascertain how the animals escaped, but we are continuing to investigate the matter. A report of our findings will follow. A list of damages, along with estimates for repairs, is appended. The condition of the lab was discovered at approximately ...

The memo went on to describe in detail how the lab had been wrecked and how many animals had been lost as a result. Morton scowled as he read. This wasn't the kind of news he liked to receive after being gone only a few days.

That lab was the responsibility of Dr. Richards. Indeed, he should have submitted this report, not Stryker, who was apparently a lowly assistant. Having a subordinate do the report was a deliberate act of defiance, in Morton's view, demonstrating the contempt Richards had for company policy and his rules.

In short, Richards was fucking up royally. He'd have to have another little talk with the good doctor concerning this newly developed propensity of his.

First he had screwed up in misjudging Myers, and now he was responsible for the lab being wrecked. Perhaps in the second case, it was only a technical responsibility and something over which the doctor really had no control, but it could help provide necessary ammunition to cause his dismissal, if Morton pressed it. In any case, he intended to use the incident against Richards when the opportunity presented itself.

Of course, canning Richards would not obviate all the trouble he was seeming to have with the project. Marian resisted progress in it, too, and if the board of directors or the major stockholders got their hands on some of the reports ... well, the project would never come to a profitable conclusion.

He ran his fingers through his reddish hair, a grim expression on his face. It was beginning to seem like the 4155A project was jinxed. His dreams of putting another psychobiological on the market were being thwarted at every turn, and its loss as a viable product would mean the loss of potential millions in revenue.

He shook his head numbly; 4155A wouldn't be terminated if he had anything to say about it. He'd find a way to get it on the market, no matter what happened. He'd think of something. He had in the past.

For the moment, though, he would have to let it rest, until he could determine what moves he needed to make.

He scanned through the next few memos, which were from various departments. One was a progress report on a new consumer product being test-marketed in the Indianapolis area, as many of Shodale's products were. Testing in the city was not just a matter of convenience; Indianapolis was an excellent test market for new products, and companies located in every part of the country conducted market tests in the city, because its inhabitants represented a mix of all types of people, a cross section of America. If they bought it in Indianapolis, it would usually sell everywhere.

In general, the new Shodale product was doing well in the test marketing conducted so far. It also lacked many of the negatives similar products had, though, as usual, some people complained of allergic reactions. It seemed there was always someone who was allergic no matter what the new product was— whether it was cornflakes, plastic bags, or insecticides. Reading further, Morton encountered an aspect of the product that jarred something in his memory. Maybe it was only coincidental, but it seemed there was some kind of connection here there shouldn't be. He reached for another report, compared some figures, then put both down. There *was* a connection.

But maybe it didn't mean anything. He wished he had paid more attention to his organic chemistry instructor in college, then he'd know what to make of it. His limited knowledge kept him from analyzing the data before him in depth. However, he had lots of people working for him who could explain just about anything—people who had listened well in college, people who could teach his old instructor a thing or two.

One thing was encouraging: The product had not been tested in a very wide area yet. However, the second tier of testing, scheduled to begin in a week, would take it statewide. He should know what to do before that level of testing began.

Before consulting any of his hired experts, he would pursue the matter on his own as far as he could. He buzzed his secretary and asked her to pull some relevant files.

"When you have them all together, lay them on my desk," he told her over the intercom.

"Yes, sir."

He pushed the other memos and papers aside. His intuition, which had served him well through the years, told him something was amiss, something he would have to take care of—and soon.

Until he had all the files together, he could only speculate. It would take a couple of hours for his secretary to gather it all.

In the meantime, he would go down and see Richards.

When Morton entered the lab, only one person was there, the Middle Eastern woman. She was busy injecting a guinea pig.

"Where is everyone?" he asked.

The woman was startled but recovered quickly, only to become visibly agitated when she recognized Morton. "They are working in other places," she said, her accent becoming more pronounced as she spoke.

"And where is Dr. Richards?" Morton eyed her closely and wondered what it would be like to have sex with an Arab—if that's what she was.

She placed the animal back in its cage and wiped her hands on her lab coat. "He went across to the other building to use the electron microscope, Mr. Morton."

"Do you know when he'll be back?"

"I don't know, sir. He has been gone quite some time."

"I guess I'll wait around for him. Where's his desk?"

"Over there, sir, but he does not like anyone to touch it."

He leaned closer to read her identity badge. "Listen, Nadjat, do you know who I am?"

"Yes, sir."

"Well, I own that fucking desk."

Her brown eyes grew wide and she flinched.

Morton patted her lightly on the shoulder and smiled benignly. He had asserted his authority and made his point, so he could make it even stronger by being suddenly agreeable. Most employees were readily controlled by such manipulations.

"Now, go about your work. I'll worry about Dr. Richards."

"Yes, sir," she said meekly, picking up a fresh syringe.

On his way to the desk, Morton observed the lab had been restored almost to its former state. Some disarray remained and there were still dried stains on the walls, but a coat of paint would fix a lot of things. The test instruments and computer equipment would be costly to replace, though insurance should cover most of it.

He wasn't really bothered by the physical aspects of the damage as much as he was by the lack of responsibility someone had shown. He also realized the premature death of some of the animals would screw up much of the data collected so far and that many tests would have to be begun anew. Which meant time had been wasted. Which meant testing of 4155A on humans would be delayed, and more to the point, introduction of the drug to the world would be delayed. Which ultimately meant delayed profits.

Again, he faced an impasse. It seemed everything that he encountered this morning required a wait-and-see attitude. But he wanted to make things happen. *Now.*

He sat down at Richards's desk. He was pleased to see it was tidy; for one of those brooding intellectual types, Richards was very fastidious. He even had his paper clips arranged neatly in one of those magnetic holders.

Idly, without even thinking about it, he started to pull the drawers open to check their contents. He discovered nothing unusual, except that the file drawer built into the desk wouldn't budge.

"Hey, Nadjat," he called over his shoulder, "do you have a key to this desk?"

"No, sir. Only Dr. Richards has the key. He will not allow anyone else access."

"Okay. No big deal."

He pretended to pass it off, but it really bothered him that the drawer was locked. He didn't like anyone to have secrets, and he felt his position in the company meant he should have access to everything. He tugged at the drawer's handle, thinking he might break it loose with brute force, but it still wouldn't move.

He glanced back at Nadjat and discovered she had left the room momentarily. Good.

He looked around for an implement with which to open the drawer and found a metal letter opener. He stuck the letter opener between the lock and the edge of the drawer and pried. The tip broke off.

"Goddamn it!"

He tucked the broken letter opener in his jacket pocket, then tried a pair of scissors, which didn't break but didn't open the lock, either.

He was becoming obsessed with knowing what was in the drawer, even if it was only Richards's lunch. No employee of his was going to keep secrets. But now he was in a dilemma. If he did anything else, it was going to be obvious someone had tried to break into the desk. A neat guy like Richards probably had every scratch on the desk memorized.

He needed time. If he knew for certain when Richards was returning, he could figure something out. He picked up a company phone directory, looked up a number, and dialed the extension of the room where the electron microscope was in operation.

"Microanalysis," a male voice answered.

"This is John Morton. Is Dr. Richards there?"

"No, sir."

"I was told he was using the electron microscope."

"He was, sir, but he left about an hour ago."

"Where did he say he was going?"

"He didn't, sir. I assumed he was going back to the lab."

"Okay. I'll talk to him later."

Morton hung up and dialed another extension.

The voice of the guard in the security shack answered after three rings. "Security."

"Morton here. Has Dr. Richards logged out?"

"Just a minute, Mr. Morton, I'll check the log."

Morton tapped his fingers impatiently as thirty seconds passed. He could hear the sounds of things being moved around—a clacking noise, then the rustle of papers. Finally, the guard came back on the line.

"Dr. Richards checked out for home at ten-fifteen. Not returning."

"Thanks."

He hung up. Now, at least, he knew he had some time, though he didn't like the idea of Richards leaving so early. His intuition told him something might be awry with Richards, too, but that was another wait-and-see.

The desk was his present challenge.

"Shit!" he exclaimed, and slapped his forehead with his palm. It was simple.

He picked up the phone and dialed another extension.

The maintenance people had not even questioned Morton when he had them bring him a key to Richards's desk. They hadn't dared, of course, and he knew they wouldn't tell Richards anything, either, not if they wanted to keep their jobs.

As soon as he had the desk opened, he took the notes and the tapes back to his office. He gave the tapes to his secretary, ordering her to have them transcribed before the end of the day. When she went to the secretarial pool to do that, he photocopied Richards's notes himself on the personal copier in his office.

It gave him a kind of thrill to be engaged in such spylike operations, for even though he hated secretive behavior in others, he felt it was his right to have all the secrets he wanted, especially from his employees. It made him more of a boss if he knew things no one else did. It also gave him special powers. Maybe that was why he liked to keep secrets from his wife, too, especially secret thoughts.

No one knew everything about him. That kept him from being vulnerable.

By the end of the day, the tapes and original notes were safely returned to Richards's desk. It had all been accomplished before quitting time.

Morton dismissed his secretary for the day and secured himself in his office. He had quite a pile of papers to sort through: the photocopies of the notes he'd found in Richards's desk; Richards's "official" report on 4155A; the transcriptions of the tapes Richards had made of the autopsies; and the files his secretary had pulled for him.

He knew he had before him the makings of a scandal—or perhaps the makings of a fortune, if he could make sense of it all. But his mind was going in too many directions at once. He would have to take it slow and easy, let the information sink in and percolate—let it brew. Then the connections and the ramifications would become obvious.

He fixed himself a martini at the wet bar in his office, settled down, and began to read.

By midnight, Morton had put it all together. Unfortunately, the scenario he envisioned as a result didn't look that promising.

He was going to need help to be certain of his conclusions, but he didn't know whom to trust. He needed to find someone who was knowledgeable, but expendable.

No matter what the ultimate outcome was, it boiled down to

a question of ethics versus profits. And, for once, the decision wasn't going to be that easy.

At the very least, he was going to have to hide a great deal.

Dr. Stephen Richards felt he was on the verge of a discovery that would change his life. It would make him or break him, depending on who rendered the final judgment. In this instance, the ultimate arbiter might be God.

He stared at the bourbon bottle he had emptied all on his own, still marvelling at his ability to drink so much liquor after having abstained so many years. The bourbon had clouded his mind, but it had also clarified some matters, such as who he really was and what he really wanted to accomplish.

He realized he now had the chance to prove to his departed Fran he was capable of the greatness she had always wanted for him, even without her there to prod him on. It was within his power to achieve some of that greatness and perhaps repair some of the past damage to his life. To do so meant playing God the Arbiter himself, but he had no problems with that. He had been trying out for the role throughout his entire career.

He would succeed, he knew it. Because he was the only one who knew all the secrets, the only one who knew everything about 4155A and its effects. With such knowledge, only he was in control. Soon, he would have to answer to no one.

What he had discovered with the electron microscope that morning had brought him to the brink of a revelation with overwhelming implications. There was only one piece of the puzzle missing, and filling in that single gap in his knowledge was his next priority.

All he had to do was to test product 4155A on a human subject, as soon as possible. Only one person would do. It had to be someone who could be monitored and trusted, someone who could not possibly jeopardize the outcome. It also had to be someone who had harrowing nightmares.

Richards knew of only one such person.

Seventeen. Marian's Dream

Marian watched the EEG wearily, occasionally jotting a note in the margin of the long paper rolling under the pens.

According to the wavy, oscillating lines on the paper, the subject in the sleep chamber, a Mr. Peter Herkimer, was going into REM sleep. He would be dreaming soon, and more than likely he would experience a nightmare. Later, she would find out for sure, when she woke him up and questioned him.

She longed for sleep herself, but she had volunteered to watch the subjects this week, and she would not shirk her duty despite her present state of agitation. Besides, even if she were at home, she was so stressed out she doubted she would get much rest.

There was always something eerie about being at Shodale in the middle of the night. Even though she knew there were other people in the building, she always had a sense of apprehension, brought on primarily by the darkness of the sleep chamber and the conditions provided to make it easier for the subjects to sleep.

Watching people sleep, with wires coming out of their heads and other parts of their bodies, was like watching dead people sometimes, too. It reminded her of something out of an old science fiction movie, so it was hard to remain totally objective and play the scientist under such conditions.

Some of her uneasiness also derived, she had come to realize, from the nature of the research itself. It was scary to contemplate what they were delving into. The dream state was such a frightening area of human psychology to explore, not only because of nightmares, but also because of the fact that they were investigating something the nature of which had eluded mankind for centuries. No one really knew why people had dreams.

She sometimes thought there was a reason—cosmic, divine, metaphysical, or otherwise—that discovering the true purpose of dreams had always proved so difficult for mankind.

There were many theories for the purpose of dreams, some of which were quite whimsical. Some theorists believed dreams were the brain's way of clearing out the mental computer at the end of the day; others felt that dreams were a means of acting out aggression. Then there were those who believed dreams were the brain's fantasy playground, that the brain was having its fun while the body rested. And in some current New Age philosophies, it was believed that dreams were a crossing over into another world, perhaps the spirit world, where the lines between the past and the future were blurred and prophecy often occurred. Proponents of this last idea even contended that if a person met someone in a dream, he *really* met that person, even if that person was dead.

No orthodox scientist, of course, would consider such an oddball theory as that. Only the alternative thinkers of the world, geniuses such as Colin Wilson, Lyall Watson, and T.C. Lethbridge, whose works she had encountered in a college philosophy course, would dare even consider such wild interpretations of the dream state.

Psychology had come a long way since Freud's work in dream interpretation, but it was still seeking answers. Whether one pursued a psychological or metaphysical course for the explanation of dreams, however, nothing could, as yet, be proved. It was all guesswork, all speculation. Nothing was firmly established, and perhaps it never would be.

Science was beginning to understand what dreams were *not*, one of the main findings being that dreams were not subject to

195

universal interpretation, so that all the dream books the common man bought were virtually worthless, except those that dealt with Jungian archetypes—which might, Marian secretly believed, have some validity.

Marian hadn't formulated any real theories for herself yet. She was glad to be involved in the research, which was one of the reasons she had worked so hard to get the grant from Shodale, but she continued to be dumbfounded by what it did and did not reveal.

If she had known what her research would entail once it got underway, she might not have been so eager for that grant. For one thing, she was worried about the drugs. The main reason she resisted having her subjects start on 4155A was that she believed drugs would not really solve the problems of nightmares. She knew the drugs were inevitable, though, since Shodale was in the pharmaceutical business, but she intended to delay their use as long as possible, which wouldn't be much longer if Dr. Richards or John Morton had his way.

The case of William Myers should have taught them something: Either the drug was not ready for human testing, or there was something wrong with the drug, or just maybe drugs had no place in the treatment of dream aberrations.

The incident in the animal lab should have taught them something, too. She had read the report on the damage and her instincts told her the drug had something to do with it, even though the person who wrote the report hadn't come out and said so.

Marian also believed autopsies on the dead baboons would reveal something, and she wondered, for the hundredth time, why she hadn't received copies of the autopsy reports. It could only mean someone wanted to hide something from her.

That was yet another aspect of this whole affair that was causing her stress. All her doubts, misgivings, and unease were increased more than ever because of Carl Nolan and the cases he had her working on.

The information he had given her regarding all the murder

suspects who claimed dreams had caused them to do things was really unsettling, because it seemed to suggest there was a factor of dreams that science could not yet explain.

It would be so easy if all those incidents could be readily attributed to drugs, but that simply wasn't the case. Only Myers was on drugs when he killed his family, but the others were not. Blood tests, expert testimony, and all other data indicated nothing that would make all those people suddenly go berserk. It was as if, for no apparent reason, their dreams had become overpowering realities that fed on the darkest parts of the people's psyches. It was a new phenomenon, as far as Marian knew, for which there was no precedent in the literature. She felt there had to be an outside influence that caused these things to happen. There had to be.

But what?

She had fed all the data Carl had given her into the computer at Shodale, and so far it had shown no common factors among any of the people who had committed the murders. All aspects of their lives varied widely: age, diet, education level, gender, and geography. The *only* thing they shared in common was that they had killed while "dreaming." Marian wanted truly to help Carl, but she was no Sherlock Holmes, and the frustration arising from these cases only made it more difficult for her to function.

To compound all this, Marian had realized only recently that Carl himself was the source of much of her stress. Much of his effect on her was due to an underlying feeling of guilt she felt whenever he was around. But that was not all of it, by any means. His very presence pulled at her sensibilities in a way she was ill equipped to handle—either as a psychologist or as a woman. The woman in her was having the most difficulty, because the woman wanted to respond to what the psychologist denied.

Thus, she not only felt guilty, but she also was in a constant state of ambivalence, trying to judge whether her feelings were caused by a surge of errant hormones or an inability to read Carl as well as she thought she could.

Could she really believe the policeman was interested in her? Or, more to the point, could she really believe she might be interested in him?

Her constant analysis of the situation provided little relief, however. Whatever she did or thought, whether controlled by hormones or reason, it made little difference. Because, after all the analysis, one fact remained: She felt good when the policeman was around.

Too good.

As a result, there was a war going on inside her, and she was unsure which side would claim the victory over her emotions or her life.

Marian shut all her thoughts off temporarily to concentrate on her work. She looked down at the EEG again and saw that Herkimer was still in REM. Glancing through the observation window, she noted his face showed no signs of agitation, so perhaps his dreams were pleasant tonight.

Herkimer was fitted with everything, including a device to measure his erections during his sleep, which would provide a reading called a phallogram. He had told her during the screening interview that his nightmares were always highly sexual, yet he claimed to be impotent. He was a young man, not yet thirty, and he was having a great deal of trouble dealing with his dysfunction.

Marian checked the line on the moving paper that represented the phallogram and blushed involuntarily. According to the present reading, Mr. Herkimer was having an erection at this very minute. That meant his impotence was psychological, not physiological. He could function while he was asleep, then, but not in his waking state.

Marian speculated that in this case getting rid of the nightmares might help him. But did that mean drugs should be given to him? And if they were, would taming the sexual nightmare cure his impotence?

Sexual nightmares: Marian wondered what experiencing them would be like. She couldn't recall ever having had a sexual dream of any kind, let alone a nightmare. If, indeed, she had such dreams, she had suppressed memory of them—which was what happened when anyone said they never had dreams. They were only denying memory of them.

The phallogram maintained a steady reading. This dream must be really something. In the initial interview, Herkimer had told her the details of a few of his dreams, and they *were* extremely erotic. She hoped he would be honest in relating the substance of this present dream.

She yawned and shook her head. Maybe a rip-roaring talk about sex with a strange man would wake her up. Unfortunately, she would have to wait for that talk; at present, though, she could ignore her drowsiness no longer. She had to do something to fight it now. Maybe a strong cup of coffee would help until it was time to wake Herkimer up.

She left the polysomnograph and headed for the outer office where a pot of coffee was always waiting. A man was sitting at the desk out front, a young research assistant. His sleep subject had not shown up, so he was collating data on the computer to pass the time.

He looked up from his work as Marian passed and nodded.

"How's your boy doing, Dr. Turner?"

"He's in REM right now." She started to add "and he has a hard-on" but decided she didn't know this assistant well enough. She grabbed a Styrofoam cup and poured it full. The coffee smelled like it was several hours old. It ought to be strong enough to keep the dead awake.

"Excuse me for saying so, but you look awfully tired."

"You sure you don't mean I just look awful?"

"No. Just tired. You want me to take over for a while?"

"I don't know. I thought I'd get a coffee transfusion and the tiredness would go away." She gulped some of the hot liquid.

"However, this foul brew may just kill me. In that case, notify the authorities."

"Honest, Dr. Turner, this stuff I'm working on can wait. Why don't you go home and let me take over?"

"I couldn't do that. It's about time to wake him up. I want to talk to him."

"You could take a nap in the lounge."

Marian considered the offer and found it very tempting. "That's a good idea. Grabbing a few zee's might fix me up at that."

"Sure it will."

"But you be sure to wake me if anything exciting develops. Wake me in an hour, in any case."

"Will do."

He shut his computer down and went to the sleep chamber immediately. Marian admired his youthful eagerness and wondered what had happened to her own. She wasn't that old.

Marian took another sip of coffee, winced, and set the cup down. Then she went back to the employee lounge at the other end of the hall. She switched off the light, kicked off her shoes, and lay down on the couch.

When Marian closed her eyes, it seemed as if her mind were a vortex of untamable images. She tossed about on the couch, unable to get comfortable, unwilling to succumb to sleep, though she knew she needed it desperately.

Then she took a deep breath and started counting backward from a thousand. Sometimes that lulled her to sleep.

The images began to swirl away, but the void that was left was not very conducive to rest, either. She tried to fill it by imagining a sexual dream, but all that would come to her was one of the dreams related to her by Herkimer.

He had told her he was running down a long hallway lined with naked women, trying to select one and . . .

. . . *there's hundreds of them, all redheads, all with large breasts. Some of them have no teeth. Some are tall, some short. Some of them look like movie actresses. They all smile at me and seem more than willing. I can tell they want me, but when I look down I can't get an erection. It's just soft down there and mushy, like there's no hardness in it at all, so I keep running and I hope I'll find the right one of these women who will turn me on so I can do it, because I'm aching, my crotch is aching, like I should have an erection, but I just don't.*

Then I get to the end of the line and waiting there for me is this very tall redheaded woman with hair that hangs down to the back of her knees. She's got huge breasts, and all of a sudden, I'm ready!

I push her down and jump on top of her, and I'm inside her now, thrusting and panting and about to, you know, orgasm, but then I realize it isn't a woman at all but some kind of plastic thing, a plastic robot, and it's not there to have sex with me, but to capture me, perhaps to eat me ...

... and Marian reached the end of the line of men, and waiting there was a tall, strong, muscular man with broad shoulders who wore a badge on his bare chest. He had nothing else on.

It was Carl Nolan.

Marian woke up, startled and embarrassingly aroused. She sat up on the couch and rubbed her eyes. Her blouse and jeans were clinging to her, pasted to her skin with sticky sweat.

"I don't want him!" she said in the darkness. "I don't want a man. I don't *need* a man! Damn it."

There were running footsteps in the hall, and a figure stuck its head in the darkened doorway. "You okay?" it inquired. It was the young assistant.

"What?"

"I could hear you moaning all the way down the hall. You must have been having a nightmare yourself." He switched on the light.

201

Marian squinted in the sudden brightness. His choice of words bothered her. Had she really been *moaning?*

"I guess I was having a nightmare," she replied. It was a nightmare all right, a nightmare of being tied down, of being stuck to another human being. "I didn't even realize I went to sleep."

"Should I hook you up to the polysomnograph?" he asked, smiling. "We need more subjects."

"Of course not." This came out with an anger she didn't intend.

"I was only joking, Dr. Turner."

"I know it. I didn't mean to snap at you. Christ, what time it it?"

"About six o'clock."

"I'm so damned groggy. It was a disturbing dream." She forced a laugh to hide her self-conscious feelings. "I'm not sure what I was even dreaming about," she told him, as if lying would dismiss the dream from her mind. "But I'm okay now."

"Do you want to go home?"

"No." She stood up. The carpet felt comforting under her bare feet, tempting her not to put her shoes back on. Then she decided she'd better. She felt naked without them for reasons she wouldn't admit, and at the moment it was very important that she feel fully clothed and not at all vulnerable. She bent down and slipped the shoes on.

Her feet safely clad, Marian walked over to the assistant to accompany him back to the sleep chamber. "How is Mr. Herkimer doing?"

"He's just out of REM. Should I wake him up?"

She started to say yes, then checked herself. She no longer wanted to discuss his dream; she dreaded the prospect of talking to Herkimer—or any man—at the moment. "No, not yet. I mean, well, you do it. I've decided to go home after all."

He gave her a look that questioned her sanity. Marian knew she deserved that look, but she didn't much care. She had to get out of Shodale, right away.

"You sure?"

"Yes. And *you* be sure the tape recorder's working before you talk to him."

"Whatever you say, Dr. Turner."

As the assistant returned to the sleep chamber, Marian went to her office and quickly gathered up her purse and a few papers. She glanced in the mirror behind the door on her way out, and what she saw made her grimace.

She tried to smooth her hair in place and rubbed at her cheeks, but neither action did much to improve her appearance. She still looked like she had just gotten off a roller coast ride.

She shook her head in dismay. "Welcome to the funhouse," she told her reflection. "If you can't take it, then you must be a big chicken."

She frowned.

"Cluck, cluck, you big hen."

She shut the door behind her, then rushed out.

Marian agreed to see Carl the next afternoon. They decided to get together at the Olive Garden Restaurant on the west side of town, more for Marian's convenience than for Carl's. He had to drive there from the center of the city, but he insisted he didn't want to eat downtown.

"And I've never been in the Olive Garden," he told her. "This gives me a good excuse to go there."

Marian had to give in. There was no denying a man the opportunity to eat at a place he'd never been before.

They met at the front entrance. They had just missed the main lunch crowd, so they had little trouble getting seated quickly. They sat at a table near the center of the restaurant, where a huge skylight illuminated the patrons. Carl ordered a meal, but Marian declined to eat, preferring to munch on the complimentary breadsticks. She still felt groggy from the night before and her stomach was not yet in synch with the world today.

Once the waitress had brought them their drinks—iced tea for on-duty Carl and a glass of Chianti for Marian—they sat a few seconds just watching each other, each waiting for the other to begin.

Marian was uncomfortable. Carl hadn't told her the purpose of the meeting—only that it was important—and his covert behavior was grating on her nerves. The main source of her discomfort was, as usual, his mere presence. This afternoon she was stimulated by him more than usual and was trying to control herself, though she wasn't sure why she should bother. What could possibly happen if she *didn't* control herself?

Maybe a lot.

He didn't help matters by sitting there staring in her eyes like an overgrown adolescent. What did he hope to accomplish by that behavior, anyhow?

Maybe nothing.

The best thing to do was to get down to business. "All right," she said, taking a sip of wine, "you've strung me out long enough. What's going on?"

Carl broke eye contact reluctantly and his face reddened slightly. "I've got another one."

"Another what?" she asked, though she had already made a good guess.

"Another dreamer."

"Another murder?"

"That, too, unfortunately."

She gulped another swallow of wine. "What happened?"

"Well, it's an old bum. Literally. A wino. The guy confessed to murdering those two teenagers we found in Christian Park last week. With a rock. It took a lot of talking, but we finally got it out of him, and as you've probably guessed, he said he did it in a dream. He said he thought the teenagers were some kind of monsters."

Marian shifted in the seat. She crossed her legs and accidentally bumped Carl's leg with the tip of her shoe. "Excuse me," she said, her face turning redder than Carl's.

"Anytime," he said. He cleared his throat. "So what do you think of this development?"

She looked thoughtful. "I don't suppose there's any connection between this man and any of the others?"

"Only that he and the little girl committed their crimes within hours of each other."

"Do you think that means anything?"

"It could—if we could place them together somehow, but I don't see how we could. The little girl didn't live far from the park, though."

"The park?"

"That's where the bum lives. I talked to a guy named Tripper down there—he works for the city park department—and he said he had to chase the old guy away a couple of times for loitering. The guy tried to attack Tripper a couple of days ago, and he called us. It was only after the old guy was in the tank a couple of days and started screaming about monsters that we got the confession from him."

"A confession? Is it any good—I mean, coming from a wino? It could be a bad case of delirium tremens."

"Might not stand up in court, but that's not our concern. I'm kind of inclined to believe him. He said a few things that fit—things only the murderer would know. And there was dried blood under his fingernails that matches the blood of the dead girl. He was there, that's for sure, or he wouldn't have got that blood on him."

He reached over and took a packet of sweetener from the ceramic dish in the center of the table. "Still, whether he did it or not, don't you think it's interesting that he says he was dreaming?" He ripped the packet open and dumped the white powder in his iced tea, then stirred it vigorously.

"Definitely," Marian agreed. "But being interesting and proving something are two different things."

"You're beginning to sound like a policemen. Or a lawyer."

"Please, don't compare me to a lawyer on an empty stomach."

He took a drink of his tea and seemed to be using the glass to hide his face as he asked, "You've talked to Cross, haven't you?"

She drew herself up haughtily. "What do you mean?"

"Talking to a lawyer like that could upset anyone's stomach. I know something about it. Didn't you talk to him?"

"Yes," she said guiltily. "Did I do something wrong?"

"No. I expected him to get to you sooner or later. Did you tell him anything?"

"Only that—" She gave him a stern look. "Are you trying to entrap me or something?"

He set the glass down and laughed. "Never say *entrap* to a policeman, Marian. It's a dirty word." He reached over and placed his hand on top of hers. "Sorry, I'm playing cop again. You don't have to tell me anything. Let's talk about something else—anything."

Marian warmed to his touch, and when she looked across at him, she no longer saw the decade that separated them in age. She saw him only as a human being, and his age was irrelevant. She also realized he was much more sensitive than she gave him credit for. "No," she said at last, "I want to tell you—if I can without getting you—or myself—into trouble."

"Whatever you say will be between us."

"Off the record?"

"Off the cuff, if you like." He fixed his eyes on her and waited.

She made a couple of false starts, then before she knew what she was saying, she had told him the whole story, everything, all she knew, all she thought she knew, and all she suspected. When it was over, she was surprised at how she felt. Instead of being overcome with the guilt and dread she had anticipated, she was experiencing a vast sensation of relief, as if a tremendous weight had been lifted from her.

It was much more than merely telling the truth; it was telling the truth to *him* that mattered, because what had been really bothering her, she knew now, was that she cared how he thought about her. As long as she had kept things from him, any other feelings either of them had were meaningless.

Carl didn't say anything immediately. He just stared past her, then he looked down at his hand and seemed to just realize he had been touching her. He pulled his hand back, as if he were embarrassed.

The waitress brought Carl his meal, a plate of steaming cheese ravioli, and he picked at it listlessly, taking only a few bites.

"That's quite a story," he said. "You think this Richards guy gave Myers the drugs?"

"I'd bet my career on it. In fact, I *have* bet my career on it," she added ruefully.

"Don't worry about that. If you're wrong, there's no harm done. If you're right, I don't see how it could affect your career adversely to tell the truth."

"Morton threatened to ruin me already."

"Mr. Morton may be talking out of the other side of his ass when I get through with him." He took one more mouthful of the ravioli, chewed it tentatively, and pushed the plate away. His second experience with yuppie food was not to his liking.

He was so serious she couldn't help but smile. "You're pretty crude, aren't you?"

"I guess I am at that," he said good-naturedly. "We fuzz are rude, crude dudes. How about you?"

"Me?"

"How are psychologists as a whole? Rude or crude?"

"Both. You haven't heard me when I'm not being Miss Professional Career Woman."

"I'd like to hear this other side of you sometime. Sounds very interesting."

He touched her hand again. "You know, Marian, when I first met you I didn't think much of psychologists—or of women, for that matter—but you've changed my way of thinking." She started to mumble a reply, but he hushed her by pressing her hand gently. "But the way you just told me everything like that—the way you trusted me, no matter what might have happened to you as a result—it makes me feel close to you in a way I've never felt before."

She nodded, then realizing the import of his speech, she said, "But—but, Carl, your wife? . . ."

He jerked his hand back. "Damn! Did you have to remind me about her?"

"I'm sorry."

"No, you shouldn't be. It's not your fault I'm married—or your fault what I'm married to."

"Carl. Let's not do this."

"Do what?" There was an edge in his voice.

"Let's not get involved."

"Is that what it is?" His expression revealed that he hoped it was just that—involvement, or the beginnings of it.

"Isn't it?"

"Are you afraid of something? Of commitment?"

"No. I . . . well, I thought we were just working together."

"We are."

"But it's more than that now."

"Maybe."

"It can't be, Carl. It just can't." Marian flinched. She couldn't decide whether she was being very courageous or very cowardly.

"Why not?"

"Because I—shit, I don't know. I can't get involved, that's all." She didn't want to be involved, did she? She wanted to go out east, where there were intellectuals.

"Because I'm married?"

"Well, that's something." She wanted to write a book.

"I'm getting a divorce. I already made up my mind about that."

"I hope I didn't—" She wanted to be on her own, unshackled to another human being. Yet she had already screwed up by telling him everything. Her career would be ruined.

208

"You didn't have anything to do with it. I've been thinking about it for a long time."

"Christ, Carl, let's just drop it." Yet dreams were sometimes prophetic, even if the prophecy made no sense.

"Okay. Anything you say."

"I want to go now." But she didn't have to marry him. A love affair would be good for her. She had been alone much too long.

"All right. You're the doctor."

That stung her. She didn't want to be the goddamn doctor. She wanted to be herself, Marian Turner, not a doctor, not a psychologist, but a person.

She followed him silently out to the register where he paid the check. Then they went outside and stood in front of the restaurant, staring at each other.

There was anger and hurt on Carl's face. Marian's face reflected the same emotions, but for different reasons. This was the turning point; something had to be done this minute, or everything would be lost.

Carl turned and started for his car. As he walked away, Marian's demon chortled in the back of her mind, taunting her with reminders of past failures—and lost loves.

Carl was already in his car, about to drive away. That made something in her mind snap, and she imagined the demon falling back in his own ordure, suffocating.

Then she ran to the other side of Carl's car, opened the door, and slid in beside him. She pressed her lips against his, and she discovered some dreams do come true.

Eighteen. A Busy Night

Chuck Tripper hadn't slept well in days, and the deprivation of sleep was beginning to tell on him. Now he had to drive to Cincinnati in the middle of the night, in a thoroughly exhausted condition. But he had no choice. He had a job interview scheduled in the Ohio city the next morning, and he didn't want to take a chance on missing an opportunity to improve his employment.

His inability to sleep had been caused by the events of the last week or so. It had started when he found the bodies of those dead teenagers behind the clubhouse in the park. The mangled mass of flesh that confronted him that morning had haunted him for nights, filling his dreams with awful bloody tableaus that seemed so frighteningly real he dreaded sleep.

The dreams did become less intense after a few nights, the dreadful images becoming less threatening if only because they had become familiar. At least he had been handling them, and he knew they would go away eventually. Then just when he thought things were returning to normal and his nightmares were about to cease, he was attacked by that crazy old drunk in the park.

The memory of that morning was still making itself felt. He was certain the drunk was going to kill him, and if he hadn't been just *slightly* stronger than the man, there was no telling what the old bastard would have done to him. He sure was a lot stronger than he looked, and there was a murderous gleam in the old man's eyes that terrified him.

So the old drunk became the new subject of his dreams, making sleep—once again—a dreaded activity to be avoided. He could barely close his eyes without seeing the man lunge at him, intent on murder.

His sleepless condition was further aggravated by the fact he had been on the verge of major illness for days. The strange smell in the park hadn't gone away, and on some days, it was such a major irritation that it made Chuck's daytime hours as miserable as his nights. His doctor had prescribed allergy medication, a rather potent antihistamine laced with codeine, but all it did was make him drowsy at the wrong times, without letting him sleep when he really wanted to. He had stopped taking the drug after only two days.

Fortunately, the further Chuck traveled from Indianapolis, the better he felt. His nose had already stopped running and his eyes no longer itched. Perhaps by the morning, he would have a clear head for the job interview.

He dearly hoped the job was offered to him. He longed to move away from Indianapolis, to escape all bad memories. And, most of all, he longed for sleep in a new environment, where murderous old bums did not jump out of the shadows.

Feeling a sudden need to make up for lost time, he pressed down on the Oldsmobile's accelerator. The old car rasped and the engine bucked against the new speed asked of it, and the entire front end began to vibrate.

"That's just great!"

Chuck sighed and let up on the accelerator. The car would do sixty, but that was about it. Anything beyond might make the engine throw a rod. He hoped he didn't get run over by a big semi doing seventy. Since the speed limit on rural interstates had been upped to sixty-five, highway travel had become hazardous.

But with this old car, the trip was just going to be slow.

Chuck resigned himself to that and forced himself to watch the road.

God, it was hard to keep his eyes open.

Richards had decided not to use the little blue capsules. Instead, he had chosen to take 4155A intravenously. That way, he reasoned, he would begin to feel its effects much sooner.

He had been injecting himself for a week now. So far, nothing had happened.

His nightmares were still occurring, and they were just as bad as ever.

Panting and sweating, Laura Nolan awoke at one-thirty in the morning.

Her left hand was between her legs. She quickly jerked it away and reached over for her husband, but her hand fell on empty space.

Goddamn him! She wanted him so badly, but he wasn't there. The son of a bitch!

Suddenly overcome with rage, she thrashed in the bed, pounding her fists into the pillow. She screamed curses at her absent husband for several minutes, but throwing a fit did not make her feel any better. It was only exhausting her.

She fell silent, then sat up in the bed. She ran the tip of her tongue over her teeth. Her mouth tasted gritty and it was uncomfortably dry. She thought about it a moment, then realized she was sick to her stomach. She got up, ran to the bathroom, and spent a distressing half hour dry heaving.

Where the hell *was* Carl, anyhow? she asked herself between bouts of sickness. Didn't he know she needed him?

"This is a nice place," Carl said, sitting down on the couch in Marian's apartment.

"It's too damn small, and you know it," Marian said, "but thank you for being polite."

"Okay, it's too damn small, but it's still nice." He wrapped his arms around her waist, pulling her down to him. "Maybe it's the company that makes it nice."

He kissed her, then looked into her eyes earnestly. "Are you sure about this?"

"Yes. I'm sure—for now, at least. And now is all that counts, isn't it?"

"Now is all we have." He started to unbutton her blouse.

The trip from Indianapolis to Cincinnati was only a two-hour drive but it was on one of the most boring stretches of road in the Midwest. Interstate 74 just went on and on for miles, with little to break up the monotony until one reached the hills a few miles west of the Indiana-Ohio border.

It was especially monotonous at night, when the intermittent white line between the lanes seemed to flash on and off in a driver's vision like some kind of hypnotic beacon.

Chuck forced his eyes away from the flashing of the white line, directing his sight straight ahead. But he couldn't turn off the clicking sound his tires made as they hit the seams in the pavement, which was almost as deadly.

Click-click.

Only thirty miles to Cincinnati.

Click-click.

He had to stay awake.

Click-click.

The damn radio in the Oldsmobile didn't work. Nothing worked in the old wreck.

Click-click.

He started humming to himself. He looked up at the rearview mirror and winced as the lights from a car behind him bounced off in his face.

The car passed him and the rearview mirror went blank.

Temporarily. Then there were eyes in the mirror staring back at him.

The first day, Richards had injected himself with 10 cc of 4155A every six hours. The second day, he increased the frequency of dosage to every four hours. On the third and subsequent days, he doubled the dose.

He had no misgivings about the effects of the drug. He knew he was the perfect test subject, not only because he had been having nightmares again, but because he was a physician and could observe the effects of the medication objectively.

He was convinced the effects Myers had experienced were not due to the drug at all. Myers was just crazy; it was as simple as that, and he had made an error in judgment by giving him the drug in the first place. He would correct that error by demonstrating the true benefits of the drug to the world.

He knew he was right, and soon he would have the proof he needed. Something told him he might have it yet tonight.

The third shift at the Shodale Chemical Facility had to shut down early that night. One of the employees went on a rampage that ended with him smashing the controller at the end of the line, effectively shutting down operations in that part of the plant.

As they led him away, he kept babbling about bugs crawling all over him.

Wrung out from trying to throw up nothing, Laura returned to the bedroom and grabbed a cigarette.

Carl's continued absence was pissing her off. The least he could have done was call. Was that too much to ask? After all, she was his wife, even if they did have their differences. He owed her something for that.

Maybe he just didn't care for her at all anymore. But she cared for him, didn't she? Why, she even dreamed they had sex together just about every night. Didn't that show she had special feelings for him?

Why did he bitch so much about money, anyhow? Money was made to be spent, not to languish in some damned old bank account. The money was just as much hers as it was his; she worked just as hard as he did, maybe harder. Laura deserved the things she bought. She deserved them because she put up with a man like him!

Why didn't he call? She smoked half a pack of cigarettes while waiting him, but by four o'clock, it was evident Carl was not coming home.

She threw herself on the bed and closed her eyes, but she couldn't sleep. Something was burning inside her she couldn't ignore.

Her hand drifted back down to the source of the fire.

Richards awoke in a disappointed and agitated state, the nightmare still lingering in his mind.

It was a replay of the nightmare he had had years before, back in the time just after Fran died. Only it was somewhat more intense.

Perhaps 4155A wasn't going to work, after all. Could all his theories be wrong?

He got up from bed, slipped into his robe, and went out to the living room. He paused to look out at the panoramic view of the city the big picture window provided.

His apartment was on the twelfth floor of a high rise right in the middle of Indianapolis. It was an expensive place to live in, but he liked being in the heart of the city, and the view of the skyline at night sometimes soothed him. Sometimes it was his only solace in life.

He watched the lights of the city for a while, but the view did not assuage his general feeling of malaise.

Part of him said he had failed—that his assumptions about 4155A were completely wrong—and he hated the idea that he might be courting failure again. He had taken risks, and now he was getting nothing in return. If anything, he might be taking a step backward in his career, especially if he were made accountable for the things he had already done. Myers's lawyer would no doubt do his best to ruin him, and if this present experiment failed, he'd be powerless to stop him.

He had to succeed—had to!

He walked over to the corner of the room that served as his lab away from Shodale. A desk and table sat there, next to the built-in wet bar that he used as a source of water for his lab station. There was a personal computer on the table and a modem, which he used to communicate with the Shodale computers.

The countertop of the bar was covered with vials and bottles of chemicals. At one end there were the jars in which he had put tissue samples from the dead animals on which he had performed the autopsies. Sitting next to bottles of vodka, Scotch, and bourbon, the jars helped to form a grotesque still life that normally amused him. Tonight, however, it only heightened his sense of disgust with life.

"Baboon dreams," he said, picking up one of the jars, "in a bottle. What a droll conceit." His grim expression showed he found no humor in the idea. He returned the jar to its place and sat down at the desk.

The top of the desk was in uncharacteristic disarray, but he had been so involved in his own experiment the last few days he hadn't taken the time to be as tidy as he usually was. An untidy desk was the sign of an untidy mind, Richards reminded himself, and he spent a few minutes arranging his papers in neat stacks. That done, he felt better immediately. He could always think more clearly when things were in order.

He started rereading his notes. He must have made a mistake in his interpretation of the data somewhere along the line. According to his theories, the drug should be doing something quite noticeable to him by now. Indeed, it should have begun to alter his thinking mechanism, actually changing the pattern of his thoughts. But he perceived no difference in his cognitive processes. Could he be immune to the drug's effects?

Maybe you had to be crazy for the drug to work.

No, animals weren't crazy, and the drug had definitely affected them. They had gone berserk, but only because the drug couldn't affect them the same way it would humans. They lacked the necessary thinking apparatus, the cerebral cortex man possessed, which would allow the drug to work the way it would in a human being.

Testing the drug on animals had been a waste of time, then. It should have been used on humans from the beginning.

With man, he theorized, the drug should provide a degree of mental control that would eventually banish nightmares, which, of course, was what the drug was supposed to do. But the exciting part was that beyond that, the drug should work to increase a person's actual mental capacity, and its effects should be lasting. At least, that's what the autopsies on the dead animals had indicated.

If his assumptions were true, then 4155A might be a miracle drug, with many applications far exceeding the control of dreams. If Richards could prove that, he'd be able to write his own ticket at Shodale. Because he planned to take his findings to the top management—bypassing Morton—and claim all the glory for himself. Morton would be left in his dust and Myers's lawyer would be faced with a much more powerful opponent in court than he reckoned on.

Theories were nice, but they remained only theories until concrete evidence was offered. And Richards did not even have empirical evidence yet. He must have overlooked something, because he was not even able to control his dreams, which he had determined was only the first indication of the drug's effects.

He needed help on this one. He thought about that a moment, then turned on his personal computer and the modem.

The computers at Shodale were on twenty-four hours a day, always accessible to top-level employees who might get inspiration at odd times of day or night. He'd let the electronic brains do some of the work.

He typed in his personal access code and was on-line with the Shodale mainframe within seconds. Then he began entering the most pertinent data for analysis.

The eyes in the mirror gleamed with malice.

Chuck blinked and looked back at the road. He gulped, then checked the mirror again.

The eyes were still there, red-rimmed eyes in which there was clear, murderous intent.

He had to be imagining them. He turned his head to look back over his shoulder quickly, trying to watch the road at the same time with his peripheral vision.

"I got you now, you son of a bitch!"

The old drunk's arms came over the seat, wrapped a belt around Chuck's neck, and pulled hard.

It had taken two and a half hours, but Richards had entered all the data he felt necessary for the computer to make its analysis. Now all he had to do was enter an encryption code to make the file accessible only to him, then he could shut down.

He leaned back in his chair and removed his glasses, laying them at the corner of the table. He massaged the bridge of his nose to ease the ache where the glasses had pinched, then closed his eyes briefly.

Working at the keyboard had eased a great deal of his tension, and he was experiencing a level of lucidity that came only in certain moments. To Richards, that feeling of supreme insight was the closest thing to being Godlike a man could ever hope for, and he relished such moments. They made him feel as if he were the center of the universe, and restored his faith in himself and his ability to succeed.

Figures and formulas floated through his mind. He let his thoughts drift, and he found himself looking into the future, at a moment when he would present his findings to the Shodale Board of Directors and put Morton in his place. That was going to be very satisfying indeed.

Well, he'd better enter that code and get on with it. The sun would be coming up soon. He opened his eyes and started to type, but was interrupted by a strange burbling noise somewhere close by.

He scanned the room, his eyes stopping at one of the jars on the countertop next to the bar. That jar contained pieces of nerve tissue he had removed from one of the dead baboons and was the same one he had looked at earlier.

The noise was coming from there. The tissue inside was pulsating. It seemed to be growing.

"What's that?" Marian asked breathlessly, her fingers tracing a purplish mark on Carl's side. The immediate lovemaking was accomplished; now it was time to explore each other in more detail.

"Bullet wound," he said matter-of-factly.

"Really?"

"Yep."

"Does it ever hurt?" Her voice showed real concern.

"No, not any more." He shifted in the bed and touched her left nipple lightly. "Actually, it was just a flesh wound. Hurt like a son of a bitch at the time, though. A young punk shot me with a cheap little twenty-two."

"Why did he shoot you?" The thing Carl was doing with his fingers was making her tingle.

"Because I was chasing him. He was a drug dealer. I wasn't working homicide then." He intensified his finger work.

"Did you—did you have to shoot him?"

"I shot at him a couple of times, but he got away. I don't think he was ever caught."

"Police work is a hazardous occupation, isn't it?" she said thoughtfully.

"Ma'am," he replied in a mock drawl, "you just don't know what can happen to you. Sometimes, you even get seduced!"

He laughed and climbed on top of her again.

I hate that son of a bitch, Laura chanted in her mind. I hate him. I hate him. As she kept repeating the phrase, its rhythm radiated through her, hammering at her awareness.

It also provided a convenient beat for the action of her hand.
I hate him.

He can't leave me like this. He can't treat me this way, when I need him so much it hurts. I'm not going to let him get away with it.

I hate him.

She kept working with her hatred, letting it provide the undulating rhythm she needed, and she found hatred was an exquisite release.

Richards remained calm. It was impossible for the stuff in the jar to increase. It was only a clump of dead cells in alcohol. Anything he saw that clump do was merely an illusion.

He set his glasses back on his nose, then stood up and reached over for the jar. It felt warm to the touch. He held it only an inch from his face, observing it with curious detachment. This could be a hallucination brought on by the drug. Was it beginning to work, after all? If so, why wasn't he able to see through the illusion and stop it?

Because it wasn't an illusion. It was real.

No, he told his mind. It's not real. You are a cool, rational individual who is not subject to mental aberrations. Think away this illusion.

Thinking didn't seem to work.

I'm not asleep. I'm awake. Everything I see is clear before my eyes. Nothing fuzzy.

Maybe it was a delayed chemical reaction of some sort. That could be it. The tissue was saturated with 4155A and the alcohol might be interacting with the drug.

See? There's always a rational explanation for any phenomenon, if only you're intelligent enough to see it.

He peered more closely. Bubbles rose from the bit of gray tissue as it emitted a gurgling sound again. He shook the jar vigorously, then watched. More bubbles. More gurgling. Fascinating.

Yet he could swear the tissue was twice as big as it had been only a minute ago, even though there was no way for its volume to have increased.

He decided to open the jar for an even closer look.

As he twirled the lid off, the stuff exploded out of the jar, splattering him with gray goo that stuck to his skin and his robe. He rubbed at the stuff frantically, but it clung tenaciously.

The stuff was alive! Strands of it curled around his fingers, crawled up his arms, and burrowed under his skin. The stench of burning flesh—his own flesh—filled the air.

He opened his mouth to yell, and the stuff crawled inside.

Filled with dread panic, he ran around the room, jumping up and down, waving his arms and clutching at his throat.

When he whirled around, he saw a vision floating outside the window, a vision that offered safety and comfort.

Fran.

She hovered in the air above the city. She beckoned to him silently, her lips moving but making no sound.

There was release from his torment in her arms.

"Yes!" he screamed. "Yes!"

He dove through the glass, trying to enfold Fran in his arms. But she had inconsiderately evaporated.

It was surprising how long it took him to hit the concrete below. It gave him time to reflect on how stupid he had been.

Just before his body made impact, it occurred to him he now knew how the baboons felt.

Early in the morning, just after sunrise, the Indiana State Police found a battered Oldsmobile halfway down the hill between the east and west lanes of Interstate 74. Its sole occupant, a young man with terror etched in his features, was dead.

When they first opened the car, the police assumed the man had merely fallen asleep at the wheel and lost control. The hill was steep and once he had gone over the edge, it would have been difficult to slow or stop his descent.

Then they discovered something around the man's neck that told a different story. It was the strap of his shoulder restraint. Somehow he had become entangled in the strap, and it had wrapped itself around his neck and strangled him.

They couldn't determine, however, if it had happened before or after his car left the road.

When Marian awoke, Carl was already gone. She stroked the place on the bed where he had been, and it seemed some of his warmth remained.

He was a good lover, a kind and gently considerate lover, the type of lover she wished she had met sooner in her life. She hoped they could carry on their affair for a little while, at least. Surely, the world would allow them that much.

She realized there was great potential for hurt in such a relationship, but pain was sometimes necessary for there to be love. She also regretted having to hurt Carl's wife, though she had never seen the woman.

She wondered what Carl would tell her. From what he had said of the woman's disposition, there was bound to be a nasty scene. But it couldn't be helped.

Carl deserved a loving relationship. If his wife was unable to provide what he needed, how could he be blamed for seeking

222

it in another woman's arms? And how could the woman who provided the love be blamed? What did his wife expect, anyhow?

Marian forced herself not to think about her. For the moment, she would be content to have part of Carl for herself. And that would have to be sufficient.

Laura had rubbed herself raw with longing, only it seemed to have happened in her sleep. What an awful thing to wake up to!

It was Carl's fault. Everything was his fault. If it weren't for him, she'd be a different person.

She called the hospital and told her supervisor she wouldn't be in today. She was sick.

After hanging up, she realized she wasn't lying.

Chapter 465 of the Sheetmetal Workers' Local met later that morning in the Union Hall on Brookside Road. After the meeting was called to order, several issues relating to work and job conditions were discussed. Very little was settled. Then the officials turned to the matter of where to hold the annual picnic. There was very little discussion regarding the upcoming event, and when they finally took a vote, there was unanimous agreement among the membership.

The company picnic would be held in Christian Park.

Nineteen. Morton on the Loose

John Morton fired six rounds at the target in quick succession. He then reached overhead to pull the target in to see how he had done. The silhouette of a man had five round holes in its chest; the sixth hole had gone in its neck.

"Not bad," Morton said. His voice sounded odd to him, since it was muffled by the ear protectors he wore. He detached the paper target from the cardboard, rolled it up, and set it aside. Then he attached a new silhouette and sent the target back down to the end of the range.

He stepped back from the firing point to see who else was on Don's Guns Indoor Firing Range tonight. It was a weeknight and close to ten o'clock, so there were only three other people around: another executive type like himself, a redneck with a rifle, and a woman.

The woman interested him. She was a trim but shapely brunette, with wide hips. She might be thirty, but not much more than that. She wore very tight frosted-pink jeans that accentuated her curves and called attention to her crack.

He positioned himself to observe her better. She was practicing with a small automatic pistol, the type easily secreted in the purse. He guessed it was a .22 or .25 caliber. When the weapon fired it produced very little recoil, shaking her body only slightly;

the main aftereffect was a small tremor rippling down her back, which caused her ass to ripple.

Very interesting.

He wished she would turn around so he could see her face. But she kept firing at the target, apparently oblivious to him.

He could wait.

He reloaded his Smith and Wesson .38 and aimed.

Early in the previous week, Morton had found the knowledgeable but expendable person he needed to help him interpet all the data he had collected regarding 4155A and Richards's experiments with it. The person was Alex Stryker, one of Richard's assistants.

It was easy to recruit Stryker. None of the people who worked under Richards seemed to have any loyalty to him, but Stryker in particular was downright hostile toward the man.

Stryker, who had written the report about the animals damaging the lab, also knew a great deal about the project and could easily comprehend Richards's notes. He explained how Richards had determined 4155A altered nerve cells, specifically the neurons that made up the brain, and had theorized this action of the drug could make it a panacea for many mental ailments, not just the sleep disorders caused by nightmares.

Richards, Stryker speculated, had been keeping his knowledge from the rest of the staff—and from Morton—so he could perhaps either steal the formula or copy it.

"That's a serious accusation," Morton had said in his office the day Stryker presented his initial findings. "Can you back it up?"

"Well," Stryker replied, "not with anything concrete." Alex Stryker was twenty-eight. He had short hair and bright blue eyes. He was six one and slender. His most charcteristic pose when talking was to stand with his hands stuck in the pockets of his lab coat.

"It'd be easier to prove if we had a document or something like that."

"We can infer a great deal," Stryker said, "by the fact that he hid everything—even those autopsy reports."

"You read the transcripts. What do you think they mean?"

"They mean that 4155A is a very potent drug."

"Anything else?"

"It seems very dangerous. If the FDA learned of its effects on the animals, I'm not sure they would give the green flag to go ahead with human testing."

"Is that your opinion, or something that can be substantiated?"

"Both, though it's a moot point. The FDA is a paranoid organization, and they've become more conservative. Consider their rulings on artificial sweeteners."

Morton nodded.

"Maybe you could try 4155A in Canada, or one of the European markets where we don't operate under such strictures."

Morton smiled at the young man. There was a touch of Machiavelli in the boy after all. Fate had sent him the right ally.

Stryker regarded him with questioning eyes that sought explanation for the smile, but Morton offered none.

Instead, he changed the subject. "That's a good idea, Mr. Stryker. I'll take it under advisement. Now, have you been watching Dr. Richards as I asked you?"

"Yes, sir."

"Your findings?"

"He's more reclusive than ever, Mr. Morton. He comes in for an hour at a time, messes around at his desk, then leaves."

"He doesn't do anything significant during that hour?"

"Nothing I can see. He's an enigma, but then he always has been."

"What do you think he's up to?"

"I have no idea, sir. If I did, I'd be only too glad to tell you."

The kid was also a good company man. That pleased Morton

226

very much; being loyal to the company was a quality he had not encountered much lately in his employees. If one to were to judge by the behavior of people like Richards and Marian Turner, one would get the idea no one was loyal anymore.

He found himself wishing he would not have to exercise Stryker's expendability once he had used him. Stryker might prove valuable for future covert activities within the company. But if the man became too valuable, he'd gain power, and Morton didn't like that idea, either. He didn't want another Richards to contend with.

Of course, he could deal with that scenario when the time came. For the moment, he still needed the young man's services.

"Mr. Stryker, you've demonstrated to me that you're a man that can be trusted. I like that."

"Thank you, sir," Stryker replied.

"No need to thank me. You're a valuable asset to Shodale, and I intend to make it worth your while. There'll be a bonus in this for you, and that bonus will be even fatter if you'll take care of another matter for me."

"Anything you say, sir."

"That's the right attitude." He removed a sheaf of papers from his desk. He had held this material back, waiting to see if Stryker could be trusted. "I have here something else that requires your expertise. You'll find data here regarding two Shodale products, one of which you'll immediately recognize. The other is a product you may not be familiar with."

Stryker nodded.

"I've gone over this a couple of times myself, but I have to be sure. I need a second opinion. That's why I want you to confirm or deny my suspicions for me."

"May I ask what your suspicions are, sir?"

"No. That might bias your findings. Just compare these two products and tell me what you think. That's all I want."

"Will do, sir."

"That's the spirit, son." He made his face a mask of gravity.

"And this, like the other things I've asked of you, has to be completely confidential. Understood?"

"You can count on me, sir."

"Let me know what you find out as soon as possible. It's important." He handed the papers over to Stryker.

"I'll get on it right away."

"That's all."

"Thank you, sir." He started for the door.

"And don't forget to keep an eye on that son of a bitch Richards, either," Morton reminded him.

"I will, sir." Stryker shut the door.

After he left, Morton felt a another pang of guilt about what he might have to do to Stryker. Fortunately, the feeling passed quickly and he was able to go about his business with a clear conscience.

Morton had fired fifty rounds and now he was out of ammunition. He looked around his partition to see if the brunette was still there. She was.

He debated with himself over whether he should buy a fresh box of ammo and continue to shoot, or just wait the woman out.

Luck made his decision for him. The woman was also finished and was heading toward the exit. Now that he saw her face, oval and pale with only a hint of makeup, he had to meet her. He quickly removed his ear protectors, stuffed them and his gun into the small canvas bag in which he carried his shooting paraphernalia, and sprinted for the door, leaving his targets behind.

He reached the woman just in time to hold the door open for her. She smiled a "thank you" at him as she walked through, and Morton returned the smile with a bow.

He followed her out to the counter and was quick to admire the target she displayed for the man sitting there.

"Nice shooting," he said, ignoring the glare of the counter man who, it was evident, had designs on the woman himself.

"Thank you."

"My name's John Morton."

"Glenda." She offered her hand and he shook it. "How did you do?"

"Not too bad. Oops, I forgot my targets. Can you wait here a minute?"

"Sure."

He retrieved his targets, returned to the counter, and unrolled them for her. She praised his shooting and even asked to see his gun.

He gladly showed it to her. Then he invited her to the Safari Bar for drinks and she accepted.

Three days had passed, and Morton had heard nothing from Stryker. He must be having some difficulty analyzing the data. He hoped the young man was being careful not to let anyone else see it.

He worried about the information that was already freely available. Marian Turner, if her curiosity were aroused, would no doubt be able to make something of it. She had already been making inquiries about the incident in the lab and had asked about the autopsy reports. She wouldn't let up until she uncovered something, and she still had that righteous gleam in her eyes that marked her as a very dangerous person.

Morton held the purse strings and could pull her grant away from her any time he wanted, but that might be foolhardy. It could cause her to act hastily, without thinking of her own welfare. He didn't want her acting at all, until he was sure about a few things.

He kept trying to think of ways to discredit her, so he would have an excuse to fire her. But she was a very careful person who did nothing to call attention to herself. Apparently, she did her job and not much else.

There was only one way to deal with such a person. Morton would have her watched. Even a nun had secrets if you watched her long enough.

He quivered at that thought and briefly envisioned an army of spies watching Marian around the clock. He saw video cameras hidden in her office and her apartment—in her bedroom and bathroom. He imagined himself watching the tapes of Marian in her most intimate moments, perhaps even playing with himself as he watched.

Being a spy was very entertaining.

But he didn't have the time to hire a lot of people. He would have to settle for much less. He would hire a private detective to see what Marian was up to.

It was a pity, because he sure would have liked to have those tapes.

The Safari Bar was located on the northeast side of Indianapolis near the Castleton Square shopping center. It was a large, very popular nightspot, decorated in a jungle motif, which offered exotic drinks and dancing in a dark atmosphere. It was a favorite watering hole for the city's young singles.

Morton liked to go there for the scenery. He always sat at a table near the ladies' room, where he could watch the parade of the city's most beautiful young women as they went back and forth to powder their noses or meet in secret to discuss the merits of the various hunks who were on the prowl in the place.

He didn't consider the young men, most of whom were of the yuppie persuasion, much of a threat. They may have had youth and good looks, but they didn't have the kind of money Morton had to throw around. Since the place was full of materialistic women who weren't necessarily looking for love, Morton often scored.

He and Glenda were making small talk at a table in the corner next to the blackjack counter, where the insidious game was played for "fun," since Indiana state law prohibited real gambling. Morton didn't like the table because he couldn't see the entrance to the ladies' room very well, and the noise of the blackjack players irritated him. However, Glenda had expressed an interest in watching the game.

She sipped a Tom Collins, and he had a double Scotch and water. He had made a big show of specifying Johnnie Walker Black Label to impress his companion, but he suspected a cheap generic Scotch had been substituted. He wasn't going to complain, though; it didn't make that much difference after a couple of drinks.

Little plastic jungle animals rode the swizzle sticks in both their glasses. Glenda was collecting them, and so far she had a monkey and a giraffe.

Loud music could be heard throughout the place. It was all modern rock, with liberal doses of Prince, Whitesnake, INXS, and other popular groups with which Morton was somewhat familiar because of exposure through his children. They listened to this kind of garbage all the time.

Glenda leaned forward constantly, offering him a view of her breasts that was quite nice, actually. She wore a quartz crystal on a chain around her neck that bounced between the two globes of flesh in a most inviting way when she moved.

Morton told her he was a doctor. This was his standard line with women he picked up, because it was much more impressive than saying he was an executive. His pharmaceutical background made it easy enough to fake medical knowledge.

Glenda was basically a space cadet or, to use the crueler current vernacular, an airhead. She worked as a space rep for a local computer magazine and had very little else to talk about. She kept referring to her big accounts and how she was going to be promoted soon, and after a while, it began to bore Morton to the point of distraction. She didn't even know anything about guns and had taken up shooting only for self-defense.

He hated this part of scoring—the small talk and the other bullshit preliminaries—but it was necessary, he supposed, when you were dealing with non-professionals. He wished they could bypass all this and just go to a motel. It rarely worked that way, however.

He continued to listen to her mindless prattle, nodding occasionally and pretending to be interested, all the while wondering how many drinks it would take to get her into the sack.

He looked away from her briefly and caught the eye of a blonde with pink streaks in her hair, sitting up at the blackjack counter. She was a woman he had met there before—a very adventurous woman.

He nodded at her, and she winked.

He turned to Glenda and said, "You strike me as a very liberal person, Glenda. Care for some adventure?"

"What do you mean, John?"

"Ever do a threesome?"

Morton had glanced up from the report Stryker prepared and fixed the young man with a piercing look. "You're sure about this, then?"

"Yes, sir."

"There's no doubt in your mind?"

"None whatsoever."

Morton sighed heavily. His suspicions had been correct after all. Now that he was sure, though, what should he do about it? If any small part of this information—or any other information related to this product and 4155A—leaked out, there would be absolute hell to pay.

It would be his head on the chopping block, too. Because he was supposed to be responsible. His career could be at an end. and there was no hope of gaining any more ascendancy in the Shodale ranks.

Stryker waited patiently for several moments, during which the only sound in the office was the faint buzz of an electric clock hanging on one wall. Then he could contain himself no longer.

"Mr. Morton?"

"Yes?"

"May I ask if these findings—do they coincide with your own speculations?"

Morton considered replying in the negative, but he could see Stryker already knew the answer. "Yes," he said at last. He felt he owed the man a little honesty.

"I'm sorry, sir."

"You don't have any reason to be sorry. It's not your fault. In fact, I'm not sure whose fault it is. Any ideas?"

"Lack of quality control, sir, and a breakdown in communications between departments."

"It always comes down to a breakdown in communications, doesn't it, son?"

"Sir?"

"That's what every fuck-up comes down to. One hand doesn't know what the other is doing. And egos get in the way, and the computer doesn't give a damn, because it's not programmed to. And it's the system, too, I guess. The proper safeguards were not in place or this would not have happened, even if people didn't talk to each other."

"I think you're right, sir."

"You're damn straight I'm right. This wouldn't have happened if everyone had his shit together." He looked across at Stryker and suddenly recognized a potentially dangerous person sitting there. This young man now knew as much as he did about this particular corporate mistake; if he were smart—and he probably was—he was already thinking of ways to use his knowledge, though at the moment he was sitting there with a very innocent look on his face.

The time to get rid of him was now, but, damn it, he still needed his expertise—for one more job, at least. "Did you share this knowledge with anyone else?" Morton asked.

"No, sir. You said it was confidential, and I treated it that way."

"You're aware of the potentially damaging nature of this . . .

233

I mean, you realize what it could do to *your* company—to Shodale?"

"I think you know where my allegiance lies, Mr. Morton." He looked hurt, but Morton wasn't sure what the man meant— whether he was loyal to Shodale, or to him. It was a fine distinction in this case. He had to find out, and the only way to do that was to ask something of him that would compromise him personally.

"Okay, Stryker, I'm going to make a request of you, which may seem strange. If you don't want to do it, I'll understand."

"I'll . . ."

"Wait until I've told you what I want before you answer. Careers—and not just yours and mine—are riding on this."

Stryker remained silent, anticipating. When it was evident he wasn't going to speak, Morton said, "I want you to take all this evidence and destroy it. Erase the disks. Shred all the documents. Go back into the files and find all references to this product and its connection to 4155A and erase and destroy them, too. When you're done, I want it to be impossible for anyone to find even the faintest trail of this anywhere."

Morton watched Stryker's face closely for signs of horror or disgust at what was being asked of him. The young man's face was blank; he seemed to be thinking.

"You want me to go back through the older files, too?" he asked at last.

Morton had him. "Yes. What you can't erase, alter."

"But I don't have access to everything."

"You will. I'll see to that. Do whatever it takes. If you run into any resistance, tell me and I'll handle it. But if you're quiet and discreet, you shouldn't have any problems."

"Yes, sir."

"Stryker?"

"Yes."

"You know what you're getting into here, don't you?"

"Yes."

"You understand this could be construed as a cover-up operation—like Watergate?"

"Sure, but that doesn't bother me."

Morton was mildly surprised. "Why not?"

"I know you'll take care of me, sir. You told me you would."

The young man smiled and left his superior alone in his office to contemplate the significance of that last remark. Morton noted he had not waited to be formally dismissed.

That had been two days ago and he was still fuming.

The motel was halfway to Noblesville, but it was a place where no one asked questions. Morton had used it often, because he never worried about running into anyone he knew around these parts. Even if he did see an acquaintance in such an out-of-the-way place, it would be one of those situations where the acquaintance would be as embarrassed at being there as Morton was.

Morton wasn't particularly worried, even if he was seen with a strange woman. The worst that could happen is that it would get back to his wife, and Kate didn't really care. Their marriage had been a sham for years. Besides, Morton knew Kate had gotten some on the side herself on occasion.

Glenda was spread-eagled on the bed. He had tethered her arms and legs with towels and now he was undressing himself while she watched, bleary-eyed and silent. She was very drunk, a condition attested to by the pile of little plastic jungle animals she had dumped on the side table. Only three of them had come from Morton's drinks.

The blond woman sat on the edge of the bed next to Glenda, drinking a wine cooler. She was nude except for her panties. Her body was well formed, her breasts very large but still youthfully firm. She looked up at Morton and smiled. She, too, was quite tipsy.

She was fascinated by the crystal hanging around Glenda's

neck. She kept toying with it and running it along the tips of the other woman's nipples.

Morton was barely feeling all the Scotch he had drunk; he held his liquor very well, and it rarely affected his sexual performance. He looked from one woman to the other, grinned, and snorted. This was going to be a lot of fun.

"Ready, Glenda?"

Glenda moved her head in a nod made awkward by her bonds.

"Ready, Diedre?"

The blonde licked her lips in answer.

Morton looked down at himself. "Well, it looks like I'm ready, too."

"Son of a bitch!" Morton told the detective the next morning. "Are you sure?"

"Yep," the raspy voice at the other end of the line answered. "Your employee is seeing a member of the Indianapolis police on a regular basis. His name is Carl Nolan."

"You mean he's fucking her?"

"Well, I don't know about that, but if I had to bet on it, I'd say—"

"Don't say it." He picked up a tape dispenser from his desk and threw it at the wall. It shattered the glass on the photo of the proposed new Shodale facility. That made him feel only a little better, and he looked around for something else to throw.

The voice on the phone demanded further attention, however. "Mr. Morton, there's something else you should know about this cop she's seeing."

"I guess he's hung like a horse."

"I couldn't say," the voice replied with no humor or surprise. He had dealt with Morton before, having followed his wife for him. "But he's working on a murder case that should interest you. It concerns that guy who killed his family— William Myers. You know, the one who was a sleep subject at your lab out there. What do you think of that?"

"What should I think of it?"

"Maybe not much, but did you also know this cop has been spending a lot of time with Ms. Turner in the lab?"

"Jesus H. Christ on a crutch!"

"I thought that might interest you."

"Anything else?"

"That's it for now. Do you want me to keep digging?"

"No. That's enough. Send me your fucking bill."

He slammed the phone down and glared at the wall. It seemed the world was conspiring against him again. Marian and this cop were probably already figuring out ways to send him up the river. Damn, how could he have been so shortsighted? How did that bitch get by him?

It was his own fault for being too smug; he had thought he had Marian totally intimidated. But she wasn't intimidated at all. Now all she and that cop had to do was get Richards to confess and that would be the end of the project. There would be lawsuits, and John Morton would be on his way out.

The more he thought about it, though, the more he realized he wasn't angered so much by Marian's apparent turning against him as he was by the fact she was screwing the cop. He had been wanting her for himself for ages, and now she had hopped in bed with the first guy that came along. That was unforgivable.

There wasn't much he could do about it now.

He had to get control of himself. Maybe things weren't as bad as they seemed. He had Stryker hard at work destroying files and records. But what if Stryker didn't get everything?

Well, there was Richards. He'd forgotten all about the doctor. Richards could take the fall. The son of a bitch deserved it, anyhow. After all, Richards had admitted giving that drug to Myers. He'd be easy to blame. All Morton had to do was lie.

Yeah, give them Richards. That would take care of things. In fact, he could turn Richards over to the police right now. No use waiting. It would be easy to fabricate a believable story about his finding out Richards had illegally dispensed drugs.

237

That would work.

Eliminating Richards would solve a lot of problems—not the big one, maybe, but only two people knew about the big one, and the other one could be handled somehow. With Richards the scapegoat, it would be easier to keep the young man in his place—once he found out what happened to rats.

And Marian—Christ, even that problem would be solved. It would be easy to discredit a bimbo who had been sleeping with the cop on the case. Who would believe a woman like that?

Things were falling into place, after all. Morton had just been looking at them from the wrong viewpoint. He'd forgotten all he had to do was lie and shift the blame elsewhere. Take care of Richards and the rest of them would fall down like fucking dominoes.

At that moment, his secretary buzzed him.

"I can't be disturbed," he told her, his mind already working on the details of how to betray Richards.

"But there's awful news."

"Oh, Christ, what is it?"

"Dr. Richards . . ."

"Yes, yes, spit it out."

". . . he killed himself."

His secretary continued with the details of how she had found this out, and what it said in the paper and on the radio.

But Morton wasn't listening. He was leaning back in his chair, dazedly watching a fly walking in circles on the window.

The fly buzzed.

Twenty. Prelude to a Picnic

"Jesus, it's hot," Jack said. "How many more houses we got today, anyhow?"

"Two," his partner Bill said, checking the list on the clipboard. "And then the park."

"Again?"

"You know the park's a big deal, Jack. If we don't spray that, the boss says it can't be billed this month. And he wants the money."

"Fuck, it ain't our money."

"It's your paycheck, ain't it?"

"I guess so." Jack continued to grumble as he turned the wheel, guiding the tank trunk through a maze of streets in one of the new housing developments on the west side of town. Most of the houses were less than a year old, and many new ones were going up. "I can't find the fucking street," he said, pulling up to the curb and letting the engine idle.

"Let me look at the map." Bill pulled a map out of the glove compartment, which he folded and unfolded several times until he found the area of Indianapolis they were now in. "This ain't no help. They don't even have this part mapped yet."

"Shit. I guess we'll have to call in for more directions."

239

"Fuck it," Bill said. "Let's go eat. We'll find the place after lunch."

"That's the best idea you've had all day."

Alex Stryker watched the baboon in the test chamber. The baboon also seemed to be watching him.

Now that Dr. Richards was gone, Stryker hadn't decided yet what to do with the animal.

There were signs the baboon was continuing to feel ill effects from 4155A. Its arms and legs were covered with scratches, cuts, and bruises from its straining constantly against its bonds. Obviously, this couldn't be allowed to go on forever.

He could take the animal off the drug, but he wasn't sure that would prove anything. He had also considered putting the animal to sleep but was afraid to do so without consulting Mr. Morton.

It was odd how Mr. Morton was suddenly so interested in everything that was going on down in the lab. Of course, now he had to be, Stryker reflected, because it was no longer safe to ignore what was going on down there. He had to worry, and the fact that Morton was forced to care gave Stryker a degree of satisfaction. He liked the idea of the ivory-tower executive having to actually get involved in the work.

Dealing with Mr. Morton was something Stryker had never expected. It just showed how one's lot in life could shift so quickly. Last week he was only a lowly lab assistant whose opinion counted for nothing, especially with the big wigs; this week he was somebody, at least to Mr. Morton, and he had become a valuable person. He was also confident that this abrupt change in status would soon translate into a better life-style; he had been making small money as a lab assistant, but he planned to parlay his new importance into not only more money, but also a much better position. In short, he now held knowledge that could change the entire direction of his career.

He smiled to himself as he observed the baboon. In a way,

Mr. Morton was trapped as much as the baboon was, only he didn't know it. Not yet, anyway.

It was funny, really. Morton actually believed he had destroyed all those files. He must have thought Stryker was an idiot. Without the files, he was a powerless and expendable nobody. With them, he was a threat—with a future.

That's why he had made a special copy of the files in the computer, encoded with his own name. And he had two hard copies of the data printed out, each of which he had hidden in a different place. When the time came, he'd show Morton who was calling the shots.

He had the power—maybe not the power of life and death as he had over this baboon, but it would do for his purposes.

Item in the Indianapolis *News:*

MORE RABID ANIMALS THIS SUMMER

A higher than usual number of rabid animals has been reported this summer, according to Kelly Stoker, chief administrator of the Indianapolis Animal Shelter.

"The incidence of rabies in both dogs and cats is up at least twenty percent over this time last year," Stoker stated. "Other agencies involved with rabid animal cases confirm this rise."

According to officials at several agencies, the number of rabies cases has increased on a citywide basis. The majority of cases, however, have been reported on the city's south side, especially around the area of Christian Park.

While people should not be unduly alarmed, they should exercise caution in approaching strange animals. Parents are urged to warn their children to be especially careful around unknown dogs or cats.

The problem is not only with stray animals. Local veterinarians say it is important to keep a watchful eye on family pets as well. Being sure pets have current rabies vaccinations is essential. If family pets show any signs of the disease, pet owners are advised to take their animals to a vet without delay.

Information concerning rabies is available from many city agencies, including the Indianapolis Humane Society.

Jack ate two Big Macs, a large order of fries, and a hot apple pie. Bill had two cheeseburgers. Their meals finished, they sat in the McDonald's Restaurant at 38th and Lafayette Road, drinking the last of their Cokes and smoking.

"Man, I can't believe how hot it is today," Jack said.

"Can't you talk about anything but the heat? That ain't going to make it go away."

"I know it. But I got to talk about something."

"Why?"

"What's the matter with you, Bill?"

"Shit, I don't know. I ain't been getting much sleep lately."

"Sure makes you grouchy."

"I keep having bad dreams, and I mean they are bad, too. Make me wake up."

"Yeah, I get dreams like that sometimes."

"No shit?"

"Yep."

"Well, I guess it means we work too hard."

"Must be." Jack drained his Coke and filled his mouth with the leftover ice. "You ready to get back to work?"

"Might as well. It ain't going to get done if we don't do it."

"Let's haul ass then."

William Myers wished they would let him have something to make the pain in his mind stop. Reality had intruded on his life again, and it was painful.

He had read in the paper that the man who had given him the little blue capsules had committed suicide, and he felt he was somehow responsible. If he hadn't been such a weak-willed

242

person, he would have turned the drugs down and maybe none of this would have happened. He would have a family, and that doctor would be alive. He was sure of that.

Why did he always have to rely on drugs to make life endurable? Why was he unable to control his emotions on his own?

But he *was* weak, and that meant he needed something to help him all the time. No one here would give him anything no matter how much he begged. He would take any kind of pill he could get.

Anything at all.

Since Walter Miller had retired, it seemed to him more and more things were going wrong in his life. It was as if his whole world was turning to shit. First it had been the roof of the house; then the furnace had to be replaced; then the refrigerator conked out. Now there was something wrong with his well, and he knew where to place the blame for that. He had determined it was his next-door neighbor's fault. He was so certain of it that he called the neighbor up and started berating him over the phone.

"You son of a bitch, you poisoned my well!" he told Dick Corley.

"Wait a minute, Wally," he answered. "What are you talking about?" Normally, he didn't mind listening to Wally's continual bitching, but this was different. He hadn't been the target of his gripes before. He had just retired himself and had hoped to spend his later years in peace. Wally, apparently, had other ideas.

"My water smells terrible, and it's your fault."

"You old bastard, why you trying to blame it on me?"

"It's you and that damn grass of yours. You keep getting it sprayed, and now that chemical shit's got into the water tables and my well is ruined."

"You're having imaginations, Wally."

"You come over here and I'll show you imagination."

"I'm not responsible for your well."

"The hell you ain't."

"Look, Wally, there ain't nothing in lawn chemicals that can hurt your well. They don't let them put stuff like that in the spray, and you know it."

"I don't know nothing of the kind, except my well is poisoned and you're going to pay for it."

"I ain't paying for nothing."

"We'll see about that. I'm calling a lawyer."

"Go ahead. Ain't no skin off my behind."

"We'll see whose behind gets skinned."

Wally slammed the phone down in a rage.

Larry paced the cell. He had lost track of how many days he had been in jail.

They told him he had killed those teenagers. They told him it wasn't a dream, but something he had actually done. But they didn't fool him with that line of crap.

He knew they were just using him, making him take the rap because he was an old alcoholic bum with no one to stand up for him.

Arnold Ray was a good vet. He had been practicing on the south side of the city for over ten years, and most of the people who came to him praised his caring manner and almost uncanny ability to diagnose their pets' problems.

Lately, however, he was beginning to doubt his abilities. Indeed, he was questioning his sanity. He had encountered eleven cases of apparent rabies in the last couple of weeks, which wasn't that unusual, except that in nine of the cases he knew the afflicted animals had been vaccinated for the disease within the last sixth months. He himself had given them the shots.

Was there a new strain of the disease going around?

* * *

"Man, we got finished just in time," Jack said, trying to see through the rain. It was coming down in sheets, and the windshield wipers were ineffective against such a downpour. Jack was piloting the truck along English Avenue by instinct. "This rain will wash half the stuff away, though."

"That ain't our fault. Anyhow, the boss will be happy. He'll still be able to bill this batch." He squinted through the windshield, watching the traffic creep by. The other vehicles on the street had their lights on, but they were still barely visible.

"Yeah, but now I'm going to be late for supper," Jack complained. "We're having fried chicken tonight. Marilyn will be pissed about me being late."

"Couldn't be helped."

"That don't make no difference to Marilyn."

"Well, tomorrow won't be so bad. We only got one house in the morning, then maybe we can just fuck off the rest of the day."

"If this rain keeps up, we won't be doing nothing."

"Well, you can fuck off all day, then."

"Maybe I'll do that," Jack said, warming to the idea. "Maybe I'll sleep all day."

Without thinking, Wally turned on the tap and filled the kettle with water. He set it on the stove to boil, while he read the newspaper.

His wife was out tonight, playing bingo at the church, and Wally didn't like the idea of her leaving him alone to fend for himself like this. She hadn't even fixed dinner for him, expecting him to make do on his own. So he had a bologna sandwich with cheese and mayonnaise, and a stack of ginger snaps with milk. Now he was going to have coffee. Instant coffee.

He hated instant coffee, but he was damned if he'd make a pot of brewed coffee to drink all by himself. That was wasteful.

He could hear the water boiling. He got up from the kitchen table and turned the burner off, then took a cup down from the cabinet and dumped a heaping teaspoon of Nescafe in it. He poured the water in on the dark brown powder and watched with satisfaction as it frothed and bubbled until it finally became coffee.

He sat down with the cup and blew on the hot liquid, then sipped. He spat it out immediately.

"God damn it to holy hell!"

He had forgotten about how bad his well water was, just as he had forgotten, for the moment, anyhow, whose fault it was—that goddamn Dick Corley.

He emptied the cup into the sink and grabbed a beer out of the refrigerator. Now, that tasted pretty good. The next beer tasted even better.

By the third beer, Wally had formulated a plan of revenge. He went to the bedroom and took his shotgun from under the bed, then returned to the kitchen to get a fourth beer.

Thus armed and fortified, Wally went out to sit on the side porch, where he had a good view of Dick Corley's house.

That evening several Shodale employees, all scheduled for the third shift, called in sick. The night supervisor, Everett Rydell, was beginning to think there was an unofficial strike going on. If this kept up, he was going to have to talk to the union about it. He would be complaining to the union steward right now, but he had called in sick, too.

This was getting ridiculous; they couldn't *all* be sick.

Myers contemplated the dark figure occupying the corner of his cell. It just stood there, unmoving, a tall shadowy thing wrapped in a shroud. Its face was obscured by a cowl draped over its head, but its eyes were faint red coals that glowed in the darkness.

"Who are you?" Myers asked the shade.

Your doctor, the thing replied. Its voice was hollow-sounding and reverberated through his cell.

"You don't look like any doctor I know."

You will know me, William Myers.

"I don't think so. I . . ."

I've come to help you. I have the medicine you need. Come closer.

As Myers approached, a skeletal hand reached out of the shroud. Bits of blue-green flesh dropped from its bony fingers, hitting the floor noiselessly. Myers was repulsed but forced himself to look, anyhow. After all, this weird vision wasn't any worse than any other nightmare he had ever had.

There were capsules in the thing's palm—little blue ones. Myers looked up into the face in the shroud, blinking in disbelief.

"It's you!" he said, recoiling in horror.

The thing pulled the cowl down from its head, revealing the ravaged but familiar face of Dr. Richards.

Yes, it's me.

"Get out of here!" Myers shouted. He could not will himself either to move or to look away.

Take these and your nightmares will go away. The fingers held the capsules up, pushing them toward Myers's face.

"I don't need those. I don't have nightmares anymore."

Yes, you do. I am your nightmare.

The Richards face scowled, then seemed to blur. One of the hands grabbed Myers about the wrist, forcing him to the floor. The other hand held the capsules right over his lips.

Take them.

"No!"

Take them and your nightmares will go away. Forever.

Myers opened his mouth to scream and the thing dropped the capsules in. He swallowed, and as he did, the thing vanished.

He ran his tongue over his lips, testing for an aftertaste. But there was none. He hadn't taken any capsules.

But there was a nightmare in his cell with him. His wife and family had come to visit.

"Don't need no goddamn lawyer to settle my affairs," Wally mumbled to himself. "Just need myself."

He shivered in the open air. The rain had started up again, causing the temperature to drop several degrees. All the cold beer he had drunk wasn't helping much.

He was too stubborn to get up and get a jacket. If he did that, he was afraid he would miss Dick Corley.

He ought to be coming home any minute now.

Larry ran to the bars and threw himself against them. He had heard that guy down the way screaming, the guy they said had killed his family. "Shut that guy up!" he yelled.

"Fuck off, old rummy!" a voice replied from the darkness.

"Nice class of people they got in here," Larry mumbled. He strained his hearing, waiting for more wisecracks from the general gloom in the jail, but there was only silence.

"Jesus, this is a scary joint," he whispered. "Lord, you got to get me out of here."

He listened for an answer, but the Lord was noncommittal. He pulled back from the cell door and moved slowly over to his bunk. He lay down and waited for the darkness to envelop him—as it always did every night.

With the darkness came the nightmares.

Dr. Ray was awakened at three in the morning. Normally, the noises coming from his little animal hospital didn't rouse him, but tonight it seemed the sounds of cats hissing were particularly intense, especially since the rain had stopped.

He hoped there was nothing amiss. People had entrusted him with the care of their pets, and he wanted always to be worthy of that trust, even if it meant his rest was occasionally disturbed.

Often, the animals reacted to external influences. After all, this was not a normal environment for them, and they missed their homes and owners. Sometimes, though, undue noise from the animals meant there was a prowler. Junkies had broken into the hospital before, looking for drugs that might provide a new high. He hoped that wasn't the case tonight. He had a gun handy, though, if that proved to be the cause of the disturbance.

But there was no way to know unless he got out of bed. He put on his robe, being careful not to disturb his slumbering wife, and went to the door that joined the animal hospital with his house. He could hardly believe how loud the hissing noise was. The cats sounded like they were fighting dragons. Some of the dogs were barking now, too.

He unlocked the door and pushed it open, then flipped on the overhead lights. He scanned the cages. The dogs, on one side of the room, were obviously barking at the cats. Nothing unusual about that.

The cats that were creating the disturbance, however, were hissing and scratching at nothing at all, as if they were fighting imaginary, nonexistent foes.

Dr. Ray went closer and checked the tags on the front of their cages. Each cat had been brought in by its owner to be watched for rabies.

Larry was not asleep. He knew that. He also knew what delirium tremens was like, and this wasn't it. Because even the worst d.t.'s didn't produce six-foot bats that smelled that bad.

The bat had black eyes and blood dripped from its two-inch fangs. It advanced on Larry, ruffling its massive veined wings as its clawed toes made disturbing skittering noises on the cold tile floor.

The bat leaned over the bunk and its fangs were only inches from his jugular.

But Larry made a fool of the beast. This time, he died before the thing could hurt him.

By six-thirty, Everett was growing extremely tired. He was proud of himself for having accomplished so much that night, though. It was really a great deal, considering that so many of his employees had failed to show.

Still, with many of his people out sick, Everett had kept one line producing all night, meeting almost two thirds of his quota. His output tonight would fill all of the tank trucks waiting out at the dock.

He went up to the shack that overlooked the plant and called down to the man on the pipeline that went over to the loading docks. Then he gave the order to fill the trucks.

It seemed the whole building rumbled as the contents of the vats rushed through the pipes.

It was a gratifying sound for Everett. It showed how well he could produce, even under adverse conditions. Even with a lot of personnel missing.

Shodale ought to give him a raise.

It was a beautiful day for a picnic.

The workers who belonged to Chapter 465 of the Sheetmetal Workers' Local expected to have a good time with their families. There was plenty of food, beer, and soft drinks. It was hotter than hell, but the trees provided sufficient shade for most, and there were occasional breezes that kept things generally comfortable.

The rains of the day before hadn't spoiled anything, after all. By noon, most of it had evaporated, and the park was basically dry. There were still a few areas where steam rose from the grass, but they didn't seem to bother anyone that much. Even the children ignored them.

And hardly anyone complained about the smell.

Twenty-One. Sleeping in the Garage

Carl knew that many men his age took the route of getting a little on the side. It was a symptom of a man's middle age, and one of his buddies on the force, Mike Tillett, had often said the only way to keep a marriage alive was to get some "strange," preferably "young stuff." That way, Tillett opined, a man could be happy and not have to go through the pain of divorce, which meant losing so many material things.

Simplistically considered, the idea of fooling around was quite attractive, but Carl also realized it was fraught with a variety of dangers.

For one thing, a man could get caught, and when that happened, it could go hard on him. Most women, even the so-called liberated type, were very possessive of their men's sexual favors and demanded fidelity no matter what. A straying male would certainly get no sympathy from any judge Carl had ever seen, either. And even if the wife decided to be "forgiving," it usually meant the remainder of married life with that woman was destined to be even more of a hell than before. Because then the estranged wife had a real weapon against her husband, which could be held back and used for as long as they stayed together.

Men like Tillett never even considered the love angle as a potential in an extramarital involvement. To such men, another woman represented only a sexual vessel, a nonentity that existed only for the purpose of gratifying the needs not met in the conjugal bed. To suggest a person might fall in love with that vessel was to suggest a heresy.

Carl found himself confronted with just such a heresy in his relationship with Marian. To him, Marian was not a "stray piece" at all; she was a person with whom Carl thought it was very possible he might be falling in love. And love made all the difference. It meant, suddenly, that the loss of material goods gathered over the course of a loveless marriage no longer had much significance. To love and to be loved changed a man's entire outlook, especially when he realized, as Carl had, that he had never really been loved before.

This new brand of love also had given Carl a false sense of courage, and that ersatz fortitude was what had made him decide to confess all to Laura.

But he knew it wasn't going to be easy, despite his resolve. He was not in a very stable frame of mind, due to the distress caused by events of the last few days. He had lost a key witness in the case with the murderous old bum, and then that Dr. Richards had apparently killed himself—just when Carl had learned he was the man most likely responsible for giving drugs to Myers. That sure blew the hell out of that case.

The Indianapolis weather had been taking its toll, too. The day before, it had rained torrentially, casting gloom over the city, and today it had been so hot and humid that it was difficult to think, let alone contemplate anything as serious as the breakup of a marriage.

Still, Carl had determined he was going to face Laura tonight—as soon as he got off work. If he waited till everything was going well and he felt better about the world in general, he might never do it. Besides, he had already called Marian and told her of his intention, so there really was no way he could back down.

He just hoped Laura would understand. After all, he had as much right to happiness as anyone else.

"Laura, I'm home," he called as he entered the house from the garage.

He found her standing in the kitchen next to the counter. Her back was to him, but he could see she was pouring herself a glass of beer. The air in the house was stifling and thick, and he wondered why she didn't have the air-conditioning running.

"It's about time," she said, turning.

After not being home for three days, Carl found his wife had changed considerably and he was shocked by her appearance. Her face was ashen, and there were deep black circles under her eyes. She had also let herself go; her straggly hair obviously hadn't been washed in days, nor had she bathed in some time. He also suspected she hadn't been going into work—they probably wouldn't let her past the door in her condition.

"Where the hell have you been for the last week?" she asked. She wore a torn flannel robe that was dotted with cigarette burn-holes. It was hanging open at the front and she had nothing on underneath. Sweat glistened off her body.

"It's only been a couple of days."

"The hell it has."

"Laura, I—"

"Don't Laura me, you son of a bitch." Her voice was raspier than usual. She started to say something else, then broke into a fit of coughing that lasted several seconds.

"What's the matter with you?" he asked, visibly alarmed by her condition.

"What the hell do you care?" she said, finally managing to control her hacking. She reached into the pocket of the robe and took out a cigarette and her lighter.

"Do you think you should smoke with that cold?" he asked reflexively.

"I'll do whatever I want." She lit the cigarette and puffed defiantly. "It's no concern of yours. Besides, I haven't got a cold."

"What's wrong, then?"

"Nothing. There's nothing at all wrong with me." Her eyes seemed to glaze over momentarily, then she blinked as if just coming awake and leered at him. "Nothing wrong with me a little old poke in the whiskers wouldn't cure." She reached down and patted the mound of her public hair.

Carl looked away. "You're not serious, are you?"

She seemed startled and jerked her hand away. "About what?"

"You don't really expect me to make love to you, do you?"

She took a swallow from the beer glass and wiped her mouth with the back of her hand, smearing lipstick all over her face. "That's a laugh! Listen," she sneered, "I don't need any of your prick, you prick, and when I do need it, you're not around, so fuck you."

He stepped closer, trying to look directly into her eyes, but she kept turning her face.

"What the hell are you looking at?"

"Are you drunk?"

"No, I'm not drunk, Mr. Police Officer."

"Don't call me that."

"That's what you are, a goddamn cop. A fuzz. A pig."

He was tempted to strike her but realized that would be a useless gesture. Instead, he felt himself temporarily filled with pity for her. He had known her so many years that it was awesome to contemplate leaving her just like that—even if living with her was sheer hell.

"I'm not a pig," he uttered, not really replying to her insults as much as trying to stall her off while he considered what he should do. He despaired of reasoning with her tonight.

"Oink," she said, then took another drink.

He watched her movements. While there was something definitely strange and quirky about the way she moved, he didn't believe she was drunk. As far as he knew, she never did any drugs, either. That didn't mean there was nothing wrong, however. Maybe if he could get her to sleep, he would have better luck approaching her in the morning.

"I'm going to bed," he said. "I think you should, too."

"Wait a minute, buster. You've got some explaining to do."

"I can see you're not feeling well, Laura. There's no point in us getting in a big argument tonight."

"I want to talk right now." She slammed the glass of beer down, making it slosh all over the countertop.

"It can wait."

"No, it can't. I want to know where you've been when you're not home. And don't tell me you were working. You would have called me if you were working."

"You get some rest, and we'll discuss it in the morning."

"Fuck that. I'm not stupid." She took a long pull on her cigarette and laid it on the edge of the counter. Then she approached him on unsteady legs. "You've got another woman. Admit it."

"Please, Laura."

She swung her arms wildly as she talked. "Who is it?"

"I don't want to talk about it."

"I bet you got yourself somebody younger. I'm not good enough for you anymore. Is that it?"

"No."

"The hell it isn't. That's the trouble with you goddamn men. A woman gives you the best she's got, then when she gets close to forty, you're ready to dump her for the first little bitch with big tits that comes along. What'sa matter? These aren't big enough for you?" She pulled her robe open, lifted her breasts with both hands, and pointed them at him. "They'd be big enough for anyone else. I'll find a man who likes them. I don't need you, Mr. Police Officer, Carl-the-prick-son-of-a-bitch!" She let go of her breasts and jerked her robe closed.

"Laura, you've got to calm down."

"Listen to me when I'm talking to you!"

She was right in his face now, and the smell of beer, nicotine, and body odor was overwhelming. He thrust his arms out to hold her away from him.

"Are you seeing another woman or not? Answer me. I want to settle this right now!"

"Yes," he answered quietly and with instant regret.

"What!"

There was no avoiding it now. He had to go on. "I want a divorce, Laura."

She fixed him with eyes that tore at his very manhood. "You dirty bastard."

"Call me all the names you want. I don't care. I just can't go on with you anymore."

He let go of her and she stood there weaving and staring at him, apparently not sure what to do. Her face showed bewilderment, and she seemed to be searching for something. She stuck her hand in her pocket, took out another cigarette, and lit it, apparently having forgotten the one she had left burning on the counter.

"I knew you had another woman. I knew it. I'm not good enough."

"It's not that. It's just that you and I don't get along together anymore. It was bound to happen...."

"Bastard!" She lunged at him, and before he could stop her, she had mashed the burning cigarette on his neck.

Carl reacted without thinking. Almost before the pain registered in his mind, he swung his right arm and swatted her across the face, knocking her to the floor. "You bitch!" He held the throbbing place on his neck where she had burned him and watched her, waiting—perhaps even hoping—for another attack.

But she was subdued. She just sat on the floor, staring at nothing, her lips working wordlessly for several seconds. "You hit me," she said, her voice suddenly dropping. "Bad enough you've got another woman, but that don't mean you should hit me ... just because ... it's bad ... enough ... divorce, my ass ... you son of a ...." Her speech slurred until it became unintelligible. Then her eyes closed and she slumped against the refrigerator.

Carl bent down and shook her, but she wouldn't respond. He put his ear to her chest. She was breathing regularly now, although with a slight wheeze. He checked her pulse, and it seemed normal, too. He concluded she had passed out.

Then she *was* drunk.

He picked her up and carried her upstairs, straining with her weight and fighting nausea all the way. The cigarette burn stung so bad it was making him sick and her smell wasn't helping the situation.

He briefly considered taking her in and bathing her, but he feared that it would overstimulate her and then they would be up all night arguing.

He laid her gently in the bed, covered her up, and went back into the bathroom to find something to rub on his burn. There was no burn medicine, so he rubbed a bit of aloe vera lotion on his burn, which did soothe it a bit.

Then he returned to the bedroom. Laura was sleeping quite peacefully now, showing no signs of illness or drunkenness at the moment. There was a slight discoloration on her jaw from where he had hit her, but it didn't look very serious. She would be able to cover it over with makeup.

If he were the old solicitous Carl, he would have sat up with her for a while, but he didn't see the point of it. He was too tired to be that caring.

He decided to take his normal refuge out in the garage. Fortunately, the cot was still out there, waiting for him.

Laura awoke to a voice whispering in her ear. At first she couldn't identify it, but as she listened to it a while, she realized it was the voice of her mother.

Her mother, however, was dead.

Still, the words made sense.

I always told you Carl was a no-account, no-good man. It's

not that you're not good enough for him, it's that he isn't good
enough for you. He's just like all men, just like your father, and
all he cares about is what he can get out of you. Then, the
minute you turn your back, he's out chasing after any old
strange woman he can find that will do all that dirty stuff.
That's all any of them want, honey—the dirty stuff. The nasties.

"I like it, too," Laura replied. She wondered why she was
not disturbed by talking to her dead mother like this. Then she
knew the answer; obviously, she was dreaming.

He won't give it to you, though. Will he?

"No."

The nasties, Laura honey, the nasties. The nasties! Do the
nasties to him!

"What?"

Don't let him get away with this. Don't let him have his way
with another woman?

"I don't understand, mother!"

Fix him!

Laura understood.

Even though he had slept on the cot many times, Carl
couldn't get comfortable. The heat was getting to him, but he
was in such a half-asleep, half-awake condition he couldn't mus-
ter the energy to get up and turn the air-conditioning on. As a
result, he felt like he was drowning in his own sweat.

He kept replaying the evening's events in his mind, trying to
determine if there was any way he could have handled it differently. Could he have said something that would have made
it go more smoothly? Was there anything he could have said
that would have made Laura take the news without flying off
the handle like that?

Probably not.

Yet he felt guilty about the way it had all turned out. True,
Laura had been drunk or ill—or possibly both—but he had

258

been in possession of all his faculties and should have been able to control the situation.

And he shouldn't have hit her. In all their married life, he had struck his wife only twice before, and both times he had regretted it. He didn't even like the idea of a man hitting a woman, no matter how justified it might seem under the circumstances, and knowing that he had done such a thing hurt him more than anything Laura could have said or done. Worst of all, it made him feel he had sunk to her level.

He couldn't take it back now, though.

Maybe he should have gone over to Marian's for the comfort she would offer him, instead of sleeping out in the garage. That was really out of the question now, though, not only because it was late, but because it would be awkward leaving there in the morning to return to the house for another confrontation with Laura.

Marian. He would have to go through hell to get the freedom to have her. But she was worth anything he might have to suffer.

Even harrowing a hell the likes of which only Laura could create.

Laura hummed to herself as she descended the stairs. It was a tune to nothing in particular. It just served to distract her from the whispering in her ears.

She wished it would shut up and let her alone. She knew what to do, for God's sake.

After all, it was her damn dream.

Carl heard a creaking noise coming from the house. He listened intently for a couple of minutes, decided it was the house settling, and rolled over on his back. He briefly considered getting up and getting his pistol, just in case, but that would require energy, and he didn't have much of that. There was no reason to be paranoid, anyhow.

"Carl."

Her voice sounded distant. She said his name again, and it was obvious she was closer than before. Then there was another creaking noise, and the door that connected the garage to the kitchen opened slowly. The light from the kitchen was dim, probably only the fluorescent tube burning over the sink, but it was sufficient to cast a strange aura around Laura's naked form.

"Carl," she called again, and this time there was a distinctive sweetness to her voice, almost a lilting quality.

"Go back to bed," he grumbled at her, propping himself up on one elbow.

"You are there, aren't you, honey?"

What was this "honey" bullshit? He realized with despair she was once again in one of her intermittent horny moods. Sex tonight was an especially hideous prospect. Did she think she could patch things up that easily?

"I'm trying to sleep," he protested.

She hesitated in the doorway, then took a couple of steps toward him. As she moved, light seemed to play off her nakedness eerily, flashing and bouncing around the dark in the garage.

That was curious. Why would light—?

Then he saw what she carried in her right hand—a long kitchen knife with a sharp, nasty-looking blade. It was the type of knife chefs on TV used to slice and dice vegetables.

Carl started to roll off the cot, but it was too late. Laura had already propelled herself on top of him.

He was able to catch her right wrist before she plunged the knife into his flesh, but he didn't expect what she did with her left hand.

She was pulling on his scrotum.

"Nobody but me can have it!" she screamed.

Realizing her intent, Carl suddenly found the energy that had eluded him all evening.

He grabbed the other wrist and slowly, painfully, wrenched it away from his most vulnerable area. He discovered, however, that Laura was very strong, though, much stronger than she had ever seemed before. She seemed to be endowed with an unreal strength that was difficult for him to overcome.

The cot was knocked over as they struggled. Carl heard one of its wooden braces snap under the weight of the two of them.

They rolled off the wreckage of the cot and landed on the cold concrete floor, both lying on their sides.

Laura was panting but fiercely determined as ever. She pressed her teeth on his bare shoulder, but he managed to twist away before she could actually bite him. He still had both her wrists gripped tightly in his hands.

The cold edge of the knife grazed the skin of his neck and he yelped.

They rolled again, and this time Carl landed on top with Laura's naked, writhing body thrusting under him as she struggled to break his grip.

Stupidly, he was realized he was getting a hard-on.

Laura sensed it, too, and glared at him.

"Don't you dare rape me, you son ... of ... a ... bitch!" She spat the words at him, her features contorting in hatred.

The ugliness of her face made the impertinent erection collapse as if it were a balloon stuck with a needle.

"No chance," he said.

Laura's right hand pivoted oddly, and he realized she was trying to hack at his fingers with the knife, but she didn't have the right angle. Insane frustration showed on her face.

She started to bring her knee up into his groin, but instinct made Carl clamp his legs on her thigh, effectively blocking that move.

But this small victory was not gained easily. He paid for the success of his counterattack by being temporarily distracted from the knife. And she had used that moment to slice the back of his wrist.

Somewhere from within him an animal screamed. That same animal was suddenly stronger than the small naked woman. And much swifter.

He released her left wrist, made a fist, and socked her solidly on the jaw.

This time he didn't feel bad about hitting her.

She made a raspy noise and a nicotine-scented belch emitted from her lips, then she went limp.

The knife clattered to the floor.

Carl picked it up and flung it across the garage. It hit a wall and bounced against his car.

He sat on his haunches, panting, trying to catch his breath, staring at the murderous woman who didn't resemble his wife any more at all.

She was extremely still.

"Jesus, I've killed her!"

He checked her body signs. She was not dead, after all, and Carl breathed relief. He wanted to be rid of her, but not that way.

The back of his wrist was dripping blood. He walked over to the scant light coming in from the doorway and examined the cut. It was three or four inches long, but it wasn't deep. The pain it had caused was disproportionate to the reality of it. However, it might need stitches.

For the moment, he squeezed the cut together and tore off a strip of his T-shirt to wrap around it as a makeshift bandage. It would hold the wound awhile, anyhow.

He picked Laura up, carried her into the house, and laid her limp form on the couch.

He draped a blanket over her. Then, wrapping himself in another blanket, he sat on the chair next to the couch, watching and waiting.

* * *

It was dawn when Laura came to again. She stretched and yawned, and seemed surprised.

"What am I doing down here?" The side of her face was black-and-blue, but nothing seemed to be broken. It made her jaw ache to talk, though.

Carl shook himself from the edge of slumber. "You remember, don't you?"

She sat up and stared at him. "I don't remember anything, except you coming home last night and—" Her expression of distaste and hatred completed the thought for her. "I also remember you hitting me, and it still hurts."

He refrained from defending his actions, knowing it was useless at best. "You don't remember later?"

"No."

"You don't remember trying to kill me?" Though her intent had been slightly nastier than merely wanting to kill him, he didn't want to remind her or himself of the reality of it. Even now, the very thought made his crotch ache.

"Look, Carl, I'm mean and I may be bitchy sometimes, but I would never try to kill anyone."

"You tried to kill me."

Accusation flared in her eyes. "You're making that up. I know what you're trying to do. You're setting it up to make it look like I'm crazy, so you can get a divorce without losing everything. It's a shitty cop trick, that's what it is!"

"Laura, be rational. I wouldn't do that and you know it, and you *did* try to kill me." He unwrapped the strip of cloth from his wrist, then extended his hand for her to see. "You stabbed me with a kitchen knife."

Laura's eyes grew wide with recognition, then abruptly glazed over with confusion. The transformation passing over her features was so dramatic Carl himself was taken aback.

"But that didn't really happen!" she said. "It was—"

"What, Laura? What was it?"

"It was only a dream. It didn't really happen."

263

Twenty-Two. Aftermath

While Carl was struggling with Laura, things had been happening in the city. That night, and for the next few days, the Indianapolis news media would have more important events to concern itself with than the rising incidence of rabid animals:

A man named Walter Miller blew his neighbor away with a shotgun and later claimed it was a bad dream.

A pregnant woman dreamed she was frying her newborn baby in a frying pan; the next morning, she discovered she had miscarried and done just that. When she realized what she had done, she attempted to commit suicide. The day before, the woman had attended a picnic in Christian Park with her husband, a member of the Sheetmetal Workers' Union.

Three people who had attended the same picnic committed suicide within hours of each other.

A man, also in the union, burned his house down, then set fire to four other houses in the neighborhood before the police arrived on the scene and stopped him. He said his desire to commit arson was inspired by a bad dream.

Jack Baldwin, an employee of a local lawn treatment company, surprised his coworker, Bill Conners, by visiting his house at about three in the morning. He beat Bill savagely, then proceeded to rape his wife and teenaged daughter. Neighbors heard the ruckus, called the police, and Bill and his family were saved, but just barely. Baldwin told investigating officers he had no recall of the assault on Conners or his wife, except for a vague recollection of a dream.

A veterinarian, Dr. Arnold Ray, entered the Winona Hospital Emergency Room at four AM, suffering from deep scratches on his face and arms. He told ER personnel his wounds had been inflicted by a cat. Pressed for further details, Ray said he believed the animal was suffering from a new strain of rabies.

A diseased, alcoholic old bum, who was alleged to have killed two teenagers, had a heart attack in his cell and died instantly.

A teenaged boy was caught running through Broad Ripple Park close to sunrise. He was naked and splattered with blood. Police continued to question him, but he refused to say what had happened to his clothing or how he came to be covered with blood. A search of the park revealed nothing.

People going to work downtown one morning witnessed a fundamentalist preacher ranting in the Monument Circle area. While this was not an unfamiliar spectacle, this preacher had a slightly different message. He claimed The Rapture had occurred at 7:35, and he was distraught because he had been overlooked by the Lord. Later, the man's wife was located, and she was finally able to convince him he had only been dreaming.

William Myers, a man accused of murdering his family, became violently insane and had to be removed from jail and taken to a mental institution. His case was judged as virtually hopeless, as the man had lost all touch with reality.

Rapes, murders, and other crimes, both violent and nonviolent, rose sharply and continued to rise. The Indianapolis police had their hands full. Almost all these crimes had two factors in common: They were committed during the night, and there was a dream element figuring in the motives of the majority of the perpetrators.

More accurately, it was an element of nightmare.

* * *

Carl had never seen Laura so vulnerable . . . and so afraid. Nor had he ever seen her afraid of herself before. But when Laura realized she had really attempted to kill her husband, he was overcome by a whole new range of emotions, which neither she nor Carl knew she possessed.

They sat together for almost an hour, Carl holding her, trying to offer comfort. There was no love involved in the touching for either of them. It was only a sharing of basic human contact, the offer of warmth, for its own sake, implying nothing else. There were only two emotions being felt: For Laura, it was fear; for Carl, it was pity.

After the pity dissipated, Carl began to consider what he needed to do. His options were limited. He could just leave and never come back, or he could have Laura locked up for her own good—which he didn't think a very good idea at the moment. Or he could use the opportunity Laura's condition presented to learn more about the dream condition. The third choice was the one he favored, but it might be difficult getting Laura to cooperate.

As a nurse, Laura's first inclination was to go to a doctor and obtain medicine that would blank her mind out.

Remembering some of the things Marian had told him, Carl argued against that solution. "What would dope do for you? It certainly wouldn't solve anything."

"It might. Maybe I'm just overstressed. . . ."

"You know that's not it."

"Maybe I'm schizophrenic then. I honestly don't remember things I did."

"I believe you, but you don't really think you're schizophrenic, do you?"

She stared at him while she thought about it. "No. But I feel sick—mentally and physically. I think I should at least have some tests, at least some blood work."

"I think you should wait on that—for a while." He didn't think blood tests would show anything, anyhow, not if his suspicions were correct.

"Then what do you want me to do? I don't like feeling this way. I know we've had our differences, but I didn't want it to come to this."

"I know that. No one likes to feel out of control."

"That's what it was, too. Being out of control, and not even knowing what you're doing." She touched his injured arm. "What are you going to do about that?"

"I'll take care of it later. Right now, my main concern is you." He realized that getting Laura to cooperate was not his only problem. The other person might not want to participate, either. But then maybe Laura wouldn't have to know who Marian was. With a little finesse, he might be able to pull it off.

"Laura," he said, "you're going to have to trust me."

"Do I have a choice?"

"Not really."

"What is it, then? What do you want me to do?"

"I want you to talk to someone. She's a person who knows a lot about the way the mind works—and she's an expert on dreams."

A hint of suspicion flickered in her face. Carl held his breath. The "she" might have alerted Laura. But her concerns lay elsewhere. "She's not one of those psychic hoodoos?"

Carl felt relieved. "No. She's a bona fide professional. A psychologist."

"I don't know. I think I need stronger therapy than that. I need medication—"

"Look, Laura, you don't have to listen to me. You don't have to do anything. But just talk to her. That's all I ask. Just talk. After that, then you can still go to a doctor, if you insist."

"I want to do what's right."

"Then do this. You'll not only help yourself, but you may help me as well." He didn't offer to explain how it would help him.

The old Laura was struggling with the newly subdued Laura, and she started to protest, but then the new woman asserted herself. "All right, Carl. I'll do it your way. For now."

"Good. Now, you go upstairs and get cleaned up. I have to make a phone call, then I'll get ready and we'll go. Okay?"

"Yes, but—"

"Everything will be fine," he said. "Trust me."

Marian watched the clock in her office with deep apprehension.

She couldn't believe what she had agreed to do. She was actually going to see Carl's wife as if she were just another sleep subject. She must be out of her mind. She had never dreaded anything more. But then, she had to expect this type of discomfort in her life if she was going to be the "other woman."

But Carl was convinced her seeing his wife would lead to some important revelation that would be useable in the cases she and he were working on together. If Carl felt that way about it, it was impossible for Marian to turn him down.

Despite all her misgivings, she had to admit she was intrigued by what Carl had told her about his wife . . .

Laura, Marian reminded herself, the woman's name was Laura.

. . . and, if it was true, then maybe they would discover something useful.

She just hoped she didn't turn into a gibbering idiot when she met the woman face to face.

She kept fretting and, ultimately, it was ten-thirty. Time passed, bringing what it would, no matter how much a person dreaded its inevitability.

Carl was, as usual, punctual. Sue announced his arrival over the intercom, and the dreaded moment arrived. Carl and the woman— *Laura, her name is Laura*—came in and were seated.

"Hello," Marian said, uncertain of whom she should be addressing. She shot a look at Carl, whose expression revealed nothing. He was evidently uncomfortable, too, but he hid it better than she did.

"This is my wife," he said, nodding to her.

"I'm Dr. Turner." She hesitated, then leaned across her desk to offer her hand to the—to Laura.

"Laura Nolan." Laura shook Marian's hand perfunctorily.

Marian noted how sweaty Laura's palms were, then realized her own were just as wet. "Nice to meet you, Mrs. Nolan."

Laura merely grumbled. There was something disturbing about her expression and the way her blue eyes seem to dart about nervously.

Marian was surprised at how fat she was—well, fat in comparison to herself—and how *old* she looked. She studied other details, too: the frosted hair, the excessive makeup, and the bright red fingernails. To be fair, though, there were other things about her that could be construed as flattering. For example, her breasts were larger than Marian's. Some men did prefer volume over sensitivity.

This, then, was the woman who was married to Carl and had claims on him. This was what she was competing with. Not only a wife, but an older wife, an older woman than she was.

She was also a woman who was very afraid. Marian couldn't help but feel sorry for her. But feeling sorry wouldn't help her, nor would it change the fact that Carl no longer loved her. It also did little to assuage her own guilt.

Marian shoved all these feelings aside. She was, for the moment at least, acting in a professional capacity here. This was her own turf; she had to be a psychologist now, not a woman.

"Would you care to smoke?" Marian asked. She had noted the nicotine stains on Laura's fingers, and the woman's perfume did little to cover up the smell of tobacco that hung on her.

"Is it okay?" She looked at Carl instead of Marian, as if it were up to him.

"I want you to be comfortable." She took an ashtray from her drawer and set it on the desk in front of Laura.

"Well," Carl said, wincing as Laura lit up, "I guess I should leave you two alone to get acquainted."

"Where are you going?" Marian asked without thinking, her

voice betraying way too much concern. "I mean, you won't be far away if I should need to question you, will you?"

Carl's expression remained impassive. Marian was thankful one of them was capable of controlling his emotions.

"Don't go far," Laura blurted. She seemed not to notice the silent exchange of emotions between the two lovers.

"I'll just be down the hall. I need to call in, or they'll wonder what happened to me when I don't show up at eleven."

"I understand," Marian said.

"You'll be okay, Laura," he told his wife. "Dr. Turner is very capable—and an expert in her field. Just answer all her questions—truthfully—and she'll be able to help you."

Laura blew smoke at him. He thought he detected just a hint of reproach in her eyes. Maybe she suspected something, maybe not. No one had any choice in the matter now.

He let himself out, and suddenly the two women were alone together.

Marian fought the urge to blush, but she could feel her ears getting red. She hoped her hair hid the telltale signs from Laura.

Be professional, she told herself. *Professional. This is only a woman—another human being—who needs your help.*

"I have a few questions for you," she said, taking a folder from a stack at her left hand. "This is a standard questionnaire, designed to zero in on your problem. From your answers to these questions, I'll be able to start forming an opinion."

"Okay, doctor."

"You may call me Marian, if you wish."

"It doesn't matter."

"I want you to be as relaxed and as comfortable as possible."

"It doesn't matter to me. I'm a nurse. I'm used to calling people doctor."

Marian started to say she was not a medical doctor but didn't feel she needed to reaffirm that fact with this woman.

"As you wish," Marian said. Then she started going through the questionnaire, beginning by asking Laura to describe her dreams.

Ten minutes into the questioning, Carl returned. His face wore a troubled expression.

"Excuse me for interrupting," he said. "Could I talk to you, Dr. Turner? In private?"

Laura turned around quickly, the expression on her face asking pointed questions. "What is it?"

"Laura, I've got to go in."

Marian gave him a pleading look. "But we just began."

"If you'll give me a couple of minutes, Mar—Dr. Turner, I can explain it. Then you and Laura can continue."

"Excuse us, Mrs. Nolan."

Laura turned away like a rejected child. She lit yet another cigarette.

Marian joined Carl out in the hall. "You can't leave me all alone with her," she said desperately. "I'm having enough trouble keeping my cool as it is."

"I've got to report in, Marian. All kinds of hell has broken loose in the city. Several murders. Rape. Arson. It's like people are going crazy. The lieutenant's calling in all available men. I couldn't stay away unless my back was broken and I didn't have crutches."

"Damn it, I can't—"

"You have to. Laura could be a link. I don't know how, but I *think* she could, anyhow. We have to take whatever comes our way."

"But without you around, she might—"

"She won't do anything. She doesn't know who you are—to me. She just thinks you're a professional acquaintance, that's all. She suspects nothing."

"The woman isn't stupid, Carl. How long do you think we can hide it from her?"

"I don't know. We'll tell her eventually." He took a deep breath.

"You're not telling me all of it, are you?" Marian's gaze locked on his eyes, seeking answers.

"No. I guess I don't know what to make of everything that's going on. It's madness, that's all I can say."

She grabbed his arm and squeezed. "Tell me the rest of it."

"Myers went crazy."

"What do you mean crazy?"

"I mean he flipped out completely and they had to take him away in a straight jacket. He kept screaming something about his wife and kids being in the cell with him."

"That's a shame," Marian said, "but somehow it doesn't surprise me that much."

"There's more. The old rummy died."

Marian's mouth dropped open in dismay. "The man who killed the teenagers? What happened?"

"Heart attack. He must have had a bad ticker."

"Wasn't anyone watching him?"

"They can't watch prisoners twenty-four hours a day. The officer in the lockup told me the old man looked like he was scared when he died."

"This is awful," Marian said. "Richards is dead, Myers is worthless, and now another person is dead. It's like something is happening over which we have no control. Like a curse or—"

"It's a like a series of nightmares—all coming true," Carl said.

"Nightmares," Marian murmured, letting go of his arm.

"Dreams, nightmares, hallucinations—whatever you want to call it, there are strange things going on right now. And you've got to be strong enough to overcome your petty woman feelings about Laura."

"It's not that," she protested. "I'm just uncomfortable."

"Our problems don't mean that much at the moment. I'm a police officer. You're a psychologist. We've got to use our talents to help people. We can worry about straightening out my life later."

Marian realized he was right because he was speaking the truth, and the truth was right under all circumstances, no matter how distressing it was to the people involved in it.

"I'll do what I can," she promised at last. "But, Carl, we've got to be careful."

"Why do you say that?"

"I don't know. It's just a feeling of dread—of apprehension I have. I don't know what's causing it. It's not just your—it's not just Laura. It's the whole thing. The murders, the nightmares—our inability to discover anything that makes any sense. It's too much sometimes."

He glanced around to make sure no one was watching, then leaned down and kissed her lightly. "I'll take care of myself—and you, too. You just worry about doing your job with Laura."

"All right, Carl. But—but you will come back, won't you?"

"If I can. Otherwise, Laura can take a cab home. In any case, I'll call you later. Now, we better go back in your office before Laura gets curious."

Carl returned with Marian to her office. He briefly explained to Laura how he was called into work and assured her he would see her later. He made sure she had cab fare, then he left.

The next hour and a half was agonizing for Marian, but by the end of the ordeal she was convinced of several things about Laura's condition, not the least of which was that the woman was somehow acting out her dreams. She had also lately become oversexed.

Laura seemed to delight in relating the details of her recently increased sexual desire, as if she wanted to see Marian squirm. And Marian *did* squirm. Despite all her efforts to maintain professional detachment, it was difficult to listen to Carl's wife describe her sexual feelings and how she found herself dreaming continually of having relations with Carl.

Marian couldn't determine if Laura was doing this because of her general bitchiness or because she knew Marian was the other woman in Carl's life. Either way, Marian found herself wanting to escape from Laura's presence. The woman was like a nasty child, saying bad words to make the grown-ups react, and her overbearing manner grew worse from minute to minute, perhaps because she no longer felt a need to be inhibited

273

with Carl gone. In any case, her sheepishness had disappeared and the real Laura Nolan had emerged in all its ugliness.

But Marian couldn't afford the luxury of examining Laura's personality right now. The overriding consideration had to be what she could learn from the woman, and that was the fact that Laura remembered everything, even the attempt on Carl's life, as things experienced in the dream state, not in reality. Marian didn't believe Laura's memories were hallucinations, either. Dreams and hallucinations were not the same, either to the perceiver or even in a clinical sense.

No, for Laura the division between dreaming and reality had somehow been disrupted, and the lines had become blurred to the point that dreaming and reality, at least at night, when she believed herself to be asleep, had become one and the same.

This malady was unfamiliar to Marian. It intrigued her, since it seemed to suggest that Laura's brain was not doing its job. Normally, the brain secreted certain chemicals during sleep that prevented other chemicals, specifically neurotransmitters, from working. The effect was a kind of bodily paralysis that prevented the sleeper from getting up while dreaming and hurting himself—or others—during the dream.

If that was what was happening with Laura, it was possible a similar thing had happened to the other people who claimed to have killed while dreaming. But how could that happen? What would cause it? Nothing the woman had told her so far indicated anything that would affect the physical aspects of the brain in any way. There was nothing unusual in anything the woman had eaten or drunk. She had been exposed to no unusual conditions at the hospital where she worked.

None of the others had anything strange to report, either. Except for Myers, who had access to the drugs.

Laura was showing signs of restlessness. But it was about time to end the interview, anyhow.

"So what do you think?" Laura asked, mashing out the tenth cigarette she had smoked since coming there.

Marian's mind flew over alternatives, considered various ways out, then settled on the inevitable. "I think you need to come here tonight and let me hook you up to the polysomnograph."

"Is that like an EEG?"

"An EEG is part of it. It also monitors eye and muscle movements. Are you up to it?" She faced another dreaded prospect if Laura agreed, but in her heart she wanted her to, if only because it would give her some real measure of control over the woman—temporarily, at least.

"I'll think about it."

"It would help me evaluate what's going on with you."

"Could Carl come?"

Marian's fists clinched involuntarily. She hid them in her lap. "Of course, if he is available."

"I'll make sure he is."

"Then I'll see you around eleven tonight. My girl, Sue, will get you a gate pass. She'll also call a cab for you."

Laura leaned back in her chair and arched her back as if stretching, though it seemed to Marian she was displaying her breasts for her approval. Then she stood up and smiled very indulgently.

"See you later, Dr. Turner."

"Later, Mrs. Nolan."

Marian averted her eyes until Laura had shut the door behind her. She waited five minutes, then called Carl.

"It's like an outbreak of 'dream alibiers,' " Carl told her, using the term he had coined himself. "We have people committing every conceivable felony and misdemeanor on the books—and they're all saying they were dreaming at the time."

Marian gasped. "This is unreal, Carl. You make it sound like an epidemic."

"It is. But an epidemic of what?"

"There has to be a common factor among all those people. There has to be something linking them together, a shared experience of some kind. It might be something easily overlooked."

"We do have one thing, but it doesn't apply to all of them."

"What's that?"

"The park. Christian Park. About half the people we've talked to in the last few hours had gone to a picnic there."

She paused to think about that. She could hear the background noise of heightened activity on the other end of the line; it sounded like the police department was very busy. Then she said, "There's something familiar about that park, isn't there?"

"Yep. That old bum I told you about lived there. And, of course, the guy from the Parks and Recreation Department worked there. He was found last week in his car off Interstate 74."

"Jesus, Carl, that's another death. How many are there going to be?"

He sighed heavily, and it was as if he were right there beside her. "I have a feeling there's going to be a lot more, unless we can come up with something."

"Carl, that park—is there anything about it that points to anything at all?"

"We've been going over it, but so far we've found nothing. The place smells bad, though. At least, that's what the guys who've been there say."

"What kind of smell is it?"

"I don't know. I was there only a couple of times and I didn't notice anything. I'll have the boys keep checking, though. Maybe they'll turn something up."

"I'm afraid, Carl. If this thing is so random, then it could strike anyone—you, me, or anyone else, for that matter. It's worse than a sexual disease."

"You talk like you've already decided it *is* a disease."

"Maybe it is. I know that from talking to your wife, we're dealing with an odd phenomenon here."

"What do you mean?"

Marian briefly explained the theory that was evolving in her

276

mind as a result of interviewing Laura. She said nothing about Laura's unseemly sexual meanderings, however.

"Whew," Carl said when she was finished. "You're talking about something that sounds pretty damn serious—I mean, something that interferes with brain chemistry. That's goddamn serious shit."

"You bet it is. And one other thing . . . I asked her to come back tonight. I'm going to hook her up to the polysomnograph and see what's cooking in her brain. Carl, you've got to be here."

"I don't know if I can. We're up to our asses in alligators here, and the phone keeps ringing off the hook. The lieutenant's giving me dirty looks right now, because I've been on the phone too long."

"You have to come, or Laura won't go through with it."

"All right. I'll see what I can do. I'll tell them my arm hurts or something."

"Did you get it taken care of yet?"

"I bought some of those butterfly bandages at Phar-Mor and stuck it shut."

"Typical man. Doesn't care how disfigured he is. That won't heal right—and you might get an infection."

"I'll go to a doctor. I promise. It won't get screwed up that quickly."

Marian made a face. She already imagined maggots squirming in his wound, but she didn't want to sound like an overconcerned mother.

"Marian, I've got to go. . . ."

"Wait. You've got to arrange something for me."

"Make it quick. The lieutenant's heading my way."

"I want you to arrange for me to be present at the autopsy of that old man who died—the wino."

"I don't know. They may already have done it."

"Then they'll have to do it again."

"Have you got an idea—I'll be off in a minute, Lieutenant— an idea I need to know about?"

277

"Maybe. Get me in on the autopsy and I'll be able to tell you more."

"I'll see what I can do. I've got to hang up. Bye."

"Bye, honey."

Marian shuddered as she replaced the phone in the cradle. Had she really just *begged* to be present at an autopsy? This whole affair must be affecting her mind.

But nothing was showing up in any of the tests performed on any living person so far. Nothing might ever be found, unless they took a dead person completely apart. The dead often revealed more secrets than the living. The old man might have been a drain on society when he was alive, but his death was going to mean something. But she wasn't sure what that meaning would be.

The idea of an autopsy made her skin crawl, though. She couldn't deny that. But if that's what it took to get to the bottom of this mystery, then Marian was prepared to go through with it.

After all, she would have been cutting *live* bodies if she had gone through with being a doctor—if she had possessed the courage she needed to succeed.

She had to find that elusive courage now. She had to do whatever was required, even if it meant delving into areas she had avoided before—and even if it meant compromising her sense of ethics.

Because she had already decided her ethics were disposable in the face of what seemed a possible epidemic. That's why she thought what she was going to do to Laura Nolan was okay—and was, in fact, very necessary.

There was too much at stake for her to do otherwise. And she assured herself repeatedly that she had no intention of harming Carl's wife.

Unless it couldn't be helped.

Twenty-Three. Marian's Risks

Marian waited till evening, after most of the workers in the research building had gone home, before she went down to the animal lab. She opened the door, stepped in, and switched on the lights. No one was working late tonight.

On the surface, it was very still in the lab, but there was an undercurrent of activity pulsating through the room that proclaimed the presence of life. The vital sounds were almost subliminal: animals breathing and moving, the rustle of fur against the wire walls of a cage, the lapping of water, the crunching of food. And, interspersed among those sounds, a tiny whimper here, a low-pitched whine there.

She hadn't been down in the lab for at least two weeks, and now that she was here again, she remembered why she avoided the place. It was because of what the lab represented: She didn't really like the idea of experimentation on animals, no matter how necessary it was. She ascribed too much humanity to the creatures sacrificed in the name of science; their suffering was too real to her.

She cringed as she passed the cage where a cat lay, apparently sleeping. Part of its cranial cap had been removed to allow the implantation of electrodes. While it supposedly did not harm the animal or cause much pain, Marian still had difficulty look-

279

ing at it. What was really served by such mutilation? Did it really benefit mankind in the long run?

Have fun at the postmortem, she thought, kidding herself. *You can't even look at a live cat.*

She shivered and continued through the lab, making her way back to the cabinet where batches of experimental drugs were kept. She unlocked the cabinet and searched along the rows of vials, stopping when she found ampules of 4155A. As added insurance, she took a bottle of the drug in capsule form.

She closed the cabinet, locked it, and started to leave. She halted when she heard a high-pitched whine coming from somewhere. It was a sound she hadn't noticed before.

She inspected the caged animals. The sound was not coming from any of the guinea pigs, gerbils, or cats. But it was still coming. It seemed to be originating from the general area of the test chamber at the end of the room.

Marian went up to the door of the chamber and pressed her face against the glass. It was dark in there, but the whining sound seemed to be coming from inside. She flipped the light switch that had been installed outside the chamber.

When the chamber filled with light, Marian drew back from the sight that assailed her senses: The lone baboon, sitting in its own filth, smeared with blood and feces and God-knew-what-else, was whimpering like a puppy. Its face was a tortured mask of bottomless despair. Its eyes pleaded for release.

Marian checked herself. This was a baboon, not a human being. Its facial expressions couldn't be interpreted in the same way as those of a human being.

The baboon might even be happy—assuming such a beast knew happiness—and the whine might be one of ecstasy.

She doubted that in her heart, though. A baboon was higher on the evolutionary scale than a cat. It might, indeed, experience true emotions, though they would, of course, be quite primitive.

If the baboon had emotions, then it might also be easily driven crazy by a drug like 4155A, because its nightmares would be as fearful to it as any human's would be to a human. Which was probably what had happened down here, she concluded. The drug had had bad side effects on the animals, and Richards had probably known about it. He had, in fact, probably been holding this knowledge back for his own reasons—perhaps on the orders of Morton. She had always suspected the two of them of collusion.

That whine was persistent in her awareness now, and she wondered how she could hear it through what was supposed to be a soundproof door. She looked up and realized it was actually coming from a speaker above the door. Someone had left the intercom on. She searched for a switch to turn it off but couldn't find one.

Fortunately, she had what she came for and it was time to go. She didn't have to listen to the animal's whining any longer.

But it echoed in her mind for some time.

Carl and Laura showed up at eleven-fifteen that night. Strained pleasantries were exchanged, then Laura went into a room to change into a nightgown. When she returned, Marian led her into the sleep chamber, while Carl waited in the observation room.

The three of them were the only people there. Marian had cancelled the appointments of all the other sleep subjects and had had all the assistants stay home. Her plan did not call for the presence—or possible interference—of anyone else.

Marian personally hooked Laura up to the polysomnograph, carefully gluing the electrodes to her scalp and skin. She arranged the wires from the electrodes so they would not get in her way, then double-checked to make sure she had not forgotten anything.

"Comfy?" she asked as she checked the wire connections going to the plate in the wall.

Laura squirmed perceptibly. "No. I don't think I can go to sleep with all this stuff."

"I thought of that," Marian replied. "I have a Shodale preparation here that will help you. Would you prefer injection or capsules?"

"What is it?" Laura asked suspiciously.

"It's just a sleep inducer. It will help you sleep and also make you able to control your dreams. It works on the pons in the brain, affecting serotonin and ..." Marian was only guessing at its effects. All she cared about was that it was a convincing spiel to Carl's wife.

"Spare me the technical details," Laura said, suddenly testy. "Give me a shot. That'll work faster."

"Your choice." Marian took an ampule and a hypodermic syringe from the pocket of her lab coat. She inserted the hypodermic needle into the ampule and drew 30cc of 4155A into the syringe. She pressed the plunger and a small amount of the fluid squirted out the end of the needle, clearing the air out. She made a face; the stuff had a peculiar, pungent smell that lingered in the air briefly.

She was taking special care to seem very professional under Laura's scrutiny. A nurse would notice if she screwed up. Apparently, she was doing okay, because Laura paid her scant attention.

Marian had even remembered the alcohol swab, applied to the skin of Laura's left forearm just before she inserted the needle into her flesh.

Laura winced slightly as the needle went in and the drug was forced into her body, but she relaxed as soon as it was withdrawn.

Marian glanced over her shoulder at the observation window. Carl's face showed surprise but he apparently wasn't going to do anything about Marian's newly assumed role of temporary physician. It was too late now, anyhow.

She swabbed Laura's skin again, then threw the syringe away.

"Feel anything yet?"

"A little drowsy."

"Good. That's what we want. I'll leave you now, so you can

get to sleep. Either your husband or I will be available at all times if you need us."

Marian started for the door.

"That's very nice," Laura said, her speech already beginning to slur. "But please promise me at least one thing, doctor."

"What's that?"

"Don't screw him while I'm sleeping."

Marian and Carl were silent as they waited for Laura to go to sleep. She watched the polysomnograph closely, and when it was evident Laura was in the first stages of slumber, she allowed herself to relax.

"She's definitely asleep," she told Carl.

"Now what do we do?"

"Now there's nothing for us to do but see what happens."

"What was that injection you gave her?"

"The sleep drug," she confessed readily. "I have to see what effect it has."

"Don't you think that's dangerous?"

"Sure it is, but how are we going to learn anything without taking risks?"

"But she is my—she's a human being, not a guinea pig."

"Of course, you're right. What I've done may be unethical. But we're here. We can handle anything she does—I hope."

"You could get into a lot of trouble for practicing medicine without a licence." He stated this as a fact, not necessarily an accusation.

"I know it. I'd be in real trouble if there was a cop around."

"Why did you do it, then?"

"I had to. We have to make progress, somehow. We already know Laura has been acting strange, and the attempt on your life . . . well, she's a ideal subject. So arrest me."

"I don't intend to, but don't expect much sympathy from her if she finds out you're not a—"

"I don't expect anything from anybody. I made my choice

and I did what I thought was necessary. If I can live with it, then it shouldn't affect you."

"What's the matter? You're awfully defensive."

"I'm on edge." She sighed; there really wasn't any reason to withhold the truth. "Carl?"

"What?"

"Laura knows I'm—that I'm the other woman in your life."

"Did you tell her?"

"I was going to ask you the same question."

"I'm not a fool. I guess she's smarter than I gave her credit for. She would've found out sooner or later."

"This complicates matters," Marian said gravely. "If anything goes wrong tonight, our relationship will make some prosecuting attorney's day in court."

He patted her hand. "Don't look for the negative and it won't come looking for you."

"Nice philosophy, Carl. But the negative *can* and will bite you in the ass when you're not looking."

He shook his head. "I'm not worried. We're all doing what we have to do. If this experiment with Laura provides a clue we need, then it was warranted. If it doesn't—if it screws up somehow—then that's the way it goes. We'll be up shit creek, but I'm not sure we're not headed there already."

"What do you mean?"

"These dream things are affecting everybody, and we're no closer to a solution now than we were a couple of weeks ago. We just have more cases to contend with."

"We can still hope, though," Marian said, not really believing her own words.

"Hope," he replied, "won't bring the dead back to life."

Laura didn't try to get up until three in the morning. When she stirred, Carl had to nudge Marian. She had fallen asleep in her chair.

"Christ, Marian," he said, "Laura's trying to take a walk."

Marian roused herself and stood up quickly to peer through the observation window.

Laura was staring at the wires connected to her skin. Then she reached down and plucked one of them off.

Marian glanced at the polysomnograph paper. "She's asleep. She's in deep REM sleep. Yet she looks like she's awake."

"How do you know she's not sleepwalking?"

"Sleepwalkers are unconscious; she is asleep."

Laura removed another wire.

"Shit, she's taken off the galvanic skin response electrodes. But the EOG is still there. Carl, look at the EEG—look at the spikes—she's dreaming like crazy."

Carl looked at the wildly oscillating line on the paper. It meant little to him, but he could tell from Marian's reaction it was significant. "Whew," he offered, having no idea of anything else to say.

"There goes the EOG. And the EEG. She's totally disconnected." She looked up over the console into the sleep chamber.

Laura was standing now. She drowsily reached into her nightgown and scratched the space between her breasts. Then she stopped and seemed to be searching for something. She squatted out of sight a few seconds. When she came into view she had the discarded syringe in her right hand, holding it up like a dagger.

She was coming toward the observation room.

"What the hell's she going to do?"

"I don't know, but if she sticks either of us with that syringe, we've had it. You've got to stop her, Carl."

Before he could answer, the door to the observation room swung open.

Laura regarded them with cold eyes that moved rapidly from side to side.

REM, Marian thought, *with her eyes wide open!*

285

"Son of a bitch," Laura said. "Son of a bitch and his whore. Caught you together. Kill you both."

"Laura," Carl whispered, "listen to me. You're asleep, but this isn't really a dream. It's really happening."

"I know what I'm doing!" she screamed, then she was on top of him, trying to stab him with the empty syringe.

Marian threw herself on Laura's back and pulled at the hand with the syringe in it. It came dangerously close to Carl's neck, but she managed to wrench Laura's arm away. The syringe clattered to the floor.

The three of them tussling and twisting in the small room resembled a kind of strange three-headed beast. It was a beast that was making a lot of noise, and Marian now wished she hadn't kept everyone else away. They could use some help.

Laura kept screaming obscenities.

Carl tried to push her away.

Marian jerked on the woman's back.

Finally, Marian let go and stood back to look for a weapon. She spied a large glass ashtray resting on top of the polysomnograph, and for once she was glad her assistants had broken the no-smoking rules. She grabbed the object, turned, and cracked Laura across the back of the head with it.

Laura jerked, then slid away from Carl's body limply—like a bug that had just been sprayed with insecticide.

"Jesus, Marian," Carl said, "I hope you didn't kill her."

Marian was staring at the blood on the edge of the ashtray. It was dark and evil-looking, with several strands of Laura's hair sticking to it. She didn't really believe what she had just done.

"Marian!"

She dropped the ashtray on the floor. Coming to her senses, she stooped down to check Laura's breathing and pulse. "I didn't kill her, but we do need to get her to a doctor. And fast."

"You think the drug made her do this?"

"No doubt in my mind."

"Then she's been exposed to the drug before."

"That I can't say. I don't see how she could have. All I can theorize is that she's been exposed to something *like* the drug. If we find out what that is, we'll be on to something. Right now, we'd better call an ambulance. And, Carl? . . ."

"What?"

"I have to see that autopsy for sure, now. The sooner the better."

"I made the arrangements—but are you sure you can take it?"

"After tonight," she said wearily, "I think I can take anything."

It was daylight by the time Laura was taken to the Emergency Room at Methodist Hospital. Carl flashed his badge and there weren't so many questions. An examination revealed Laura had suffered a slight concussion and needed a few stitches in her scalp, but otherwise she was going to be okay. After that was established, Marian held a small conference with the doctor and a lab technician.

"What was that all about?" Carl asked her when she met him in the ER lobby.

"I asked them to do some tests on her. If I'm right, there will be a high level of certain chemicals in her system—chemicals that wouldn't necessarily show up in the standard battery of tests. I think our drug—or whatever it is that's affecting her— alters the balance of these chemicals in the brain."

"How can you be sure?"

"I'll know more after the autopsy. Did you get it set up?"

"Yeah."

"Where is it going to be?"

"Right here. They just remodeled, and their Autopsy Room has the latest technology available, if you need it. That's why I wanted to bring Laura here."

"It's good to see you can plan ahead. I like that in a man."

"Thanks. I hope you have a chance to appreciate some of

my other good qualities someday." He checked his watch. "We have an hour and a half before the M.E. comes in. You want some breakfast?"

Marian made a face. "Just coffee. I'm not happy about viewing an autopsy with my stomach full of food."

"You'll want some *real* coffee then. Let's go over to that pancake house."

"Sounds great to me. I need to get about half a pot in my blood. Give me enough caffeine and I can conquer the universe."

The pancake house was located at 16th Street and Meridian, just a block or so from the hospital. Carl and Marian sat in a booth, drinking coffee together for forty-five minutes. Carl had a couple of doughnuts with his.

They spoke very little during their time together in the restaurant, despite the fact that Carl was anxious to hear anything Marian had to say about the drugs. He had decided to let her handle everything, trusting her to tell him what she had discovered once it all fell into place.

He wasn't sure he would understand much of it, anyhow. All he understood was that a great many people were doing crazy things, and it was up to them to do something about it.

The medical examiner performing the autopsy was a man in his late fifties, stockily built, with close-cropped silvery hair and gray-blue eyes. His shaggy moustache was salt-and-pepper and appeared to have been hastily pasted on. He practiced a no-nonsense, follow-procedure-by-the-book attitude that was somewhat refreshing. He was one of the old time professionals who didn't consider anything but the bare truth worthy of his notice.

His name was Lewis Collins. His shoes appeared to be as old as he was, and they were stained with blood and possibly other substances of the body. He was assisted by a young man, formally called a *diener,* whose function was to hand him various implements necessary for dissecting the human body. Both wore disposable latex gloves and plastic aprons. Marian had been given an apron, too. Performing autopsies—or being close to one—was messy business.

Carl sat in the corner of the room, just far enough away that he really didn't have to watch but could participate in the pretense of watching. Marian didn't think he was chicken, but if he was, she would not have blamed him. It took a strong stomach and an even stronger nerve to endure an autopsy.

The old man's body, as it lay on the gurney, seemed shrunken and pale to Marian, and his face in the repose of death seemed barely human, so she didn't empathize with him as much as she thought she would. That didn't prevent her from feeling she was going to faint several times. She avoided it by drawing upon an inner reserve of strength, forcing herself to observe every detail of the autopsy as it proceeded from one point to another. She did have to look away a few times when internal organs were removed from the trunk of the body and weighed, but she remained fairly steady.

She wondered how people who did this sort of thing every day lived with the smell of it. The human innards were extremely malodorous after death, and the fluids seeping from various places stank a great deal as well. Adding to the pervasive stench were the aromas of various chemicals used in the Autopsy Room—for preserving tissue, cleaning, and other functions.

Despite the ghoulish sights and the ghastly smells, after a few moments, she found herself more interested in the procedure than she needed to be. It reminded her of her earlier desire to become a physician, and instead of conjuring up the old regrets, it showed her the ambition was still there. Perhaps, if everything came out all right, she could yet pursue a medical career, assuming no one sued her—or jailed her—for the various risks she had taken since it all began.

Collins recorded every detail fastidiously and worked at his own pace. Finally, he was finished with the major organs, which revealed the man had many maladies: tuberculosis, cirrhosis of the liver, diabetes, and the beginnings of other diseases, including a kidney ailment. The man would have soon succumbed from one thing or another in any eventuality, but what had actually brought him down was cardiovascular arrest—a heart attack.

But they had already suspected that; this finding only confirmed the obvious.

What really interested Marian was what the M.E. would find when he opened up the skull.

She gritted her teeth and choked back something foul that rose in the back of her throat as Collins cut the skull from ear to ear with a vibrating bone saw. He used a chisel and metal hammer to complete the cut, then turned the hammer around to use the hook on the end of the handle to pry the skull cap away from the head.

Marian almost fainted again. She took a deep breath and looked away briefly, spying Carl out of the corner of her eye. He was observing the many patterns in the floor tile with great studiousness. She guessed he wished he had not eaten those doughnuts.

Turning back to resume watching, Marian edged up to the end of the gurney, positioning herself at Collins's left elbow so she could get a better view.

Collins's assistant stepped back to let her in. He grinned maliciously, and she guessed he had lots of fun whenever amateurs were around. He probably would be a lot of fun at a wake, too. His face was covered with pimples that seemed on the verge of popping at random.

"I'll be damned," the old man said. "That's not supposed to be there."

"What? What is it?" Marian asked breathlessly, leaning even closer.

"Look." He took a probe and indicated a purplish growth at the base of the brain, near the brain stem and pons. "It's a lesion of some kind." He peeled away sticky flesh with a knife. "No, it's more like a boil. Get me a couple of slides, Thomas."

"Yes, sir," the assistant said, and quickly brought two glass slides from a nearby table to the examiner.

Collins took one slide and scraped some tissue off on it. Then he punctured the boil and collected the stuff that oozed out of it on to another slide. He handed both slides to the assistant. "Run these down to Pathology for analysis."

There was a pungent, familiar odor in the air that asserted itself through the other smells in the room. After the young man left, Marian asked, "What is that stuff?"

"I have no idea. It's not a tumor, though—at least it's not like any kind of tumor I have encountered. I don't think it's a congenital deformity, either. My best guess is that it's a growth, though I reserve judgment on that until the lab results are back."

Marian had her own suspicions. "When will that be?"

"A couple of hours at least. Maybe more, if they have trouble identifying the substance."

She didn't want to wait—and she had access to high technology herself. At Shodale. "Dr. Collins, could I get some of that ... fluid?"

He gave her an odd look, then nodded. "If it's okay with our representative of the police department."

She looked to Carl, pleading with her eyes.

His glance told her he understood and that there was no need to beg. "Give her whatever she wants, doc. She's helping the department."

"As you wish, then."

He prepared a small vial of the fluid, labeled it, and gave it to Marian.

"Thanks, Dr. Collins," she said, removing the plastic apron and tossing it on an empty metal table. "You may have given me the solution to a very big problem."

"Indeed?" he said, his voice indicating skepticism.

"We'll let you know what develops. Come on, Carl. I've got a lot of work to do."

Carl dropped Marian off at Shodale, then went home to sleep a couple of hours before reporting into work. He anticipated there would be much for him to do at the office but promised to contact her later.

Nothing could induce Marian to sleep, however. Her mind was charged with possibilities—and problems that had to be approached immediately.

She had no difficulty finding assistance from the personnel in the analysis lab at Shodale. One young man in particular, who had been Dr. Richards's assistant, was especially helpful.

Analysis soon confirmed what Marian's nose had already told her. The stuff from the dead man's brain not only smelled like 4155A, the "nightmare" drug, but it was essentially the same substance. But what was it doing in the body of a man who surely had never come near Shodale?

The answer was obvious. Somehow, Shodale had come near him.

Twenty-Four. Ambition

John Morton had developed a case of paranoia in the last few days. As a result, he had started carrying his Smith & Wesson pistol with him to the office. He didn't know if he would ever need it, or even why he might need it, but he felt considerably better with the gun within reaching distance. There were too many possibilities in the air—too much potential for things to go wrong.

This morning in particular the shiny pistol's presence was a source of comfort, because of what he had just read in one of the production reports from Shodale's agrichemical division.

It seemed the night supervisor there, Everett Rydell, had become very efficient, managing to up his production of a new product despite such problems as a higher-than-usual absentee rate among the employees on his shift.

Because of Rydell's accomplishment, distribution of the new product for nationwide testing had already begun—well ahead of schedule.

And why shouldn't it be going nationwide? Morton reflected. It had proved itself an efficacious product in the Indianapolis market. There was nothing wrong with it, was there? Of course not. It was just a new entry in the long line of products for better living through the magic of chemistry that Shodale was providing to the public.

It was going to be difficult to cover this up. But Morton had already started doing just that—this time without the aid of anyone like Alex Stryker.

Marian compared the spectrographs of 4155A and the mystery substance from the dead man. They confirmed again what the other analyses had shown.

But the problem still remained: How had an old derelict ingested enough of the substance for it to form a boil in his brain? Did it have something to do with the park? She couldn't make sense of it. But she did have access to computers, and she felt she knew how to use them well enough to gain the knowledge she needed.

She went to one of the computer rooms on the third floor and commandeered the use of a CRT terminal that linked into a Shodale mainframe. She sat before the amber screen of the Compaq and began typing in data. At first, she was slow, since she hadn't fingered a keyboard in a while, but when she stopped thinking about it, entering the data became easier and faster.

First, she called up directories of all files relating to 4155A. She scanned each directory and discovered most of the files were already known to her. She explored a couple of the unknowns, neither of which yielded anything new, then went back to the directory. Then she went into subdirectories and came across a curiously titled file with the name "RICHAR."

Could that be a form of Richards?

There was only one way to find out. She typed in the file name, hit the return on the keyboard, and waited.

The file came up on the screen within seconds and proved to be one of Richards's files, as she had guessed. The date on the disk directory indicated it had been entered the night he had died. It was strange that he had not encrypted the file, limiting access to it. A man with his personality would not have made it so easy to get to. Unless he died before he had a chance to encrypt it.

Marian realized she had stumbled upon a very elaborate suicide note.

"He'll see me," Stryker said. "He has to."

Morton's secretary balked. "But he has left instructions not to be disturbed."

"Buzz him. I'll take full responsibility."

She pushed the call button on the intercom and told Morton Stryker was there to see him. She was surprised when her boss asked her to send the young man in immediately.

"I told you," Stryker taunted as he went through the door. "I'm getting to be pretty important around here."

She shook her head and went back to work.

"I hope this is good," Morton said, directing an icy stare at Stryker. "I've got a lot on my mind."

"I thought you'd like to know what Dr. Turner is up to."

Morton's studied impatience turned abruptly into rancor. "Well, what's she doing now?"

"She's been busy on the computers—putting two and two together—and the result is 4155A."

"What do you mean?"

"She's right on the verge of discovering something."

"But you were supposed to erase everything. . . ."

"I did erase the things that would show the connection between 4155A and the other product," Stryker lied. "But I had to leave some data behind. There'd be too many questions if it all disappeared, especially since so many people know about it."

"Goddamn."

"There's more to it than that, I'm afraid. Dr. Turner brought in a strange fluid sample this morning for analysis. It turned out to be very similar to 4155A. Of course, I neglected to tell her it was *exactly* like another substance."

"Do you think she'll find out?"

"Possibly. She's a very intelligent woman. The actions of both substances are, of course, very much alike."

"You don't need to remind me of that."

"Oh, but I think I do, Mr. Morton. I read that production report, too. The stuff's on its way."

Stryker noted how Morton squirmed in his chair; that was a rare sight for any subordinate Shodale employee to witness.

"How'd you know about that, Stryker?" Apparently he hadn't acted quickly enough this morning or Stryker wouldn't be so smug.

"You gave me access to all the files, Mr. Morton. I have all the computer passwords, all the encryption keys, all of it. I can read anything I want, anytime I want."

"Not if I have the passwords changed." Morton glared. He hated being made uncomfortable by an inferior. He *would* have to change passwords now and double up on other methods of making company knowledge secure from prying eyes. Bills of lading, invoices, and stacks of printouts would have to go through the shredders.

"That would be unwise. With my new position in the company, I think I should be privy to all the secrets, don't you?"

"What the hell are you talking about?"

"You made certain promises, Mr. Morton, based on my doing some things for you. I've upheld my part of the bargain."

"I didn't promise to give you the fucking company."

"I didn't say I wanted the company. But I do want—let us say—greater status. Much greater status. I'm very tired of being a lackey for Shodale."

As Marian began reading Richards's file, she soon understood that he had not intended to commit suicide, unless one considered his ambition the killing force behind it. But he was certainly responsible for his own demise.

The speculations and revelations in the file confirmed many of Marian's suspicions about 4155A. Only, Richards had not realized just how strong the drug's effect was. He had theorized the lesions on the brains of the baboons had developed because they were lower animals, and that on man, such lesions would not appear. That's how he had justified injecting himself with massive quantities of 4155A.

He had been wrong there. It was because baboons were higher animals that the lesions had developed. So on man, they were even more likely to appear.

Richards had sacrificed himself to a wrong idea.

Morton found himself thinking of the Smith & Wesson. A .38 slug between the eyes would put Mr. Stryker in his place very nicely. There wouldn't even be that much blood.

Damn! This was what came of consorting with inferiors and letting them in on secrets. Inferior people had inferior minds and mediocre visions, and they made unreasonable demands. Why couldn't Stryker be content with a little money under the table? Hell, he'd even give him a new car to keep his mouth shut. What was the purpose of this grandiose bullshit, anyhow?

But, of course, he knew its purpose. And he smiled, because what irked him so much about this young man was his ambition, which Morton recognized as his own most powerful trait reflected back at him. It was that quality of himself he saw in the young man—the ambition of the grasping, avaricious businessman bent on climbing to the top by whatever means presented themselves.

In short, it took one to know one. In this case, it took a Morton to know another Morton.

What a laugh. This twerp actually thought he could manipulate John Morton.

Right between the eyes. That would do it.

But, wait a minute, he could still put the twerp to work and put him in his place at the same time. Let him know he didn't hold all the cards at that. All it would require was a little finesse, and Morton had plenty of that.

He clasped his fingers across his stomach and leaned back in his chair, displaying a broad grin for the young man. "Stryker, I admire your gall. It takes balls to play in the big leagues, and you've got them. In fact, a ballsy guy like you deserves to get ahead."

"Thank you," Stryker replied uncertainly.

"Tell me something, Stryker. Do you think this drug—4155A—do you think it can kill?"

"How do you mean, sir?"

"Let's put it this way. . . . How much would be an overdose?"

"What are you getting at?"

"Come on, you know all about it."

Stryker gulped, suddenly wary of what he was getting into. "Any drug is deadly in a large enough dose. From our experiments with the animals, I would guess 100 cc, given in one dose, would be quite dangerous and potentially fatal. Even if it didn't actually kill the person thus injected, it would most certainly plunge them into a fit of madness not unlike that induced by a strong hallucinogen. . . ."

"That's enough, kid."

Stryker stared at him, trying to read his thoughts. When it was evident Morton wasn't going to reveal those thoughts, he pressed ahead on his own.

"What are you getting at, Mr. Morton?"

That was what Morton wanted—for Stryker to ask the question that would lead to his entanglement and ultimately his own downfall.

"Stryker, we're in very deep shit here. That bitch Turner is about to blow this wide open. She's balling a cop who's bound to know almost as soon as she does. And, even if we recall those trucks Rydell so thoughtfully filled up for us, the least we can expect is about a billion dollars in lawsuits."

"I can see that sir, but—"

"But, Stryker, we can still cover this up. If—and this is the big if—if we eliminate the goody-two-shoes that might go blabbing things around before we have a chance to straighten things out."

"Eliminate?"

"Would you prefer something politer? How about 'snuff'? Or 'off'?"

"Mr. Morton, you're not seriously contemplating—suggesting that I ..."

Morton leaned forward, his expression as serious as he could make it. He was becoming excited about the idea; he had never seriously plotted another person's death before, and it imbued him with a sense of power he had never experienced. It was almost tantamount to sex.

That was it, he realized, almost gleefully. If he couldn't screw Marian, then he would dispose of her. There was a handy proposition for a man to put to a woman: *Do it or die!*

"Stryker," he said, "either you're big-league material or you're not. If you really, *really* want to succeed, you sometimes have to do things other people would not do."

"But why me?"

"You can get close to her, because she doesn't suspect anything from you. You'd have that needle up her ass before she knew what hit her."

Stryker blanched at Morton's imagery.

"I couldn't ..."

"Hell, man, do you want to be a part of this company or not?"

"I don't need to commit ..."

"It wouldn't be that bad. It would be easy to fabricate a story about how Marian—Dr. Turner—decided to test the drug on herself. We could falsify records, put spurious notes in the computer banks, forge diaries...." Realizing he was getting carried away with his own fantasy, he stopped abruptly, then glanced up at the pale face before him. "The decision is yours, Mr. Stryker."

"I don't know if I can ..."

"A needle discreetly pushed under the skin ...

". . . it's too . . ."

". . . and *snap!* No more Dr. Marian Turner. No more Miss Goody-Two-Shoes. No more hassle while you and I . . ."

". . . awful . . ."

". . . orchestrate the cover-up. We'll save millions for the company. And Stryker . . ."

". . . sir?"

"I'll be pretty goddamn grateful. You don't know how grateful I can be when I want to."

Stryker looked down at the carpet. "I'll try, sir. I really will."

"I knew you had it in you, Stryker. Get it done."

"Now?"

"As soon as possible. Damn it, we can't wait until she starts blabbing to that cop."

"I see your point, sir." Crestfallen, he turned to leave. He couldn't understand how he had come here merely a blackmailer and was leaving a potential murderer.

"Don't fuck this up, Stryker. This is your one and only chance to save the company—and yourself. Get it done, and let me know as soon as you do it."

Stryker nodded mutely. He seemed numb. But Morton was reasonably certain he would do what was asked of him.

When the young man was gone, Morton laughed out loud. Inferior people were so easy to manipulate. And if Stryker succeeded in taking care of Marian, he'd be even easier to take care of. Morton had many plans for the young man, none of them particularly pleasant.

He pointed his finger at the door and made a *pow* noise with his lips.

Right between the eyes.

The computer screen blurred before Marian's eyes, but she forced herself to continue reading Richards's file until she reached the end. When she read his last entry, she hung her head sorrowfully.

300

Richards's notes indicated for certain that 4155A did block the neurotransmitters in the brain that kept people from acting out their dreams, but in his twisted understanding, Richards saw that as a way of expanding human consciousness. Like so many men before him, he had been enticed by visions of attaining divine wisdom—as induced by a magic potion.

"You fool," she found herself lamenting. "You stupid fool."

He had let his own egomania drive him to taking the drug, because he had deluded himself into thinking it would make him godlike. Instead, it had succeeded only in calling up the demons of his own mind.

She wondered which demons had pushed him through that window.

Ambition, Alex Stryker considered, was a perverted thing. At least it was when it became an end in itself.

John Morton was a good example. Here was a man for whom ambition had become the overriding factor in life, and he himself was as perverted as his ambitions were. He was a twisted person whose sole interaction with other human beings consisted of manipulating them to his own desires.

But Morton had also attained a high station in life by making ambition his creed. He had power and material wealth.

Stryker wanted those things, too. And perhaps more. After all, if he could never be recognized as a scientist, then he might as well become someone important—with money and power. But it had never occurred to him ambition might require following convoluted moral precepts. He was not a Machiavelli or a Raskolnikov. Maybe he *was* a Morton, but had Morton ever murdered anyone?

Stryker nodded grimly to himself. If Morton hadn't actually killed, he was certainly capable. Directing someone to do the deed was almost the same as doing it. The man's heart was cold as stone.

"The big leagues," Morton had called it. Being in the big

leagues meant you did anything that was necessary. You took full advantage of every opportunity presented to you, and you didn't look back. You just kept climbing.

Stryker reached up into the cabinet and took down four ampules of 4155A.

Above all, you didn't look back.

Lack of sleep was beginning to tell on Marian. Every bone in her body ached and her eyes were burning. How long had it been since she slept? Thirty hours?

She checked the clock on the wall in the computer room. It was almost three in the afternoon. That made it close to forty hours without sleep, not counting that catnap she'd had the night before—out of which she was rudely awakened by Carl's wife.

She closed her eyes briefly and the scene in the sleep lab replayed itself in her mind. It seemed so vague and distant now. It was hard to believe that was only twelve hours ago.

The most vivid part of the whole incident was when she had hit Laura in the head with the ashtray. She could still see the ring of blood rising from the woman's skull.

Guiltily, she tried to recall if she had felt any pleasure in splitting the woman's head open like that. She didn't think she had, but she wasn't very sorry about it, either.

Nor was she sorry about giving Laura the drug. It had proved her point, hadn't it?

Still, she had hit her awfully hard.

Well, maybe the bitch deserved it.

Alex darted into the computer room, glanced around, and turned to a young woman sitting at the terminal nearest the door.

"Where's Dr. Turner?" he asked nervously.

"Who?"

302

"Dr. Turner, the woman who was using that terminal over there."

"Oh, I guess she went out. She said something about coffee."

"Great."

"Shall I tell her you're looking for her?"

"No, damn it." He rushed out without bothering to explain himself. The syringe in his lab jacket seemed to be getting warm. He could swear it was going to burn a hole in his pocket.

Marian put another quarter in the slot and pressed the button for "black." She leaned against the coffee machine and watched as it spat a beige paper cup into the little door in its middle, then filled it with steaming black liquid.

Yawning, she reached for the cup and brought it up to her lips. The stuff was way too hot to drink, but it smelled okay. Maybe inhaling the fumes would pump a few hits of caffeine into her blood.

She fumbled in her pocket for more change. It was time to call Carl and let him know what she had found out so far.

John Morton suddenly realized he had overlooked a variable in his zeal to have Marian killed. The cop.

No matter what happened to Marian, the cop was bound to show up. And Morton wasn't sure what the cop knew. He would have to deal with him somehow. Maybe he could get Stryker to—no, that guy was barely able to take care of the woman.

He would have to figure something out on his own. A cop would require a very special plan.

He called down to the guard shack out front. All visitors and employees had to pass that point before entering the Shodale complex.

"If a police officer named"—he glanced at a scribbled name

303

on his desk pad—"Carl Nolan wants in, let me know. *Immediately*. You got that?"

"Should I detain him, Mr. Morton?"

"No. Just let me know when he comes. Understand?"

The guard did not understand, but he wasn't one to argue with the boss.

Marian finished drinking the brackish coffee, then crumpled the cup and tossed it in the tall waste can next to the bank of vending machines against the wall. She considered buying a snack, but her stomach grumbled at the thought of a vending machine pastry. The coffee was insult enough.

The clock said four-thirty.

It didn't seem like a whole hour had passed. That meant she was really getting tired, because time was compressing. What next? Hallucinations?

Having hallucinations was the ultimate effect of sleep deprivation, but it took days to get to that point. She didn't have to worry about really spacing out. Yet.

A little nap would feel good, though. Carl wouldn't be out there till around six. But if she allowed herself to sleep now, she would probably sleep round the clock.

Maybe a little more coffee would help, a little more caffeine to get her along till the adrenaline kicked in again. She spent another quarter and, clutching the caffeine fix tightly in one hand, made her way back to the main hallway.

Instead of returning to the computer room, she decided to visit the animal lab. She wanted to see the baboon again, if only to make sure he was safe.

Besides, there was a terminal up there she could use.

Stryker had checked the computer room twice and Dr. Turner's office three times, but he still hadn't found her. He knew

304

she was still in the building somewhere. She hadn't signed out with the security guard.

Frustrated, Stryker decided to return to his regular station and try to plan things out in greater detail.

The animal lab wasn't that far away.

It was five o'clock. Many people were going home and John Morton was having a lot of fun pretending to be a sniper. His vantage point in the building was perfect, because he could see most of the company from the big window.

The hordes of employees moving along the walkways below presented a vast ocean of potential victims.

He singled out an employee, aimed the Smith & Wesson, then *pow!* Old, young, male, female, short, tall, fat, and thin. He was no respecter of types. He was killing them all.

It was too bad Marian wasn't down there. If she were, he might be tempted to really pull the trigger.

With the knowledge Marian had gained reading Richards's file, she thought finding the source of the mystery substance that so resembled 4155A would be easy. Instead, it was frustrating. Every inquiry so far had led to a dead end, or worse, to an encrypted file for which she had no passwords.

She had even tried entering the name of the park into the computer, and all she learned from that was that the Department of Parks and Recreation used Shodale cleanser in its bathrooms.

She even compared the formula of the cleanser to 4155A and discovered no similarities whatsoever—but then she had expected that inquiry to go nowhere. She was grasping at straws.

She was going to have to solve this mystery the hard way— by using a three-way program designed to compare the substance from the dead man with 4155A, and then compare all other products made by Shodale with both in the hopes that something would match, or come close to matching. Since there were hundreds of Shodale products and the formulas for most all of them were very complex, analyzing the data was very time-consuming, even on the computer.

Screen after screen of numbers, arcane symbols, and polysyllabic word configurations flashed before her eyes. This job might take hours.

Hours—what did they mean to her anymore? They flew by like minutes. So, what was one hour more or less? One more minute. One hour. It was all the same. Time was compressed into a little knot in her mind that kept shrinking and shrinking.

The amber screen disgorged more numbers. More symbols that seemed to dance in Marian's vision.

Was that a minute that slipped by just then? Or an hour?

Another screen. More figures.

Was the baboon whining again? Didn't anyone ever clean his environment?

Another screen. If only that animal could talk.

There, that was only a minute. A short minute, but no more than that.

Of course, it couldn't talk. The only way it could tell anyone what was needed to be known was if it were put to sleep.

Strange euphemism, that. Being put to sleep was not the same as going to sleep. That was for sure.

Sleep was a nice word.

That was an hour. Yes, it was.

Vending machine coffee was worthless. No potency. No effect. Just a bad taste in the mouth.

So sleepy.

Hello, Mr. Baboon.

Stryker was careful to note the time: *five-thirty-five*. Attention to detail was extremely important now. One slipup and all his ambition would be meaningless.

The lab was very quiet. The animals remained silent, as if

they too were caught up in the human drama unfolding before them.

Stryker ignored the pounding of his heart, the throbbing in his temples, and the sweat pouring down his face. He had to be steady if he was going to join the big leagues.

He took soft, measured steps across the lab, slowly moving toward the woman who had fallen asleep in front of the computer terminal. Her face was bathed in amber light, and she was really quite pretty.

He reached in his pocket for the syringe.

Twenty-Five. Messy, But Neat

Morton took his handkerchief out and rubbed the stainless steel surface of the Smith & Wesson. Then he hefted it in his right hand a few seconds, deriving pleasure from the sheer mass of the weapon. When it was loaded, as it was now, it felt much heavier than it did normally, even allowing for the weight of the cartridges. It was as if the killing potential of the bullets added the extra weight. Perhaps death had substance, even before it was perpetrated.

Morton laid the pistol on his desk and sighed. It had been a busy day for him. He had taken precautions to hide the facts of the agrichemical shipment, making sure much of the paperwork was destroyed. It was possible someone could still uncover what had happened, but by then he would have everything under control and there would be no reason to suspect him. He would have the loose ends represented by Marian Turner, her cop, and Stryker all taken care of, and a very quiet recall of the product would be underway. At least, he hoped it worked out that way.

If things didn't work out, he might have to flee the country, but he was prepared for that—but only as a worst-case scenario. He was confident his behind-the-scenes manipulations would ultimately remove guilt from him and from Shodale.

Of course, a great deal depended on Stryker doing his part.

He was getting tired of waiting to hear from the man. Surely, there had been ample opportunity by now for him to have performed his task. Why hadn't he contacted him?

The phone rang, startling Morton so much he almost fell out of his chair. He grabbed it.

"Stryker?"

"No, sir, Security."

"Well, what is it?"

"That police officer you left word about is here. Carl Nolan."

"Let him pass."

"Yes, sir."

He set the phone in its cradle with a worried look on his face. Now the shit was about to hit the fan. The cop had arrived and there was no word from Stryker about Marian.

He was going to be one sorry individual when Morton was finished with him.

It was six-fifteen when Carl pulled up to the guard shack at Shodale. The guard took his time clearing him for entrance, but Carl was patient. After a day spent interviewing countless witnesses and suspects, a few minutes spent waiting was like a small vacation.

Finally, the guard waved him on and Carl drove the police-issue Ford to the area of the parking lot closest to the research building. He parked, locked the car, and headed toward the front doors.

In his jacket pocket he had a plastic bag full of soil from Christian Park. He hoped Marian could do something with it.

Marian kept staring at the needle jutting from the syringe. Viewed from the business end, it was not a very pleasant sight. Even lying on the table, where it was less threatening, it seemed ready to bite her.

The computer terminal's amber face provided the only light

in the room. It cast an eerie glow over the side of her face, causing the corner of her left eye to twitch, and it rendered the figure sitting in the chair opposite her in strange hues, as if he were an old tintype of a person, and not real at all.

He was no less pathetic, however.

"You were going to try to kill me with that?" she asked, still incredulous.

Stryker buried his face in his hands. "I lost my nerve," he said. "Lost my nerve at the last minute. I guess I'm not as ambitious as I thought."

He was sobbing. It was his odd, racking cries that had awakened her.

"But why would *you* want to kill me? I don't understand."

"That's just it," he said, lifting his face. Tear tracks stained both cheeks. It was difficult to tell if he was more upset over the idea of killing or the idea of failing at it. "I didn't want to. It was Mr. Morton's idea."

Marian gasped. She knew Morton was a monster, but she never thought he'd go this far.

He didn't even have the courage to do it himself, sending, instead, this confused young man. That made him seem even more monstrous in Marian's eyes. She could only guess at the manipulations by which he had caused Stryker to become an attempted assassin.

Though she already had some ideas, she asked, "Why did he want you to do this?"

"He was anticipating that you'd find out the connection between 4155A and 4155."

Marian let that sink in a minute. "I know about 4155A. What's 4155?"

Stryker took a deep breath. He had apparently decided to tell all, regardless of the consequences. "4155 is an early formulation of 4155A, with only slight differences. It affects dopamine production in the brain, inhabits serotonin, and increases levels of acetylcholine and—"

"My organic chemistry is pretty rusty, Mr? . . ."

"Stryker. Alex Stryker."

"Mr. Stryker. You're losing me. What's the bottom line on its effects? In somewhat simple terms, please."

"It stimulates nightmares while allowing the free flow of neurotransmitters that control movement. In short, a person exposed to this substance . . ."

". . . will get up and act out his dreams."

"Correct."

Marian glanced back at the computer screen. It was blank, the program she had been running having apparently exhausted all possibilities while she was asleep—with nil results, she noted. "Why didn't my program show me the similarity between these two substances?"

"Because of what I put in the files. Any inquiry about 4155 compared to 4155A caused the program to go into an endless loop that is unresolvable, though the program will seem to go through the motions. That's all Morton wanted me to do at first—just fix the computer references and destroy some files. But when he found out you were snooping, he decided to—that is, he decided I should—well, you know the rest."

"What's the difference between the two substances, then?"

"Not much. It was decided a buffer would offset the effects the drug had on the reticular activating system in the brain, but the buffer chosen evidently wasn't strong enough. Mr. Morton—and Dr. Richards—both believed human testing would point out what fine tuning needed to be done to make the product more effective without the side effects.

"It seems to me both substances should have been shelved permanently."

"A lot of money had been invested. Neither Morton nor Richards thought the side effects were unmanageable. I don't think Morton even understands them."

"I still don't see how the first product got on the market—or why."

"That's where things get complicated, Dr. Turner. The original substance—4155—was made available to other divisions of

Shodale, as all failed products are, to see if it had any other uses. It's standard procedure, designed to minimize losses. There have been cases where a product that was no good for skin rash, for example, turned out to have applications in controlling weevils. In those instances, profits are sometimes greater than if the product had been marketed for its original use."

"But it seems unconscionable to put a potential hallucinogen on the market—in *any* form."

Stryker made a face that showed he agreed. "Somewhere along the line, the pharmacological actions of the substance were either minimized or overlooked. As far as we could tell, one department did not read all the data available from another department. That is, the right hand did not know what the left hand was doing. The result was that 4155 was tested by the agrichemical division and found to have an effect on the control of certain noxious *poas*—that is, unwanted grasses and weeds."

"You mean 4155 was to be used as? . . ."

". . . a herbicide. It's the major component in Shodale's new lawn treatment products."

Morton was on his way to the research building. He had the Smith & Wesson in the inside pocket of his jacket, where it bounced awkwardly as he walked.

He hoped the bulge was not too obvious.

"Where are you?" Marian spoke the question into the phone.

"Down in the lobby," Carl answered. "I've been looking all over for you. That's why I had you paged. The guard didn't want to do it, though."

"They have trouble with motor skills, you know, such as tying their shoelaces and working an intercom button."

"Are you implying cops are dumb?"

"Only rent-a-cops." Out of the corner of her eye, she saw Stryker watching her with a critical expression. Now was not the time for repartee. "Carl, hurry up here. I've got someone here who's just about unraveled the whole mystery for us."

"Where is 'up'?"

"In the animal lab on the second floor." She gave him quick directions.

"I'll be there in a flash."

She hung up and faced Stryker again. "He'll be up here in a minute or two."

"He's the cop, right?"

"Yes, an officer with IPD, the homicide division."

"I guess that means I'm going to jail."

"Not necessarily. If you help out, I'm sure they'll go easy on you. After all, you haven't really committed a major crime. . . ."

"You don't count attempted murder?"

"I won't mention it, if you don't."

"You have a generous nature, Dr. Turner. I only hope the authorities are as understanding."

Carl opened the plastic bag and dumped the soil sample on the laboratory dish. Marian picked some of it up, rubbed it between her fingers, and sniffed it.

"I don't even have to analyze this," she said. "This dirt is loaded with the substance. Where did it come from?"

"Christian Park."

"That was one of the places where the herbicide was being tested," Stryker said. "I remember reading it on the list of test sites."

"What list?" Marian asked.

"It's in the computer. Everything is in there, in a backup file I made—for insurance purposes."

"Not a bad idea when dealing with a man like Morton," Marian said.

"It's encrypted with a file name only I can access, but I'll be happy to print it out for you."

"We'll need that later," Marian replied. She wondered again

313

how Morton had so perverted this young man's thinking. Perhaps it was because Morton had the ability to appeal to the darker side of anyone's nature. That was one of the many qualities that made him so hateful.

"What are you two talking about?" Carl asked.

Marian explained the basic problem to him.

"Lawn chemicals?" His features twisted in a grimace. "Laura had *our* lawn sprayed at least twice. I guess that's why I didn't notice the smell in the park. I was used to it."

"That explains how she was exposed and—oh, Carl! That mean's you've been exposed, too."

Carl paled. "But nothing's happened to my dreams."

"Maybe he's immune," Stryker offered. "Or the effects are so minimal on him as to be unnoticeable."

"Or, the drug hasn't kicked in yet. The effects could be delayed with some individuals. It took several days for anything to happen to Richards. In any case, Carl, we'll have to get some tests made."

"What kind of tests?"

"I think the lesion might show up on a CAT scan. That's a special X ray of the brain. We'll have to get CAT scans on everyone who might've been exposed."

"But, Dr. Turner . . ."

"What?"

"Even if you find the lesion, we don't know how to counteract the effects of the drug. We have no antidote . . ."

". . . or any idea for one," she added.

"We've got to do something," Carl said. "All hell is breaking lose on the streets. Criminal activity in this city has tripled in the past few hours. And we have no way of knowing how many people have been exposed. From what you've told me, there must be walking time bombs everywhere in Indianapolis."

Marian's mind was racing, seeking answers and possibilities. "The baboon," she said at last.

"The baboon?"

"Right," Stryker said, picking up on the idea. "He's full of the drug. We can start by working with him."

"There's no time like the present." Marian said. "We'll start with taking a sample of spinal fluid, then we'll do blood tests. Now that we know what we're looking for, maybe we can make some progress."

"I'll have to sedate him," Stryker said, and hurried over to the test chamber.

He was glad to be of help. He felt fate had given him a second chance by preventing him from committing murder. If he came out of this unscathed, he vowed not to let ambition lead him to the verge of such folly again.

He took a key from his pocket and opened the door. He was about to enter, when he was stopped suddenly and forever.

A slug of hot lead had penetrated his brain.

The animals in the lab raised a ruckus, squealing, hissing, and screaming at the sound of the shot. Then they hushed, and the absence of their noises was just as terrifying.

Morton stared, momentarily hypnotized, as the young man's body dropped to the floor. He had never realized death could be so sudden, but now that he had actually shot a living person, he discovered it was not as bad as people made it out to be. In fact, it felt pretty good.

"Mr. Stryker won't give us any more trouble now."

Carl and Marian turned to see Morton standing in the doorway, a smoking .38 in his hand. Marian emitted a strangled cry when she saw what the bullet had done.

"That was an easily solved problem," Morton continued, now addressing the two of them calmly. "But the problem you two represent is a bit more complex."

"What are you going to do?" Marian asked, getting control of her emotions.

"It's obvious I have to kill you, isn't it?"

"You're dealing with the police, here," Carl said.

Morton was not intimidated. "So?" he replied.

"You are an evil bastard," Marian said, careless of the consequences. "You knew about the drug and the lawn chemicals, yet you let them spray the stuff all over the city."

"Ah, but you're wrong there. I didn't know at the time. When I found out, though, it was too late to stop it. The damage had been done."

"You can stop it now."

"That still leaves the problem. Because I don't intend for my career to end or for this company to go bankrupt because of a silly mistake."

"You'll be held accountable, no matter what happens," Marian said, righteousness evident in her voice.

"You can't cover this up," Carl said. "We know about it. And the authorities aren't stupid. They'll—"

"They'll be ignorant of the whole affair. Stryker already erased most of the data, and I've taken steps . . . well, you have no need to know the details. You both are going to be the victims of a nasty accident."

"It won't work," Nolan said. "Too messy."

"Maybe even messier than you think, Mr. Nolan. Would you please remove your pistol from its holster?"

Nolan hesitated, then reached inside his coat and brought out his .357 Magnum. He held it out, reluctant to let it go.

"You cops carry big ones, don't you? They make nice big holes, too. Toss it this way."

Carl threw the gun a few feet in front of them. It slid across the floor, landing close to where Stryker lay.

Morton moved across the room toward Stryker's body. "I guess I'd better make sure this fellow is quite dead. By the way, Marian, I've decided *you* killed him."

"Your bullet is in his head," Carl pointed out.

"Thank you, Mr. Nolan." He leaned down, keeping his eyes on Carl and Marian, and picked up the other gun while dropping the .38 in his pocket. He went to Stryker, put the barrel of the .357 against the hole his shot had made, and fired. The result to Stryker's head covered Morton's shoes and trousers with blood. He reacted with distaste, then stood up.

Marian and Carl both flinched. The animals went crazy again.

"Now it's not my bullet. I challenge anyone to find anything in this mess. This boy is very dead now."

"You can't do this," Marian said.

"I can do anything I please. Would you please pick up that syringe I see there?"

"No."

"Did you forget I have a gun?"

She did as she was told.

"I believe it's full of 4155A. Convenient. Stryker was going to do his job, after all. I suppose he lost his nerve—or did you dissuade him with your charms?"

Marian didn't honor that remark with a reply.

"I could see how a nice pair of tits would stop a man from doing his duty. It never stopped me, however. It's a pity to waste a body like that." He sighed. "But it can't be helped."

"You son of a bitch!" Carl growled.

"She is a nice piece, isn't she? Did she come for you?" He laughed. "You two will make a nice couple—in hell."

"You'll be there first," Marian said.

"No. You'll inject yourself with the drug, and then you'll go berserk—or it will be assumed you did—and you'll kill your lover and yourself. There will be awfully large holes in your heads. You're right, Mr. Nolan, it will be very messy indeed. Messy, but neat."

Carl gritted his teeth. He could think of no curse strong enough to express his feelings. Marian threw the syringe back on the table, then stepped closer to Carl, wrapping her arms around his waist.

"Do your own dirty work," she said defiantly.

Morton sneered. "It makes no difference. I'm just as happy to inject you before or after you're dead." He aimed the gun at her but hesitated a moment. His eyes were suddenly moist. He hated killing Marian, hated the idea of never being able to

317

spend his lust on her. The opportunity would soon be gone forever.

"Good-bye, Marian . . ."

A hairy arm reached out and jerked him backward. He dropped the gun.

Morton's screams echoed throughout the lab.

Carl raced across the room, stopping to pick up the .357 on the way, and darted into the open door of the test chamber.

The sight he beheld turned his stomach. The baboon had Morton down of the floor, tearing him to pieces.

There was so much blood on both man and beast it was difficult to tell where Morton began and the baboon ended. His left arm had already been ripped from his shoulder, and now the animal was working on the rest of him.

Its mouth was wide open, displaying blood-dripping fangs, and it was about to bite into Morton's head. Its razorlike nails were already digging into the man's throat.

Carl raised the .357 and aimed.

The baboon's head was transformed into a spray of blood and flying gore as its body was propelled backward against the wall.

Marian came in as Carl went over to the mangled thing that was now John Morton. He kneeled on the floor and lifted the man's head under his arm.

Overcoming her revulsion at the bloody scene, Marian approached and bent down beside them. She looked to Carl, then shook her head; it was obvious there was no saving the executive.

Morton's eyes moved from on face to the other. "Baboon got me." Blood-flecked spittle ran from the corner of his mouth. "Goddamn baboon."

"At least we stopped you," Carl said.

"You stopped nothing," Morton said, smiling triumphantly.

Then he died.

Epilogue.

The Shodale trucks kept rolling, hour by hour, day by day....
A little girl named Sue Bundy sat in the corner of the white room all day. She knew people were watching her. Big people who asked her too many questions. She wondered why Mommy and Daddy didn't come and take her away from this awful place.

And a teenager kept dreaming of chainsaws.

And an elderly woman kept dreaming of killing her cat.

And a retired man kept wondering why he had killed his neighbor.

And scores of other people could no longer tell the difference between reality and dreams.

There was something in the air to precipitate nightmares.

Marian Turner and Carl Nolan wondered a long time what Morton meant by his last words. When they tried to find out where the lawn chemicals had gone, they found out.

The man had covered his tracks well.

Alex Stryker also took secrets with him when he died. His list was never recovered from the computer files.

So it was days before they knew for sure some of the places where the chemicals had been used. They still weren't certain

319

they knew them all, for every day another shipment was discovered. Shodale's distribution network had efficiently and quickly carried the deadly substance to its destination in many cities.

But they had clues:

Such as the rioting in the suburbs of Detroit.

Such as the high incidence of rape and murder in Henderson, Kentucky.

Such as the terrorism on the outskirts of Memphis, Tennessee.

Such as the increased occurrence of suicide in Miami, Florida.

The nightmare stuff had been sprayed in suburbs, in parks, in retirement villages, and in playgrounds. It seeped into the ground water, poisoning wells; it got into city water supplies; and whenever it rained, its influence spread even further.

Even knowing where the trucks had been made little difference. Without an antidote, all the authorities could do was lock up people and offer warnings. But the jails and asylums couldn't hold everyone.

No one thought much of it anymore when television programs were interrupted with news bulletins of new acts of violence and horror, often perpetrated by a child or another unlikely person. People were learning to live in fear—of themselves and of each other.

The Shodale trucks kept rolling, hour by hour, day by day, through the landscape that was America, through the landscape that was turning into the nightmare plains.

Soon, there would be a nation of zombies out there—waiting.